"Camp out with me tonight," Mac said.

Maggie stared at him. "I'm not sleeping with you."

"I'm not suggesting you do. We'll have separate sleeping bags." He wouldn't come on to her. Sully knew trouble when he saw it. "Look, Scouts camp in more remote places than this," he reassured her.

"You're insane. I'm not going to spend the night with you."

"Suit yourself. I won't sign the contract, then."

"That's blackmail!" She glared at him. "You're saying if I sleep with you tonight, you'll sign."

"No, it's not about sleeping *with* me. If I wanted to make a move on you, I'm smart enough to do it in a soft bed in a fancy hotel."

"You couldn't seduce me anywhere."

"Then we understand each other. You stay in your sleeping bag, I'll stay in mine. If you last until daybreak, I'll sign the contract."

He let her sputter and protest a few more minutes because they both knew she was going to do it. He'd probably feel safer sharing his tent with a bobcat, but Maggie Sanders was *going* camping.

For more, turn to page 9

Isn't It Romantic?

"You call that romantic, Charlie?" Liz questioned.

She moved toward him and the story he'd been creating on his computer. "Charlie, you've got the heroine ripping meat off a bone with her bare teeth. And you're right, the detail is vivid. So vivid, in fact, I could almost hear her doing some territorial growling. You even had the hero dabbing grease from her face. In romance novels the hero might wipe away a tear or brush a smudge of dirt, but not grease, and certainly not with the sleeve of his shirt!"

Charlie frowned. Liz continued.

"Maybe he cuts her a bite of food from his plate and feeds it to her with his fork, or fingers. Fingers are good, Charlie, and the sensuality of a finger slipped between her lips should never be underestimated."

"Like this?" Charlie raised his index finger to her lips. At first he traced the line of her bottom lip slowly as if to memorize every contour. Then he moved to the top lip and followed the delicate outline from corner to corner, hesitating over every detail of the curves. "Is it romantic enough, or would she prefer something more like this?"

Hmm, how romantic...

For more, turn to page 197

HARLEQUIN DUETS

ISBN 0-373-44172-X

Copyright in the collection:
Copyright © 2003 by Harlequin Books S.A.

The publisher acknowledges the copyright holder
of the individual works as follows:

DESPERATELY SEEKING SULLY
Copyright © 2003 by Pamela Hanson and Barbara Andrews

ISN'T IT ROMANTIC?
Copyright © 2003 by JJ Despain

Desperately Seeking Sully

Jennifer Drew

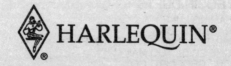

HARLEQUIN®

TORONTO • NEW YORK • LONDON
AMSTERDAM • PARIS • SYDNEY • HAMBURG
STOCKHOLM • ATHENS • TOKYO • MILAN • MADRID
PRAGUE • WARSAW • BUDAPEST • AUCKLAND

Dear Reader,

Maggie Sanders, the heroine of our latest book, writes extreme adventure guides from a comfortable chair in front of her computer. She's all about researching via the Internet, not about doing any real traveling. Too many bad road trips!

Hunky hero Mac Sully, on the other hand, is a real-life adventure guide. On hiatus from hiking, kayaking and mountain climbing, he encounters the biggest challenge of his career: Maggie!

Whether you're the adventuresome type or the stay-at-home type or a combination of the two, we (Jennifer Drew is the pseudonym of mother and daughter Barbara Andrews and Pam Hanson) hope you enjoy Mac and Maggie's excellent adventure!

Happy reading!

Jennifer Drew

P.S. Please look for our first Temptation novel in December 2003.

Books by Jennifer Drew

HARLEQUIN DUETS

*Bad Boy Grooms

To Joan, this one's for you!

1

"PLEASE, PLEASE, PLEASE, pick the guy with the fake snake around his neck," Rayanne Jordan begged.

The office receptionist stared out beseechingly from under her thick false lashes and tucked a long strand of hair—blond this week—behind her ear.

"You have a thing for snakes?" Maggie Sanders teased, knowing perfectly well why Rayanne wanted her to hire the acting student with smoky-gray eyes and thick coal-black hair curling on his shoulders. He'd caught Maggie's eye, too, when she'd ushered out the previous applicant she'd interviewed.

"I loathe anything that crawls on its belly! Okay, I admit the rubber reptile is a silly prop, but he'd be perfect to pose as the author of the *Extreme Adventure* guides."

"It's how he sounds, not just how he looks," Maggie said. "So far I've only interviewed two applicants. How many more are there? A dozen or so?"

"Closer to thirty," the receptionist admitted. "Some are lined up in the hall. They've practically crowded me out of my space. If that guy in the bush jacket doesn't get his beefy buns off my desk, I'm getting my staple gun. How many signs did you post for the job?"

"Just a couple. I put them where the dramatic arts students at Carnegie Mellon would see them," Maggie said, surprised herself by the big turnout.

"Oh, they saw, all right!"

"Send in the next one, please."

Rayanne was the third young woman to have Maggie's old job as receptionist, and Maggie enjoyed her enthusiasm and sense of humor—most of the time. Maggie had been working for the Pittsburgh-based Granville Publishing Company since she'd graduated from West Virginia University nearly six years ago, but Rayanne had been hired last June, almost a year ago. They'd hit it off and were good friends, sometimes sharing rides home since they'd both grown up in small towns not too far apart across the border in West Virginia.

Maggie loved working at the small publishing company, mostly because Mr. Granville was a great employer. He'd hired her as a temp at the reception desk with the promise of "something better" when the opportunity arose. After only a few months he'd made her an assistant editor, but her big chance had come when he let her write Granville Publishing's first *Extreme Adventure Guide.* The first edition exceeded his expectations and was followed by three more, all wildly successful. Maggie had written them all doing the research on her trusty computer.

Until the *Adventure Guide* series, Granville Publishing had been a modestly successful small publisher specializing in local history, bed-and-breakfast guides and poetry. The firm occupied the top two floors of an old, narrow three-story brick building in downtown Pittsburgh, not far from the Carnegie Museum of Natural History. Mr. Granville's spacious office occupied the third floor along with a storage area. Everything else was crowded on the second, and the outer office across from the antiquated elevator was far too small for the thundering herd Maggie had to interview. She belatedly wished she'd insisted on appointments instead of inviting eager young acting students to show up anytime that afternoon.

The next applicant who came into her office was dressed in jeans and a black Pirates T-shirt, refreshingly ordinary compared to the safari jackets and camouflage outfits crowding the outer office. One jobseeker had even showed up as a jungle boy in a fake leopard-skin loincloth. She'd interviewed him first and quickly sent him on his way when he started calling her Jane.

Maggie sighed and asked the pinched-face blond boy now in front of her the first question on her prepared list.

''Are you free to do publishing tours and book signings whenever needed?''

''You can be sure of it, mate.'' He elaborated on his availability in the worst imitation of an Australian accent she'd ever heard.

She groaned inwardly and managed to shoo him out after a few agonizing minutes.

The office was a zoo, and it was all because the *Extreme Adventure* guides she'd written were so successful. They'd boosted the profits of Granville Publishing and given Mr. Granville an opportunity to sell out to the Pierpont Corporation. Maggie's boss was approaching seventy and wanted to retire without liquidating the firm his grandfather had founded. When the deal was finalized, though, he'd agreed to stay on as a consultant for up to a year during the transition period.

There was one little thing Mr. Granville had neglected to mention to the prospective new owner.

M. S. Stevens, the pseudonym she used on the adventure guides, was really a five foot two, hundred-and-ten pound female whose total wilderness experience was one disastrous week at Girl Scout camp as a kid. There she'd managed to get lost in the woods, burn mulligan stew over a campfire and get poison ivy on her butt in a way she preferred to forget.

She looked around her cozy little office, the gray steel desk, swivel chair and computer softened by bits and pieces of home. Her parents and sisters—Annie, a year older and recently married to an air force pilot whose adventurous nature matched hers, and Laurie, three years younger and still finding herself—smiled out from a family photo in an ornate gilded gesso frame Grandma Sanders had given her. A huge bouquet of Mom's homemade silk flowers was squeezed between books on one of the wall shelves, and Maggie's collection of ceramic elephants, which were each an inch to two feet high and in a rainbow of colors, made themselves at home wherever there was space.

Granville Publishing was a low-key house that had depended on local sales and word of mouth until the *Extreme Adventure* guides became surprise big sellers nationwide, mostly through web sales. It hadn't mattered that Maggie quietly researched and wrote them from her little office until the soon-to-be-new owner, Peter Pierpont, dropped his bombshell: M. S. Stevens was going on the road.

Pierpont wanted to promote the guides with an author tour of the eastern seaboard, and that was only the beginning. He wanted to make M. S. Stevens a publicity sensation with maximum media coverage. He didn't have a clue that the star of his new acquisition was a twenty-eight-year-old computer addict who thought a walk in the park was enough of a wilderness trek. Worse, Maggie loathed public speaking, had an absolute horror of microphones and tended to freeze up when she was the center of attention.

It was one of life's little jokes that she was so successful telling other people how to be adventurous. She was a travel agent's nightmare. If Maggie booked a flight, the plane was sure to be held up by a blizzard, hurricane or engine trouble. Her parents loved family vacations, but their big trip west when Maggie was eleven almost put them off travel for life. She got lost at Disneyland, came down with chicken pox the next day and discovered she was allergic to bee stings. This was before the transmission in their station wagon died in Trinidad, Colorado, and Maggie's pox-marked face was so violently red she couldn't leave their motel room for the three days it took to get the wagon fixed. And that was one of her more successful expeditions.

A fifty-mile trip home to Beaumont, West Virginia, was her equivalent of going into battle.

Afraid of ruining the sale, Homer Granville had let Pierpont believe what he wanted about the author of the guides. Now the new publisher was expecting to send a macho outdoor type on tour.

Mr. Granville had come up with a simple solution: hire a stand-in for Maggie to do the publicity. Which was why she had plastered job notices where college drama students would see them. Who knew Pittsburgh was a hotbed of wanna-be wilderness survivors? The outer office was wall-to-wall with hopefuls. They were sitting on the worn beige tiles of the floor, lounging against the rattan-textured walls and occupying the few chrome-legged chairs with brown faux leather seats.

How on earth was she going to pick one from among the thundering herd?

If she weren't so darn grateful to Mr. Granville, and if she didn't like him so much, she'd dust off her journalism degree and look for a nice sane job working on a small newspaper. Or would she? She loved writing the guides and having imaginary adventures she'd never dare try in real life. Probably a lot of her readers felt the same way, vicariously enjoying a risky lifestyle through her books.

Her office door opened and another candidate stalked in, this one a tall, lanky woman with dark auburn braids and a khaki jumpsuit. Maggie's first reaction was positive. Why not hire a woman? Then the applicant yanked on something bright yellow she was carrying and half the office was filled with a large inflated raft.

"Ohmigosh!" Maggie gasped as the pink-striped elephant on her desk toppled on its side.

"I believe in making a dramatic entrance," the young woman said, beaming like a kid who'd just pulled off a clever trick. "When your name is Mary Smith, you have to do something to make people remember you."

"I will remember you," Maggie said, righting her china elephant, which now had a chipped ear.

She hastily asked a couple of questions, glad of the interruption when her phone rang.

"Maggie Sanders," she said, picking it up.

"Yes, yes, of course."

With his pointy gray beard and wire-rimmed, half-lenses, Homer Granville reminded her of a stereotype of an English butler. But his tiny, squeaky voice didn't match his dignified girth. He sounded uncharacteristically flustered, which only made his voice somewhat shrill.

"I'm parking the car," he said into his cell phone, his voice pregnant with innuendo.

She hadn't even known he'd left the building.

"Mr. Pierpont is with me. He's eager to meet the staff."

"Oh, oh!"

"Yes," her boss agreed.

"Stall as long as you can. I'm swamped with job applicants."

"I certainly shall."

The line went dead.

"Thank you, I'll get in touch, Ms. Smith," Maggie said, racing around her desk and giving the inflated raft a shove toward the door.

She didn't give the woman a chance to plead her case.

"Rayanne!" she called, summoning the receptionist to her office.

She whispered the bad news to Rayanne, who quickly went into action in the outer office.

"I'm terribly, terribly sorry, everyone," she said loudly, "but we have an office emergency. Everyone will have to leave now. We have everyone's résumé and application, and I promise you'll all hear from us by the end of the week."

"Today's Thursday. That means tomorrow," the man perched on Rayanne's desk said.

"Thank you for sharing that with us," Rayanne replied in a dangerously sugary tone.

The crowd grumbled but started to disperse while Rayanne rushed out to the corridor to repeat the bad news. Maggie felt a little guilty letting the receptionist do the dirty work, but she was a big chicken when it came to confrontations. There wasn't time for a lot of apologies, and Rayanne was tough.

The first bunch of candidates crowded into the small cage of the elevator while the rest of the herd stampeded toward the stairs, urged on by Rayanne.

Mr. Granville would park in his reserved spot off the alley behind the building, put his cardboard sun shield across the front window of his classic black Cadillac, and step delicately around the Dumpster in his black wingtips, avoiding the numerous potholes in the crumbling concrete. When he got to the rear entrance, he'd fastidiously brush the sleeves of the dark business suit he wore in all seasons and pull out the heavy ring of building keys. Even allowing for the pokey ascent of the elevator, he'd get to the second floor with his visitor in another minute or two tops.

Mr. Pierpont didn't know about the stand-in idea, and the sale hadn't been finalized. The lawyers were still nit-picking, and she didn't want to do anything to jeopardize Mr. Granville's retirement plans. There was nothing wrong with letting someone else front for her to do publicity since M. S. Stevens was a nonexistent person, but an office full of pseudo survivor types would be awkward to explain. She trusted her boss to explain about the stand-in before he let Pierpont sign on the dotted line.

She stood beside Rayanne in the corridor and watched the last job applicant saunter over to the fire door at the top of the staircase.

"Whew!" Rayanne said.

"Whew," Maggie echoed, opening the glass-paneled door with the company name and an Art Deco design etched on it.

"What was with the raft?" the receptionist asked.

Maggie opened her mouth to answer and saw—trouble.

"I'm sorry but we're not doing any more interviews today," she said to a tall, darkly tanned man standing beside the office's potted rubber plant.

"I'm trying to see Maggie Sanders," he said in a deep, distinctive voice.

"Yes, I understand, but we'll get in touch with you tomorrow if your phone number is on your résumé."

This man was older than the student applicants, maybe thirty or so, with dark blond hair sun-bleached on top as though he spent a lot of time outdoors. She immediately liked his startlingly blue eyes with the sexy little crinkle lines in the corners. His nose had once maybe been broken, but being slightly off-center made his face seem more rugged without distracting from his drop-dead good looks. He was wearing khaki bush shorts and a matching short-sleeved shirt with the top buttons open to reveal a scattering of fine hair. He soared to the top of her list on appearance, but co-operation wasn't his strong suit. He stubbornly stayed where he was.

"I don't know what's going on here," he said in a voice that gave her shivers, "but I'm not part of it. All I want to do is see Maggie Sanders for a minute. I promised a friend I would."

This was getting complicated. Rayanne sat behind her desk and pretended to be doing something, but Maggie sensed her avid interest in the conversation.

"I'm Maggie Sanders, but I can't possibly see you right now. I'd really appreciate it if you'd come back later."

"Gladly, but I promised Ann Cartwright I'd hand-deliver this to you." He held out a fat manila envelope.

"Who are you?" Mr. Granville and Peter Pierpont could be in the building, on the elevator, but the man had her full attention.

"Mac Sully. Ann was on a white-water expedition I led. She knew I was coming here and insisted I give you this."

"She's a friend of my mother's," she said, not that he wouldn't already know that.

Ann Cartwright was a self-appointed critic and cheerleader for the *Extreme Adventure* guides. An old school friend of Mom's, she lived the kind of life Maggie only researched. Single and comfortably supported by an inheritance, Ann spent a good part of her time traveling and having real-life adventures. She also studied every guide as soon as it came out, applauding or criticizing in the misguided belief she was being helpful. Maggie liked her, and she was a good supporter, but no doubt the bulky envelope Mac Sully handed to her was a critique of the newly issued fourth guide.

"Well, she asked me to give it to you," he said in the tone of a man who's done his duty. "Nice meeting you, Ms. Sanders. I heard a lot about your guides from Ann."

"You haven't read them?" It was a dumb thing to ask, but she blurted it without thinking.

"Not to speak of," he answered blandly, leaving her to guess whether he thought her books were valueless to a real outdoorsman.

"Oh, I didn't mean to…"

The door from the corridor opened, but at least she could explain that—what was his name?—Mac Sully was a friend of a friend or something.

"Peter, I'd like you to meet two indispensable members of the Granville team," her boss said. "This is Rayanne Jordan, our receptionist. She's only been with us a year, but her work has been exceptional."

Rayanne stood for the new owner's inspections, taking his hand when he offered it, and Maggie gave Mr. Granville points for trying to keep their jobs secure after he was gone.

"And this is my right-hand assistant and the editor of many of our best books, Maggie Sanders."

"A pleasure, Maggie." Peter Pierpont took her hand firmly in his, held it for a few seconds longer than necessary and smiled broadly. He had ramrod posture under a rumpled yellow linen jacket, white tank top and white trousers, not what she'd expect in a corporation head who was past the age of fifty. He also had sharp eyes of an indeterminate color, a long face and thin lips that made his smile somewhat sinister. His iron-gray hair was cut in a short buzz, and he wore tan loafers without socks. He didn't at all fit her idea of a CEO.

Mac hadn't gone away. He was standing beside her, looking interested, and she felt she had to introduce him.

"This is Mac Sully—" she said.

"M.S., glad you're here," her boss said, cutting her off. "I want you to meet the future owner of Granville Publishing, Mr. Peter Pierpont."

"Oh, no, he isn't…" Maggie tried to say, but again she didn't have a chance.

"M.S. as in M. S. Stevens, I assume," Pierpont said, exchanging one of the bone-crushing handshakes favored by alpha males.

Sully frowned and tried to catch her eye.

"No, I just stopped in to make a delivery for a friend," he said.

Granville thought Mac was the actor she'd hired for the publicity tour, and why wouldn't he? Sully certainly looked the part.

Obviously that meant Pierpont thought Mac was the real author. She didn't have a clue how to set them both straight without jeopardizing the sale of Granville Publishing and her boss's long-awaited retirement.

She felt a little queasy.

Apparently, Pierpont was one of those people who only heard what he wanted to hear. He ignored Sully's denial.

"I have my staff working on your tour," Pierpont said. "Marketing agrees you've only scratched the surface on sales potential."

"You've got the wrong guy," Mac said. "I lead wilderness tours...did, anyway."

"That's why you did such a wonderful job on the guides," Granville said. "You don't need to be secretive anymore."

Pierpont checked a wristwatch that did everything but make coffee. "You don't have to keep up the charade with me, anyway. Granville can explain. I have a plane to catch, but someone will be getting in touch with you as soon as the legal eagles finish the paperwork. Glad to have you aboard."

Sully gave her a look that asked if he was the only sane person in the room and was out the door before she could think of anything to say.

Pierpont frowned. As a big-name publisher, he obviously expected some fawning from anyone he believed to be an author, but Mr. Granville guided him away to meet the rest of the staff and inspect the third floor.

The simple plan to hire a stand-in for the publicity tour had turned into the stuff of nightmares. As soon as the two men were out of sight, she sprinted into the corridor trying to think of a way to salvage the situation without jeopardizing Mr. Granville's retirement...or her job.

MAC PUSHED the elevator button, unimpressed by the fancy gold-and-black geometric design on the closed doors. When, predictably, they didn't open, he headed toward the exit sign by the stairs.

He should've known Cartwright's little favor would land him in a loony bin, not that he didn't like the eccentric old girl. He'd had some serious doubts when she signed up for his British Columbia trek a few years ago, but she ran circles around a lot of the yuppies who thought all they needed in the wilderness was pricey gear. Better still, she didn't complain about everything from grounds in the coffee to sand in her shorts the way some of his clients did.

He grimaced, knowing he wouldn't miss the neo-phytes who didn't know a canyon from a cow pasture, but he hadn't planned on retiring at thirty. He had a woman to thank for that—his own favorite relative—but he didn't blame his grandmother for refusing to sell her mountaintop home near Eighty Four, Pennsylvania, and move to Florida where his parents would coddle her to death.

Cora Sully had helped her husband build their house board by board, and turning eighty had only hardened her resolve not to leave it. Mac was the only one in the family who would help her stay there. His older brother, Todd, worked in suits and had his life planned like paint-by-number art. He lived in a suburb of Chicago with his pretty, somewhat bland wife and two immensely spoiled kids. He thought their grandmother should sell out and start acting her age, which meant no more splitting logs for the huge stove that heated her house, no more wandering in the woods to gather wild mushrooms and berries, and no gardening to raise all her own produce and supply half of her neighbors, all comfortably distant from her home.

Mac was the only one who stood between Gram and the old folks' home, at least until her broken wrist healed. She probably shouldn't have climbed on the roof over the porch to nail down some loose shingles, but at least she hadn't, as everyone else in the family predicted, broken her neck.

The metal steps in the stairwell resounded under his heavy hiking boots, but he reached the main floor quicker than the elevator would have. He stepped into a 1920s-style lobby with a black-and-white checkerboard floor and a jungle of potted trees that didn't quite disguise how shabby the old building was. He'd expected the publisher of the *Extreme Adventure* guides to be more high-tech, a glass-wall type of operation. But what did he know about the business?

He had a pretty colossal problem of his own. He and Gram respected each other's privacy too much to live in the same house for long, but he had a plan. He was going to use his savings to build a cabin on part of her property, but when the money was gone, how the heck was he going to make a living? He knew how to live on the cheap, but he wasn't ready to give up his SUV or the habit of eating. He'd blown off college after a couple of years, but he couldn't see himself penned up in an office for the rest of his life even if he had the necessary credentials.

The elevator opened behind him just as he started to head toward the door to go outside, and he heard his name echo in the high-ceilinged lobby.

"Mr. Sully! Please wait a minute. I need to talk to you."

Oh boy, he didn't need this. Maggie Sanders had followed him. He'd picked up on something fishy in the office, and he definitely didn't want to get involved in her problems. Why did helpless little females always think he was put on earth to play hero? When—if—he ever found a woman of his own, she had to be as tough as Gram and as self-reliant as he was.

He half turned and tried to put her off without seeming like a total oaf.

"Sorry, I've got another appointment," he said, which was true only in that Gram knew he was coming to visit, and patience wasn't her long suit.

"I'll just take a minute. I'll walk you to your car."

He had another excuse on the tip of his tongue when he made the mistake of looking directly at her. She had eyes a man could get lost in, so brown they were almost black. At the moment they looked moist and shimmering. He hoped she wasn't a crybaby. He couldn't stand tears, and he'd seen his share from panicky campers who were afraid of their own shadows. He wouldn't miss that part of his wilderness excursions.

"If you can keep up," he said, still hoping to discourage her.

"I can." She sounded miffed. "You're probably wondering what was going on up there."

"No, not really."

The only thing he was wondering was how to avoid hearing her explanation, but he held the door for her. Score one for chivalry.

He'd had to park nearly four blocks away in a pricey lot, another reason not to dawdle. He tried not to look at the woman by his side, but it wasn't necessary. He'd pretty much memorized the whole package on first sight, she was that impressive. She had a fair, indoors complexion—not usually a plus with him—but she went easy on the makeup. The pink on her cheeks was real. Her hair went with her eyes, a rich dark brown cut a few inches below her cute little ears. She wore it tucked behind them, but she didn't have the annoying habit of constantly fussing to keep it in place.

She did keep up, but it didn't leave her much breath for chattering. Still, he was impressed. She was about a foot shorter than his six foot one, but her shapely legs really pumped to keep pace.

He liked her outfit, a yellow polo shirt that only hinted at full, lush breasts and a dark green skirt that brushed the tops of her knees. Her clothes made her look sexy without making a guy hot and bothered. She had class, but she was still trouble. He could sense it.

"The thing is," she said, when they were forced to stop on a curb to wait for traffic, "I wrote the *Extreme Adventure* guides."

"That's what your friend Ann told me."

"She's a good friend of my mother's—my older sister is named after her—but that's not important now. My boss is selling the company to the Pierpont Corporation."

"The dude with the fancy watch?"

"Yes, and he wants to promote the guides with a big author tour."

"Guess that's the way the game is played." He started to cross the street.

"Will you slow down for just a minute?" She did have a bit of a bite.

"Here?" He gestured at the busy street they were crossing.

"There." She led the way to the relative safety of the walk on the other side.

"I can't do the tour!" she shouted over the noise of a delivery truck turning the corner next to where they were standing on the sidewalk.

"Why not?" Okay, she had his attention.

"Look at me."

He did, and he liked everything he saw from the firm natural line of her brows to her pert chin. Her face was heart-shaped and her skin was flawless. She was about as cute as a girl could be without being a raving beauty. He'd always been a sucker for the pixie look, but not this time. He could not solve her problem, whatever it was.

"Do I look like a wilderness survival expert?" she asked.

He shrugged. She had him there. He'd probably screen her out of his rougher trips.

"Do these look like hands that chop through jungles with a machete and skin squirrels to eat?" She grimaced and showed him the smooth pink palms of her hands. "Who would believe I'm M. S. Stevens?"

"You do write the books, don't you?"

She had him puzzled, and he didn't like it.

"I research everything on the computer, research it thoroughly, but I don't do it."

"Ah."

"Don't say 'ah.' I'm good at writing them. Everything in the guides has been proven in the field by experts.''

He started to walk toward his car again, but she put her hand on his arm so he had to stand there on the sidewalk or rudely shrug her off. She flushed when he looked pointedly at her grip.

''Where is this leading? I really do have to get going.''

''All those people in the office were acting students. Mr. Granville wants me to hire a stand-in to do the tour, someone the new owner can promote after the sale goes through.''

''Ah.''

''You said it again! Mr. Granville thought you were the one I'd hired. Worse, Peter Pierpont thinks you're the real M. S. Stevens, even though I am.''

''So why not do the tour yourself? The guy who signs your checks will have to know you're writing the guides.''

''I can't,'' she replied with downcast eyes.

''Can't?''

''Don't want to. I hate public speaking. I have a microphone phobia. I'd feel like a complete idiot signing books. It just isn't me.''

''I'd think you'd have people lining up in the streets to buy your guides.'' He meant it as a compliment, but she didn't seem to notice.

''I want to hire you as my stand-in for the tour.''

He laughed then regretted it. She was deadly serious, and if he didn't handle this carefully, he might have to deal with tears.

''You'd be perfect,'' she went on. ''Do you have a wilderness tour scheduled this summer?''

"No, actually I'm getting out of the business. Family concerns."

"Oh, you're married?" she asked.

"Not even close. Are you?" Oddly enough, he was interested in knowing her status.

"No, but…"

"Then you're free to go yourself. You don't need me."

They were blocking the sidewalk. A big group of Japanese tourists passed on either side of them headed toward the big white museum building.

"It will pay really well. The guides have made a lot of money for Granville Publishing."

"How well?" He didn't want to be tempted, but money wasn't a minor consideration at this point in his life. If he could buy time to look around for something he really wanted to do… Wait a minute, what was he thinking?

"No." He said it to himself as much as to her. How could he parade around the country pretending to be an author? The whole idea was silly.

"If you don't do it, the sale to Pierpont might not happen. Mr. Granville isn't young. This may be his only chance to keep Granville Publishing alive after he retires. He's invested his whole career in it."

Mac had an injured grandmother and a career that was on hold. He didn't need to take on her problems, too.

He took a deep breath and looked into her eyes. No tears. One plus for her.

She mentioned a dollar amount for his services, and he felt as if she'd punched him in the solar plexus.

"You're kidding? What do you get from me for that? Body, soul and seven years of servitude?"

"Not quite." She giggled, probably in relief because he was weakening.

"Let me think it over," he said reluctantly, starting to walk again.

"How long?" she asked, doggedly staying by his side.

"Until I decide."

"How about tomorrow?"

She was tougher than she looked.

"Don't push," he warned.

"Can I at least call you tomorrow?"

"My cell phone number is 555-2626."

"I won't forget it," she promised.

"I bet you won't."

He walked away, leaving her behind, all too aware that her gaze followed him.

2

─────────

"GRAM, I'M HERE," Mac called as he opened the front door of his grandmother's isolated home.

As usual it was unlocked, but Sheba, Gram's aging Shetland, sounded an alarm with loud, sharp barks.

"Hey, remember me, Sheba," he said, stooping to let the brown-and-white miniature collie sniff, then lick his fingers.

He petted her bony but softly furred head and ran his hand through her thick ruff. The long hair was immaculately white in spite of the dog's habit of roaming the woods hunting for rabbits. Sheba kept it clean herself by licking it like a cat.

"She remembers you, all right," Cora Sully said, coming into the great room that ran the length of the house. "Sheba's older than I am in dog years, but her mind is as sharp as a pup's. Mine, too, as far as that goes."

Gram wasn't much for hugs and kisses, but Mac stood and planted a kiss on a darkly tanned cheek deeply scored by wrinkles.

"How's your wrist?" She wouldn't like the question, so he wanted to get it over with now.

"It's just cracked, no big deal, but Doc Ross put me in this plaster. Said he didn't trust me to wear one of those new things with straps. Don't know why his father had to retire. He was only seventy-one."

"Well, it's good to be here," Mac said, meaning it and ignoring her good-natured grumbling.

He loved the old house his grandparents had built themselves when they were newlyweds. As a kid, Sully had envied his father growing up here with his older brother, Walt, even though Richard Sully didn't have many fond childhood memories of the place. Dad had hated the hour-long bus ride to school and the way the town kids looked down on "backwoods" kids. Uncle Walt loved hunting, fishing and being out in the woods so much he'd become a forest ranger, but Mac's dad mostly remembered the chores and hardships of living in the remote wooded hills of southern Pennsylvania. Grandpa had eked out a living by selling the furniture he handcrafted and by driving a school bus. Gram had kept them fed by raising chickens and tending her huge garden, now greatly scaled down in size.

To Mac, the place had been his boyhood paradise. He loved the knotty-pine great room with Mission-oak furnishings his late grandfather had built. Gram had woven the braided rug on the floor using castoff clothing, and big muslin cushions and curtains had been dyed saffron and orange-brown from dye she made herself.

Behind the great room there used to be three small bedrooms, but a few years ago Sully's father had insisted on converting one of them into a bathroom with indoor plumbing. Most of all, Mac liked the big back room his grandfather had used as a workshop. The walls and floor were unvarnished planks warped and discolored by age, and the only furnishing was a long, battered workbench. But in his imagination, Mac could still smell his grandfather's pipe tobacco and freshly cut lumber, each board salvaged from fallen trees on their many acres of woodland.

"Are you hungry?" Gram asked. "I made you a sweet potato pie."

That explained the spicy smell coming from the kitchen at one end of the room where Gram still cooked on a wood-burning stove.

"I'm starved. How did you make it one-handed?"

One of his parents' big worries was that Cora wasn't eating enough.

"I broke my left wrist, not my back," she said.

He tried to help her with the midday meal, but she shooed him away with a wooden spoon, a threat he'd taken seriously as a kid.

"Nothing here I can't handle," she said, "including you."

He perched on an oak chair, the seat amazingly comfortable considering the hardness of the wood. Everything Grandpa had made was marvelously functional and comfortable. He had found a ready market for his work with a handcrafted-furniture specialist in Pittsburgh. Trouble was, Grandpa had often spent many weeks on a single piece, so the high prices his work commanded were never enough to relieve the couple's tight finances.

Gram served huge slices of homemade bread with jam she'd made from wild berries, thick creamy chicken soup and her sweet potato pie. Looking much like a little elf in her faded jeans and rusty orange tunic, she sliced the bread, holding it steady with her elbow. Her hair was silvery and tied in a long tail, and her small, triangular face was dominated by an impressively large nose and ears that looked like little wings on either side of her head. She'd never been a pretty woman, but Mac had always thought she was beautiful.

She didn't talk while she worked, and Mac's thoughts kept coming back to M. S. Stevens. It was hard to believe that such a gorgeous, delicate woman as Maggie Sanders had authored the *Extreme Adventure* guides. He'd expected someone like Ann Cartwright, who was tougher than ninety-nine percent of the people who signed up for his wilderness tours. Ann had iron-gray hair cut shorter than his—a lot shorter since he had a habit of not bothering to get a haircut— and legs like telephone poles.

Sheba rested her head on his knee and submitted to some absentminded petting while he tried to figure out what to do about Maggie's offer. He had some money in the bank since he'd learned frugal living from Gram, but he wanted to use it to build a cabin for himself near her. It would give him an excuse to keep an eye on her without the strain of two people as independent as they were trying to live in one house. He had almost enough cash for materials, and it was something he'd always wanted to do. Grandpa Charles had left him a couple of acres of wooded tract on the northern fringe of what was now Gram's property because Mac loved the outdoors even more than Uncle Walt. It was Grandpa's way of making sure part of his land stayed in the family.

"That skunk, Oliver Bronson, has been bothering me again," Gram said as she put a bowl of soup thick with homemade noodles on a woven orange-and-brown place mat in front of him. "Wants to steal my land and build fancy places for a bunch of city folks. He calls them 'gentlemen farmers.'" She snorted with derision.

"Over my dead body. I should oil your granddad's rifle and scare the pants off him."

"I'll have a word with him," Mac promised, sinking his teeth into a slice of whole-wheat bread so good he moaned his approval. "I've missed your bread."

"I'll bake some for you to take when you leave."

Here was the tricky part. If Gram thought he was there to baby-sit her, she'd have a fit.

"Maybe I'll hang around for a while."

"What about your job?" she asked suspiciously.

"The company went belly-up."

They'd folded without paying him for the last expedition he'd led on the Colorado River, but he didn't tell Gram that. If he built a halfway decent cabin, his money crunch would be real. Which brought him back to Maggie's offer. But damn, he couldn't see himself posing as a writer no matter how good the pay was.

"I think I'll look into building a cabin on the land Grandpa left me," he said, holding his spoon over the best chicken soup in the world.

"What do you want to do that for?"

"I'm thirty years old, Gram. Time I had a permanent place to stay between expeditions."

She sat across from him, her lip pursed in concentration.

"Makes sense, I guess."

"Maybe I'll go over to the lumberyard in Eighty Four," he said. "See what it might cost me. Want to come along?"

He knew a trip to the oddly named Pennsylvania town of Eighty Four wouldn't appeal to his grandmother, but he wanted her to know he was serious about a cabin.

"I'll pass. Older I get, the less use I have for towns."

"How's the cell phone working?"

His father had insisted she have one after she turned seventy-five. It was still a sore subject, although it had enabled her to call for help when she'd fallen.

"Dang stupid invention. That skunk Bronson calls me pretty near every month."

"I'll speak to him," Mac reassured her, although he knew the greatest threat to her independent living came from her own family.

His father was pressing her to move to Florida where he owned a boat dealership, turning a hobby into a second career after his retirement. Todd, Mac's lawyer brother, was pressuring her to go, too, partly because a gun club had offered a huge sum of money to turn her land into a private hunting preserve. Gram's sister-in-law, who'd never understood her brother Charles's lifestyle, was pushing, as well. Mac was the only one who understood and supported Cora Sully's determination to continue living in the house she'd helped build.

"If you didn't have a cell phone, you couldn't have called me," Mac reminded her.

If Gram made one phone call a year, she was really talking up a storm—by her standards.

"Surprised you weren't off in New Zealand someplace," she said, then took a tiny sip from the miniscule amount of soup in her bowl.

"Not this year. Anyway, you know I always love to come back here. Remember, I used to spend every possible day here when I was growing up in Pittsburgh. Who else would let me mountain bike down a real mountain?"

"Damn fool wild kid," she said, but her smile told her how much she adored him.

"Without you and Grandpa, I would've grown up a couch potato."

"Not you. You always loved the outdoors. It's in the genes, although your dad must take after my great-uncle Bill. That man lived alone over the family grocery store and didn't step foot outside from one year to the next."

"Don't get mad, Gram," Mac said cautiously, approaching a subject that was probably none of his business, "but are you okay on your doctor's bills?"

"I've got that government insurance."

"Did medicare cover all the expenses for your wrist?"

"Pretty close." She got up and cleared away her bowl, her soup barely touched.

"You should've let Dad buy you supplemental insurance."

"No damn sense in that. Why pay out money for nothing? I sold a little bitsy throw rug for seventy-five dollars last month. People are plain crazy to spend big bucks on things they could make themselves if they weren't so lazy. I can take care of my own bills."

Mac would have to call Doc Ross and settle her unpaid balance himself. Maybe he was just as stiff-necked as his grandmother, but he wouldn't go running to his father to get it paid. He didn't want Gram to get an I-told-you-so lecture about additional insurance. Anyway, she would toss him out on his ear if he tattled. Helping a person who didn't want to be helped was complicated and expensive.

He loved his rootless, nomadic lifestyle, but he was going to have to stay put for a while, he thought, watching Gram get up from the table and head for the couch. Maybe when the cabin was built, he could hire someone to live there and keep an eye on his grandmother in exchange for a rent-free place.

This still left the problem of a temporary income. He couldn't see himself driving a school bus, not that he could even get the position during the summer. Maggie Sanders's offer was looking better—and worse. If the job involved wearing a starched bush jacket and cutting his hair, he wouldn't touch it for any amount of money.

Gram nodded off on the bed of cushions and pillows on the couch, the first real sign of her slowdown. Mac went outside on the long wooden porch that ran the length of the front of the house. Later he'd have to climb up to the roof to see what repairs were still needed, another expense he'd have to handle.

Meanwhile, he had to do something much harder, and possibly more hazardous to a rootless bachelor if he let himself get interested in Maggie Sanders.

He dialed the number for Granville Publishing on his cell phone.

MAGGIE PATTED HER HAIR, adjusted the waist of her lime-green capri pants and smoothed her matching sleeveless sweater. Rayanne said this outfit made her look hot, but Maggie fervently wished she'd worn one her conservative suits, maybe the heather-gray. She looked like something people squeezed into a drink. What had made her think she could be more persuasive with Mac Sully if she dazzled him with neon-green?

But then, when she'd arranged to meet him for lunch, she hadn't been thinking like a successful professional. His voice reminded her of honey and melted butter—sweet, mellow and mesmerizing. If she'd been thinking straight, she would have insisted they meet in her office, but before her brain caught up with her tongue, she had a date to meet him at Deanna's Dinette.

It was a favorite lunch spot for people who worked in the area and only a few block's walk from her office. Ideal, except their meeting felt too much like a date. They could order malts and fries in the replica of a 1950s diner decorated in chrome and steel with red-leather banquettes. But could they hammer out a deal that would send him on the road to promote the guides and possibly cinch the sale for Mr. Granville?

Mac was late. Most of the diner's clientele were finishing lunch and leaving, so she and her guest wouldn't have trouble getting a table. She'd planned it that way, but she hadn't counted on cooling her heels while he took his own sweet time getting there.

"Honey, I'm saving the back corner for you," the owner said. "Do you want to be seated now?"

"Thanks, but I'll wait for my—" she nearly said "date" "—my business appointment."

Deanna snapped her pink bubble gum, her ode to the 1950s, and waved brightly polished pink nails toward the far end of the diner.

"Seat yourself whenever you like," she said, probably recognizing Maggie as a familiar face even if she wasn't a regular.

"Thanks."

Maggie was starving. She'd been far too nervous about meeting Mac to eat breakfast, and the huge slices of fluffy lemon meringue pie sitting under glass on the counter looked luscious enough to make her mouth pucker in anticipation.

The pie gave her a plan. She'd ply Sully with food until he'd agree to anything, all on the credit card Mr.

Granville was letting her use. She hoped Mac had a thing for half-pound burgers, crinkle-cut French fries and milkshakes topped with whipped cream and cherries, each one big enough for a family of four.

First he had to show up. Her wooden platform sandals were fine for walking, but not what she would have chosen for standing rigidly in place trying not to look as if she'd been stood up.

Then he walked through the door and her heart did the oddest little flip-flop before she remembered to smile.

"Sorry I'm a bit late," he said. "Traffic was heavier than I expected."

"No problem," she lied. "We can sit at the banquette back there in the corner."

She led the way, wondering whether the platforms made her hips wiggle. It wasn't a good start to a strictly business luncheon if he thought her buns looked like two limes bouncing against each other.

He waited until she was seated, then sat across from her with lots of room between them on the curving corner seat. Deanna hurried over to hand them menus and told them their server would be right over.

"Order anything you like. It's Mr. Granville's treat," Maggie told him.

He glanced briefly at the menu, then looked at her so intently she pretended not to notice. Could he be a throwback to the Neanderthals—a man who couldn't stand it if a woman picked up the check?

"Their cheeseburgers are famous," she said, looking into the little bits of brilliant blue sky captured in his eyes.

He hadn't shaved, and the stubble made his chin look even more manly. She'd always thought a strong chin was a sign of character, but that wouldn't necessarily make him easier to deal with. His face was rectangular with lean cheeks. His hair looked windblown, the top highlighted by the sun, and dark blond strands fell across his forehead.

He hadn't dressed for success. His black T-shirt had bluish-gray patches from countless washings, and his khaki trousers carried nondescript to a new level. She suspected he wanted to look too scruffy to be considered for the job.

Think again, Mr. Sully, she thought. You'll clean up just fine. She knew animal magnetism when she saw it, and his voice sent shivers down her spine. If a cool, rational woman such as herself was turned on by his bedroom eyes and seductive voice, he'd have women lining up for blocks to buy her latest book.

Mr. Granville could retire, Mr. Pierpont would be delighted by his successful acquisition, and Maggie could write more guides hiding behind Mac Sully's appealing presence.

"Did you hear a word I said?" Mac asked.

"Oh, sorry, I was concentrating on lunch."

"Were you?" He smiled in a teasing way.

She was busted but darned if she'd let him know he could trip her just by existing.

A round-faced, chubby boy came to take their order. Mac passed up all the luscious entrées calculated to tranquilize him into ready acceptance of her deal and ordered grilled fish filets with garlic-roasted vegetables. Maggie ordered a junior-size cheeseburger she didn't especially want just to show him he couldn't influence her with his healthy eating habits.

"Now, Mr. Sully…"

"Mac. I intend to call you Maggie, so you might as well call me Mac."

"Mac, I have a tentative agreement here." She dug into her oversize white canvas shoulder bag and pulled out a sheath of papers.

"I expected you to be more like Ann Cartwright, not such a dainty little thing."

Dainty? Ha! She'd show him how tough Maggie Sanders could be when it came to contracts.

"First, would you like to be represented by an agent?" she asked as a matter of fairness.

"Whatever for?" His scornful laugh gave her the shivers.

"This could turn out to be quite lucrative for you, but, of course, your attorney can advise you if you want to do your own negotiating."

"You mistake me for someone who wants a long-time commitment."

"No, I'm only authorized to offer a one-year contract. Then it will be up to the new owner to renew your contract."

"I go around pretending to be you for a whole year?"

She was losing him. She had to talk bottom line before he flatly refused.

"No, you'll be M. S. Stevens. It shouldn't be too difficult since you live what I only research and write about. There will be several appearances throughout the year, most of them only for a weekend. Why don't you read this for the specifics?"

She shoved the tentative contract toward him, watching his hands as he picked it up. He had long, tanned fingers with clean, neatly rounded nails, confirming that his unkempt look was mainly for her benefit. In fact, she couldn't force her eyes away as he held the papers. The fine sun-bleached hairs on his arms made her think of spun gold, and she wondered if his hair darkened as it spread to more secretive places.

Maybe she should have her head examined! Mac was the last man on the face of the earth who should trigger her fantasies. If she had it in her to live a rugged outdoor life like his, she wouldn't need him. She could get over her dread of public speaking, but she couldn't fill in the gap left by her lack of adventures. She'd lose credibility every time a potential reader asked a question she couldn't research on the computer before answering.

He did read fast. She didn't know if that was good or bad for her purposes.

"Let me get this straight," he said, pointing at the payment clause of the contract. "All I have to do is make the specified number of appearances wherever and whenever the company decides to send me, and you'll pay me this amount?"

Mr. Granville's generosity surprised her, too.

"Plus a small percentage of future royalties if you remain in the publisher's employ. Of course, you can do your own thing between appearances. Most will be on the eastern seaboard, and we'll try hard to work around your schedule."

"Damn! I hate this!" He reacted so angrily, she thought he wanted more money.

"It's a generous offer…" she began.

"Too generous. I'd be a fool to turn it down."

She slumped with relief, hardly noticing the server who was putting gigantic platters of food in front of them. She wasn't even sure she'd be able to open her mouth, let alone eat any of the golden-brown fries or three-cheese burger.

"Is that a yes?" she asked weakly.

"I'm still thinking about it."

"Did you notice the part about being a research consultant on the next guide? You'd be paid extra on an hourly basis."

"I read it."

"Then you won't mind giving me a little backup and possibly some personal insights on the next guide?"

"Be specific."

He started eating, acting as though becoming a future celebrity was as bad as making a dentist's appointment.

"Just let me pick your mind about your real adventures and use anything of value to enhance the next guide. I'm eager to learn anything you can teach me."

"Anything?"

He raised one expressive eyebrow. It was dark brown, so she probably could forget about golden hair sprinkled in unseen places.

This wasn't how a business meeting was supposed to go. She took a big bite of burger to give herself a moment to think. His "anything" sounded like a proposition. Maybe it was time to follow Rayanne's oft-given advice to get out more and meet some sexy devil.

"I would appreciate hearing about your wilderness experiences," she said primly, "with the aim of incorporating what you've learned firsthand into a new guide.

He chewed thoughtfully. He kept his long, inviting lips closed and didn't talk with his mouth full. Funny how she was noticing all his little characteristics, and she didn't even much like him.

"How appreciative would you be?" he asked.

He was too much! She should have left the negotiating to her boss. It wasn't just what Sully said; it was the way he made his words sound like a challenge. Lots of guys undressed women with their eyes. He made her wish he would do it to her for real.

"It's all in the contract!" she said, exasperated more by her own reaction to him than anything he actually said.

"I'll read it again and let you know."

"Fair enough." *Yeah, keep me in suspense, as if I have nothing to do but think about you.* "Will I hear from you soon?"

"Probably."

"Tomorrow?" No harm trying to pin him down.

"When I decide." He blotted his lips on one of the diner's huge paper napkins.

"It's really important to start working out the details of your tour." She had to stop watching his lips.

"Is that your job?"

"Well, I'll sort of supervise it, I guess." She didn't know what her responsibilities would be when Pierpont took over, but she didn't need to tell Sully that.

"Are you going on the tour, too?"

"That hasn't been decided. We have a small staff, lots to do."

"If I agree to let you throw me to the wolves, I expect you to come along as backup."

"I don't think that's Mr. Granville's intention." It certainly wasn't hers.

She was interrupted by the ringing of a cell phone. Not hers. Mac took his out of his pocket and answered it.

"Sully here."

There was a long pause. Someone had a lot to say to him.

"Hold on. I'll take care of it on my way home. He won't bother you again. I guarantee it."

He broke the connection without saying anything else.

"The woman in my life," he said with a grin. "Thanks for lunch. I'll be in touch."

And just like that, he left the diner without a backward glance, carrying the tentative contract with him.

Whoever the woman in his life was, she must be pretty special. He hadn't even finished his roasted potatoes, celery, carrots and onions. She slid his plate next to hers and tackled lunch in earnest, but it was his platter she cleaned.

3

"MAGGIE, HAS YOUR MAN signed the contract yet?"
Mr. Granville asked.

This Friday morning her boss looked more than ever
like an old-fashioned English butler. His neatly trimmed
beard came to a point above a starched white collar and
a small black bow tie. He wore a charcoal-pinstriped
suit and a vest with a gold watch chain.

"I'm sorry, not yet," she said, apologizing even
though it wasn't her fault Mr. Granville had jumped to
conclusions about Mac.

"Better hurry him along. It's been a few days since
Peter Pierpont met him."

Maggie understood why her boss was antsy. The sale
was coming down to the wire, and he wanted the family publishing firm to survive after he stopped running
it. Unfortunately he didn't have children or a close relative to take over.

"Give him a little nudge," Mr. Granville advised as
he moved away from the open doorway of her office.

Easier said than done! She hadn't been able to get
in touch with him even though she'd been calling his
cell phone. The address part of the contract was still
blank, so she couldn't go see him either. If he hadn't
been in such a rush to leave after his "woman" called
him, she might have gotten an answer about the job
then and not be stewing about his significant other now.

Scratch that! Mac's love life was no concern of hers unless it kept him from accepting the job. Drop-dead gorgeous men didn't walk around unattached and fancy-free, at least not the few she'd met. Of course, Sully might not appeal to every woman. She already knew he was stubborn and opinionated. Anyway, what woman in her right mind wanted a man who only dropped in between treks to the wilderness? Sometime in the future she wanted a mature, settled man, not an aging Boy Scout.

Maggie sat in front of her blank computer screen and fumed. She was an expert researcher. She should be able to find Sully. All she had to do was locate the company for which he worked.

An hour later she was stymied. His employers had passed into the never-never land of failed businesses, and it would take a master hacker to track down Sully based on what she knew about him. She wasn't even sure Mac was his given name.

One possibility remained, but it would cost her a lot of phone time.

Her parents, Len and Gayle, had recently retired from their combination hardware-locksmith business to discover the joys of nomad life. They'd bought a motor home and taken to the highways unencumbered by their car-sick, rash-covered, accident-prone daughter. Maggie tried their cell phone with predictable results. They'd either turned it off or, more likely, forgotten to charge it.

She couldn't call Annie, her older sister; she was with her airforce husband in Guam, where, hopefully, she wouldn't meet up with any of the horrendously long and dangerous tree snakes rampant there. Only Maggie was worried about it.

She could and did call Laurie, her younger sister, who was still living—she liked to call it house-sitting—at the family home in Beaumont, West Virginia. Laurie groomed dogs in the time she could spare from writing a romance novel and holding parties to sell candles.

Maggie wanted to ask her "little" sister—four inches taller and two decades younger in spirit—if she'd made any progress in "finding" herself, but she didn't have time for an argument.

Her phone call woke Laurie up.

"You know my muse is a creature of the night," Laurie protested sleepily. "My gosh, it isn't even noon."

"Do one tiny favor for me, and you can go back to your beauty sleep," Maggie said.

"Oh, don't tell me you want me to mail something!"

Two years ago Maggie had asked her to send a parka she'd left at home. Laurie still hadn't recovered from the trauma of finding a box, sealing and addressing it, and taking it to the post office.

"Nothing that complicated," Maggie assured her. "I just need Ann Cartwright's phone number. It's unlisted, but Mom will have it in her green address book in the top left drawer of her desk."

"She probably has it with her," Laurie whined, never one to wake up cheerful and helpful.

"It will be in the desk." Maggie had had years of practice being reasonable with her younger sister, who was as lovable as she was aggravating.

"Oh, okay."

Maggie logged onto her e-mail and worked through her messages while Laurie searched.

"I found it!" Laurie came back on the line sounding awake and triumphant. "Although why you want to call her, I'll never know. She scares me."

"That's silly. You're twenty-five and you should be over that. She just likes to play mother and tell you what to do because she doesn't have kids of her own to micromanage. Give me her number, please."

Maggie spent another ten minutes extracting the number from Laurie and catching up on family news before she could hang up and call Ann. Surprisingly, the frequent traveler was home.

"Maggie, good to hear from you," her mother's friend said. "I gave you a good review this time, didn't I? I'm going to post it online for my wilderness-adventure chat group."

If Maggie told her she hadn't read it, Ann might insist on finding her copy and reading the whole thing to her on the phone.

"The reason I'm calling, Ann—"

"Your advice on snakebite was a hoot!" Ann said with a roar of laughter. "Remember when you saw that tiny garter snake in your backyard? You wouldn't go outside for a month!"

"I was five years old!" Maggie protested. "Anyway, I confirmed my research by talking with an emergency-room doctor and a paramedic who'd been in the military."

Enough of the remember-when game. She needed Sully's number now.

"About that man you sent here—"

"Isn't Sully a cutie? If I were thirty years younger, I'd give my eyeteeth to snuggle down in his sleeping bag."

"Ann, can you tell me how to get in touch with him?"

"I can, but I don't know if I should. There's no taming that boy. He won't settle down until the next ice age, which, by the way, may come sooner than you think."

Besides wilderness treks, Ann's passion was predicting disasters. She and Maggie's mother had been friends since grade school, but their friendship was something of a puzzle given how different they were. Gayle Sanders was calm, serene and family oriented. Ann had tried marriage briefly—something like eighteen months—then tossed her husband's clothes on the front lawn and called it quits. Fortunately for her, a comfortable inheritance allowed her to do almost anything she wanted, including writing long critiques of the adventure guides.

Maggie liked her in spite of her reviews. She'd been the first to take the three Sanders girls to the Pittsburgh zoo and the first to buy them tubes of luscious lipstick, blush and eye shadow. Unfortunately, Ann's conversations were like meandering paths through dense woods with lots of detours.

"Mr. Sully dropped something in my office. Could you give me his address, and I'll mail it to him? Or I could call him if I knew his phone number."

"Dropped what?"

There was a reason why it was a bad idea to tell fibs to Ann.

"Just an envelope." Maggie tried to sound indifferent, but her lying skills needed work.

"Isn't it addressed to him?"

"No, it's just a plain white envelope."

"Well, open it. See if it's important," Ann said.

"I can't do that!" This, at least, was the truth, since there was no lost envelope.

"Well, let me dig around. I must have his address because I mailed him some photos I took on our first expedition together. Hold on."

She put the phone down with a clunk before Maggie could ask her to call back when she found it.

Twenty minutes later Ann gave her Mac's phone number and the address she'd used to mail the photos.

By then it was lunchtime, and Maggie had to meet an author she wanted to sign for a how-to book on water gardens.

She spent a lovely two hours talking about flowers with a charming, gracious Southern woman who wore a straw hat and white gloves for lunch at the diner. They settled the terms of her contract so easily, Maggie hated to press her luck by tackling Mac the same day.

At three-fifteen Mr. Granville poked his head into her office again.

"Did you sign our 'M. S. Stevens'?" he asked.

"I haven't been able to reach him yet, but we have the water garden book."

"Good, good, but make Sully the top priority. We need a successful tour to encourage Pierpont."

Maggie got up, closed the door after him and stabbed her finger at the phone to punch out Mac's number. It rang seven times, and she was about to give up when a woman answered.

"I ain't selling, and you know where you can stick your offer," a belligerent voice said.

"Maybe I have the wrong number," Maggie said. "I was calling Mr. Sully."

"Mr. Sully? That's a good one." The woman

laughed, and Maggie tried to guess her age. Definitely on the upside of fifty.

"Is he there?"

"Nope."

"Do you know when he'll be back?"

"When he gets hungry, I reckon. You a friend of his?"

"Well, I haven't known him long."

"Mac makes friends fast. Always did. When he was little, he'd charm the pants off everyone who met him. Still does."

"Can I leave a message for him?" The image of Mac charming her pants off was unsettling, to say the least.

"Sure, you can tell me anything. I'm Grandmother Sully."

Was this the woman in his life who'd called him away from their lunch?

"Mrs. Sully, this is Maggie Sanders…"

"You can call me Cora, Maggie. I don't hold with that Mrs. Sully business."

"Cora, I'd really appreciate it if he'd call me. I'll give you my number…"

"No need to go to all that trouble."

Trouble? She was beginning to believe "trouble" was Mac Sully's middle name.

"I really need to talk to him." If she sounded a little desperate, it was because she was.

"Just come on out for supper."

"Supper?" Invited or not, she couldn't drop in on him. The idea was preposterous!

"Be here at six or thereabouts. I promised Mac some venison stew."

Venison? She wouldn't dream of eating deer meat. In her world, people didn't put Bambi in a stew pot.

"I've no idea where you live," Maggie said.

"You can find Washington, Pennsylvania, can't you?"

"Yes, but I really don't think…"

"Well, write this down. The directions get a little complicated seeing as how the roads snake around in these hills like a drunk copperhead."

Reptiles get drunk? Maggie was out of her depth here, but she picked up a pencil and started scrawling directions just in case they came in handy sometime.

She used part of her brain to make a sketchy map and tried not to feel jubilant that Mac had rushed away from their luncheon for his grandmother's sake. How silly was it to be interested in a man she barely knew and wasn't even sure she liked? All she wanted from him was a temporary professional relationship.

What would happen if she showed up on his doorstep—well, his grandmother's doorstep, but her place might be his home base when he wasn't trekking in the wilderness.

"Got that?" Cora asked none too patiently. "You'll be fine as long as you fork left a quarter mile beyond the barn some addle-brained city folks painted purple. Probably thought it would look cute."

Maggie repeated the older woman's directions, wondering if she had enough nerve to follow them. The midsummer evenings were long. She could easily have dinner, get Mac's signature and be home before dark. Well, maybe "easily" was a bit optimistic since she'd have to pick venison out of the stew, convince Sully to sign and find her way back on roads that sounded like the stuff of her nightmares.

"See you." Cora hung up.

Was she brave enough to go? No, but what were the alternatives? Mac wasn't going to waltz into her office ready to do her bidding. He needed some persuading. If he didn't agree to front for her on the guides, she'd have to interview more drama students. But could she do that after Pierpont had already seen him? The corporate head obviously didn't need to add one small publishing company to his financial empire. He just seemed to like the idea of being a literary patron, especially for a macho series like her adventure guides.

To go or not to go? She made her decision and hoped she wouldn't get a flat tire on the way.

On the drive there she had time to wonder why Cora had been so hospitable. Maggie could be a bill collector or a process server for all Mac's grandmother knew. Did she think they were an item? No. Cora had no reason to believe she was Sully's girlfriend or even a potential one. Maggie tried to remember every detail of their conversation, and she was sure she hadn't shown the slightest hint of personal interest.

Once she left the highway, she had to navigate roads so winding and narrow, two-way traffic seemed impossible. She dreaded meeting another car head-on and was horrified when a dingy blue pickup raced toward her on a sharp curve that didn't seem wide enough for even one vehicle. The unsavory character driving it managed to get past her with all of a half-inch to spare.

Her heart was beating normally by the time she turned off onto a dirt road that threatened to ruin the shocks on her aging hatchback.

The drive was scary, but Maggie really felt as if she'd dropped off the planet when she negotiated a hairpin turn and pulled up in front of a rustic home that looked like something out of a history book.

Her nerve nearly failed her. She got out of the car debating whether to hightail it home when the screen door opened and an elderly woman with her arm in a cast stepped out onto the porch.

Growing up in West Virginia, Maggie had seen people who lived in hollers and didn't venture into a coal town like Beaumont more than twice in a lifetime. The stooped woman in faded jeans and green muslin tunic had the look of a mountain woman though apparently held little wariness or suspicion of strangers. "Come on in and make yourself at home," she said, holding the screen door open when Maggie got to the porch. She smiled broadly and Maggie started to forget the hazardous drive she'd made to get here.

"It was nice of you to invite me, Mrs. Sully."

"Remember I told you to call me Cora. I don't hold with formalities."

Maggie was a little surprised to hear the word *formalities* coming from a woman who lived in such primitive surroundings. She didn't know what to expect from Mac or his grandmother, but she couldn't fault the woman on her hospitality.

Cora ushered Maggie into a rustic but cozy great room as if she were visiting royalty.

"I love your colors," Maggie said, genuinely impressed by the warm woodsy hue of the knotty-pine walls and the rich natural tones in the braided rug and couch cushions.

"Make my own dyes," Cora said, obviously a statement of fact, not a ploy for more compliments. "Where did you meet my boy, Mac? One of his expeditions?"

"No, no, I'm not the outdoor type. A friend of my

mother's sent him to my office to deliver something.'' When Cora looked blank, she added, ''In Pittsburgh. Where is Mac?''

''Expect he'll be back anytime now. Sit yourself down. I gotta give the stew a stir.''

''Can I help you with anything?''

For a brief instant Cora looked offended, as though Maggie wanted to intrude on her territory.

''I run a one-cook kitchen,'' she explained. ''Don't be fooled by this cursed cast. There's nothing around here I can't handle except maybe finishing the roof repairs.''

''If you even think of going up on the roof again, I'll hog-tie you and deliver you to Dad in Florida,'' Mac said with mock severity as he came into the room, letting the screen door slam shut behind him. ''I didn't know we were having company.''

He didn't sound delighted by Maggie's presence.

''Your grandmother asked me—''

''I bet she did.''

His voice was flat, but there was no mistaking the frown lines on his brow. His welcome was as cool as his grandmother's was warm.

''No reason why your lady friend shouldn't have a plate of stew with us,'' Cora said, her faded blue eyes watching both of them with undisguised curiosity.

''Miss Sanders isn't my lady friend.''

The way he said it made Maggie want to run for her car. If she irritated him that much just by being here, what chance did she have of getting him to sign the contract?

''I'll be putting things on the table,'' Cora said, but she was obviously much more interested in them than dinner.

Mac seemed taller than he had in her office now that he was standing under the low, painted boards of the ceiling. He was wearing old jeans, threadbare at the knees, and a black T-shirt that exposed impressive muscles on his shoulders and arms. He had smooth, sun-bronzed skin and a lean, athletic build that made him look invincible. He was a hero type if she'd ever seen one, but he was scowling at her with hooded eyes.

"Go take care of dinner," Mac told his grandmother.

Cora scurried over to the kitchen end of the big room with an indignant little sniff.

"You never bring your friends to see your old granny," she said.

"My old granny is the number one woman in my life, and she'd better keep that in mind the next time she tries to play matchmaker."

Their banter was good-natured. Maggie relaxed a little, but she still didn't know whether to run for her car or to launch into her spiel about the advantages of the job she was offering.

Cora was playing Cupid for her bachelor grandson? That must mean he was unattached, which, of course, had absolutely nothing to do with her. She was here on business. She wasn't the least bit attracted to Mac. Lots of men had unruly hair touched with gold and melodic voices that gave a girl the shivers. It was only natural for a woman to admire a flat stomach and the impressive bulge above his powerful thighs. Sure, he had a spectacular rear with round, tight buns, but that didn't mean she was at all interested in him as a man. There was no chemistry between Sully and her. Even his grandmother must realize that.

"I came to offer Mac a job," she said, feeling she owed Cora an explanation.

His grandmother looked up from stirring the contents of a big yellow-enameled pot with a wooden spoon.

"What kind of job?"

"A consultant position with the publishing company where I work."

"Consultant?"

Cora seemed to be pondering the word while storm clouds gathered on Mac's face.

"We need his expertise on a series of wilderness adventure guides."

"You need my body," he said.

Cora dropped the spoon into her pot and came back to the living area where Mac stood in front of Maggie, his feet apart, fists clenched at his sides.

"Exactly what are you two up to?" Cora asked. She looked like an adult poised to break up feuding children.

Maggie was embarrassed. She shouldn't have come, not without explaining why she wanted to talk to Mac.

"Miss Sanders," he said, without trying to conceal his irritation, "writes a series of extreme adventure guides, although her idea of outdoor life is walking to her car."

That was so unfair—and true—that Maggie stood to her full five-foot-two-inches and glowered at him.

"She wants me—"

"My publisher wants you!"

Mac sighed. "They want me to pretend I wrote the guides. That means going on a promotional tour, giving talks, signing the damn books…"

"Watch your mouth, young man. You know I don't hold with cussing," his grandmother warned.

"It pays a whole lot better than playing nursemaid to a bunch of wanna-be explorers," Maggie said, not pulling her punches since she suspected he'd say no regardless of her arguments.

"It pays?" Cora sounded a lot more interested than Mac.

"Some people don't want to live their lives with their butts glued to chairs. If you ever got out from behind your damn computer..."

"MacDonald Horatio Sully! You're not too big to have your mouth washed out with soap!"

The tiny octogenarian's threat was so ludicrous, Maggie laughed. Even Mac grinned, maybe more in exasperation than amusement.

"MacDonald Horatio?" Maggie asked.

"My father has a nautical obsession. Horatio Nelson, Horatio Hornblower..."

Cora was chuckling, and Maggie let her tension dissolve with a good belly laugh. She didn't stop until a heavy knock shook the screen door.

"Hi, neighbor."

Cora scurried over, apparently energized by anger.

"Oliver Bronson, you drag your worthless carcass back to your automobile." She turned to Mac. "You told me you warned him off."

"I went to his office twice and tried his house. He's hard to find."

The newcomer came inside without being asked. He wasn't someone Maggie would invite in. He was taller than Mac by a few inches, maybe two or three, and "portly" was a polite way to describe him. The man seemed to be all stomach, a fancy snakeskin belt that circled his middle like the line marking the equator on a globe separated dull gray pants and a wrinkled white dress shirt. He had thinning black hair, beady brown eyes and plump, wet lips.

Maggie glanced at Cora's face and hoped the little woman never got that mad at her.

"Oliver," Mac said, sounding calm and reasonable, "my grandmother has no intention of selling any of her land. If she ever decides differently, we'll give you a chance to bid on it, providing you don't bother her with more unwanted offers. Now, I have a contract to discuss with Miss Sanders, my editor at Granville Publications." He nodded at her by way of introduction. "So you'll have to excuse us."

"Nice to meet you, miss." He held out a moist palm, and she reluctantly let him shake her hand while she acknowledged the introduction.

"I understand, Mac," Bronson continued. "Sorry to be a pest, but I do have buyers clamoring for prime land like your grandma's. I'll go now."

"And don't come back," Cora warned. "I've still got my husband's deer rifle and don't think for one minute I can't use it."

She shook her cast at him as he left.

Mac had told the man he intended to discuss a contract. Did that mean he planned to take the job? Maggie waited in suspense while Mac followed Bronson out to a white Cadillac that looked too huge to turn around on the hilltop trail. He was backing away when Mac returned.

His scowl didn't bode well for contract negotiations.

4

MAC WATCHED his unexpected guest push aside the chunks of venison in the stew and fervently wished she wasn't so darn cute. Her dark brown hair curled over her ears no matter how often she pushed it behind them. Her eyes were the color of bittersweet chocolate and her luscious lips were a natural pink that was more flattering than any artificial color could be. Even her cheeks had only a slight pink tinge. She was wearing tight-fitting tan slacks with a silky black top that revealed a slash of pale skin between her breasts. Her shoulders and arms were bare and untanned. She was a hothouse flower if he'd ever seen one—definitely not his kind of woman. But she was gorgeous. She'd be easier to deal with if he wasn't distracted by her good looks.

"How's the stew?" he asked, wondering if she were a vegetarian.

"Delicious." She put a chunk of carrot in her mouth to demonstrate enthusiasm.

"Are you saving the meat to eat last?"

He was being evil, of course, but Maggie was here to turn his life upside down. He didn't like it even though he needed the job. It would allow him to help Gram and to build his cabin without much financial strain, but he hated the idea of pretending to be M. S.

Stevens. He'd feel like a sideshow freak. He hated even thinking about it.

"I'm not used to wild game," she said primly.

He'd like to show her what wild was. Six weeks away from civilization, living in a tent and eating off the land would teach her how silly it was to write adventure guides without getting up from her computer.

"Then you haven't actually tasted any of the emergency food you wrote about in your last book? Grubs, grasshoppers…"

"No! I mean a writer doesn't have to experience everything firsthand. People write about Mars, but no one has been there."

"Taste the meat in your stew," Mac said.

"What?"

"If you want me to talk contract, eat a piece of the venison."

Gram came back from the stove where she'd refilled his bowl. She put the heavy white stoneware dish in front of him.

"Some folks aren't meat-eaters," Gram said.

"Are you a vegetarian?" he asked.

"No, but…"

"Try the venison."

It was like coaxing a stubborn child to eat, but he wanted her to refuse. He wanted an excuse to turn down the job. Gram would call it cutting off his nose to spite his face.

"All right, I will."

She was mad, but she spooned a little chunk of venison along with a big piece of onion.

He wanted to point out that it didn't taste bad, but Gram was giving him the evil eye.

Maggie chewed, but, he suspected, swallowed the little piece of meat whole.

"There," she said triumphantly.

"Okay, I guess you can have dessert," he said, trying not to snicker.

They finished the meal with dishes of spicy applesauce Gram had preserved in mason jars the previous year.

"I'll help you clean up," Maggie offered, "but I can't stay much longer. I want to drive back before it gets dark."

"And the bears come out," Mac teased, beginning to think of a plan.

"You two have your talk," Gram insisted. "I don't need help."

Maggie made a token protest, then gave in. Mac didn't suppose Gram would actually whack her with a wooden spoon if she invaded the kitchen space, but he was glad Maggie hadn't insisted on helping; it riled Gram to have anyone else in her territory.

"Let's talk on the porch," he suggested.

Maggie thanked his grandmother for the meal and followed him outside, taking her purse for a quick getaway. Mac felt challenged to keep her there awhile, if only to show her he wasn't easy to buy. It wouldn't be fully dark for another hour and a half, so there wasn't any chance she'd get lost in the mountains unless she was a total klutz. He knew from years of leading expeditions that some people should never leave their own backyards. If she was one of them, she shouldn't be giving advice to people who actually experienced outdoor life.

"It's nice here," she said.

No doubt she was only making conversation. He'd

seen her check her watch twice in the last couple of minutes.

"A lot of people don't realize places like this exist fifty miles from Pittsburgh," he said.

He wanted to get on with the contract business, if only to be done with it, but he was curious to see how she'd bring up the subject. How did she plan to convince him to sign? He was tired of small talk and would be relieved when she finally got to the point of her visit.

"About the book-signing tour…"

"What's the itinerary?" he asked.

"Well, it's not set in concrete yet, but Philadelphia, Baltimore and Washington, D.C., are on the list."

"You're the one planning it?" He leaned against one of the porch supports and watched her with narrowed eyes.

"I have input. Mr. Granville's secretary will handle the details."

"I'm not sure I should leave my grandmother alone right now."

Maggie nodded her understanding. "How did she break her wrist?"

"Fell off the roof—" he pointed upward "—trying to do her own repairs. She was lucky it wasn't her neck."

"Oh." She sounded skeptical.

"Are you going on this tour?" he asked.

"It hasn't been decided. I'm not much of a traveler."

"Why not?"

"I'm a jinx. Things happen to me when I travel. Storms, floods, accidents, illnesses, rashes, bug bites, motion sickness. The list is endless. I'm a walking case of bad luck."

"I don't believe in luck." Not entirely true. Maggie could be bad luck—or good. He didn't know which yet.

"If I go, you go," he said.

He hadn't planned to say that, but it made sense. If she got him into this, she could tag along as his coach. He knew squat about writing books and was no actor, but he could earn as much in a year as he could leading expeditions. He liked the idea of her going even though he still hated the necessity of taking the job.

"I don't think I should go," she said.

"Don't think about it now. Come on, I'll show you where I'm going to build a cabin."

"I really don't have time."

"Sure you do. If it gets dark, I'll lead you to the highway," he promised.

He grasped her hand and squelched any more objections by taking her off the porch. At least she was wearing little canvas shoes with ties. Maybe she could walk to the cabin site without stumbling, but to be sure, he planned to keep a tight grip on her hand.

She tried to jerk it away and he was surprised by her strength. Her palm was soft, but her fingers were long, lean digits that nearly slipped from his grasp.

"You don't need to hold my hand," she protested.

"Okay, grab my arm. The trail is a little rough, and I don't want to take care of two women with fractures."

"Your grandmother seems to take care of herself very well."

"Yes, when she doesn't try to do everything herself."

Sheba followed them, and Mac let the dog race ahead, nose to the ground, doing what she lived to do. Canines and humans were either adventuresome or they weren't.

"What about ticks?" Maggie asked, gripping his bicep so hard her nails dug into his skin.

"Don't worry. Our ticks don't lie around waiting to be stepped on. They climb trees and dive-bomb intruders."

"You're kidding."

"You're the wilderness expert. Am I kidding?"

She sputtered and let go of him. He checked his arm for marks where her nails had dug into him, then grabbed her hand again.

"I'm kidding. With Sheba leading the way, all we have to worry about is bears."

"Bears! I really think it's time for me to go home."

"I'm not coming to your office to sign a contract. Of course, you could come back here tomorrow. If you leave around seven in the morning, you might catch me before I go to the lumberyard."

"You're really going to build a cabin here by your grandmother's home?"

"My grandfather left me a part of the property. I've always planned to put up a little place. It gives me an excuse to keep an eye on Gram. My dad wants her to sell out and live in an old folks' community in Florida, but she'd hate it."

The sun hadn't set yet, but the path was dark in the shadow of the trees. Maggie stumbled on an exposed root and went down on one knee. His grip kept her from sprawling on her face.

She said a few choice words when she saw the stain on her pants. The girl had quite a vocabulary when she was mad. He pulled her to her feet, then bent to brush the dirt off her knee.

"Never mind! I don't need your help!" she said.

"Funny, I thought that's why you came."

"I didn't come for a back-to-nature tour."

"Okay. Be sure you take the right fork going back, not the left. If you come to a little brook, you're lost. But I guess a wilderness expert like you can find her way back."

"Take me back!"

"I'm not ready to go back. I loved your chapter on the wildlife of the mid-Atlantic region. I pictured the author running with wolves, staring down bears…"

"I research the *Extreme Adventure* guides on the Internet, then interview experts. That's why I need you to front for me."

"You do need me. That's why you're going to have a look at my cabin site."

She muttered something he didn't catch and started gingerly picking her way forward on the path as it went uphill. The way up to the ridge was steep and she had to work hard to keep from sliding back down. He grinned, glad he could have his lumber trucked in on an old logging road not far from the path instead of hauling it up to the site this way.

For the moment he was enjoying himself immensely. He was partial to strong legs and sexy butts on women, and Maggie was giving him an immensely satisfying view of hers. He would prefer stronger light since it was getting darker and fewer clothes—make that no clothes—but a man had to take his pleasure where he could.

She was panting now. On an especially steep stretch she paused, gasping for breath. He gave her a push from behind to get her going again, liking the way her buttock tightened under his hand.

"Stop that!" She reached behind and slapped his hand away.

"If you want to get home soon, you'd better keep moving."

Her answer was an anguished wail, but she scurried up to the top of the ridge. He came up behind her and put his arm around her shoulders, but she didn't seem to notice.

"This is—" she gulped air "—spectacular."

He loved the spot with its dramatic view overlooking miles and miles of rolling hills and unspoiled forests. The sun was low in the west and he wanted to stay there until the sky was streaked with pinks and oranges. He wanted her to see the fiery ball of sun disappearing behind Sully's Ridge.

"It's my favorite place," he said.

Words weren't adequate for the way he felt about his land. When he was here, he forgot about all the other places in the world he wanted to see. He didn't mind putting his wanderlust on hold to build his cabin.

She was quiet for several minutes. Sully's Ridge, his name for it, had that effect on people, not that he'd shared it with many others. When he did bring friends here, he was too often disappointed in their reactions, maybe because no one loved it quite the way he did.

"I can see why you're building here," she said at last. "But will you have water, electricity, heat, things like that?"

He laughed. "You'd be surprised how unimportant the comforts of civilization are."

"You have to have water. You'll freeze in the winter without heat."

"I'll haul water until I can pipe some in from a stream about three hundred yards away. I thought of building a fireplace, but I think I'll settle for a cast-iron stove. I know a guy who has one stored in his barn. If he needs the cash, he may sell it to me."

"Is this going to be your home?"

"When I'm in this part of the country. I did rent a room in a boarding house in Washington, Pennsylvania, but I gave it up to build the cabin. All my stuff is stored at Gram's now, but that's only temporary. Neither of us needs or wants a permanent roommate."

"But it's so isolated."

She scuffed her toe in the dirt and weeds underfoot as though testing the soil.

"It's too rocky to dig a foundation, although I might like a root cellar someday. Depends on how much time I spend here."

"I can see why you like to come here. It's so unspoiled."

"Wait until you see the sunset."

He put his hand on her shoulder and pointed to the ridge where the sun was starting to disappear.

"What time is it?" She checked her watch, for maybe the eleventh time since they'd left the house. "I have to start home."

"Why not camp out here with me tonight? You've never seen stars until you watch the night sky from here."

"I can't do that! I have things to do and—"

"Tomorrow's Saturday. What do you have to do that won't wait?"

"That's not the point. I can't camp out. I don't have equipment, clothes."

"Sure you're not afraid? Maybe afraid of me?"

"Of course not! But I don't even have a tooth-brush."

"Gram has spares of everything. She hates to go into town, especially since she has to get someone to drive her when I'm not here."

"I cannot spend the night here!"

Mac heard the alarm in her voice. He'd shepherded enough novice adventurers to recognize panic when he heard it. Knowing how to steady a nervous camper, he especially relished the challenge of making the *Extreme Adventure* author's experience a little of what she wrote about.

"I'll put up a tent and zip us inside. No reason to be frightened."

"I'm not sleeping with you."

"I'm not suggesting you do. We'll have separate sleeping bags. You can trust me not to crawl into yours in the night. I do this kind of thing for a living."

Of course, while he was rarely tempted by a body like hers, he wouldn't come on to her. He knew trouble when he saw it, and she was definitely not his type. She wasn't the kind of woman to take life as it came with no commitments. He'd tried relationships several times, but had never found a woman who'd follow him anywhere without strings.

"Why do you want me to sleep outside in a tent?" she asked angrily.

"You want me to work in an alien environment—big-city bookstores. I wonder if you have enough guts to step outside your little cocoon."

"It's not the same thing at all. I'm offering you a job. I don't have to prove anything to you."

"I'm not trying to strand you on a desert island.

Scouts camp in more remote places than this. We can get everything we need at my grandmother's."

"You're insane! I'm not going to spend the night with you."

"Suit yourself. I won't sign the contract."

"That's blackmail!"

"No, it's fair play. You want me to pretend I write advice books about surviving in the wilderness. You know zip about outdoor living. If M. S. Stevens doesn't have enough guts to sleep out on a perfect summer evening—not a cloud in the sky—I don't want anything to do with it."

"So you're saying if I sleep with you tonight, you'll sign the contract." Her voice was so low and angry, he had to strain to hear.

"No, it's not about sleeping *with* me. If I wanted to make a move on you, I'm be smart enough to seduce you in a soft bed in a fancy hotel."

"You couldn't seduce me anywhere! You're arrogant and high-handed and..."

"Then we understand each other. You stay in your sleeping bag, I'll stay in mine. If you last until daybreak, I'll sign the contract. Refuse, and you blow the deal."

"That's despicable!"

He shrugged.

"You don't have to like it. Just prove to me you're not a total phony."

"Phony!"

He let her sputter and protest a few more minutes because they both knew she was going to spend the night. He'd probably feel safer sharing his tent with a bobcat, but Maggie Sanders was *going* to camp out on Sully's Ridge.

5

THIS WAS A NIGHTMARE. Maggie wanted to wake up in her own little bed with the pillowcases her grandmother had embroidered years ago.

She watched as Mac took out a bundle he'd carried up to the ridge. She was hoping his tent had been chewed by the dog or shredded by mice—anything so he'd cancel their camp-out. Unfortunately he set it up as easily as if he'd opened an umbrella.

"As promised," he said with satisfaction. "Big enough for two sleeping bags, rainproof and cozy."

He unzipped the front flap and invited her inspection. She popped her head into the low, domed cubicle, not quite believing she'd agreed to spend the night in it.

"Nylon floor and a window with a fine mesh so we can open it if the tent gets stuffy. All the comforts of home."

"If you happen to be a raccoon," she said.

Sheba investigated the tent, sniffing all sides until she was satisfied with her inspection.

"Is Sheba sleeping with us?" she asked hopefully.

"No, she'll go home when the novelty wears off. She knows her job is watching Gram."

"How did she get here? She didn't come up the path with us."

Maggie's calves ached from making the steep climb twice, the second time with a pack on her back.

"It's easier for her to cut through the woods. Not as steep."

"Here, Sheba," Maggie called, stooping to pet the dog when she came.

She played with Sheba for a couple of minutes while Mac put the rest of the gear in the tent. She didn't see how there'd be room for both of them and their packs, not without... Well, they certainly wouldn't be snuggling.

"Ordinarily everyone pitches in to set up camp," he said.

"This wasn't my idea. You can pitch away by yourself."

"Lazybones usually find sand in their boots and their clothes tied in knots," he teased.

"Lucky for me I don't have boots and I'm wearing all my clothes."

"That flannel shirt of mine will feel good tonight when it cools down."

She loved the outdoorsy smell of the shirt he'd taken off the clothesline behind the house, but wouldn't admit it to him. As far as she was concerned, he was blackmailing her into this overnight ordeal.

She couldn't fault the sunset, though. The horizon was streaked with vibrant pinks and oranges as an incredibly large sun dropped behind a distant ridge. The two of them stood, watching the sky, and some of her hostility ebbed away.

"Now what do we do?" she asked when the colors smeared and lost their brilliance.

"I'll dig a little pit while you gather some sticks. I cleared the brush on the ridge last time I was here, so it's safe to make a small fire."

"It's warm. We don't need a fire."

"Are you ready to sleep?"

She wasn't going to close an eye until she was safely back in her own bed, but Mac didn't need to know that.

"I suppose it's too early," she said.

"Didn't you write a segment on fire as a camper's friend?"

"I guess."

Why did he make her feel like a kid caught telling fibs?

"Well, I like a campfire. Go find fuel."

He took a small fold-up shovel out of his backpack and started digging.

"You brought a shovel for one night?"

"Never know when a hole will come in handy. There are no powder rooms up here."

She'd taken care of that back at the house when she'd brushed her teeth with a new toothbrush Gram had provided. If nature called, she'd cross that bridge when she got to it.

The woods behind them were dark and uninviting, but she managed to find a handful of twigs and sticks without going too close to their murky depths.

"Is that all?" Mac asked, frowning at her meager handful. He walked to the closest tree and snapped off a few dead branches, reducing them to convenient size for their fire.

"This should do." He knelt and piled the sticks, using a few dry leaves to fuel the flames. At least he used matches from a metal container. She'd half expected him to strike sparks with flint just to show her how hard it was to follow the advice she'd given in chapter six of the last guide.

The sky gradually became a canopy of midnight-blue, and the first stars became visible as pinpricks of twinkling light.

He gallantly produced a plastic garbage bag for her to sit on so she wouldn't stain her slacks, and he didn't make a big deal out of draping his flannel shirt over her bare shoulders. He even came up with some bug-repellent cream.

"You must take good care of your clients," she said.

"I bring them back alive and hopefully uninjured. The ones who think they know everything are the real problems."

"I still think it stinks that you're making me do this."

"Relax. You might enjoy yourself."

"I don't call this an adventure," she rumbled.

He was sitting so close his knee pressed against hers. He'd changed into sweatpants and an old sweatshirt, and she had to admit the ridge cooled quickly after the sun went down.

"There are different kinds of adventures," he said.

He wasn't whispering, but his voice was low and soothing. The meager firelight didn't reach his face. All she could see was a dark profile, but the blaze did illuminate his hands resting on his thighs. He was sitting the same way she was, the way school kids sat when listening to a story. She was uncomfortably aware of his pants stretched taut over his upper legs and the dark hollow between them. She couldn't imagine spending weeks in the wilderness with a man who could turn her on just by blinking his eyes.

"Well, what do we do now?" she asked.

How on earth could she crawl into a tiny tent with this man? She had butterflies in her stomach and a jumpy feeling right below her navel just thinking about it.

"Watch the stars come out. Enjoy the peace and quiet." His voice dropped to a sexy whisper. "Or I can suggest something else."

"Um, do you know the names of the stars?"

"Do you want a lesson in astronomy? I thought all you wanted from me was survival tips."

"I want you to tell me things, not demonstrate them."

"Too bad. I'm pretty much a hands-on instructor."

"Let's play a game," she suggested with feigned cheerfulness. "How about truth or dare?"

There were some questions she'd love to ask him and they had nothing to do with back-to-nature stuff.

"Okay, I'll ask first. How many men have you slept with?"

"I'm not going to answer that!" No way would she admit her total was two, one a not particularly pleasant experiment in college and the other a short-lived affair with a stockbroker who got so depressed when the market was down he stayed down, too.

"Okay, your dare is to dance naked around the fire."

"That's not fair! I'm not going to do either."

"Okay," Mac said. "Here's an easier one with no dare. Why are you living your life vicariously? You're obviously fascinated by extreme adventures, so why no adventure in your life?"

"I have a very interesting life." At least she'd thought so until she'd met Sully.

"I don't think so. You go to work, come home. Then what?"

"I do things. I have friends." She didn't want to talk about this.

"Men friends?"

"Not at the moment, but I keep busy."

"Keeping busy isn't living. Where's the passion in your life?"

"Mr. Sully, your questions go way beyond any possible professional relationship we might have. I'm only here to take care of signing the contract."

"Are you telling me to mind my own business?"

"Emphatically yes."

She wanted to go home. This wasn't the right time in her life for adventure—or romance. She'd know when she was ready. She should ask him some personal, embarrassing questions to see how he liked it. For instance, why was his grandmother the main woman in his life? Why was he living day-to-day instead of making plans for his future?

"Then let's tell spooky stories," Mac suggested. "I'll go first."

"It sounds like something kids would do."

"My story begins when Sid and Amy wanted a place to be alone," he said.

"Who are Sid and Amy?"

"A nice young couple. Don't edit my story."

"Sorry." She wasn't.

"They drove to a heavily wooded area outside of town."

"What town?"

"Oliver, Ohio. They turned off on a rutted dirt road where couples like to park."

"A make-out spot?"

"Yes." He took a deep breath and sighed in exasperation.

"Thank you. I like specific details."

Mac threw a few more sticks on the fire. They flared

up, letting her see his face. He was looking directly at her with an expression that told her to shut up.

"Sid turned on the car radio. He wanted some romantic mood music, and it must have worked. He had Amy's panties off when—"

"This doesn't sound like a spooky story to me." She shifted, telling herself she was only trying to get more comfortable.

"Be patient, that part is coming…. A voice interrupted the music on the radio to warn that a serial killer with a hook for a hand had escaped. Two sheriff's deputies had been transporting him to an institution where he'd be incarcerated for life. He'd left them both horribly mauled and near death."

"Were they taking him to prison?"

"No, an insane asylum."

"I don't think they still call them that."

"That's what I'm calling it. Amy and Sid were pretty wrapped up in each other, so they just turned the radio off and got on with it. The killer was supposedly somewhere in their county, but they were more interested in each other."

The fire got lower, and so did Mac's voice.

"Until they heard an odd scratching noise on the roof of the car. They ignored it at first. It could have been the wind shaking a branch or a raccoon on night patrol. They were young. They were in love. It had taken Sid six months to get this far."

"I wouldn't call this a scary story."

"Then the scratching got louder. Sid was going to get out to have a look, but Amy freaked."

"I would, too. It sounds like a lousy place to—"

"Amy didn't want him to get out, but he was really unhappy about the interruption. He made sure the car was locked up tight, the windows up. He wanted to go back to where they'd left off, but Amy was too spooked."

"Why is it always the woman who gets the wimpy part?"

"Then there was a terrible squeal of metal on metal. Sid didn't need any more convincing. He gunned the motor, spun the wheels in the dirt and reversed the car at top speed until there was a spot where he could make a U-turn."

"So they high-tailed it out of there."

"Yes, but the evening was ruined and Sid felt like a damn fool for panicking because a branch had scraped the car. When he got Amy home, he came around to her side of the car to open the door."

"At least he was a gentleman about that," Maggie mumbled.

"He was horrified to see a hook caught between the door and the frame. The serial killer had tried to pry it open like a can of sardines."

"And the killer's name was Captain Hook," she scoffed. "Really, one-handed men haven't worn hooks since pirate days, if then." It took a lot more than an urban legend to send her down the mountain.

"Well, see if you can tell a better one," he said, leaning back with his arms behind his head.

"I only went to summer camp once. I don't know any campfire stories. Do you mind if we go to sleep now?"

The great outdoorsman would probably fall asleep right away, but she expected to be wide awake until dawn. How could she possibly close her eyes with nothing but a flimsy tent as shelter.

"Sure. Anything you need to do?" he asked.

"Let me go first and slip out of my shoes and slacks. They're a little snug for sleeping."

"I'll be on guard out here," he teased.

She noticed that Sheba had deserted them. The dog wasn't dumb. She probably had a nice soft bed waiting for her in Cora's house.

The tent seemed even smaller with two sleeping bags laid out side by side. Maggie sat in the dark and wiggled out of her slacks, folding them and putting them in what she hoped was the backpack Mac had loaned her. His shirt came to her knees, modest enough by anyone's standards. She was glad he'd made her take it, which did not mean she wanted to be out in the wilds sharing a tent with a man she hardly knew—or with anyone else.

She couldn't believe Mac had told her such a silly story. A hook for a hand and a horny hero? She'd heard better ones at slumber parties when she was a kid, and they hadn't included a panicky woman who lost her panties.

"May I come in?"

Mac stooped outside the entrance where the closure was unzipped. He'd extinguished the campfire so the dark form could've been anyone, but his voice was distinctive, low-pitched and masculine, with an irresistible twang that gave her the shivers. This man was going to crawl in beside her in a space the size of a doghouse.

"Just a sec."

She fumbled with the zipper on the sleeping bag and managed to open it enough to slither inside. When she was covered from toes to neck, she told him to come in.

"Comfy?" he asked.

"Fine," she lied. She could feel every lump, pebble and stick on the ground under the plastic floor of the tent.

"I'll tuck you in, tell you a bedtime story if you like."

"No, thank you!"

She expected him to pop into the other sleeping bag, but instead he seemed to be—yes, he was! He pulled off his hiking boots and stripped off his sweatpants, tossing them in the general direction of the packs nestled together beside the tent opening. When he raised his arms to peel off his sweatshirt, she couldn't hide her alarm.

"What are you doing?" She was annoyed when she heard the tremor in her voice.

"I like to sleep naked, especially on a nice summer night like this. Don't worry, I'll leave my underwear on. Don't want you to get the wrong idea."

Everything about this sleep-out was wrong!

"You're going to get too warm zipped in like that," he warned.

"You don't need to worry about it," she said crossly, surprised at how well she could see him with only natural light from the sky.

He was wearing perfectly ordinary white briefs, low-cut and snug, as far as she could tell. She closed her eyes, but what she imagined was more disturbing than what she could see in the dark interior of the tent.

"I'll close the door," he said.

This maneuver involved crawling to the end of his sleeping bag and zipping shut the flap. It gave her a whole new view of Sully, not one that would lull her to sleep.

The tent was dark with the flap closed, but she didn't

need eyes to know her roommate was settling down in the sleeping bag without zipping himself inside.

"Sweet dreams," he said.

"Fat chance."

"I hope you're a morning person."

"I'm not."

When she was around him, she felt grouchy morning, noon and night.

Apparently he had a clear conscience and a tranquil mind. In only minutes she could hear soft, regular breathing from his side of the tent. He was sound asleep.

She tried to fill her mind with soothing images, first visualizing the ocean on a calm day. A shark broke the surface and snapped his razor-sharp teeth at her. She imagined a lovely flower garden, then it was filled with angry yellow jackets.

She was hot. That's why she couldn't relax—not that she wanted to fall asleep out in the wilderness. What if a bear came? It could easily rip open the tent and she'd be nothing but a hairball in its stomach.

Whether she slept or not, she was going to melt into a puddle in this sleeping bag designed for the Arctic. She wiggled out, not sure whether to lose the flannel shirt or to put her slacks back on and lie on top of the sleeping bag. The tent had heated up since Mac had come inside; it felt like a steam bath.

Her panties were riding up uncomfortably. She yanked on the elastic leg bands, trying to rearrange them so they wouldn't cut into her skin.

"Are you ever going to be still?"

His voice made her jump.

"I thought you were asleep."

"I'm a light sleeper. You'd be more comfortable if you stripped before you got back in the sleeping bag."

"In your dreams!"

"Didn't you write a chapter on sleeping gear? Follow your own advice, but quit wiggling."

"I am not wiggling." Squirming was a more accurate description.

"If you're scared, you can share my sleeping bag," he teased.

"Oh! Go back to sleep!"

He thumped and resettled himself in a new position, then conked out again. Maggie sat spacing out, trying not to look in his direction.

Even sitting on the lumpy ground was hard on her bottom. She tried lying on her stomach, but that was worse. She'd never realized how many tender spots her body had.

She didn't want to sleep, but she couldn't help thinking about Sully's offer. She could cradle her head on his chest and drape her legs over his. His soft spots could be a buffer against the hard ground.

"Yeah, sure," she mumbled to herself in a whisper.

If she went for an idea like that, she was a candidate for his mythical lunatic asylum. Starting anything with Mac would give a whole new meaning to extreme adventure. She definitely didn't want to go there.

Weren't the woods supposed to be quiet at night? Sure, there were night hunters, but how could a noisy animal catch anything? Things weren't nearly as silent on the ridge as she'd expected. She could recognize a cricket's song—well, maybe—but what were the other hisses and buzzes? She didn't want to meet whatever was making that scraping sound.

Scraping?

"Oh, dear." Was any contract worth this?

She pulled up her knees and hugged them, listening intently. She wasn't imagining it. There was a distinct scrunch, scrunch, scrunch sound.

The tiny window vent—flimsy mesh between them and whatever was out there—was unzipped. She froze, hoping it would go away.

"If you won't let me sleep, I'm going to expect some entertainment," Mac said in a groggy voice.

"I hear something."

"Nothing you need to worry about."

He turned his back toward her, his shoulders muscular and bare in the dimness. His musk reminded her of hot sun and newly cut fields.

"Mac, I'm serious. There's an awful scratching noise. Don't you hear it?"

He groaned. "This is what I get for telling you a spooky story."

"It was a true story, wasn't it?"

"No." He sighed. "Just an urban myth."

"Well, I hear something—and that's not a myth."

"Just a loose branch," he said, sounding sleepy but not reassuring.

"Where have I heard that before? The least you can do is go out and look around. Coming here was your bad idea."

"Camping doesn't get any safer than this. My brother and I slept up here before either of us was twelve."

She got up on her knees, wanting to shake some sense into him.

"There it is again!"

"Where there are trees, there are animals. Nothing will bother us." His words were muffled because he'd turned over onto his stomach and had buried his head into his pillow.

"At least stick your head out and really listen!"

He grunted his lack of enthusiasm but crawled to the door and unzipped it.

"Nothing," he insisted.

"You're lying. You must have heard that."

"You won't be satisfied until I get into my boots and look around, will you?"

"No." She crossed her arms and stared at him to show how serious she was.

"If I do, will you settle down and go to sleep?"

"I'll settle down," she said, miffed because he wasn't taking her alarm seriously.

He located his boots, pulled them on and crawled to the door. Her own breath sounded as loud as a drum roll while she watched him go out into the night.

She dug her nails into her palms while he stood and looked around. Through the tent flap all she could see were his calves, compact and muscular. Rummaging in her pack, she found the flashlight he'd loaned her. Shining it on him, she saw more of his legs and narrow half-moons of white flesh where the tan line on his upper thighs ended. She was almost too scared to appreciate the way his briefs sagged a little over round, sexy buttocks. Almost.

"There's nothing here," he said. "You're just spooked because I told you that story."

"I certainly am not!"

She bounded out of the tent, too annoyed to take his word for anything. He turned just as she stood and she collided into him. His arms went around her as she knocked him backward several steps.

"Are you trying to knock me off the ridge?" he demanded.

The drop-off was covered with brush and not steep enough for homicidal purposes, but she was embarrassed. She'd nearly knocked him to the ground.

He didn't hurry to remove his arms, and she felt the silkiness of his chest against her cheek. She liked tall men even though she was only five-two. His six foot, one inch lean, muscular body qualified.

"Sorry, I just wanted to see what was out here."

"Well, look around," he said, sounding exasperated. "Do you see anything menacing? Enraged bears, poisonous vipers, serial killers, rabid raccoons..."

"Rabid raccoons?"

"They can be mean. Try to stop one with a shovel and it will climb up the handle and savage you."

"Another bedtime story?"

"You should know. You're the wilderness expert. Are you still hearing things?"

"No." Darn him, she wasn't.

"Is there any other reason why you can't get into your sleeping bag and go to sleep?"

She could mention the hard ground or the close quarters in the tent. She could complain about being too hot and too nervous. Or not.

"I won't disturb you again," she said, trying not to sound as irritated as she felt.

"Unlikely, but I'll settle for no talking. Get in the tent."

She'd lie down, but dang if she'd sleep a wink. Mr. Granville owed her for this nightmare.

DAWN CAME EARLY on the ridge, but by the time the small mesh square that served as a window showed a patch of gray, she'd changed position a thousand times without getting any sleep. Maggie stretched, settled on a new patch of lumpy ground inadequately softened by the sleeping bag and closed her eyes again. This night was a total loss. She wasn't going to get a minute of sleep.

The next time she opened her eyes, she saw the unmistakable glow of sunlight illuminating the tent. She had fallen asleep! When? How? Had that noise come back? She reached over to Mac's sleeping bag and flattened her hand on the quilted surface.

He was gone. He'd deserted her! She was too tired to panic and, besides, something was teasing her nostrils. The aroma of coffee wafted through the tent, making her realize it really was morning. She'd survived the night.

"Breakfast will be ready in a couple of minutes."

Mac bent and looked through the opening in the tent, making her realize the borrowed shirt was bunched around her waist.

"Don't look!"

"I already have." He laughed. "You have a B-plus butt and A-minus legs."

"B-plus!"

She rolled over and sat up, tugging the shirt to cover anything he hadn't already graded.

"I lied. It's A-plus, but I got you moving. Hope you're hungry. I've been slaving away over breakfast."

"Breakfast? Did you make cappuccino?"

"No, good hot Colombian to wake up you up."

"I smell bacon."

"You smell right. Bacon and pancakes with maple syrup Gram boiled down herself. If you need to run into the woods, you can't get into any trouble behind that tree.''

He pointed to where she had to go. It was primitive, but maybe not as complicated as she'd supposed.

When she got back, she insisted on putting on her slacks in the tent before she succumbed to the heavenly smells coming from a pan sitting on the fire pit.

''How long have you been up?'' She was awed by the pancakes and bacon, not to mention the best coffee she'd ever tasted, even served in a metal cup.

''Not long. I'm an old pro, remember? Breakfast for two is a snap.''

''Did you go back to your grandmother's for food?'' What she really wanted to know was if he'd left her all alone.

''No, I brought an insulated sack in my pack. You were never unguarded.''

''I really did hear something last night.''

''I heard it, too, but believe me, it wasn't anything more threatening than a loose branch.''

He handed her a metal plate, warning her not to set it on her legs. She wasn't just hungry, she was ravenous, using her fingers to eat the bacon when the plastic fork proved inadequate. He sat opposite her, watching her as he ate.

''I hate you for blackmailing me into staying, but this is the best breakfast I've ever had,'' she said.

She accepted a second pan-size pancake even though she felt greedy doing it.

''You've kept your part of the bargain. I'll sign the contract back at the house before you leave,'' he said after he'd finished his meal.

''Is there any coffee left?''

She hadn't seen a blue-and-white enameled pot like his anywhere but in antiques shops.

"Yes." He poured for her. "I expected you to be thrilled that you can leave now."

"Are you going to eat that piece of bacon?"

"Help yourself." He grinned.

"I'll help you pack up," she said, chewing the last crunchy strip. "Then we can go back to the house and sign the contract."

"That's my intention," he said.

"Good."

She snagged a few scraps of bacon left in the pan and gobbled them up. One thing in her guides was certainly true. Outdoor living gave a person a tremendous appetite.

6

GRAM WAS GIVING HIM the look. Maggie had left nearly an hour ago and still his grandmother hadn't said a word about her. It didn't bode well. When Gram focused her pale blue eyes that way, it usually meant he was in big trouble.

When he'd returned from the ridge, Mac had stowed the camping gear, had washed his and Maggie's breakfast dishes and had taken a quick shower. Now he wondered if the lumberyard closed early on Saturday. He wanted to make arrangements for materials to be delivered to the cabin site on Monday, but Gram obviously had something to say.

"I took the job," he said, trying to sound casual. "That's why she came here."

Gram didn't say anything. He knew her technique. She wouldn't say a word until he'd talked himself into trouble. Well, he wasn't a rebellious kid anymore, and it wouldn't work.

"Don't expect me back for lunch." He started to leave.

"What did sleeping out on the ridge have to do with a job?" she asked, sounding reluctant to ask the question.

"It's complicated."

If she wanted information, she'd have to pump him for it.

"I'm not senile yet."

She was bringing out the heavy ammo. When Gram mentioned her age or infirmities, it was only to make him toe the line.

"You're a long way from it, sweetheart."

He walked over and touched his lips to her heavily creased brow.

"She's a pretty girl," Gram said, ignoring his affectionate kiss but not dropping the subject.

"She's a city girl. Never camped out before. Not my type."

"You spent the night with her in that little tent."

Was Gram on a morals kick? He was thirty years old. She must assume he'd slept with women, so why the concern about Maggie Sanders?

"We slept in the same tent, but that's all we did. Sleep."

"That part's not my concern," she sniffed.

"The only concern you have is to keep out of trouble while I'm gone. Whatever you want carried or fixed, I'll do it when I get back."

He headed toward the door.

"Your grandpa was no damn good until I married him."

That got Mac's attention. He stopped in shock. Not only had Gram never before made a negative comment about her husband, she'd used a cuss word.

"He was always carousing in bars, running with a bunch of hoodlums. Even got himself arrested a few times for drunk and disorderly. He only worked when he needed whiskey money. I changed that."

He didn't doubt her, but he was still stunned. His grandfather had been sober, hardworking and quietly devoted to his wife and family. Mac couldn't imagine him drunk or in jail.

"So it's time you settled down," Gram said decisively.

"You think Maggie and I... Oh, no! Believe me, it won't happen. I don't have a problem with booze and I've never been in jail. And I certainly don't need Maggie Sanders to keep me on the straight and narrow. Forget it, Cora. Don't play matchmaker with me."

"You could do worse," Gram insisted stubbornly.

"I doubt it. She's afraid of life. She can't tell the difference between a loose branch and a bear, and her idea of a long trip is going to the mall. It doesn't matter though. I'm not the settling-down type."

"You'll get over that wanderlust of yours someday. Then what will you have? That cabin you want to build will be mighty lonely."

"*You* prefer being alone. You could move to Florida and live near Mom and Dad if you wanted company."

"I belong here. My memories are here. You're just starting out. You need a good woman to keep you in line when I'm gone."

"You'll be around a long time yet."

He said it, but didn't believe it. Neither did she.

The prospect of losing Gram was bleak, but that didn't mean he was ready to give up his freedom. He'd learned the hard way how much he valued his independence. Whenever he started to get close to a woman, she expected more commitment that he was ready to give. It had happened twice with live-in girlfriends, and he didn't want any more emotional turmoil in his life.

"Well, that Maggie is a sweet little thing," Gram said. "Had the good sense to stay out of my kitchen."

"I'll be back this afternoon," Mac said, walking to the door. "Don't worry about me. I don't need a woman to take care of me."

Gram snorted her disapproval, but he didn't stick around for more lecturing. He still had a hard time picturing Grandpa as a hell-raiser.

It rained for the next two days and Mac spent the time studying the cabin plans he'd bought, wondering when he'd be called to make the first author tour and doing inside jobs for Gram. She hinted from time to time that he was ready for a domestic arrangement, but he ignored her unless she mentioned Maggie. Then he emphatically denied having the slightest interest in her.

He was more honest with himself. Maggie was cute, no question about that. He thought about her quite a bit, but it didn't signify anything. He liked women and she was as womanly as they came. He got hot whenever he remembered her on the sleeping bag with bare legs and only skimpy pink silk panties covering her bottom. He'd love to have those shapely legs wrapped around him. He'd like to know if she tasted as sweet as she smelled. But he was too sensible to get involved with someone who was totally and completely wrong for him. Even if he wanted a wife—and he emphatically did not—he'd choose a woman who loved the outdoors the way he did, one who would share his lifestyle with pleasure. That wasn't Maggie Sanders.

On the third day the sun finally came out, hot and brilliant. He worked all morning on the ridge, anticipating the delivery of his lumber the next day by way of the old logging road. When he went down to the house for lunch, he was hot, sweaty and exhilarated. He'd never built anything big before, but Grandpa had taught him all he needed to know. He was excited about the challenge.

Gram met him on the porch.

"You got a call about that job. It wasn't Maggie who phoned." She sounded disappointed. "I wrote down the name and number."

He didn't want to talk to anyone at Granville Publishing, but Gram's pointed silence over a lunch of chicken-vegetable soup and fresh cracked-wheat bread goaded his conscience. He'd signed that infernal contract before Maggie had left. He might as well find out when they wanted him.

He connected with Miss Mason, Granville's secretary. She sounded as old as Gram, but considerably more prim.

"We have your itinerary, Mr. Sully. Do you have a fax machine so I can send it to you?"

"No, ma'am. Just drop it in the mail."

"I could send it by overnight express. There isn't enough time for regular mail delivery."

That sounded ominous.

"I get my mail at the post office. They don't deliver up here. When do you need me?" he asked.

"The first part of the tour starts the day after tomorrow. I've made all your reservations."

"Maggie's going with me, right?"

"Oh, no. Miss Sanders has too many other responsibilities. Her editorial assistant, Miss Jordan, will accompany you."

"Who's Miss Jordan?"

"Rayanne Jordan. She was the receptionist before her promotion." Miss Mason sounded disapproving.

"The blonde with the pierced eyebrow?"

"Yes. Now, about the schedule... Would you like me to read the highlights?"

"No, thank you. Let me talk to Maggie."

"Miss Sanders is working at home today on a manuscript she's editing." Mr. Granville's secretary seemed exasperated by Mac's request.

"Give me her number, please."

"I'm sorry, Mr. Sully. I'm not allowed to give out personnel information."

"Let me talk to Granville then."

"*Mister* Granville is out for the day."

"Who is working today?"

"I can connect you with Miss Jordan."

He groaned, remembering the dippy receptionist he'd seen when he delivered Ann's envelope to their office. She'd been pasty-faced and dressed all in black. If Maggie thought he was going to go on a tour with a freaky-looking young kid, she was mistaken. He'd told her she'd have to go or it was no deal. He'd assumed it was part of their deal, but cursed himself for not getting it in writing.

"You look as if you've swallowed a burr," Gram said when he hung up.

"Worse, the lumber's coming tomorrow and I'm supposed to go on a book tour the next day."

He'd told Gram roughly what his new job entailed when he'd decided to take Maggie camping.

"I guess you gotta go since you signed that paper," she said with no trace of sympathy.

"I'm going to Pittsburgh. I'm not sure when I'll be back, but I'll call you."

He showered but only because he'd been sweating like a pig. He always splashed a little men's cologne on his face when he went to the big city. It had nothing to do with the possibility of seeing Maggie. Gram noticed his efforts on his way out.

"Hafta say you smell good," she said. "Pittsburgh. That's where Maggie lives, isn't it?"

"Granville Publishing is there. That's why I'm going."

He was too old to have any female keeping track of where he went. The sooner he got his cabin built, the better, but first he had to make a few changes in the travel arrangements.

VISIONS OF WATER GARDENS swam in her head, but Maggie couldn't seem to concentrate on the pages she was trying to edit. The author, Eve Wiltshire, had the unfortunate habit of going off on tangents that had nothing to do with her gardening book. Maggie hoped Eve wasn't as fragile as she'd looked in white gloves and hat at their luncheon because the revisions were going to be brutal.

Maggie had thought working at home would be productive, but she'd also wanted to avoid Mr. Granville. He wanted her to go on the tour with Mac, and she knew that was just asking for trouble. Even though she'd talked him into letting her newly promoted editorial assistant go, he'd been known to change his mind.

Promoting Rayanne had been her idea. The pay raise had been miniscule, and the duties were virtually the same since Mr. Granville had no intention of hiring Maggie a new receptionist. But having a new title would make her friend seem more important when a new owner took over. It also made her a more suitable escort for Mac. Rayanne was friendly and gregarious. She'd do just fine on the road.

Maggie read the same paragraph for the third time. When the phone rang, it was a welcome interruption. She didn't wait for her machine to screen the call.

"Maggie, hi. This is your editorial assistant." Rayanne loved titles. Her dream was to marry a count or a baron.

"What's up?" Maggie asked. "Are you still at work?"

"Yes, I'm talking in your office with the door closed."

"Why?"

"You should know the gargoyle let something drop."

Mr. Granville's secretary insisted the younger women call her Miss Mason. Leave it to Rayanne to nickname her after a grotesque medieval stone statue. Maggie loved Rayanne like a sister, but she'd be glad when her Goth phase was over.

She smiled, wondering how Mac would like traveling with the Queen of the Damned.

"Is it going to make me happy?" Maggie asked. "If not, I'd just as soon not hear it."

"Mac Sully called and the gargoyle talked to him. He wanted your phone number and address."

"She didn't give it to him, did she?" She fought to keep the anxiety out of her voice.

"Well, actually, that would be me."

"You gave him my number? That's not what editorial assistants are supposed to do!"

"Well, he convinced me it was urgent. He said he'd get it one way or another. I'm sorry, Maggie. That man could charm the pants off…"

"Never mind! Are you telling me he plans to come here?"

"Good guess."

"From now on all my editorial assistants have to work two hours overtime on Friday."

"I'm your only editorial assistant. You're kidding, right?"

"I'll tell you when I know whether Mac shows up here."

Maggie hung up, trying to calculate how long it would take him to get to her apartment if he came directly from the office. On a good day she could drive to work in fifteen minutes, but he'd probably get caught in rush-hour traffic. She had time to leave her apartment before he got here.

Purse in hand, she was poised for flight, then realized she was being silly. Sully didn't scare her. Maybe she had agreed to go on the tour with him, but there was nothing about it in the contract. He hadn't brought it up again when he signed. Anyway, she didn't owe him anything after the way he'd blackmailed her into spending a night in a tent.

She abandoned the manuscript. So much for working at home. It didn't matter how she looked, but she ran upstairs out of habit to check herself in the full-length mirror in her bedroom. She fluffed her hair with her fingers, wondering why she looked pale. Must be the light. The sky-blue walls weren't a good backdrop for her coloring, although she loved them. Her apartment was small, one of hundreds in a large brick complex, but having two levels made it feel less cramped. The landlord had let her repaint, and this room was her favorite with its sheer white curtains, thick, soft comforter with big swirls of cobalt and aqua across the bed of the secondhand bedroom set she'd painted in white enamel and decorated with sprigs of hand-painted bluebells.

Okay, she passed inspection, more or less. She had a spot on the front of her white shorts where she'd dropped a piece of lettuce with French dressing from her lunch. Her halter top had long ago faded to a wishy-washy peach, but she'd dressed to work, not to entertain. Darned if she'd change whether Mac showed up or not.

But she didn't want to see him. Wasn't it bad enough she couldn't stop thinking about him? He hadn't shown any personal interest in her, so why did it matter that he was built like a statue of Apollo, all rippling muscles and firm, tanned flesh? After all her trouble to avoid him, getting Rayanne promoted and assigned to go on the tour, she certainly didn't want to confront him.

Mac was trouble. She fervently wished she'd hired the kid with the rubber snake. Better an idiot she could control than a man who made her crazy.

"Okay," she said, trying to get perspective. "Maybe he won't even show up. If he does, I don't have to answer the door. If I do decide to let him in, he probably isn't dangerous. I'll give him a reasonable explanation about why I'm not going, then he'll leave.

What if he didn't go quietly? What if he left and she wanted him back so badly she chased after him?

This was horrible! She trusted herself less than she trusted a man she'd just met who made his living tramping around in the wilderness.

She went downstairs still wondering if she should leave while she could. How long had it been since Rayanne called? Maybe ten minutes. If she left, would Mac camp on her doorstep, forever barring the way back into her apartment?

In spite of expecting him, she was startled by a loud knock on her door. She didn't doubt who it was. Who else would pound instead of using the door buzzer?

She looked around her living area, a cozy space decorated in warm fall colors, with a rust-colored couch, two Boston rockers and a round braided rug on top of the drab tan carpeting that came with the place. At the far end, her kitchenette and table were partly blocked from view by a counter and the cupboards suspended above it. For the first time she realized there was no place to hide. Everything was open, and Mac could see into the whole place because her beige blinds were open.

He pounded again.

Wait, she could hide in the coat closet. The front door was solid except for the peephole. She could duck in there without being seen and—

"I know you're in there, Maggie. Your car is in your spot," he yelled loud enough for half the tenants to hear.

Forget the closet. She wouldn't be able to sleep tonight anyway if she didn't settle this now. She flung open the door and frowned to show him she wouldn't take any guff.

"You don't know where my parking spot is," she accused.

"Not a clue, but you opened the door, didn't you? I thought maybe that weird girl warned you I was coming and you were hiding somewhere."

Her face felt hot and flushed, but she wouldn't admit he was right. She stepped aside to let him in, the only alternative to a shouting match on her doorstep.

"Now," he said, pulling the door shut and crossing his arms over the black T-shirt that covered his broad, near-perfect chest. "What's this about reneging on our deal? You're supposed to go on this circus tour with me."

"You're making too big a deal out of it. You go to some bookstores, sign books and smile like a chimpanzee. It's simple, really."

"What about speeches?"

"Just radio and TV interviews. Maybe a little reading. Rayanne will give you a few sheets of possible questions and the answers. You'll be able to wing it better than I could, great outdoorsman that you are."

"There's one hitch in that plan."

He was standing, legs apart in faded jeans, his hiking boots making him look even more macho than he was. Did he ever comb his hair? It went every which way, a disorderly spill of dark blond waves tinged with gold. His face was shadowed by dark bristles, and she wondered how scratchy they'd feel rubbing against her tender skin. The men she knew shaved before dates and had their hair cut at chichi salons, not local barbershops, so why did Mac look so good to her?

"What hitch?" she asked cautiously.

"You agreed to go."

"That was before you made me camp out to get you to sign the contract. Blackmail nullified any previous agreement."

"That's what you think!"

"You can't coerce me into risking my life in the wilderness and expect—"

He snorted derisively. "Camping on my ridge is safer than walking to your car after dark."

He was probably right, but she'd touch a big hairy spider before she'd admit it.

"I took you at your word," he insisted. "Let's put it this way. You go or I don't."

"You signed the contract. Our attorney—"

"So sue me."

"Don't think I won't! You'll be in breach of contract." Let him worm his way out of that one, Maggie thought.

"Sweetheart, you're not a party to the contract, and I doubt Granville would involve the firm in litigation, given the possible adverse effect of the negative publicity. Good luck selling the company if that happens."

Sully said that? What happened to his laconic tone and slight Southern accent that could send ripples down her spine? She realized her mouth was open and clamped it shut.

"Now let's get packing," he said.

He looked around, then headed up the stairs.

"Where are you going?" she asked, following close on his heels.

Sully looked into the spare bedroom she used as an office and catch-all room, then walked into her bedroom.

By the time she caught up, he was inside her walk-in closet shuffling through her clothes.

"Stop that, Mac! You can't—"

"Pack this." He tossed her favorite little black dress on the bed. "But lose the jacket."

"That's too dressy for daytime—not that I'm going."

"A big-time author like M. S. Stevens wouldn't drag along a frumpy female. This will do, too."

He put a black leather miniskirt beside the dress. She'd bought it on sale years ago and worn it maybe twice because she'd never lost the requisite five pounds to make it fit well.

"This is ridiculous! If I were going, I'd be perfectly capable of picking my own clothes."

"Where's your luggage? Never mind, I can see it."

He grabbed her wheeled navy suitcase from under the bed, dropped it next to her clothes, then went back into the closet.

"Too much black. This red outfit might do." He held up a pantsuit in a plastic bag.

"It would do fine in December. It's wool. That's why it's in a storage bag."

"This will go with the skirt." He held up a white camisole. "Does it show a little midriff? Guys will buy a carload of your guides if they think it will help them share a tent with a hottie like you."

"You're awful! I'll quit my job before I go anywhere with you."

She angrily grabbed the camisole and hung it up again, then realized she was crowding Sully in space the width of an ironing board.

"I can't go without you," he said.

His arms closed around her from behind and she let out a squeal of surprise.

"You do smell good." His voice was low and mellow again.

"You have to go without me."

She tried to wiggle free, but he held her close, her back to his front, not a good position for resistance and definitely not a good time for her spine to tingle and her knees to go weak.

"Nope."

"Why not?"

She tried not to sound squeaky, but his chin was

brushing the back of her neck. The beard was scratchy, deliciously so. She'd never realized why some men went to a lot of trouble to keep their stubble just the right length.

"I'm scared to go without you," he whispered.

"What?"

She managed to twist away and escape from the closet.

"You heard me. I'm no celebrity. I'd rather wrestle a bear than try to fake my way though some literary get-together."

"But you're not scared of anything!" she protested.

He was big. He was strong. He was macho. He went down raging rivers and hiked through deserts and forests. It had to be a ploy. She looked into his face, the deep blue eyes riveted on her, and saw only sincerity.

"You wanted the truth, didn't you?"

"Rayanne could—"

"Rayanne is a flake. I doubt she's even read your books."

Maggie couldn't refute that. She didn't think Rayanne had read them, either. Her taste ran to vampire novels and Gothic horror.

"It's your decision. If you're not at the airport packed to go, I won't get on the plane."

He walked to the bedroom door, then turned around.

"I need you, Maggie."

He smiled shyly and she suspected he was embarrassed by his admission. She had an almost overwhelming urge to comfort him and tell him she understood, but before she could go after him, he was gone.

When the shock of seeing a new side of Sully wore off, she felt trapped. How could she go on a weekend trip with a man who made her weak in the knees? Sure, he'd been a gentleman in the tent, but she couldn't trust *herself* alone with him again. How awful would it be if she fell in love with a modern-day Tarzan? She couldn't live his way. He'd never live hers. This was bad, bad, bad.

Mac wasn't the only one who was scared.

7

"THIS ISN'T WHAT I expected," Mac muttered.

Maggie had to hustle to keep up with him as they walked toward Brown's Book Emporium, an independent store in the heart of downtown Philadelphia.

"They've done well with my guides—that is, your guides, Mr. Stevens."

"I don't see any point in this. And I don't know why you're dressed for an undertakers' convention."

"You're the one who pulled black clothes out of my closet."

"Not that outfit you're wearing."

Maybe her black pantsuit was a little too conservative, especially with a man-tailored white shirt buttoned to her throat, but there was no way she was going to follow his advice on what to wear.

Anyway, she wanted to stay in the background, which wouldn't be hard if there were women at the signing. Mac looked luscious in crisp tan slacks that were either new or carefully ironed. His blue Oxford shirt brought out the color of his eyes, and it didn't hurt that he'd left the top three buttons open to reveal an impressive patch of golden brown hair. He'd even left his hiking boots at home in favor of cordovan loafers and appropriate tan socks. Not only was he gorgeous in his natural state, he cleaned up spectacularly.

"I probably should've gotten a haircut," he said.

She could tell by his tone he was nervous. Maybe he'd told the truth about being scared about the signings, although she had some doubts.

"Your hair fits the image Mr. Granville wants for the guides," she reassured him. "It's all right."

It was better than all right. Long, unruly hair suited him perfectly. Women would get itchy fingers wanting to comb through those gold-tinged locks.

"If it's any consolation, I hate this as much as you do," she whispered as he opened the dark red door of the store.

Brown's Book Emporium looked small from the outside, just a hole-in-the-wall with gray stucco exterior walls over old red bricks, a few left deliberately exposed. A jaunty red-and-white awning shaded the front and kept the sun away from a display of travel books in the bay window to the left. The last two *Extreme Adventure* guides were tucked to one side. A tiny white card taped to the window announced an author would be doing a reading and signing today.

Mac held the door open for her without noticing the understated announcement. Good thing. He'd been so grouchy about the whole situation, she hadn't mentioned the reading part again.

They stood in the front of the store on worn wooden flooring. The place appeared to be old-fashioned by design with tall, dark-oak shelving, an embossed tin ceiling painted pale gray and a circular checkout counter decorated with floral wood carvings. The outside was deceptive. The building was long with lots of display space on three stories and an elevator to service them.

"Can I help you folks?"

They were approached by a laconic young man in a

long-sleeved white knit shirt and faded brown corduroys too hot and heavy for the heat outside. He had a scraggly brown goatee, a small gold hoop in one ear and pointy-toed black shoes.

"We're expected," Maggie said. "This is M. S. Stevens, and I'm his assistant, Maggie Sanders."

"Oh, sure, the author." He only nodded at Mac. "I'm an assistant, too, assistant manager here. Gordon Petrus."

He offered Maggie his sweaty palm for a limp handshake. She resisted an urge to wipe her hand on the side of her slacks.

"We set up back here," he said, leading the way through a maze of shoulder-high periodical stands and circular racks of paperback books. "It's a joint signing with Amanda Riddle. You've heard of her, haven't you?"

"Sure," Maggie lied, not wanting to admit she'd never heard of that author.

"I haven't," Mac said in a disgruntled voice.

Obviously he wasn't going to play the book game by anyone's rules but his own.

"She's done fabulously well with *Ghosts of Philadelphia.*"

Spiffy, Maggie thought. Nothing like a joint signing with a ghost hunter. They'd do well to sell half a dozen books if the people who showed up were supernatural buffs.

"Amanda Riddle, this is A. M. Stevens and his girl Friday, Maggie," Gordon said.

"M. S. Stevens," Maggie corrected him. Just because she hadn't come on this tour willingly didn't mean she wanted it off to a bad start.

"M.S., how charming." A whippet-thin woman with

silver cropped hair smiled broadly at Mac. "What does M.S. stand for?"

Mac looked blank. How could she have forgotten to coach him on that?

"Mark Steven," she said quickly, cringing that she didn't come up with something better.

"Isn't that cute. Mark Steven Stevens."

The ghost hunter giggled, an odd sound that made it hard to guess her age. Maggie thought the silver hair belonged to a fifty-year-old, but there wasn't a line on the woman's face. Either she had a good cosmetic surgeon or she was forty or younger.

Amanda Riddle offered her hand to Mac and held his for considerably longer than necessary. He looked bemused, maybe because she was wearing a flowing black tunic with celestial signs embroidered in gold and a dark violet skirt that hid her feet.

"Have you had a chance to take the ghost tour of Philadelphia?" she trilled.

"I may have to pass that up," Mac said. "We're on a tight schedule."

"Oh, you mustn't miss it. Haven't you ever wondered if Ben Franklin's ghost still haunts the city?" Amanda asked in a low, conspiratorial voice. "It's a candlelight walking tour. I'd be happy to come along to run interference with the spirits. They get cross if they suspect you're an unbeliever."

Oh, brother! This woman was old enough to be Mac's—well, not mother, but certainly his aunt. Didn't she realize how silly she sounded coming on to a young stud like Sully? Maggie had had enough of this signing, and it hadn't even started yet.

Two tables were set up at the rear of the store with the history section as a backdrop, while off to the right there were mounds of frosted ghost-shaped cookies and paper cups for the pitcher of orange punch. Someone should tell Gordon it was July, a tad bit early for Halloween treats. At least the authors' seating areas had glasses of ice water making moist circles on white tablecloths. One of the tables held a hundred or so copies of *Ghosts of Philadelphia*. The other had four even stacks with three copies each of the *Extreme Adventure* guides she'd written.

She wanted to complain about the number of books, but instead decided to check the outdoor section herself when people started to line up for autographed copies. Surely there were more guides available somewhere in the store.

A middle-aged couple in matching lemon-colored walking shorts and snug white T-shirts wandered over to their table. The woman looked down her rather sharp nose at the guides, then eyeballed Mac.

"Have you done everything you write about?" she asked.

"Pretty much." Mac grinned like a schoolboy with a candied apple. "And I always take a bunch of real nice folks along with me."

His accent was as thick as molasses, the big phony. He was probably exaggerating it just to annoy her.

The female browser giggled and picked up one of the guides. "Will you sign this to Lorraine?" she asked.

"I'll be happy to." Mac flashed a thousand-dollar smile. Just what part of this job couldn't he do without her?

Gordon came back, his cords rubbing together loudly between his legs as he walked.

''We'll do the readings in about five minutes. Which one of you wants to be first?'' he asked.

Mac looked over at Maggie, who was standing off to the right so she was out of the way. If looks could vaporize, she'd be a bunch of unconnected atoms now. She looked away quickly and pretended to gaze at books on macramé.

''Ladies first,'' Mac said.

''Oh, please, no,'' Amanda said. ''I'd so appreciate it if you go first. I need to gather my wits together and make sure I'm in harmony with the spirits before I begin.''

Mac deserted his post behind the table and walked to Maggie. He looked ready to throttle her.

''Read page eighty-seven in the mid-Atlantic states guide,'' she said, backing away. ''I thought a description of white-water rafting would be good. The trip begins at Ohiopyle and goes west on the Youghiogheny. That's pronounced Yoo—''

''I can pronounce it,'' he whispered angrily. ''What I want to know is why you didn't tell me I'd be reading today.''

She'd been afraid he'd bolt if she hit him with too much at once, but it didn't seem politic to say so.

''Sorry,'' she squeaked.

A few people were milling around, and Gordon was belatedly setting up some folding chairs in a semicircle in front of the two tables. A willowy blonde helping him yelped when she put a table leg down on the top of her own foot because she had her eyes on Mac.

She wasn't the only one. Female customers who were wandering around the store and got a glimpse of Mac hovered for a better look. The chairs filled up quickly and a standing crowd formed behind them.

Gordon, radiating self-importance, stood in front of them and introduced Mac by reading the fictitious biography on the book jacket. Maggie fervently wished she'd written a book on quilting or home decorating or even ghost-hunting instead of the guides. She felt like a fraud. She couldn't even take credit for her hard work.

Mac read beautifully. His voice was lyrical as he read her description of picturesque rocks and rushing currents.

A woman in the front row raised her hand, jiggling it excitedly until Mac noticed and stopped reading.

"Did you have a question?" he asked.

An experienced speaker would've said he'd take questions at the end of his reading, but Mac didn't lose the attention of his rapt audience by pausing.

"I wonder what you wear white-water rafting," the woman asked, giggling.

"It's all in the book." He didn't sound too sure about that. "The important things," he said, "are a helmet with an adjustable strap, rafting sandals and, of course, a life jacket."

"Do you wear anything under the life jacket?"

She-with-all-the-questions was too old to giggle like a teenager, at least in Maggie's opinion.

"It depends on who I'm with."

Mac got a big laugh.

"Do you do private tours?" Another woman in the audience spoke up without bothering to raise her hand.

Why were all these women vying for his attention? Sure he was eye candy, rugged, handsome and heart-stopping when he turned on the charm, but this was only a book signing. Did they expect him to toss his room key to someone in the audience?

Maggie was still annoyed he'd insisted on dragging her on the tour. She was just a spectator here, not the least bit important. Nothing good ever happened when she hit the road—or the airways. All she had to do on this trip was to watch Sully, the superstud, and worry about when disaster would strike.

"Yes, ma'am, I certainly do," Mac said in answer to the private tour question.

No woman in the audience could resist him now. He finished reading to an entranced, mostly female audience, then they stampeded to his table, making it impossible for Amanda to begin her part of the program.

Gordon, who'd been dozing in the back, awoke from his comatose state when he heard the ruckus. Maggie followed behind him as he rushed to get the books from the window display and those left on the shelves. He made an emergency call to another independent bookseller, then went back to the crowd where the ghosthunter still hadn't done her reading. In fact, she was in line to have Mac sign a book for her. Gordon promised to have more guides in twenty minutes and eventually managed to get the book buyers to listen to Amanda Riddle's reading.

The bookstore closed at five. They were still there when Gordon started shooing people up to the counter to pay for their selections.

"Thanks for coming, Mr. Stevens," he said. "I didn't expect your books to sell like that. Sorry I didn't order more."

"It surprised me, too," Mac said.

Easy for him to play the modest author, Maggie thought. He believed the whole book tour was a waste of time.

"What do we do now?" he asked when they were

out on the street walking toward the Royal Point Hotel where they'd checked in earlier and left their luggage.

"We could visit Independence Hall, see the Liberty Bell. Or maybe a trip to the zoo. At least, we could have if we hadn't spent the entire afternoon at Brown's Book Emporium."

"I thought that's why Granville was paying me the big bucks."

It was, of course, but having Mac remind her only made her more irritated. Those book buyers had treated him like a rock star. They'd given him lingering handshakes and sizzling looks. She wouldn't have been surprised if they'd tried to rip off part of his clothes as souvenirs.

Mac grabbed her arm to stop her from stepping off the curb against a traffic signal.

"I didn't expect them to mob you," she muttered.

He laughed.

"It's not funny. I want M. S. Stevens to be dignified, polished, sophisticated..."

Pedestrians flowed around her and Mac gave her arm a little tug to get her moving.

"You want to be M. S. Stevens yourself," he accused. "You didn't like it when I got so much attention."

"That's not true!"

"No?"

He let go of her arm, but took her hand to propel her along the pavement. A big raindrop landed on her forehead. She hadn't even noticed how gray and forbidding the sky had become.

"It's starting to rain."

"We won't melt," Mac said, picking up the pace so they were practically running toward the hotel.

"I just don't like feeling superfluous," she said as several more drops pelted her face. "You didn't need me tagging along. You could've done the whole thing without me."

"You were my inspiration," he teased.

"You were so busy with your adoring public you didn't even know I was there."

"Oh, yes, I knew."

"We're going to get soaked," she said.

At least the sudden shower was an excuse to change the subject.

"Let's run," he said.

The rain came down harder, splashing up to soak her pant legs and drip down from her hair. It was a warm deluge, and she couldn't help laughing as they skipped over puddles and dodged around better-prepared people wearing plastic raincoats or carrying multicolored umbrellas.

Traffic was snarled at the next intersection, and they dashed between vehicles that weren't going anywhere at the moment.

She was short of breath, more from giggling than running. Mac dropped his arm across her shoulders as though he could shelter her from the downpour.

There was one more street to cross, but they had to wait as rain pelted their faces. His hair was darker when it was wet, making him look more rugged but no less handsome. Ordinarily she'd hate looking like a drowned cat, but Mac was making it seem like an adventure.

"There it is!" he said, gesturing at the dark green awning in front of the Royal Point Hotel. A doorman in a burgundy coat with gold braid was trying to flag down a cab without any success.

They sauntered arm-in-arm toward the dripping edge of the canvas shelter, too wet to bother hurrying. Mac used the edge of his hand to squeegee water from his face and to push back his soaked hair just as a swimmer would. His now-translucent shirt clung like a second skin, revealing dark hair under it. Maggie brushed her face and hair, trying to pretend she wasn't enjoying his soggy physique and the way his slacks clung to his thighs.

"That was fun," he said.

"Oh, yeah."

No way would she admit it was a hoot. She stamped her feet and nearly got bowled over by a burly man wheeling his suitcase out toward the curb where he joined a file of hotel guests who couldn't get cabs.

"Come on." Mac took her arm again. "Why stay in a posh hotel if you can't drip in their lobby?"

He propelled her through a revolving door, both of them in the same section.

"Why are we staying in such a fancy hotel?" Mac asked.

They walked into the elegant lobby, all dark wood, burgundy furnishings and potted trees, leaving wet footprints on the highly polished floor.

"I guess Mr. Granville wanted this to be a first-class tour. Miss Mason lives to serve, so it wouldn't have been her decision. I don't know what she'll do when he sells out and retires."

She followed him onto an elevator that stopped first on his floor, the ninth. Her room was on the eleventh. Did the gargoyle request rooms well apart to satisfy her own sense of propriety? Maggie thought of the floors between them as a safety zone.

"I'll call you when we've had a chance to dry off."

He grinned at her, holding the otherwise empty elevator open. "Although I like you wet," he said, letting the doors shut between them.

She didn't dare check herself out in the mirrored hallway until she was behind a closed door in her room. Tastefully decorated with seafoam-green carpeting, muted beige wallpaper with gold stripes and floral bedspreads, Maggie was reminded of a Monet painting.

Seeing herself in the tall dresser mirror made her squirm. Walking in the gusty downpour, she'd gotten thoroughly soaked. Her nipples poked out, highly visible under her wet cotton shirt and lacy bra. That was why Mac looked so amused when he got off the elevator, but why were her nipples so swollen and hard? She couldn't be...excited? By Mac?

No way! She remembered being annoyed at his cocky attitude and the way he'd let women fawn all over him at the book signing. It was just the cold dampness, not excitement.

After stripping out of her soggy clothes, she took a long shower. Then, rather than dress to go out, she slipped into a pink nylon nightie and her practical blue-striped cotton robe. She was ready for Mac to call. The phone rang only minutes later.

"Do you want to meet me in the lobby? Or can I come to your room?" Unlike most people, his voice sounded almost as good on the phone as in person.

"None of the above."

"I thought we could have dinner here. There's an English-style pub—"

"Thank you, no. You go ahead without me."

"You have to eat."

"I'm going to order room service. That way I can

get some work done. I brought along a manuscript to edit.''

''I'll join you.''

''I don't think so, Mac.'' .

''If that's what you want.''

He sounded indifferent, which didn't exactly give her ego a boost. Did she want him to insist, maybe storm up to her room and try to convince her in person?

The line went dead in her ear, and that was that.

Or was it? The phone rang again almost as soon as she stepped away from it.

''We could meet later for a drink,'' he said. ''I hate to leave you on your own.''

''I'll manage just fine. Too bad you didn't come with Rayanne. She loves nightlife. Anyway, we have an early plane to catch for Baltimore. I'll meet you in the lobby at seven tomorrow morning.''

''See you then,'' he said, again hanging up abruptly.

Darn that Sully anyway! If he hadn't smirked at her... If he hadn't enjoyed himself so darn much with all those women...

No, it wouldn't have mattered. She'd made the right decision. With Mac, it had to be all business. He was much too dangerous for up-close and personal encounters. Or was she a coward, afraid of risking her heart with a man who lived the kind of adventures she only wrote about?

8

YESTERDAY Maggie's outfit had been too severe for a judge, at least until it got wet, but today she was adorable—not a word that usually crossed Mac's mind. She was wearing a bright yellow dress that hugged her in all the right places. He recognized it as T-shirt material, but her snappy little dress bore no resemblance to that prosaic piece of clothing. Her arms were bare and the neckline scooped down to create a major distraction. Her cleavage was sensational when she didn't hide it in mannish clothes. Best of all, he could see her legs from midthigh to slender ankles.

They were rushing to the day's signing on the outskirts of Baltimore, behind schedule because their plane had been stuck on the runway behind a plane with a problem that delayed takeoff.

"Big mall," he said as they pulled into a huge parking area to go to the next bookstore on their itinerary.

She didn't answer; he supposed she was still mad.

She'd insisted on driving the rental car from the airport, which was okay with him. He loathed big-city traffic. But she'd gotten in a wrong lane and had to get off the highway for directions, then find her way back. She didn't exactly blame him, but she was testy.

Or maybe she was tense for the same reason he'd lain awake for hours last night. Separate rooms had been as hard to take as separate sleeping bags, especially since the longer he knew her, the more he wanted to be with her.

Maggie parked and got out of the car, leaving him to catch up as she race-walked toward the building. She could really move fast, even in flimsy flip-flops. Her big toes were surprisingly sexy. He'd like to feel them wiggling against his thighs.

"We're not late," he said, confirming the time on his wristwatch.

"No, but the media will be there. Yesterday was just a warm-up so you'd know the drill. The bookstore here is right across from a really huge outdoor outfitter. Their customers are a big target market for the guides, so we'll be attracting the right kind of attention."

"What was that part about the media?"

They reached the main entrance, and she yanked open the door, not giving him a chance to hold it for her.

"TV."

"I have to do this dog-and-pony show on television? Do you have any more surprises in store?"

"Not that I can think of."

She hurried past a big glass signboard displaying a map of the mall. He stopped to locate the bookstore.

"Wrong direction," he called after her.

"I see a bookstore right down there," she argued, pointing to the left.

"Religious bookstore. We have to go right, then jog left at a fountain. Didn't you give this advice in your book? Always consult a map before you plunge into unfamiliar territory."

She backtracked to his side, obviously not pleased to take instructions from him.

"It's a mall, not a jungle," she said.

"There are similarities. Exotic species prowling for food and sex."

Maggie just stared at him. "Never mind! We have to get there."

They found it easily enough by going in the right direction. Mac figured one bookstore was much like any other, but Maggie was so thrilled she forgot she was annoyed with him for being right.

"This is great!" she said as they walked into the open front of a huge bookstore.

"Looks like a supermarket," he remarked, enjoying his banter with Maggie but not the prospect of a repeat of yesterday's carnival.

"Oh, look, there's a man with a TV camera!" She nodded toward a cameraman with a bushy black mustache and a bored expression who was lounging near a high counter with half a dozen checkout stations.

A no-nonsense woman in blue slacks and matching tunic approached them and introduced herself as Dorothy Kroger, the bookstore manager. At least she didn't wear a single earring or noisy corduroy trousers.

The place was busy, Mac noticed, but he didn't know if the huge sign on the easel outside the store had attracted the crowd. Apparently M. S. Stevens was the main and only attraction today, but people were browsing everywhere.

Dorothy was explaining the setup, which interested Maggie a lot more than it did him. He was more concerned about whether she would hide in her hotel room to avoid him again tonight.

The manager turned to him and started enthusing about how well the guides had sold in her store. She was thrilled that Granville Publishing had responded to her invitation to hold a signing there. Mac lost sight of

Maggie, who'd wandered off for some unknown reason. Now that he had a handle on what was expected of him, he could do this, no sweat; he didn't need Maggie's help. He wasn't quite the wimp he'd pretended to be to get her to come along on the tour, but he wanted her with him. He didn't like it when she was out of his sight, and that was scary. She was maddening and totally not for him, but he had a hard time concentrating on anything but her. He wondered what was the matter with him. Why was he obsessing over a woman who'd never be comfortable with his lifestyle? Talk about doomed relationships. There was no way he and Maggie could be a couple. She hated travel, had no fondness for the outdoors and preferred a sheltered life with a nine-to-five job. He knew all this, but he still couldn't stop thinking about her.

"I'd like you to meet Georgia Gainsborough from Channel 84, a local TV station," the manager said.

"Nice to meet you." He shook the hand of a fluffy-haired blonde in a skimpy red dress.

He wondered if her crimson nails would hold up on one of his excursions. They were dangerously long and looked as sharp as daggers.

They chatted a bit about the books and Mac's adventures. Apparently that's what authors did on tour, a lot of small talk and self-promoting. The reporter stood too close, not that she didn't smell nice, but she was really crowding his space. Where was Maggie when he actually needed her?

Between talking to the manager and the reporter, they seated him at a book-laden table at the front of the store, as exposed as possible to everyone who passed by the entrance. He felt doubly conspicuous because he was wearing his one and only safari jacket, a gift from his brother and sister-in-law several years ago. It felt pretentious even though it was drab khaki cotton. He'd never worn it and was only doing so now because Granville's secretary had pointedly suggested that jeans and shorts would be inappropriate, effectively scrapping his whole wardrobe.

Georgia Gainsborough told her cameraman to haul his butt over to Mac's table. When the tape started to roll, she launched into a sugary introduction of him as an exciting new reality-based author. Mac did his imitation of an author with a hearty smile and silently vowed never to, in his entire life, do anything that would make the evening news. Her attention made him feel like an alien species.

The interview was relatively short and didn't hold any surprises, let alone any intelligent questions. Then the bookstore manager gave a short speech to launch the signing. The cameraman started to leave, but Georgia called him back with more colorful language. The reporter was a nice girl, if a guy was into foul-mouthed bleached blondes.

Where the heck was Maggie? He knew she'd felt superfluous at yesterday's signing. Is that why she'd disappeared?

"Where did you learn everything you write about?" a plump grandmotherly woman asked.

"Mostly from my experiences," he answered. The more vague, the better, in his opinion. It was at least the twentieth time in two days he'd fielded that question. He signed a book "To Grace" as per her instructions. He was hopeless at coming up with clever little sayings to go with the signature so he didn't even try.

Where *was* Maggie? She was supposed to stick around and be his inspiration. If he didn't have all of these people dying to hear about M. S. Stevens's adventures, he'd get up and go look for her.

Two young guys with dark tans and the look of outdoorsmen approached him, and each bought a copy of the latest guide. One didn't want to bother with Mac's signature.

"If I don't lose it in the river, I'll probably drop it in a campfire when I'm through with it," he explained.

"That would be my choice," Mac agreed, pleased that someone was buying it to learn more survival skills. The whole concept of coffee-table books seemed silly to him.

The two guys left his table, but didn't go far. They latched on to Maggie who'd just reappeared from wherever she'd been hiding.

"Oh, I see you both bought the fourth guide," she said cheerfully to the pair.

"Yeah, I've read the first three," the potential book burner said.

Although Mac wanted to hear the rest of the conversation, he was distracted by a woman who was too old for the ponytail and belly-button-baring top she was wearing. She wanted three books to give as Christmas presents, each one inscribed to a whole family of names spelled in peculiar ways.

When Mac surfaced from that, Maggie was still standing off to his right. So were the two jocks with muscles bulging in their tank tops. They were laughing, coming on to her like a couple of horny baboons.

"You must be really strong to paddle through white water," a woman gushed at Mac, leaning across the table to within inches of his face.

If she patted his biceps, he was out of here. There were things no man should do for money.

What about for love?

That uncomfortable thought made him scrawl M. S. Stevens twice as large as usual. He'd better concentrate so he wouldn't slip up and sign his own name.

The manager had her minions keep him supplied with ice water, and the book buyers kept coming. Maggie and the two guys had wandered off, hopefully not together, while he was busy. Mac didn't like feeling jealous. It was dumb to be annoyed by a couple of studs chatting up Maggie. She wasn't his girlfriend. They were oil and water, too different to get seriously interested in each other, not that a relationship was anywhere on his list of priorities.

The blond bombshell reporter was back without her cameraman, or maybe she'd never left. He hadn't noticed.

"You really kicked butt today," she said, bending over his table so far her breasts jiggled in his face.

"I sold a few books."

"I thought maybe we could talk over dinner. You know, discuss your amazing success," she purred.

"I'm afraid we have another commitment this evening," Maggie interrupted, coming up behind gorgeous Georgia.

"My manager," he said, then wondered if he should have said agent.

"Authors have managers?" the reporter asked.

"They do if they're wildly successful like Mr. Stevens," Maggie said with saccharine sweetness, apparently forgetting the power of the press in career building.

"Give me your business card. I'll call you if there's a break in our schedule," Mac said.

He winked at Georgia, hoping his leer would smooth over any rift between M. S. Stevens and the media.

"Anytime," Georgia trilled, then sauntered away, putting all she had into her sexy walk.

"You've made a new fan," Maggie said dryly.

"Isn't that why I'm here?"

"Yes, but I don't know why I had to come along. You're better at public relations than I'll ever be."

"Don't sell yourself short." He moved a step closer, but the few inches that separated them seemed like a huge gulf.

What would he have to do to get her out of his system? He knew what he wanted in life, and it wasn't a wage-slave existence with a woman who didn't share his passion for outdoor adventure. He fervently wished she wouldn't wear perfume that clouded his mind and made him want to nuzzle her throat.

AFTER THE SIGNING—two hours of pure hell watching women fawn over Mac—Maggie wandered the mall with him. They had lunch and took in a matinee movie to kill the afternoon.

Just when she thought they'd said all there was to say about signing books and dealing with the media, she got a surprise. Mac brought up the bookstore again.

"You got pretty cozy with those young guys while I was signing. What were they, college kids?"

"One is an orthodontist, the other works for a shipping company, something to do with computers. I didn't get cozy. They were interested in the guides. I may have mentioned I helped with the research."

"You may have mentioned?" he asked skeptically.

"They were friendly, that's all. Not like that barracuda from the TV station."

"She seemed like a nice girl to me," Mac teased.

"It's not too late for you to call her." It was the last thing Maggie wanted him to do, but she was trying to be cool and to pretend she didn't care.

"She's not my type." His eyes said more than his words. Maggie averted her gaze, afraid he'd be able to read her too easily.

Whatever she'd expected on this tour, it wasn't the tension that sizzled between them whenever they talked about anything more controversial than the weather.

"You can drive if you like," she said as they approached the white rental car.

"If that's what you want."

"It doesn't matter to me either way."

"Okay, I will."

"I don't usually get lost, you know. It's just my traveling jinx."

"There's no such thing as a jinx." He took the key she offered and opened the door on the passenger side for her.

"Whenever I travel, bad things happen."

"Missing an exit on the expressway has nothing to do with luck. You'd never driven it before, and maybe you weren't paying enough attention."

"Yes, I was. You'll find out before this tour is over," she warned. "I'm jinxed whenever I leave home. I can't even go to the supermarket without having a cart rammed into the backs of my ankles. I wish I were kidding," she said sadly, knowing she could never be the kind of woman Mac deserved.

She was serious. He laughed. They were both quiet on the drive to their lodging, a good thing since Mac apparently loathed big-city traffic as much as she hated being in bear-and-snake infested woods.

"Why do we have to drive into the city for a room?" Mac asked, fortunately driving with more skill than enthusiasm.

"According to the gargoyle..." She had to stop using Rayanne's name for Granville's right-hand woman. "According to Miss Mason, there's a lot going on this week, some historical stuff and a big convention that gobbled up the rooms in major hotels and motels. She found us a bed-and-breakfast near the Inner Harbor where we can soak up some local color and enjoy the waterfront, the marina and stuff. It sounds quaint."

"Quaint." He chewed on the word, apparently not liking it.

"It has to be better than sleeping in a tent," she muttered.

Maggie wasn't at all disappointed when she saw the King's Row Inn. It was a gigantic Victorian-style mansion converted into a bed-and-breakfast with twenty-five rooms for guests. The storybook house had a round corner tower, a widow's walk and more alcoves and fanciful peaks than she could take in at first sight. The owners had highlighted the odd-shaped windows, the front door and the gingerbread trim with white and periwinkle blue to contrast with the dove-gray siding.

"It looks like a lopsided wedding cake," Mac commented when a young man who introduced himself as the owners' son had driven the car away to park it.

"It's convenient. We can walk to the waterfront and restaurants." Maggie sniffed the fresh breeze coming off the water, a welcome change from the air-conditioned confines of the car.

"I hope that means you'll join me for dinner," he said.

"It's a bed-and-breakfast. The only meal they serve is breakfast."

What would they do until it was time to go to bed? Part of her loved being with Mac, but she had serious reservations about getting closer to him. He wasn't her type, no way, never, impossible. But when she looked at his face, her resistance was at low tide. She loved the deep blue of his eyes and the tiny sun lines beside them that crinkled when he smiled. She'd never seen whiter teeth or a more pleasing nose and chin. His lips were broad and sensual, full of promise and...

And she was losing it! Sully was unhappy with her for getting him into this author charade, and she wasn't exactly pleased with him for insisting she go along. So far, she'd been useless. He didn't need her any more than he needed one more adoring female hovering over him. When the sale of Granville Publishing was finalized, she wouldn't allow herself to be roped into any more road trips.

"This place is different, anyway," he said after they'd climbed a tier of steps beside a ramp that made the long front porch accessible to everyone. "Let's see if it's as fancy inside."

They went in and found it totally different from the cheery facade outside. The decor in the front hallway paid homage to the city's most famous literary light, Edgar Allan Poe. His portrait, a dark amateurish effort done in thick oils, hung in gloomy splendor on dark paneling. The carpet was midnight-blue with faint dots of gray. A curving staircase with a heavily carved banister seemed like an ascent into gloom. To the left, through an arched doorway, the long, narrow windows of the parlor were draped with heavy crimson velvet. Victorian love seats and side chairs with carved walnut legs and needlepoint seats were scattered around the room in conversational groupings.

A spacious room to the right served as an office, and a tall, slender woman with graying red hair greeted them with a gracious Southern accent. She introduced herself as Mrs. Chamberlain. Maggie thought the woman's long black skirt, gray blouse and pale complexion matched the ambience of the entryway.

"I'm so pleased you chose to stay at the King's Row Inn," she said before getting down to the business of signing them in.

"Our pleasure. This is quite a house," Mac said, smiling.

He charmed their hostess, of course. Women doted on his combination of boyish charm and masculine ruggedness. Maggie hated going along with a crowd. She couldn't let herself succumb to him the way casual strangers did.

The house had a little elevator, an iron cage that labored up to the third floor where they were booked into the last available accommodations. There were only two rooms for guests on that level, and the owner apologized because the bathroom was down the hall. She pointed out an emergency exit, a narrow staircase once used by the female servants. The men, of course, had been housed over the stable, she explained.

Maggie was surprised to see that her room was connected with the one next door. She heard a key click on Mac's side.

"I guess if you want to keep me out, you have to slide home the bolt on your side," he said, sticking his head through the doorway and pointing at a simple safety lock, the kind her grandmother used to have on the inside of her kitchen door.

"High-tech security," she said dryly.

"Your room is even weirder than mine." He came in and looked around at the silver-striped wallpaper, heavy black-velvet bedspread and drapes and the white lace doilies on a chair back, dresser and small desk. A cross-stitched sampler of a red heart hung over the bed with prints of ravens on either side, obviously more homage to Poe and his chilling tales.

"Do people come here to be scared?" she wondered out loud, thinking of what she'd read about Lizzie Borden's house where guests could sleep in a supposedly haunted atmosphere, *if* they could sleep.

"Look at my room," Sully said.

He'd dropped his duffel on a blood-red velvet spread. Matching drapes drawn back by heavy black cords framed a long, very narrow window that went almost floor to ceiling.

Maggie laughed. A less-than-skillful artist had rendered "The Pit and the Pendulum" in thick, garish oil paints.

"If you're scared, we can look for something else," he teased.

"Don't be silly. It's just a gimmick to decorate like this. Poe never came here. It was built after he was dead. Anyway, I always thought his personal life was more pathetic than scary. He had major substance abuse problems before doctors identified them as that."

"Let's forget Poe and the writing business and find a place for dinner," Mac said.

They walked, ate and walked some more, holding hands as though they were lovers, which, of course, they were not. The summer sky had deepened to dark blue by the time they got back to the bed-and-breakfast.

Maggie had stuffed herself on New England clam

chowder, crab cakes and bites of Mac's lobster, hoping a huge dinner would make her too sleepy to remember he was sleeping only feet away behind the dark connecting door.

Not that she didn't trust him. She had doubts about herself, and their delightful dinner together made her even more aware of how much she'd like to be in Mac's arms. Yet the risk was too high. She could so easily fall in love with him, but she couldn't live the way he did, river rafting one month, climbing some remote mountain or dashing off to a South American jungle the next.

"Good night," he said when they reached her door, looking at her in a way that made her fumble to unlock it.

"Good night."

"I won't lock the adjoining door on my side. You know, just in case you find Poe's ghost an uneasy bedfellow."

"Don't be silly. I don't believe in ghosts."

The single ceiling light in the hallway was muted by a yellowish frosted-glass globe. The place was a little spooky after dark, but the owner, Mrs. Chamberlain, had mentioned that every other room in the house was booked. No switching to less Gothic digs. Rayanne would have loved staying here!

Maggie waited until she was sure Mac was in bed before going down the hall to the bathroom. When the light under the crack of the adjoining door went out, she decided the coast was clear.

The bathroom was huge by modern standards with both a big claw-foot tub and a more recently built shower stall. Maggie opted for a long soak in the tub, pouring in lavender-scented oil and staying in the water until her toes were puckered. Dressed in her nightie, she quietly crept back to her room, although Mac was undoubtedly asleep. He hadn't been bothered by the lumpy ground under his tent. He'd probably zonked out instantly in a real bed. She should be so lucky!

She'd wasted gallons of hot water hoping she'd be relaxed enough to doze off immediately. Instead her joints were as jumpy as springs, and her nerves were hot-wired. She knew the reason but couldn't go through the door to Mac's room, not even if her sanity depended on it.

Turning out the room light, she went to the window and raised the old-fashioned canvas shade covering the single pane. The draperies, she'd learned, were strictly ornamental. Beyond the glass, the sky was star-studded, lessening the gloom in her room. Cities glowed at night. She liked the illumination that radiated out from populated areas even on cloudy nights. Maggie knew she belonged in a city, so why was she thinking about a deserted ridge with dark woods behind it?

She turned back to the room, intending to go to bed, but something had changed. There was no band of light from the hallway in the gap between the door and the bare boards of the floor. No red letters were glowing on the digital bedside clock. The phone was lost in the darkness, no little green message dot marking its place.

This was a dang creepy place for a power failure. She was alone in a third-floor room that had probably been home to underpaid, overworked serving girls in the house's heyday. If ghosts stayed around because they'd had miserable lives...

Was the exit sign still lit above the entrance to the narrow stairs at the end of the hall? She couldn't find her way out of here if it wasn't. She closed her eyes, counted to twenty and opened them hoping the black-out would be over.

Just when she'd decided to hop into bed and pull the covers over her head, she heard a soft tap, tap, tap. It took a moment to determine it was coming from the door that joined the two rooms. Drawing on her memory, she navigated her way toward the raps without bumping any body parts or tripping over the end of the bed.

She'd slid the bolt shut, but hadn't bothered to lock the old-fashioned lock with her key.

"Is that you, Mac?" she asked in a low voice appropriate to the dark room.

"Of course. Are you all right?"

"Sure, why wouldn't I be? I thought you were sleeping."

"Bed's too soft," he said.

"Should we call someone and report we don't have any electricity?" she asked.

"No doubt the owners already know."

"What if the power is only out on this floor?"

"Do you need light right now?"

"The clock…we need to drive to D.C. in the morning."

"The sun will be up long before we have to leave. It always wakes me up."

"What did you say?" She hadn't caught all his words; it was as though he'd turned around and started walking back to his bed.

"Open the door," he said loudly enough to be heard.

That was a really bad idea, but her hand didn't pay any attention to her brain's red alert. Her fingers crept over the jamb then froze when she found the bolt.

She couldn't think of a single good reason to let him

into her room, but she was tingling from head to toe wondering what would happen if she did.

"Ah, sweetheart," he said, using the term of endearment with hesitancy. "I think my room is haunted."

"No, it isn't!" She giggled nervously.

"Yes. I'm shivering all over, and the image of a beautiful woman is keeping me awake." He made his voice sound sexy even though he had to shout through the door.

"It's only your imagination." She hoped. "A dark, strange room can do that to you."

"What I'm feeling is very real," he cajoled. "Would you keep me locked out if Poe's ghost were sitting on the end of my bed?"

"I guess I couldn't do that." Her fingers were possessed. They were unlocking the door in spite of her better judgment.

She stepped aside and let Mac into her room.

9

NOW MAGGIE WAS REALLY scared, but not of the darkness or ghostly spirits. She was afraid of making a mistake with Mac.

His arms circled her and his bare chest was so close it tickled her cheek. She loved being held by him and didn't feel jittery anymore. His touch calmed her as no hot bath could, but was this the start of something that would hurt both of them?

"You couldn't sleep?" she asked. "After that night in the tent, I thought you could sleep anywhere."

"I faked it. I wanted to crawl into your sleeping bag so badly I hardly dozed all night."

He pressed his lips against her forehead, a feathery touch that made her knees buckle. She brushed against his leg and remembered how he slept—stark naked.

"Oh, oh."

"What's wrong?" His lips caressed her eyelids, which were closed because she was remembering more of him than she could see in the darkness.

Was he naked? Did she want him to be?

She reached out, only intending to check for a waistband with the tips of her fingers. He picked that moment to move. Not only did she find the elastic, confirming that he wasn't in the altogether, but two fingers accidentally slid under his briefs where they had no business being.

He made a little sound, more gasp than moan, and found her lips. There'd never been a first kiss like this. She saw light burst inside her closed lids and felt tingles from her nose to her chin. She wanted Mac even if she had to live in a tree house and launder his loincloth in a river filled with crocodiles.

"Oh, my!" She gasped for breath and rose on bare toes, bracing herself against his body for a kiss that rocked her foundation.

"If I'd known this would happen, I would've cut the power myself," he murmured between kisses.

"Are you sure you didn't?"

His hands were under her nightgown, rubbing her back, then performing sorcery with his thumbs on the back of her neck.

"I didn't think of it."

His breath was warm in her ear, and he kissed the sensitive spot where her jaw ended and her throat began.

"Oh, that's wonderful."

Her fingers were still trapped under his waistband. She plunged her hand downward, sure that nothing in the world was sexier than his lean, sleek hip.

Whatever she'd expected, it wasn't to be swept off her feet and lifted into his arms. He carried her through the door into his room, darker than hers because the shade was pulled down to the sill.

She tried to think of a reason not to be here, but couldn't come up with a single one. He lowered her to the bed, finding it by instinct and luck because the room was as murky as the inside of a cave.

"We shouldn't do this," she said, kissing his jaw.

It was a token protest. She wouldn't let him stop, not when her whole body was on fire with desire. She raised her arms and tossed aside her nightie, probably the most wanton thing she'd ever done.

He left her, fumbling around in the dark, and for a panicky instant she was afraid he was having second thoughts.

"What are you doing?" She sat up, but could only see a faint outline as he stepped out of his briefs.

"Promise you won't get mad and kick me out?" he asked.

"It's your room."

She'd dance naked at noon on the widow's walk above them before she'd let him go. This was why he'd insisted she come and why she'd agreed to it. The spark that had ignited when he'd first come to her office was a raging inferno now. She hadn't known she had it in her to be this aroused.

"I was optimistic," he said, doing something she couldn't see.

He found his way back to the bed and handed her a strip of foil-wrapped packets.

"You thought I was easy," she accused, not too seriously.

"Easy! You wouldn't even have dinner with me in Philadelphia."

"I wanted to," she admitted. "Too much."

"You were afraid this would happen?"

He pulled her down beside him and gently kissed her face, stroking her breasts while she held her breath in anticipation. She wanted to go fast and feel him moving inside her. Mostly she wanted to know if the world would rock on its axis when Mac made love to her.

"I wish we had a light," he murmured, kissing her nipples and stroking her tummy and thighs, but treating the area lower as a forbidden zone. "You're beautiful. I'm dying to see all of you."

Sure that she'd die of happiness, she explored his body with her hands and lips, loving the soapy scent of his skin and the short, sharp growth of new beard on his chin.

Red and green dots flickered in her consciousness. She'd been too drugged by sensation to notice when the lights on the phone and clock came on again.

"You're even more gorgeous than I imagined," he said.

He propped himself up on one elbow beside her. Far from being uncomfortable under his intense scrutiny, she returned it, fascinated by the hard muscles in his torso and the golden tan of his chest and arms. Most enduring was the pale white skin where the sun never touched him. It made a strong man seem vulnerable.

His visual appraisal was so openly admiring, she let her eyes dwell on his erection, huge compared to anything in her limited experience.

For no reason at all, she started giggling, or maybe she was so excited and happy it had to come out somewhere.

"Are you laughing at me?" He sounded more bemused than offended.

"No, I just don't know how to deal with everything I'm feeling."

"Let me help you."

He entered her with his hand until she was frantic and impatient. When he finally joined his body to hers and began an effortless rhythm, her world exploded in a dazzling climax.

Later, much later, when she didn't think she'd ever

be able to make herself leave Mac and this bed, the sun burst into the room around the edges of the shade.

"We have to go," he said, kissing her shoulder and caressing the swell of her hip.

"Go without me." Getting up seemed beyond her.

"No chance."

She let one arm drop over the edge of the black-sheeted mattress. She didn't have enough energy to pick her way through all the condom packages on the floor.

"I didn't want to go on this tour, but I'm glad I did," she said.

"I am, too."

He gave her a wet kiss on the ear, calculated to rouse her from a stupor induced by satisfaction.

"We'll be back in Pittsburgh tonight," she said, "but there will be more tours. This one was only a warmup."

"Yeah, we'll have to hustle to make our flight after the signing."

"Then where will you go?" She rolled over to face him.

"I'm a little worried about Gram. I called her after we got back from dinner, but she wouldn't tell me if anything went wrong. I'd better go check on her directly from the airport since you have your car there, too."

He stood and stretched, his back toward her. He was beautiful. Maybe men didn't like to be called that, but he was. Beautiful but not really hers. He'd be off hiking the Grand Canyon or dog sledding in the Yukon, and she'd sit at home thinking of tousled hair, sleek, tanned muscles and adorable white buns.

She wanted to cry, very much afraid the unthinkable had happened and she was in love with Sully.

MAC WAS EARLY for his noon appointment with Granville on Monday. He parked three blocks away and walked slowly to the publisher's office so he wouldn't get there too soon. He didn't want to look as eager as he felt, not about the meeting but about seeing Maggie again. It had been less than twenty-four hours since he'd left her at the airport after their two-day tour, and it seemed like ages.

He stopped for a second when he realized he might not see her at the office. Maybe she wouldn't be involved in the meeting with Granville. It'd be safer for him if she wasn't. He didn't know where this thing with her was going. Worse, he felt befuddled and confused, an unusual state of mind for him. His body still hummed with well-being after the best sex of his life, but he was mature enough to know it had more to do with how they felt about each other than how they clicked in bed.

What he didn't know was where to go next. Maggie was a hothouse flower. He couldn't transplant her to a cabin in the hills. On the other hand, he'd tried living in a city apartment and had hated it. He needed to wake up in the morning with fresh air in his nostrils, not the stale stink of other people's cooking.

Maggie was worth any sacrifice, but she wouldn't be happy saddled with a civilized Sully. It had been an eye-opener to learn his grandfather had been a troublemaker and a misfit until he found the right life for him. Would Mac go the other way if he gave up the outdoor life he loved? Would he become a misfit himself, bitter and not worthy of Maggie?

He went into the publishing company and rode the elevator to the third floor for his appointment, torn between eagerness to see her and indecision about what to do.

The cage stopped with a jolt typical of old elevators, and the door slid open. Mac walked out into a much fancier corridor than the ones below. Gleaming butterscotch floor tiles enhanced the art that crowded the walls, mostly oil portraits of whiskered men in formal wear. Some could have been relatives of Homer Granville, and most looked dignified and self-important.

"They're my ancestors and other great men of their day," Granville said, coming out of a golden-oak door with geometric carving. "It's been a little hobby of mine to assemble portraits of Pittsburgh's past leaders."

"Interesting," Mac replied, thanking his lucky stars he'd never have to sit for hours posing in a high-starched collar and a frock coat. He was too busy living to worry about being remembered.

"Peter Pierpont is here," Granville said, lowering his voice. "We're very close to concluding our deal. I can't tell you how happy I am someone will keep the family firm afloat after I retire. Well, come in, Mr. Stevens. We have luncheon reservations at the Renaissance Club, and Peter's dying to talk to you."

Mac walked into a spacious office with thick beige carpeting, paneled walls and green leather furniture. The mahogany desktop was empty except for an ornate antique silver pen and inkwell set and a laptop computer.

"Peter, you remember M. S. Stevens."

Mac wouldn't be thrilled handing over a business of his to a guy dressed like a yacht captain. Pierpont's cap was loaded with gold braid, and the silver buttons on his navy blazer were polished to brilliance.

"I hear the trial run of your publicity tour went splendidly," Pierpont said. "We'll be scheduling more in the near future."

Mac was too disappointed that Maggie wasn't there to do more than nod his head. Pierpont and Granville exchanged some sales statistics about the guides without paying any attention to him, then the door opened. Mac turned and saw her.

Maggie inclined her head. He was speechless. The woman gave new meaning to gorgeous. She looked demure and sexy at the same time in a pink suit with a short jacket, a formfitting short skirt and little white pumps with not very high heels. He wanted to touch her, if only to shake her hand, but she kept her distance, walking around the desk to lay a folder on it.

"Well, if everyone's ready, we'll leave now," Granville said.

After a short ride in the long gray limo Pierpont had hired for the day, they entered one of Pittsburgh's newest skyscrapers, the Jurgen Building, a tower of glass and steel. An express elevator carried them to the top floor, and they got off in the Renaissance Club, a businessman's restaurant with windows overlooking the river and the new stadium.

Mac was uncomfortable when the maître d' provided him with a jacket to wear with his jeans and madras cotton shirt. The club's employee was wearing a tux, and he held out a jacket that smelled vaguely of smoke as though it—or Mac—were contaminated.

"Sorry about that. I should've warned you to wear a coat," Granville said.

Pierpont tried to be gallant and offered Maggie his

arm. She took it without looking at Mac. The jerk seated her at a cozy table for four, the better to rub knees, no doubt. Mac had a sour taste in his mouth, but at least he managed to sit across from Maggie. Eventually she'd have to look directly at him over the white linen tablecloth.

She seemed to be pretending not to be impressed by the elegance of the place, dark wainscoting, creamy embossed wallpaper, strategically placed trees in pots and waiters who looked ready for a military parade. Mac didn't have to pretend; he wasn't impressed.

The menu was written in French with, of course, no prices. Mac was good at languages, and his college French came back to him well enough to order grilled salmon, a spinach salad and a beer with a passably good accent. Pierpont tried and sounded as if he had a mouthful of mush. Maggie did okay, admitting high school French hadn't been her best subject, but Granville could pass for a Parisian, at least in Pittsburgh.

She still hadn't looked at him, which puzzled him even more than it annoyed him. That was the way the meal went.

"I understand you're researching the next guide," Pierpont said to Mac. "What's the title again?"

"*Scenic Gems Most People Miss,*" Maggie quickly said. "At least, that's the theme."

"Well, be assured, I'll be one hundred percent behind it when Granville Publishing is part of my conglomerate."

"That's good news," Maggie said.

Mac ranked Pierpont's statement right up there with garbage strikes and political campaign promises. The last thing he wanted was a permanent job pretending to be a nonexistent writer.

At least Pierpont had other pressing business, and
the lunch didn't drag on. Mac was happy to surrender
the ratty jacket when it was over, but he still hadn't
had a single private word with Maggie. He had no
choice but to follow her inside Granville Publishing
after the limo dropped the two of them off and continued on with Granville and Pierpont.

"Lunch was fun," he said dryly, following her into
her inner sanctum without invitation. "You did a great
job of ignoring me."

"It was a business meeting," she said primly.
"What did you want me to do?"

"What business? All we did was listen to Pierpont's
bragging."

"That's true." Finally she smiled at him.

He shut the office door and took her in his arms for
the kiss that had been waiting to happen.

"So we're writing another book," he said, reluctantly releasing her.

"Pierpont is in a big rush. The other guides took six
to nine months each. He wants another one done in
three. It would serve him right if I wrote it for another
publisher." She crossed her arms over her chest, thinking of the possibilities.

"Would you do that?"

"Not to Mr. Granville, but he'll be out of the picture
if the deal goes through. He was generous in the terms
of my contracts. I control my own pseudonym. All I'd
have to do is change the title to something besides a
guide." She sighed. "Mac, I'm so stressed! Three
months! I really need your help now. You've probably
been to places I've never heard of."

"What kind of help?" He looked skeptical.

"You know, share your experiences with me. You promised."

"I could probably write a book myself," he mused.

"You wouldn't! Isn't it enough that the public thinks you're M. S. Stevens? Would you do a book to compete with mine?"

"Probably not. About our collaboration—"

"We're not collaborators. I just need to tap into some of your real-life adventures."

"Like the one in Baltimore."

She blushed. He loved it.

"Tell you what. We'll get together on the weekend. You can pick my brain all you like. Save both days for me."

"I don't know."

She was trying to pace, but her office was too small to go more than a couple of steps in any direction.

"I'll give you the details later in the week. Meanwhile I have a load of lumber waiting for me." He started to leave.

"Mac."

"What?"

"Baltimore was all right, wasn't it?" The flush in her cheeks became brighter.

"Oh, yes!"

This girl made her living with words, and "all right" was the best she could do?

"I mean, we're just good friends, right?" she asked. "It's not as if we have enough in common to be more than that."

Good friends who'd generated enough electricity to light up a ball park for a night game, he thought. He had to get out of here before he was too aroused to get on the elevator.

"We'll talk on the weekend," he said, backing out of her office.

He closed the door before she could come up with an excuse not to see him. He had a plan.

10

MAGGIE REPLAYED Mac's message on her answering machine for the tenth or eleventh time, still mystified by what he had in mind. They were going someplace to do something. Knowing Sully, it could be anywhere or anything.

He'd thoughtfully provided her with a list of things to pack for an overnighter. Apparently pajamas were optional. She had a small suitcase stuffed with jeans, sweatshirt, bathing suit and the usual travel necessities. No worry there, but he'd emphasized sunscreen and bug repellent. She had a bad feeling about this mystery trip.

Should she call him and cancel? Of course she should, but every time she picked up the phone, she had second thoughts. She desperately wanted to see him again. Still, it was a very bad idea.

She was ready to go when he came for her at six sharp Friday evening, not even waiting for him to come to her door. She rushed out like a teen on her first date because she was so eager to see him.

"Okay, Sully," she said, trying to sound cool and detached even though she was a seething bundle of raw nerves. "This is as far as I go unless you tell me what's up."

He didn't pay the slightest attention to her, but

opened the rear hatch of his vehicle and loaded her suitcase.

"I mean it, Mac!" She crossed her arms and planted the soles of her running shoes on the pavement.

"Haven't you ever been on a mystery trip? The object is to be surprised."

"I'm not sleeping in a tent!"

"Absolutely not." He grinned, clearly enjoying Maggie's reaction.

"If I don't want to do what you have planned, I'm not obligated just because I came along to satisfy my curiosity."

"I wouldn't have it any other way."

He smiled and opened the passenger door for her. His hair was unruly, and he hadn't shaved this morning. His faded blue T-shirt and khaki shorts had been worn a few too many times, but he was still outrageously gorgeous. She wanted to hug him with every ounce of strength in her arms. She wanted to grab his bottom and squeeze those delectable buns. She longed to taste the saltiness of his skin and to inhale the erotic musk of his body.

She was bloody loony! Mac was stupendously wrong for her. She should make a beeline for her door and lock it before he could persuade her to go.

Instead she meekly slid onto the seat and fastened the belt. Besides being curious, she wanted to spend time with Mac, even though a lasting relationship with him was beyond hope. They just lived in two different worlds. That didn't mean she couldn't enjoy the fun while it lasted, though.

Cora had packed a picnic dinner for them: fried chicken, homemade biscuits and big slices of cinnamon-apple pie. They stopped at a highway rest stop outside of Pittsburgh and made fast work of the feast. Mac still refused to tell her where they were going.

"Trust me," he said, grinning in that maddening way of his.

She wanted to kiss the smile off his face.

A couple of hours into West Virginia she dozed off. Conversation had been awkward. There were too many things she didn't want to discuss with Mac, for instance the fate of the guides and the great sex they'd enjoyed in Baltimore. He seemed distracted, answering her questions in an absentminded way when they didn't involve his annoyingly top-secret plan.

When she woke up, they were on a dark and twisty road in the mountains. She'd been dreaming the kind of dreams that left her edgy and aroused.

"Where are we?"

"Almost to Decora, West Virginia. That's where we'll be sleeping tonight."

Just sleeping? She didn't ask. Her dream had faded, but she still felt achy and sexy.

Would Mac drive all evening just to spend another night with her like the one they'd had in Baltimore? Why would he, when she had an apartment all to herself and they could spend time there? Anyway, he hadn't said or done a thing to suggest he wanted a repeat of the night in Old Edgar's shadow.

The town, if it could be called that, was a collection of small homes and a block-long business section with a tavern, beauty parlor, café and gas-and-grocery stop. To the east and the west, round-topped, forested mountains sheltered the settlement. The dark waters of a swift-flowing river went past only yards from the road.

Mac turned onto one of the few side streets and pulled up in front of a rambling rectangular house with a porch and a balcony, both running the length of the house. A small white neon sign indicated it was Charlotte's Bed-and-Breakfast.

"We're staying here?"

"Don't worry. I booked separate rooms."

That wasn't her worry. It was why they were driving into the backwoods of West Virginia at all that concerned her.

After grabbing their things out of the car, they made their way to the entrance of the B and B. A sheet of cardboard tacked beside the front door directed guests to walk in.

They walked into a big common room with pegged plank flooring worn down by millions of footsteps. Maggie guessed the house was as old as they came in this part of the state. The owner hadn't tried to renovate it or to redecorate in some cutesy country style but had preserved it as a historical structure. The massive fireplace was made of giant rough-hewn rocks, and the boards of the wall glowed honey-gold under an electrified wrought-iron chandelier.

"Have you been here before?" Maggie asked.

"No."

Mac's answer was anything but informative.

The owner wasn't the care-worn mountain woman Maggie was expecting. He wasn't even a Charlotte.

"Herb Quinn. What can I do for you folks?"

Their host was lanky, bearded and extremely thin. He could be forty or sixty. It was hard to tell since the skin that showed above his drab gray facial hair looked like tanned leather.

"We have reservations. Two rooms for Mac Sully."

"Two rooms." Quinn chewed on that as though he didn't quite understand it.

He wasn't alone. If Mac didn't want to share a bed with her, why bring her all this way?

"You have them, don't you?" Mac asked, not quite hiding his impatience.

"Yup, sure do. I collect up front, cash only. That's two nights you'll be staying, isn't it?"

Two nights? Mac hadn't been at all clear about that in his phone message. Maggie now wondered if she'd packed enough.

Quinn put the cash Mac gave him in his pocket and handed them a couple of old iron keys chained to rectangles of wood. He then directed them to the stairs at the end of a hallway that bisected the back of the house.

"Breakfast is from six to eight," Quinn told them.

That said, he went into a room on the side of the hall and left them to find their own way.

The stairs were so narrow Maggie's hips brushed against the crudely plastered walls on either side. They were so steep, Mac carried her suitcase in his arms, his own duffel over his shoulder and hanging down his back. He bumped an elbow more than once on the climb.

Upstairs an upper hallway ran the length of the B and B with a row of doors on either side. This part of the house was perhaps a hundred years newer than the lower level, which still made the wallpapered walls antique.

"Have you ever tried a hotel? You know, swimming pool, exercise room, newspaper in front of the door in the morning?" she asked when she caught her breath from the climb.

"Yeah. I don't like swimming in chlorine."

"But where do you find these places? Is there a guide to the bed-and-breakfasts time forgot?"

He laughed. What made him think she wasn't serious? She'd toyed with the idea of a guide that rated bed-and-breakfasts. Until now, she'd assumed the research would be enjoyable, but the collection of wicked metal animal traps hanging from the ceiling at one end of the upper story gave her doubts.

Mac unlocked the first of their two rooms and snapped on a floor lamp with a fringed shade seventy-five years out of fashion. An iron bed painted white was covered by a crazy quilt made of hundreds of small snippets of old cloth, the first homey touch in the place. There was actually a washstand with a blue-and-white-flowered bowl and pitcher. She hoped they were only ornamental.

"We'll look at both rooms, and you can take your choice," he said.

"Big of you. I don't seem to see a bathroom."

"Must be one somewhere unless that's it." He pointed at a chamber pot beside the bed.

She was ready to go home.

Sully was the explorer. He found a bathroom the likes of which she'd never seen before at the end of the hall. The commode sat on top of a wooden platform like a throne, and the water tank for flushing was mounted on the wall above it. The tub had claw feet and looked as if nursery-rhyme characters should be rowing in it. A flimsy hook on the inside of the door was supposed to assure privacy.

There were six rooms on the floor, and at least three were occupied by people who played the radio, snored or made the floorboards creak, hopefully by doing vigorous exercises.

"Well, which one?" Mac asked, throwing open the door of the second room.

"The other one!" she said quickly.

Was it possible this mattress was stuffed with corn-cob husks? She didn't know what else would account for the thin, lumpy mattress covered by a faded pink-and-purple blanket with baskets of flowers woven into the threadbare design.

Mac still had her suitcase, rolling it on the worn green, tan and red linoleum in the hallway toward the first room. It sounded like the echo of cannonballs, and she expected Herb Quinn to come up and tell them to pipe down.

"It could be better," Mac admitted as he hoisted her suitcase onto a fragile-looking wooden luggage rack.

It'd be a whole lot better if he'd sleep in here, too, she thought. The space was adequate enough, but Mac made it seem tiny. When he was in a room, his over-whelming presence filled it to the exclusion of every-thing and everyone else.

"Do you think I deserve a good-night kiss for haul-ing your case up those stairs?" he asked, sounding al-most shy.

"I'm not sure what you deserve. Can't you tell me why we're here in Motel Hell?"

"You'll find out…" He winked when she stuck out her tongue.

He inclined his body in her direction, but she had to take two steps to connect. Okay, maybe she was too eager, giving him the impression she was desperate to kiss him, but a girl deserved something for checking into this backwoods hovel.

She well remembered Mac's kisses, but this one was different, sweet, gentle and lingering. She parted her lips, welcoming penetration by his tongue. He cupped her face softly but firmly. This truly was a good-night kiss.

"We have to be up early in the morning," he said.

"I'm not getting up at dawn to eat breakfast here."

"Trust me," he said. "Set your alarm to be downstairs at six."

He pressed his lips against her forehead, which hardly counted as a kiss, and left the room, closing the door behind him. She locked it, wishing she hadn't slept in the car. Now she was wide awake and dying to spend the night in Mac's arms.

What was with him? Why had he changed so much, holding her at arm's length even though this weekend together was his idea?

"Drat!"

She sat on the edge of the bed, the only place in the room to sit, and stared at yellow wallpaper with faded orange flowers and moped. Her life had been so simple B.S.—before Sully.

WHEN MAGGIE LEARNED what was scheduled tomorrow, she was going to kill him. He probably deserved it.

For a long time Mac lay on the lumpy mattress thinking about her. Remembering Baltimore was no way to lull himself to sleep, but his memories were so vivid he could smell the natural perfume of her skin.

He would've stayed with her tonight, maybe should have. The trouble was he didn't know how to reconcile what he felt for her with the impossibility of being with her all the time. His wanderlust wasn't plaguing him now, but it was only a matter of time—and Gram's health—before he'd need the kind of adventure that made him feel fully alive.

He tried to imagine Maggie in the Australian Outback or the Arctic, both places he longed to visit. He could easily conjure up a vision of sharing a sleeping bag or a narrow bunk with her, but he was sure she'd hate roughing it. She really believed she was jinxed when she traveled. Even if he could persuade her to take a chance on his way of life, she'd be miserable.

Mac wanted Maggie, but he didn't want to make her unhappy. He felt obligated to give her some experiences she could use to make her writing more realistic, but there wasn't any future for the two of them together.

What he should have done was keep his distance, stay away from her from the beginning. He didn't know why he hadn't. He looked his weakness squarely in the face, and her name was Maggie.

His only chance was to share something he loved with her. If she hated it—and she probably would—the gulf between them would be too great to bridge.

WHEN MAGGIE FIRST WOKE UP, she wished she hadn't agreed to come with Mac. She wanted to wake up in her own bed and not face what this day would bring. She lay staring at the network of cracks in the ceiling and wrinkled her nose at a musty smell in the room. It was hard to believe many people paid to stay here. What on earth would bring them to Decora, West Virginia?

She joined Mac and a couple of sleepy-eyed, middle-aged guests in the dining room and had a breakfast of pasty gray oatmeal and a grocery-store donut several days old. Afterward she walked down to the riverfront with Mac, who was still being mysterious about his plan.

"You're going to learn a lot for your next book," he said grinning to himself.

"Our deal was for you to tell me about things you've done and places you've been for research."

"I've never been here, so it's a first for both of us."

Why did he sound so darned chipper? It was inhuman to be out on the street before 7:00 a.m., and what a street it was. If it wasn't for the service station with garish yellow-and-green pumps and a pickup truck in front of a weathered wooden house, the area could have been a set for a depressing movie about backwoods life a century ago.

The air was cool for midsummer, but temperatures were usually lower in the mountains. To fight off the chill, she was wearing jeans and a Pittsburgh Steelers sweatshirt over her T-shirt. Mac was dressed the same way, but his sweatshirt was gunmetal gray with no logo.

"Why won't you tell me..."

She didn't need to finish her sentence. A small black-and-yellow bus pulled out from a side street, and Maggie knew she'd been had.

"'The New River Rafters,'" she read from a sign on the side of the bus, which was pulling a trailer with inflatable rafts. "Is this your idea of a joke, Sully?"

"No joke."

He took her arm as if he expected her to make a break for safety. She considered doing just that.

"You hated the book tour, and you want to get even," she accused him.

"I enjoyed some of it," he said, squeezing her hand.

"Well, I'm not going."

"Okay, but you may be bored back at the bed-and-breakfast with Quinn. I expect to be gone all day."

"You'd leave me stranded here while you play around in a rubber boat?"

"I'm betting you're not the big chicken you think you are. You may get wet rafting on the river, but you'll have fun."

"I don't think so."

"And when you give advice on white-water rafting, you'll know what you're talking about this time."

"I consult experts. I research thoroughly," she argued.

"You're a phony."

"What?" She stopped in the middle of the street they were crossing.

"You heard me. You wouldn't need me to pretend to be M. S. Stevens if you weren't afraid to try things yourself."

"I am not afraid! I'm just not lucky. Things happen to me. Every time I travel, it's a disaster."

"Was Baltimore a disaster?"

"That's not what I mean, and you know it."

"I know you got in the wrong lane on the expressway and had to get off for directions. No big deal. It happens to people all the time."

A big black pickup came down the road, forcing them to finish crossing to the other side.

He walked ahead to a dock where the bus had parked. Several people who had been waiting came out of a shelter with a small New River Rafters sign over the door. The driver of the black pickup parked in a gravel lot and got out.

"It's so foggy back there I thought we'd miss the bus," a lean man with a gray crewcut said.

"I told you we should have left before four," his female companion said. "See? The bus that will bring us back is already here."

Her hair was a mop of bright yellow curls, and her face was weathered to a dark tan crisscrossed by fine wrinkles.

Would an outdoorsy woman like this buy the survival guides? Maggie wondered. Maybe Mac was right. She was a phony. She should give up on them. Maybe she could write a gardening book or concentrate on a bed-and-breakfast guide.

She wasn't going to start her B and B research here in Decora, though. Herb was scary, and she was afraid of losing her breakfast if she inspected his kitchen. She didn't trust a man who wore the same clothes two days in a row.

She was trapped. If she didn't go rafting, Mac would think she was an even bigger chicken than he already thought she was. Unfortunately, he might not want anything else to do with her after this. Judging by his actions last night, maybe he didn't anyway, but for once in her life she had to take a big risk.

"So tell me what to do," she said, capitulating with less than good grace.

More people arrived while Mac helped her adjust a helmet from a chest in the trailer. A pair of guides, a young man and woman who looked young enough to be in high school, were using a compressor to put more air in the rafts that had been released from the trailer while Maggie tried to figure out how to wear a life jacket. Mac helped her, and Terry, the female guide, gave her a paddle with a white plastic blade. Jeff, the other guide, sorted out people by their experience level so each of the rafts had people who knew what to do.

Maggie and one teenager were the only ones who'd never rafted before.

She and Mac were assigned to Terry's raft, which tested all her beliefs that women were the equal of men. Terry might know a lot, but Jeff's brawny arms were more reassuring.

"You've signed up for a class-five run," Terry said. "Class one and two are easy. You could take the trail by canoe. Six is the most difficult. We'll do everything a six does except for one waterfall at the end of our route."

"Gee, I'd hate to miss falling over a wall of water onto jagged rocks," Maggie whispered to Mac.

She was making herself go, but she was still peeved at him for not giving her a choice before they came.

Terry gave the group more information than Maggie could absorb all at once, even though most of it sounded familiar from her own research. The guide would sit in the center at the back and shout instructions to the other participants. All Maggie had to do was to follow orders, paddling forward or backward on command. She could handle that. Maybe. It was the part about big rocks and swift currents that made her nervous, not to mention following directions on what to do if she went into the water.

"We'll toss out a throw bag with a rope on it. Just grab it and we'll tow you back to the raft," Terry said.

Maggie felt the way she had when she'd had her tonsils out at the age of twelve. She had to do it, but she steeled herself for a really horrible experience and fervently wished it was over.

"You'll do fine." Mac patted her shoulder and made her feel like a big baby.

She took her place in the raft as directed by Terry.

The water was calm, the sun was rising behind the eastern peaks, and the first few bends in the river took them between beautifully wooded slopes that seemed primordial in their serenity.

Mac made paddling look like kids' play, his shoulders broad and powerful as he gracefully stroked the water. She was behind him in the middle of the raft where she could do the least harm. She was glad he couldn't see her awkward strokes, but gradually she got the rhythm of it.

One minute the river was serene, then they rounded a bend and the water boiled with the force of the current. Their raft was the first to plunge into the rushing white water. Terry shouted above the noise, and Maggie didn't have time to worry about the raft ripping apart on jagged rocks. She had all she could do to follow orders.

Then, quicker than she'd believed possible, they were through the turbulent waters. She was alive. The raft hadn't sunk, and she'd helped save it—well, at least a little. She'd never felt so exhilarated. She wanted to hug Mac for making her come, but the river grew turbulent again and there wasn't time. She was rafting for real, and she loved it even more than a roller-coaster ride.

At noon they rowed ashore at an area where the rocks along the shore were flat and dry. The New River Rafting company had provided lunch. It was luscious, even though it was just cheese and bologna sandwiches, apples and store-bought cookies. Maggie was having so much fun she avoided Mac, reluctant to let him know it yet, instead eating lunch beside a couple of women who'd driven from Alexandria, Virginia, to go rafting. There would be plenty of time after the excursion to thank him for bringing her. She was curious why the others enjoyed this type of adventure.

"I think the New River will be the place to go when more people hear about it," one of them said.

She was a family practice lawyer who could've made it as a fashion model with her golden hair, almond-shaped eyes and long, lean body. Her companion for the day was her aunt, older and shorter but still pretty stunning. Mac didn't pay any attention to their little group, instead eating lunch with Jeff and talking white water with the guide.

Maggie took off the sweatshirt and jeans she'd worn over her swimsuit and tucked them inside the waterproof bag that had held their lunch. Terry secured it to a ring in the raft, and they were off again.

By early afternoon, Maggie's arms and shoulders ached. Every stroke hurt, and the rapids didn't let up. They went over a small waterfall, maybe only five or six feet, but it felt like Niagara when the raft plunged downward at a dizzying speed.

She was soaked. She hurt. Her face was sunburned in spite of layers of sunscreen, or maybe it was windburned. Despite all that, Maggie had never had more fun in her life. She caught herself laughing out loud after a scary rush around a wicked rock. Mac looked at her over his shoulder, and she didn't have it in her to scowl at him.

It never occurred to her to worry about how they'd get back upriver.

Eventually it got so hot she couldn't wait for the next onslaught of water to spray over her. She wasn't sure she'd be able to get her hands loose from the paddle she was gripping so hard, but her soul was singing. No wonder people bought the adventure guides. There was nothing in the world like the challenge of the wild.

MAC HAD PREPARED himself for the worst: Maggie hating the river ride so much she'd never speak to him again. He'd expected her to argue, protest and vilify him. In his worst scenario, she might scream, cry and walk away.

She didn't do any of those things. Except for being a little cool and aloof when they stopped for lunch, she seemed to be having a great time. She laughed, talked to other rafters and put her all into learning how to paddle.

Who knew she had the makings of a white-water woman?

When the bus they'd seen earlier met them at the end of the trip, she was pink-faced with a wild halo of dark hair and a grin that didn't fade all the way back to Decora, a shorter ride by road than by river.

"It was fun," she said when he sat beside her on a worn black seat at the back of the twenty-four-passenger bus.

"I'm glad you enjoyed it."

He wanted to gloat a little and to point out how silly it was to avoid new experiences, but even more, he wanted to make love to her.

She brought the scent of the river and woods into the bus with her. The blue spandex of her swimsuit had dried fast, and she wiggled back into her jeans as the bus pulled out, a maneuver that threw her onto his lap.

"I can't believe how much fun I had."

She said it more to herself than him. He was enjoying her perch on his lap too much to say anything.

"I did give good sound advice in my river-rafting

chapter," she continued, slipping onto the seat beside him. "I knew I could trust my sources."

He didn't want to hear about books or research. He especially didn't want to risk saying anything that would ruin her mood. He laid his hand on her thigh, glad he'd been able to grab a back seat.

He loved touching her. Her legs under the taut denim were fantastic, not like the stork legs on the blond lawyer at the front of the bus. Good breasts were a gift, but a woman had to earn great legs by walking and keeping in shape.

Taking his hand away, he stared out the window. The bus was following a narrow, curvy blacktop road with as many dips as the river ride. He had to cool it for now. He wasn't into public displays of affection, but already he was aching for Maggie. He'd been fighting his feelings ever since Baltimore, but like it or not, he was falling for her. He needed her and wanted her, even though he couldn't see a future for them. When the urge to see new places got too strong for him to resist, would she leave her job and comfortable life to go with him? He was sure she wouldn't. One day's fun wouldn't change that.

"I've never been so hungry," she said, laying her head on his shoulder.

He laughed softly and covered her hand with his. Her fingers were long and slender, and he locked his with them, gently stroking the hollow between her thumb and palm. Who knew holding hands could give such a rush?

It was dusk when the bus got back to Decora. The couple who'd had trouble with fog left right away, but the rest of the group walked the short half block to

Shorty's Tavern for a pizza party that was included in the cost of the outing.

The place wasn't much to look at, a dilapidated building with tar-paper, fake-brick siding and high, small front windows with blinking red-and-pink neon beer signs. Inside, the bar was little more than a battered wooden counter with stools upholstered in cracked green leather. Some wooden tables had been pulled together at the rear to accommodate their group. The chairs looked like remnants of defunct kitchen sets, either salvaged from a junkyard or bought cheap at a country auction. They'd never been painted to match, so the cracked, peeling paint was a dozen shades of white, blue, green, orange and yellow.

No one faulted the pizza, though. It had a thin, crisp crust heaped with stringy mozzarella, spicy sausage, pepperoni, mushrooms, onions, green pepper and the best sauce in the world.

Olive oil ran down Mac's arm when he took a bite, and Maggie wiped it away with a thin paper napkin. A waitress in pink shorts and a skimpy white top brought pitchers of beer and bottles of wine with screw caps.

Everyone who'd made the trip was a best friend now. It was a phenomenon Mac had seen often, instant friendships based on a shared adventure. What surprised him was that Maggie joined in wholeheartedly. She called everyone around the table by name, learned their life histories with conversational ease, switched from beer to wine and got silly, giggly and even more desirable.

When the party broke up, it was past midnight, and some rafters headed for home or better accommodations elsewhere. A pair of college boys from Maryland and a married couple who commuted between their separate jobs in Pennsylvania and West Virginia walked back to Charlotte's Bed-and-Breakfast ahead of Mac and Maggie. She had even learned who Charlotte was. Quinn had inherited the place from an unmarried aunt and hadn't changed a thing in the twenty years he'd had it.

Mac was tired, but it didn't lessen his need to be with Maggie.

They kissed outside Charlotte's when they arrived. They hugged and kissed some more on the stairway, nearly getting stuck when they tried to stand side by side. He cradled her against him and put his hand on her breast while she fumbled with the key to her room. He came inside with her. She giggled a lot and rubbed against him, sliding her knee up to his groin.

"I have to go to my room for a minute," he said, nuzzling her ear.

"I won't let you."

She stroked him and fumbled with the zipper on his jeans.

"Remind me not to let you drink cheap wine with anyone but me," he said.

"I never have."

She giggled some more, and he kissed her to quiet her, not wanting the college kids across the hall to get any vicarious thrills.

"I'll be right back," he insisted.

He pulled the crazy quilt to the bottom of the mattress and turned back the sheet. She sat on the edge of the bed, smiling up at him with liquid brown eyes. It took all the willpower he had to leave for his room for his things. Another two minutes of touching her, and he would have forgotten he'd come prepared.

He rushed to his room and got his duffel and the

precious foil packs. Maggie's door was closed but not locked when he returned from his quick errand.

He eased it open and went inside. She was curled up in the middle of the bed, still fully dressed except for her shoes, and dead to the world. He locked the door and sat beside her, stroking her hair and softly kissing her cheek.

She didn't wake up.

He stretched out beside her, which wasn't easy because the bed was narrow for a double and she was squarely in the center. He hugged her next to him, but she moaned and rolled away.

His frustration was growing, so he whispered her name close to her ear. It had no effect on her slumber.

Some planner he was! He'd been thwarted by fresh air, strenuous exercise and cheap red wine. Maggie wasn't going to wake up unless he shook her. Even then she'd be too out of it to respond the way she had in Baltimore.

He'd wanted Maggie to have fun, and she had. Now he just plain wanted her, but she was sleeping so soundly he took it as a signal to slow down. One enjoyable excursion didn't change anything. He still couldn't imagine her sharing his life with him. How could he possibly make her happy if she hated the way he lived?

He wasn't into brooding, but he'd like to take to the woods for a couple of months and get over Maggie.

11

"I'M SWEARING OFF MEN and sour red wine," Maggie said Monday at lunch.

She picked at her spinach salad, trying to fake interest in it. Rayanne had insisted they go to the diner for lunch, and Maggie appreciated her friend's efforts to cheer her up.

"Let me get this straight," Rayanne said. "You had a wonderful time. You loved white-water rafting, but you don't think there's any possibility you and Mac will get together again."

She was wearing a red tank top with her black skirt, hopefully a sign her Goth period was on the wane. She'd even abandoned black and dark purple lipstick in favor of cherry red, possibly a sign she was a little worried about her job, which was not a sure thing under the new ownership.

"That sums it up." Maggie poured more vinaigrette dressing, but soaking the salad didn't give her an appetite.

"He wouldn't have asked you to go if he wasn't interested."

"Separate rooms in Motel Hell? Our deal was he'd share some of his experiences for the next guide. I'm kidding myself if I think it was a real date."

"Mmm." Rayanne dipped a French fry in ketchup and nibbled thoughtfully.

"Now Pierpont will take over in a few weeks, and he insists M. S. Stevens go on a nationwide tour. How awkward is that? Will Mac insist I go again? He certainly doesn't need me. I'd go in a minute if I thought it would bring us closer together, but Mac doesn't want a city girl. I don't camp, trek or travel. There's no place for me in his life. He doesn't want me."

"Maybe he does."

"Not to sign books. Not in his life. He's probably planning to winter in the Antarctic even as we speak."

"A little cold, but bracing weather wouldn't hurt you. You could go with him. Check out the polar bears."

Rayanne's commonsense advice was well meant, but Maggie knew it wasn't counseling she needed. Only a miracle would help her get over Mac.

"That's not the point. Sully is a lone wolf. He doesn't need or want me hanging around. Do you know what we talked about on the way home yesterday?"

Rayanne shook her head.

"The weather! The geology of the Appalachian Mountains. Snowboarding."

"Not very romantic, although I like ski lodges. I went once with Harvey Huntley. Who names their kids Harvey anymore? Everyone in his family has a name beginning with *H*. Poor Harv was the youngest of a dozen or so cousins. At least he didn't get stuck with Herbert. Imagine the nickname kids would give him for that."

Maggie smiled and was grateful to discover her face didn't crack. Rayanne's babble was just what she needed to perk up, if that was possible.

"Hey, we only get an hour for lunch, but I have a

great idea. The Shoe Box at the mall is having a big sale. Let's go after work and buy some funky shoes. No one can stay depressed with happy feet.''

"Sure, why not?" Maggie agreed.

At least shopping was better than suffering alone. She couldn't survive another tour as Mac's girl Friday, and she didn't know whether Pierpont would fire her if she flat-out refused to go with him. If the truth about the guides came out, she'd probably be fired anyway for deceiving the new owner.

The prospect of job hunting was grim, but it wasn't what really mattered. She was in love with Mac, and she might as well be obsessed with a movie star for all the good it was likely to do her.

After work Rayanne drove them to the mall. She'd take Maggie to get her car later. Riding on the expressway in rush-hour traffic with her friend was an adventure, to say the least, but it didn't distract Maggie from thoughts of Mac. What would've happened if she hadn't fallen asleep after the rafting party ended? Why hadn't he woken her? Why had he been so cool on the ride home? He must have had second thoughts and regretted bringing her. Instead of being pleased that she'd loved white-water rafting, he'd avoided the subject.

How would Sully react when Pierpont insisted he go on another book tour? Maggie had visions of mushroom clouds and erupting volcanoes.

They arrived at the mall in spite of Rayanne's peculiar brand of road rage. She assigned the name of a barnyard animal to every driver who annoyed her and made appropriate noises. Donkeys were at the top of her most-despised list. She'd brayed a lot on the way there.

"My parents sent me a birthday check," Rayanne said. "I'm going to blow it all on neon platforms. I met a guy in my pool league who's crazy about psychedelic art. We have a date next weekend. I'm going as a flower child."

Maggie didn't try to visualize that. Rayanne was sometimes scary but never dull. Maggie knew she was the boring one. She researched life instead of living it, at least she had until she'd met Mac.

They went into the mall and found the Shoe Box by wandering until they'd walked a mile or two. She'd shopped before with Rayanne, who left no store unexplored in her quest for the weird and wonderful.

The Shoe Box was huge with high shelves and little room between them. There were no chairs or harried salespeople rushing around trying to please customers. It was strictly self-serve, all shoes guaranteed at least until the customer got them out the door. Maggie, who was addicted to brand-name shoes that lasted for years, felt a little overwhelmed by plastic sandals and rainbow-colored pumps. Rayanne was so excited to try on every shoe in the place, Maggie joined in.

"These aren't too bad," she said, showing Rayanne a pair of ginger-brown platforms with cork soles at least three inches high.

"Try them on." Rayanne rejected some purple pumps and found a pair of neon-pink sandals.

A pair of preadolescent boys with buzz haircuts ran down the aisle, one in hot pursuit of the other.

"Don't children have parents anymore?" Rayanne asked.

Maggie slipped out of the practical beige flats she'd worn to work and stuck one foot, then the other, into the platforms. They were aptly named. She felt as if she were standing on scaffolding, towering above her usual height. It was a good feeling suddenly to grow a few inches, but she wasn't at all sure she could walk in them.

"How are they?" Rayanne returned the pink shoes to their box and picked up a pair with transparent straps embellished with gold stars.

"Too high. Scary."

"They look terrific. I'd swap the tattoo on my butt for ankles like yours."

"No deal! I don't know why you got a bumblebee tattoo where no one sees it."

"Optimism. Try walking."

Maggie did. The shoes made her feel tall and willowy. She walked to the end of the aisle on the dingy tan carpeting then turned around.

"I may buy them," she said, a little surprised by her decision. "What do you think?"

She lifted one foot and stuck it out for her friend's approval just as the rambunctious little monsters with the buzz cuts rounded the corner at a run. The first one plowed into her and knocked her off balance. She grabbed at a row of shoes in open boxes to catch herself just as the second boy knocked into her. She went down in a heap with shoes raining down on her.

"Maggie!"

Rayanne rushed to help her as the two boys streaked out of the store into the mall. A clerk who looked like a high-school student came over to see what was happening, and Rayanne told him without mincing words.

"Little brats," he said. "They're always sneaking in here to race around the stacks. I should've called security."

"You should've told them to leave before they barreled into my friend," Rayanne said, trying to help Maggie up.

Pain shot through her right ankle as if a red-hot knife was stabbing through flesh and bone. Maggie couldn't help whimpering. The boyish clerk hurried off to find the store manager. Rayanne gave up trying to help her up and started tossing aside the boxes heaped around her, stuffing the loose shoes in without matching them in pairs.

A red-faced, potbellied man in a pale blue dress shirt, drab necktie and mud-colored trousers came over to them with an undertaker's expression.

"Do you want me to call you an ambulance? Your ankle might be broken."

"Don't be silly," Maggie said, in too much pain to be tactful.

The thought of a stretcher, flashing lights and screeching sirens was worse than the pain.

"The mall must have a wheelchair," Rayanne said. "I'll bring my car up to the entrance by the food court. You can wheel her there."

Maggie didn't like being left to the care of the heavily perspiring shoe-store man, but it was the best plan since her ankle hurt so much she couldn't get up. Rayanne hurried off to get her car, the clerk produced a wheelchair, and Maggie endured being heaved into it like a tackling dummy.

The manager found her own shoes and the ones she'd been trying on, boxed both and handed them to her along with her purse and a gift certificate for two-hundred dollars worth of merchandise at the store.

She couldn't imagine suing the Shoe Box because a couple of little ruffians had knocked her over, but she was in too much pain to reassure the panicked manager.

Hours later, after a long wait in the emergency room, Maggie was home on her own couch, her badly sprained ankle propped on pillows and a pair of rented crutches within easy reach. She finally persuaded Rayanne to go home and hoped the pain medication would lull her to sleep.

The bad news was that she had to stay off her ankle and keep it elevated for the next forty-eight hours. The other bad news came via a phone message from Mr. Granville. Pierpont had arranged an interview of M. S. Stevens on a New York TV station for the day after tomorrow to promote her recently issued guide. She and Mac were supposed to fly there tomorrow. There was no way she could go. She looked at her ankle, swollen under the hospital wrapping, and wondered how Mac would react to the abrupt summons. Would he go without her or would he refuse and blow off his contract?

Her whole world could come crashing down, but she was too groggy from the pain pills to sort things out.

WHEN MAC GOT THE CALL from Granville, he raged inwardly but didn't refuse to go. He was a man of his word, and he had signed that infernal contract. The kicker was he couldn't get Maggie off his mind no matter how hard he tried. He'd sign books in the monkey cage at the zoo if it gave him an excuse to be with her, but he couldn't bring himself to pick up the phone or to drive to her place. What could he say that wouldn't mislead her?

He should forget her. One night of fantastic sex and one day of white-water rafting didn't change the basic differences between them. He couldn't imagine life with a wife, but Maggie didn't deserve anything less.

Marriage! Where had that idea come from?

His reluctance to go to New York had grown to flat-out repugnance by the time he got to the Pittsburgh airport the next day. The only bright spot was that Maggie would be flying with him.

He checked in and went to the security check with his one carry-on bag without seeing her. Just before his turn came to toss his luggage on the conveyer belt, the receptionist from Granville Publishing rushed up to him.

"Maggie can't go. She sprained her ankle trying on shoes and has to stay off it for a couple of days. I'm going in her place. Rayanne Jordan, editorial assistant. I met you the first time you came to the office."

"I don't need a nursemaid, Rayanne." Especially not one dressed totally in black except for a neon-green vest.

"Of course not, but I have your script. We can practice on the plane. You know, go over a few jokes and pithy comments you can work into the interview."

Pithy comments? He gave up his place in line.

"Tell me about this sprained ankle."

A couple of minutes later he sent Rayanne to the gate, swearing he'd get there in time to get on the plane. He'd heard some lame excuses from people who'd found his excursions too demanding, but Maggie's was too much. He went to a bank of pay phones, dropped some coins in one and punched in digits, glad he'd memorized her number.

"I heard you sprained your ankle," he said as soon as Maggie answered the phone.

At least she was home, not at work, but he still didn't buy Rayanne's improbable story about young boys knocking her over in a shoe store.

"Where are you?" She sounded a little panicky.

"At the airport."

"You're still going, aren't you?"

"What choice do I have? What's your real reason for not coming?"

"My real reason! My ankle is the size of a cantaloupe. I'm supposed to elevate it today and tomorrow."

"More of your bad luck?"

"You make it sound as if I'm making it up."

"I don't remember saying that."

"No, but you sound skeptical."

"Are you sure you're not afraid of going with me?"

"Why would I be afraid of you?"

"Maybe you're just afraid of living life to its fullest."

"Isn't your plane leaving?" She sounded as angry as he felt.

"Yeah, in an hour."

He'd been eager to get to the airport—no, eager to see her. He felt deflated and depressed. There was no point in seeing her, but he ached from missing her.

"Well, have a nice trip."

"Not likely."

He hung up, still not convinced she was incapable

of making the trip. Would Maggie lie to him? He didn't know her well enough to be sure.

He walked toward the security check with a hollow feeling in his chest. When this thing he had for Maggie ran its course, he'd be glad she hadn't come with him today.

Meanwhile, she left an emptiness in his life that he was hard-pressed to understand.

12

MAGGIE HAD A LOT to answer for.

Without her on the trip to New York, the media circus had spiraled out of Mac's control. The smart-ass TV interviewer, a pompous Ivy League type who wouldn't be caught dead in a tent, tried to make Mac look like an idiot. Rayanne's "pithy comments" were about as much help as wet matches to a freezing camper. She'd tried too hard to coach him and had driven him nuts by talking nonstop all the way to New York and back. Didn't she know a woman's greatest gift to a man was a little silence once in a while?

They caught a plane after the interview and were back in Pittsburgh before seven in the evening. Mac had only one thing on his mind. He was going to Maggie's place to check on her sprained ankle. First though, he wanted to make sure Gram was all right.

He went to pay phones wishing he had his cell phone. He'd left it with Gram's nearest neighbor, Josh Taylor, a crusty old mountain man who refused to have one of his own. He'd wanted Gram to be able to call someone close while he was gone.

She didn't answer her phone. He tried to call his own cell number, but Josh didn't answer that.

He could think of all kinds of reasons neither of them was answering, none of them good.

Maggie would have to wait. He'd better go home and check on Gram.

Worried as he was about his grandmother, Mac couldn't get Maggie out of his mind on the drive home. The story Rayanne had told him was too improbable not to be true, and he was worried about her. What did the future hold for them? Could he handle never seeing her again?

As soon as he got to Gram's place, he saw a rusty green pickup parked on the track. Josh Taylor was there, so why hadn't either of them answered the phone?

Mac walked into the house, and his worst fear was realized. Cora was sitting on the couch, one side of her face covered by a big bandage pad. Josh was sitting at the table sipping Gram's homemade blackberry wine from a jelly jar.

"What happened? I tried to call both of you."

"Just a few scratches," Gram said without getting up. "We musta been down at the hospital."

"She fell off a ladder," Josh said laconically.

He was a big man with two braids in his white beard and not a hair on his head. A widower as old as Gram or older, he'd been a friend of Granddad's. He poached deer out of season, didn't believe in paying income taxes and was proud of not accepting social security.

"What were you doing on a ladder?" Mac asked.

He knew what his parents would say. Dad might try to have her declared incompetent and deported to Florida.

"There's a wasps' nest in the eaves," Gram explained cheerfully. "The little devils have been buzzing me every time I go out. I was going to smoke the nest and knock it out with a stick. Your granddad did it lots of times.''

Mac groaned. ''I would've done it for you. How many times did you get stung?''

''Just a couple. Hurt like sin, but nothing I can't handle.''

''That's why she fell,'' Josh said, refilling the jelly glass and sniffing it like a connoisseur.

''Where are you hurt?'' Mac asked.

''Didn't fall far. Got scratched up a bit, is all.'' Gram looked him straight in the eyes without a trace of penitence.

''I'll be going,'' Josh said.

''Take the bottle, Josh. I surely do appreciate your help,'' Gram said.

''No trouble,'' the big man said, taking the cell phone out of his pocket and leaving it on the table. ''Take care, Mac.''

Mac walked him to the truck, but Josh couldn't tell him much. Gram had cuts, scrapes and stings but no broken bones. Knowing Josh had done his best, Mac thanked him and watched as his neighbor drove away.

She was dozing on the couch when he went back inside, looking old and frail with one cheek covered by the stark white bandage. His life kept getting more and more complicated. He was the only one standing between her and internment in a senior citizens' home. Add to that, he wanted Maggie so much he was half crazy when he wasn't with her and filled with doubts when he was.

He woke Gram and got her to go to bed, then dialed Maggie's number.

''How's your ankle?'' he asked when she answered.

"About half the size it was, but it still looks like an elephant's. Rayanne said the interview was nasty, but you handled it like a pro."

"She reported to you?"

"She's my editorial assistant," Maggie said.

Mac took a breath before talking again. "This isn't working for me, pretending to be an author."

He couldn't leave Gram again to pose as M. S. Stevens. She wasn't senile by any means, but she refused to rely on anyone but herself.

"But you're doing a good job," Maggie said.

"I can't traipse around the country like a half-baked celebrity. My grandmother needs me, and I can't be here if I'm on tour." Frustration made him angry.

"The interview wasn't that bad."

"Easy for you to say. You found a reason not to be there."

"Do you want a letter from the doctor who took care of my ankle?"

"Don't be sarcastic. You aren't good at it," he said.

"Apparently you don't think I'm good at anything."

This was getting personal, and Mac didn't like emotional phone calls. If they were going to have it out, he wanted it to be face-to-face.

"I'm coming to see you tomorrow." He'd just decided.

"I won't be home. I'm going to work. Pierpont is holding a press conference at noon to announce his acquisition of Granville Publishing. I have to be there. Now that the deal is finalized, I'm going to tell him the truth. If he fires me, I can't help it. Unfortunately it means you'll be out of a job, too."

"I hate being M. S. Stevens."

"Well, you won't have to be anymore."

They ended their conversation because there wasn't anything else to say.

MAC AWOKE at dawn the next morning. He'd heard a noise in the kitchen, but it was early for Gram to be up. He pulled on jeans and opened the door of the cozy, paneled room he'd been using since he was a kid.

He hadn't imagined the sound. He moved silently on bare feet and saw Gram in a flowery wrap filling the enamel coffeepot with water.

"You're up early," he said.

"MacDonald Sully, you scared me out of my wits! What are you doing up so early?"

"I was going to ask you the same question, but I have a better one. Where's the big bandage you had on your cheek? Why cover one little sting with a yard of gauze?"

"You noticed, eh?"

"Hard not to."

"You've probably figured out I didn't fall yesterday."

"The thought crossed my mind."

"You think I'm a silly old woman."

"Never, but I am curious." He was sure Gram had a perfectly rational explanation.

"I did get stung. Hurt like the devil."

"I seem to remember a remedy for stings in your bag of tricks."

"Of course! That's why I rolled around on the ground a bit and got dirty to look like I'd had another tumble. The sting gave me the idea."

"Why on earth—"

"Josh isn't much, but he's reliable. Came right over as soon as I called him."

"You went to the emergency room because you wanted a reason to call him?"

"'Course not. I didn't want the doctor to think I'm a silly old woman. Josh helped me inside, then I sent him off to put gas in his truck. Gave me enough time to clean up in the ladies' room and buy a bandage pad at the hospital pharmacy."

"What are you up to, Gram?"

"Not what you're thinking. I wouldn't want that old coot around all the time. No one can take your granddad's place, but every once in a while I ache to talk to someone about the old times. Josh helped Charles build this house, and his wife was my second cousin. I cried for days when she passed on."

"She was a nice person," Mac said.

"I'm not exactly lonely. Charles is still alive in my heart, but sometimes I need to hear someone say his name. Now you probably agree with your dad. You think I should sell out to that vulture, Oliver Bronson, and go vegetate in Florida."

"I don't think that." He walked up behind his grandmother and put his hands on her frail shoulders. "And I don't intend to let it happen. From now on when I'm not here, I'll ask Josh to check on you. If you've laid away a good supply of blackberry wine, he'll be tickled pink to hang out here."

"You're a good grandson." She reached up and patted his cheek.

Gram insisted on cooking a special breakfast of pancakes, deer sausage Josh had given her and eggs sunnyside up. Mac needed time to think more than he needed a lumberjack's breakfast, but he ate enough to satisfy his grandmother.

He climbed the ridge afterward, intending to work

until dark that day. Summer was waning, and he hadn't made nearly as much progress on the cabin in the last three weeks as he'd hoped. The framing was done, and he had insulation on the rough siding, but the rest of it would take a whole lot more effort. He didn't mind hard labor, but he didn't love working with his hands the way his grandfather had.

After an hour or so on the ridge, he'd accomplished almost nothing. Gram had shown him a new side of herself. In spite of being so damn independent, she did need people. She was living on memories, and the long, happy life she'd shared with her husband was sustaining her, but she needed more.

What if he lived to her age? He valued his independence as much as she did, but what memories would he have? What could he do with the rest of his life that would matter fifty years from now? He felt an unusual stab of loneliness and something much more intense—longing to be with Maggie.

MAGGIE'S MAIN RESPONSIBILITY at the press conference was to pour wine at the buffet table. His big announcement over, Pierpont was treating the press to a fancy luncheon in Mr. Granville's spacious office. Miss Mason was supervising the harried caterer while Rayanne carried a tray of cheese puffs to the guests.

As nervous as she was, Maggie couldn't talk to her new employer until the TV cameramen and the reporters were gone. With each passing minute she had more doubts, but her mind was made up. Nothing she did could hurt Mr. Granville now. She'd more than fulfilled her debt of gratitude to him. It would be far better for her to confess the truth now than to let Pierpont dis-

cover on his own that she was the author of the guides
and a sham.

Peter Pierpont was a master politician. She had to
give him that. Even the crabby business writer for the
Pittsburgh Sentinel was lapping up every word along
with the free lunch. Pierpont stood out like a tropical
orchid in a bed of daisies. Today he was wearing a
raspberry jacket with chocolate-brown trousers and a
brown silk shirt open at the collar. On him it worked,
although her first impulse had been to laugh.

She felt downright drab in her lavender skirt and
long-sleeved black blouse. Rayanne was almost demure
in a butter-colored dress and jacket, except the skirt
was slit to reveal a whole lot of thigh. Mr. Granville,
dressed in a dove-colored frock coat and gray-striped
trousers for the occasion, would stay on for a year as
consultant, but the new regime had begun.

At last the press was stuffed to capacity on tiny bar-
becued wienies, roast beef and smoked salmon. Pierpont stood at the office door and glad-handed the media
on its way out. Now all Maggie had to do was to pick
an opportune moment to approach him. It had to be
soon. His limo was probably waiting for him.

"Mr. Pierpont, can I speak to you for a moment?"
she asked.

"I always have time for my employees," he said
expansively. "What is it?"

She had in mind a cozy chat in a quiet corner with
no witnesses. Pierpont was poised for flight. He
checked his watch and called over to Rayanne, praising
her for the good job. Miss Mason looked sour in an
olive-green suit that made her complexion even more
sallow than usual, but he complimented her, too.

"It will only take a minute, Mr. Pierpont." Maggie

managed to put herself between him and the open door, her back to the hallway. "There's something I need to tell you about the guides."

"I appreciate the good job you've done editing them. This is only the beginning, Maggie."

"What I'm trying to tell you is—"

"She's my ghost writer," a wonderfully familiar voice said from behind her.

Her heart skipped a beat, and she forgot her carefully rehearsed confession.

"Without her there wouldn't be any guides," Mac said.

He was wearing faded jeans and a navy T-shirt, looking as different from Pierpont as two men could be, but they confronted each other eyeball to eyeball. Her new boss backed up a step.

"From now on, her name should be on the cover," Sully said.

"Mac, no—"

"Granville, did you know about this?" Pierpont said to the older man who was standing behind the desk looking distressed.

"Does it really matter, given the success of the guides?" Mac asked. "Maggie is a great writer, but she doesn't like the spotlight."

"I guess it doesn't," Pierpont said slowly. He seemed to be weighing the ramifications before saying more. "I've already had an offer from a major New York publisher to reprint the guides. It could lead to all kinds of spin-offs."

"The name of the game is profit," Mac said.

Was she the only one who knew he was mocking Pierpont?

"Exactly," her new boss said decisively. "I have a plane to catch, Stevens. You'll be hearing from me."

He and Mac tried to crush each other's fingers doing what men call a handshake. Pierpont patted her shoulder and left.

"I guess we're still a team," Mac said quietly.

She forced a smile. It wasn't the kind of partnership she wanted with Sully, but he left without saying anything more. She was shocked—and bereft.

Two long weeks passed after Mac's stunning announcement. Mr. Pierpont had a lot of new ideas for Granville Publishing, including a much more aggressive marketing plan. He created a new position and brought in his own man. Maggie got a new title and a raise, but from now on, she'd have nothing to do with promoting her guides. That job was all Mac's. If he ever came to the office for meetings, she didn't see him.

Her life should've undergone some life-altering change, but, in fact, nothing much happened after Mac saved her from committing career suicide. She fell into a routine so much like her old one she scarcely noticed the change in ownership. Rayanne wore her black outfits a couple of times, then, bored with her old look, started dressing for success in preppy suits and ironed blouses.

Maggie moped when she wasn't working. Did Mac call? No. Did he suggest getting together after she gave in and called to thank him for saving her? No. Did he let her know when he was scheduled to make a few short book tours? No, Mr. Granville told her that.

She went home to Beaumont for a weekend. The sleepy little West Virginia coal town never seemed to change, but she had. She didn't even feel like calling old friends. They were mostly married with kids, and Maggie couldn't work up any enthusiasm for long discussions about diapers and teething.

Her parents were home, but Len and Gayle were already planning their next trip. They were going to Ontario, around Lake Superior to Minnesota, then through the Midwest following the fall colors. Unless they changed their minds, they'd be home for Thanksgiving.

Laurie had sold a story to *Heartbeat* magazine for the princely sum of fifty dollars. As an old pro in the publishing business, Maggie strongly advised her sister not to give up the dog-trimming job. She didn't see much of Laurie this trip, something to do with a new vet who'd gone into practice with old Doc Ferris.

Her family wasn't much interested in the goings-on at Granville Publishing, not that Maggie was, either. Where had the fun in her life gone? She knew the answer, but she had to forget about Sully. What choice did she have?

It was the Friday following her trip home when she finally heard from Mac late in the evening.

"Hope I didn't wake you up."

"Oh, no," she said, trying to sound casual and disinterested.

"How are you?"

Dumb question! How did he think she was? She was withering away because she missed him so much.

"Great." Keep your lies short and simple, she warned herself.

"I wonder if you can come for dinner tomorrow."

"At Cora's?"

She was surprised, but there was nothing romantic about an invitation to his grandmother's. She absolutely could not get her hopes up. Mac probably wanted to talk about the tour schedule.

"I'm not sure I can find the place again."

"You don't need to. I'll pick you up around four. Plan on bringing your overnight bag."

He hung up before she could ask questions. What was this overnight business?

Mac came for her as promised. After the initial shock of seeing him, her heartbeat slowed to something approaching normal, and she managed to pretend mild indifference. She didn't bring an overnight case. No need for him to know she had a toothbrush and clean underwear in her purse, just in case. He probably only suggested it so he wouldn't have to make the long round trip to Pittsburgh twice in one day.

When they got to his grandmother's, Cora welcomed her like an old friend. She'd made dumpling stew, no venison, and treated Maggie like a long-lost daughter. Her attentions were almost embarrassing, especially since Maggie didn't understand them.

"This is Josh Taylor," Mac said, introducing her to a big man with a Santa Claus beard and baggy overalls. "Josh has been helping me with the cabin. He helped my grandfather build this place."

"Me and half the county," Josh said, acknowledging her with a friendly smile.

Mac was pleasant during dinner, but his conversation was as impersonal as it had been on the drive. She didn't have a clue why he'd wanted her here.

"Days are getting shorter," Cora said, after they topped off the meal with the best bread pudding Maggie had ever tasted.

"Gram…"

Mac flashed his grandmother a warning frown.

What was going on here? Maggie didn't know whether to be excited or apprehensive. If Mac had some big pronouncement to make about what now seemed to be their mutual career, she didn't want to hear it. She didn't want Mac as a business partner. It hurt to think about the way she did want him.

"I've got something to show you," he said almost shyly. "If you're through eating...."

Apparently they were leaving.

"Everything was delicious, Cora. Thank you. Nice meeting you, Josh."

She automatically shouldered her purse and followed Mac outside. It was dusk already, the shortened day a harbinger of the winter to come. Mac took her hand and wordlessly led her up the path to his ridge.

When they got to the top, she couldn't believe her eyes.

"It's a house!"

"I made it a little bigger than I intended at first."

"Mac, it's adorable! I love the redwood stain with the green roof. Can I see the inside?"

"That's why you're here."

He put his arm around her shoulders and started enthusiastically explaining what he'd done.

"I hired some expert help. I discovered I'm not the builder my granddad was. The generator should give us all the power we need."

Us? She held her breath. Nothing seemed real, not the first star twinkling above them or the soft whispering noises in the woods. Was she hallucinating because she desperately wanted to be with Mac?

"I finished it as fast as possible." Mac was leading her around the outside of the house. "Josh got all his relatives to help for the price of beer, pizza and some ammo for deer season. I think it turned out fine.''

Maggie's eyes got misty as Mac led her inside and showed her his home. It had pale green walls, a delicate shade that enhanced the terra-cotta floor tiles and the pine kitchen cupboards. The only furniture in the living area was a pair of aluminum lawn chairs with yellow-and-green webbing.

''There's the bathroom, running water and all the conveniences. The bedroom's in here. I did get a bed, but I thought you could help pick out the rest of the furniture— I guess I'm getting ahead of myself,'' he said sheepishly.

The room was small, dominated by an old brass bed with a warm patina. The patchwork quilt looked new, bright squares of green, yellow and red in an intricate pattern.

''Did your grandmother make the quilt?''

''She worked on it for two years. All sewn by hand. It was her way of telling me it was time.''

''Time?''

She was breathless with anticipation, and Mac's arm around her shoulders was all that was holding her up.

''I want you to live here with me,'' he said solemnly.

''Live here…''

Her brain wasn't fully functioning. All she could do was repeat his words.

''Not all the time. We'll keep your place in Pittsburgh. I don't expect you to give up your career, but Pete said there's not much you can't do at home with a computer. The company will spring for whatever you need.''

''Pete?''

''Pierpont. I'm taking him fishing in Alaska, just a

short trip. I won't be gone long. I guess you know I have to go sometimes. I've started doing the wilderness tours again when I'm not M. S. Stevens. I'll hate every minute away from you, and any time you want to come with me, I'll love it.''

"You call him Pete?"

"It's a guy thing." He grinned and pulled her close, finally kissing her the way she'd been imagining day and night since last seeing him.

"Marry me, Maggie," he said, holding her so close she could hear his heartbeat.

"You want me to marry you," she said with wonderment and joy.

"I'll get the path from the logging road graded before winter. It won't seem so isolated when we can drive up here without wrecking the springs on our cars."

"Mac, no more construction details now."

She put her arms around his neck and kissed him with every fiber of her being. He tasted of cinnamon, vanilla and everything good. Maggie thought she'd die of happiness.

"Is that a yes?" he murmured into her hair.

"Where will we go on our honeymoon?"

"Tangiers, Tibet, Timbuktu. Your choice."

"I choose there." She pointed at the bed. "Then I'll follow you to the ends of the earth if that's where you want to go."

"I may make a camper of you yet."

He lifted her in his arms and carried her to the bed. She'd never believe in bad luck again.

"I love you, M. S. Stevens," he said, lying down beside her and pressing soft, sweet kisses around her mouth.

"That's what I should say to you."

"Then I love you, Maggie Sanders-soon-to-be-Sully."

Words failed her, but she had a lifetime to show him how much she loved him.

Isn't It Romantic?

Dianne Drake

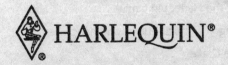

HARLEQUIN®

TORONTO • NEW YORK • LONDON
AMSTERDAM • PARIS • SYDNEY • HAMBURG
STOCKHOLM • ATHENS • TOKYO • MILAN • MADRID
PRAGUE • WARSAW • BUDAPEST • AUCKLAND

Dear Reader,

Welcome to my latest Duets novel! This one was fun for me, because like my first, *The Doctor Dilemma*, it's based on a true story. Years ago I hired an ad firm to run a professional campaign for my association, and the owner was a "closet" romance fan. He read them, but of course he didn't tell anyone because...well, real men didn't read romances. But friend Charles not only read them, he got himself mixed up in a bet to write one.

I'm not going to tell you that Charles had a long and illustrious career in romance, because he didn't. His book was published as his one and only. He went back to ad writing, which was where his heart was. But he wrote the book, and had the courage to send it out into the publishing world at a time when men weren't recognized in the field. And in a sense, his determination opened new doors for many new readers and writers— the men of romance.

Besides being a writer of romance, I'm a devoted reader. I always have been, starting with the great du Maurier and Holt classics, then eventually the Harlequin books. I was thrilled beyond words to meet Charles, my very first published Harlequin author! Then years later I became one, and now my deepest appreciation goes to Charles, for the inspiration as well as the twig of an idea that grew into a story, to my own husband—who reads *my* romances—and to Kathryn Lye, who allows me to be part of the Harlequin family!

Wishing you much humor and happiness!

Dianne Drake

Books by Dianne Drake

HARLEQUIN DUETS
58—THE DOCTOR DILEMMA

For my buddy Charles,
who had the courage to write a romance.
And, as always, for Joel.

Prologue

"ANYONE CAN DO IT." Charlie Whitaker bestowed one of his legendary know-it-all grins on his sister, then picked up his martini, triple olives, and sipped.

"That's what they all say." Charlene lobbed the smile right back to him, but it was demure. That is, until the instant she picked up her car keys and jingled them at him, then her smile turned to pure, jubilant devilishness. "And they're wrong, Charlie, just like you are." She jingled her car keys again, just to rub a little salt into his oh-so-new wound, then tucked them away in her tiny, black crocheted purse.

"I could do it in my sleep," he snorted, "and I'll guarantee that it would be as good as anything you've ever seen come across your desk."

"Promises, promises." She slid her purse slowly across the table at Charlie and watched his eyes follow the hypnotic movement. "Been there, brother dear, and I've heard it all before. Got the proof, if you know what I mean." She wrinkled her nose at him, then snatched the purse away, and tucked it under her arm, completely out of his sight. "If I were you, I'd give it up. Save yourself the embarrassment…again."

Charlie blinked, shook his head, then refocused his attention on his twin. "Embarrassment? You've got to be kidding. I'll write it with one hand tied behind my back, no sweat." He took another sip of his martini and signaled the waiter to bring a second round. "Make that my right hand, since I'm right-handed. Don't want to take any unfair advantages."

"Yeah, right. Same old song, second verse." Charlene leaned back in the booth and folded her arms across her chest. "So what's the offer this time—I'm assuming an offer is coming, isn't it? And it had better be good, because I'm beginning to get bored with this whole thing. Not enough challenge to it anymore."

"Anything your little heart desires, sis. Anything at all."

"Sounds a little arrogant, if you ask me. Especially with your track record." She patted her purse to emphasize her point.

Charlie plucked the plastic skewer full of olives out of his fresh martini and, out of habit, passed them to Charlene. The two of them may have been on opposite sides of their betting game for years, but apart from the competition, he loved her dearly. Loved her more than anybody else he could think of, actually. "You can call it arrogant if you want to, but I'll call it confident because this one's as good as won."

Charlene laughed. "Won, but by whom?" She studied the olives for a moment, then continued. "You know, Charlie, I should probably be insulted, but I'm not. In fact, I'll take you up on the bet just to show you how wrong you are this time—just like you were last time. And you know what I want—what we both want."

Charlie sucked in an excited breath, and let it out slowly before he responded. "Are you kidding? *The sword?*" Saying the words almost made him choke, he wanted it so badly. "The sword," he repeated, just to make sure.

Charlene nodded.

"Well, don't get your heart set on it, sis. It's as good as in *my* trophy case, permanently."

"Shouldn't I be saying that to you, especially since, well…I wouldn't want to humiliate you by bringing up how many times I've won lately. So are you absolutely sure you really want to go that far, because we can do something simple like a cruise."

He nodded his acceptance before he even thought about it. "Dead sure. Are you?"

She nodded back. "And I won't even make you tie one hand behind your back, because I don't want you complaining later on that I took unfair advantage of you." Charlene chuckled, and stretched out her hand to shake his. "Now or never, little brother. Deal?"

"Fair and square? You won't change your mind?"

"I won't change my mind."

"For sole ownership." Charlie reached across the table to shake his sister's hand. "Deal. Now, let's work out the details."

1

JONQUIL SAUNTERED INTO THE ROOM and stood quietly, gazing wistfully at him as he read. It was a magnificent... imposing...wonderful...great...magnificent... It was...he was a magnificent sight in his boxers...briefs... nakedness...red brocade smoking jacket. Her nipples protruded through the filmy fabric of her sexy, black, low-cut, clingy, see-through negligee as she contemplated the many ways in which she would gratify...satisfy...pleasure him. "Wouldst thou fancy my companionship tonight, Irwin...Ralph...Igor...Ralph?

She flounced away from the door, out of the shadows, and pranced across the room to his desk...divan... balcony...to his desk, her bosom heaving in excitement with every step. "I wouldst fancy that you would take me as you would have me, kind sir," she panted breathlessly. She ripped the negligee bodice away from her ample bosoms and offered her pinkish, stimulated peaks up to his self-assured...dominating...experienced...to his proficient touch. "Now, kind sir," she gasped. "Take me now, I beg of you. Acquaint me with your steely, eager manhood. Restraint and virginity are such dreary conditions, and I beseech thee...you...pray thee...entreat you to take me before I die of my carnal, demanding, wanton need of your pleasures."

Beep.

Charlie Whitaker grabbed a tissue from his drawer and dabbed the droplets of perspiration from his face, then picked up the phone. "What is it, Dolores?"

"Your eleven o'clock, Charlie. With Liz Fuller—Jackie's assistant."

"Give me two minutes, then send her in." He looked at the words on his computer screen and smiled. Not a bad start, and Charlene thought he couldn't do it. Well, he'd show her. This was one competition she was going to lose for sure. And at the rate he was going, she'd be eating a little crow inside of two weeks or so. After all, how hard could this be?

"You wanted to see me, Charlie?"

Charlie glanced at the door. He knew Liz in passing. Had lunch with her once or twice. Just casually—a chance meeting—may I join you? kind of thing. She was pleasant enough, and all work. Definitely all work. But pretty. Gorgeous in fact, if she softened some of that starched formality. And a great smile—wide, and sometimes on the verge of downright sexy...even without lipstick, which she never wore. He thought about her lips in red for a moment—moist, glistening, succulent red...red-hot red...a provocative contrast to her fair skin...then his appraisal trailed down to her bosoms. Not large like Jonquil's fantasy bosoms, but not bad in a modest sort of a way. Not bad at all. Suddenly, the palms of his hands began to sweat and he brushed them on the legs of his jeans. "Why don't you prance right on over here, Liz, and have a seat," he suggested, trying to find his real voice, instead of the one that was making him sound like a hormonal, pubescent boy. "Slowly. I need to capture the full image."

"I beg your pardon," she said quietly. "You asked me to prance?"

"Did I?"

"You did. And excuse me if this sounds a bit blunt, but why?"

Charlie cast her an ill-at-ease smile and started to drum his fingers on his desk. "I'm trying to get a visual fixed in my mind for this thing...um...project I'm working on. And prance is the only word I can think of at the moment that comes close to what I'm describing. That's all.'' He shrugged, still clearly ill at ease.

"For an ad campaign?'' Liz stepped forward, sans prance, and closed the door behind her. "Because if you want it from a woman's perspective, which I'm assuming you do since you asked *me,* the word prance brings to mind one of Santa's reindeer, or a show horse on parade.''

"Good point.'' He readjusted his reading glasses, looked back at his computer screen, hit a few keys, then asked, "So if prancing across the room isn't a good choice, what is?'' He cleared his throat. "In terms of what a woman might do if she's…um…eager to fall into her lover's arms? Does she spring, maybe? Or trip.'' His eyes stayed glued to the screen. "Either one of those work for you?''

"Only if she's a klutz and there's a lot of furniture in her way. How about trying something straightforward like running or rushing? Sometimes the more direct words create the best image, don't you think? I mean, the goal is to get the public to notice and understand a product, and if you have the woman prancing across the room I'll guarantee half the audience will think Prancer. And if you have her tripping, floating, flying or shooting, the images you'll create with your word choices will cause readers to think of some things you don't want them thinking. At least, that's my opinion.''

"You're right again,'' Charlie agreed, hitting the save button. "Please, sit down.'' He motioned to the chair across from his desk.

"And I'm guessing you want me to run over there?'' she replied, refusing to budge from the door. "Or rush.''

"Those were your word choices. Remember?'' To take in Liz's best angle, Charlie twisted in his chair, then reared back in an attentive, ready-to-watch pose, his hands cupped behind his head, one leg crossed over the other. "So is there a better word? Bolt? Dart? Dash, maybe?''

"And if I bolt, dart, dash, run, or rush, what's in it for me?" She reached up and brushed an impatient hand through her hair, pushing a few straying strands back from her face. "Will I get credit for an assist on the campaign, since that seems to be what I'm doing? Or at least, what you want me to do."

"I understand you've been churning out some pretty good things as Jackie's assistant," he hedged. No way he was going to tell her what he was up to. No one at Whitaker knew, and he wanted to keep it that way. Office gossip was a Whitaker and Associates way of life he religiously avoided, and this little bet would make the tales of the file clerk, prim Miss Pettigrew's off-hours healthful wine sipping, as she called it, tame by comparison. "She's given you a generous recommendation. Raves, as a matter of fact." Liz was actually much prettier than he remembered. Definitely prettier than Jonquil. Less makeup. Softer. Blue eyes. Jonquil's were actually...well, he hadn't decided yet. Sometimes they were green, other times nearly black. Never blue, though. And definitely not ice-blue like Liz's, although on Jonquil ice-blue might not look bad. He scribbled a note to himself on a yellow legal pad, then looked up. "And you've been working here how long now?" Nice hair, too. Soft, almost blond. It reminded him of honey. Jonquil's was wild and red, frizzing halfway down her back. Liz's sprang loose from the clips that pulled it up and created a fringed frame around her face. Delicate, feminine, definitely pretty, it was almost angelic. Maybe he'd tweak Jonquil's hair later on. Tame it down some. Do away with a little of the wild and unfettered and add a smidgen of angel. Maybe even pull it back from her face to see how she'd look. "A year?"

"Two years, Charlie. As an assistant."

"No accounts of your own, yet?"

Liz shook her head. "Nothing to speak of. A couple of grocery store single-shot promos, an image-builder for a retirement center. Nothing to shake the world." Or even her little corner of it. "But Jackie's been great about the amount of responsibility she hands off to me."

"So I've heard. And I've also heard that you take that responsibility and run with it. Which brings me to this offer. Are you ready to take over Jackie Pollard's position temporarily, while she's out on maternity leave?"

"Absolutely," she declared without hesitation. "I know the accounts, I understand what the clients want and I'm ready to deal with them right now, if that's what you decide."

Charlie smiled. She was confident. He liked that. Maybe he'd add a little dab of that to Jonquil, too. "So you're ready to jump in with both feet? Good, since Jackie's blessed event may happen any minute and she's heading to the hospital as we speak."

"And this doesn't involve Marc Wells?" Liz drew in a stabilizing breath. Marc Wells, the man who, according to the water cooler scuttlebutt, was next up on the senior ad executive promotion list, had been gearing up to take over for Jackie. No one, including Liz, expected anything else.

"Marc's still out of town, and Dad left a memo saying you were second in line, if Wells didn't get back from his book tour before Jackie left. And he's not back, which means it's yours, if you want it. So what's the word?"

2

_____

"IF I WANT IT?" Liz smiled, but not so much that she
looked eager or excited. Calm, steady, in control—that
was her image, the one she'd rehearsed for this event,
and she refused to show him anything else. "The word
is absolutely!" Ideas were already beginning to effer-
vesce. They had been for months, from the moment that
Jackie first mentioned her maternity leave, even though
common office knowledge was that Marc would be
tapped posthaste. Even so, she'd planned ahead, made
herself ready just in case. And just in case had just
landed in her lap! "So, will I get a shot at the next
promotion when a position opens?" At thirty, she needed
the next promotion. Being an assistant was fine for starters, but it was time to start moving up, time to get her
career on the fast track. Especially since she was a come-
lately to the working world.

Charlie shrugged. "That's Dad's call. I don't do management, and don't want to do management. Not my
style." He grinned at her. "But if you do a good job,
maybe he'll notice you."

"Notice me? He can't even remember my name. His
eyes glaze over when he passes me in the hall and he
gets that _I know I should know her name_ look, then he
nods so he doesn't have to say anything. He nods, Charlie...professionally, not personally. A brief, ambiguous
jerk of his head without ever meeting my eyes. And
that's the man who's supposed to notice me so I'll get
promoted?"

"So do a good job with Jackie's accounts, and see

what happens." He picked up a manila file folder and opened it. "It says here that Sporty Feet is due up next week. Are you up to speed?"

"Yep," she gulped. She was up to speed on which PowerPoint points to push during the presentation. She was up to speed on how Barry Gorman, the Sporty Feet veep in charge of advertising liked his coffee. She was up to speed on how to arrange the chairs in the conference room for the best view. But about the actual campaign...her speed was a passing familiarity with what Jackie had been working on, namely the associated grunt work. But she knew that grunt work inside and out— facts, figures, competition, trends—the kinds of things no one else wanted to do, but that she was glad to tackle in the event that someone who mattered to her career noticed her efforts. Dues paying, she called it. "I'm ready," she stated, not convinced her voice was convincing. "And I can't wait to get started."

"Then welcome to your first senior account." Charlie took off his reading glasses and set them aside, then gave her a long, contemplative stare. "It's a tough business, Liz. You don't wait for the breaks to come to you, you make them happen. This is your shot, maybe the only one you'll get. Who knows?"

"My shot," Liz murmured. She'd treaded water for years in a go nowhere, do nothing marriage, and sucked in more than she should have in the way of an upwardly mobile hubby who wanted his showpiece at his side, at his convenience. But after nearly five years of marriage, she waved goodbye to a husband who was threatened to find that his wife had set out on a quest for a little personal fulfillment. Consequentially, Liz was a late arrival to a real life, but that didn't matter because it felt so darned good just to get there. The long delay was of no significance now that she was finally on track. "I'm ready." This time her voice was a bit more convincing. "And Sporty Feet will be ready, too. I'm not going to let you down, Charlie," she said solemnly, even though she was sure her voice still sounded more like a feeble warble than anything packed with self-assurance. "You, or Whitaker and Associates."

Charlie nodded absently, his attention once again fixed on his computer screen. "Good. I'll let Dad know you're good to go when I talk to him tonight. He may want to call you, or have a meeting when he gets back. So would you mind running across the room and sitting down so we can hack out some of the details?" He gestured to the chair again, and grinned, but this time quite comfortably.

Liz didn't budge. "Only if I get credit. Another account in my portfolio can't hurt."

"Credit…no, yes…I mean…" He shook his head. "Guess I need to be honest here, don't I?"

"If you want my input *in any form.*"

"That's just it. It isn't really input, not in the way you think. I need to…well…I need to observe feminine movements…um…bosoms," he said, his trademark sunshine smile erased by an awkward frown. "It's reality-based curiosity, actually."

"Bra campaign?"

Shaking his head, "Not exactly."

"Clothing? Maybe something athletic? Running… you're not trying to horn in on Sporty Feet are you?"

"I don't want Sporty Feet. Didn't want it when Dad offered it to me, and I certainly don't want it now. This is something different altogether. Not even a campaign, really. Just an observation for a description I'm writing, and it doesn't have anything to do with Whitaker and Associates. It's a private deal, not even advertising."

Liz glanced down at her chest, then back up at Charlie. "And for this *private deal* you want to observe my…"

"Bosoms. You know, the whole…" He gestured toward his chest, moving both hands in a circular motion. "The whole, um, you know…area. In general. Nothing personal." He cleared his throat nervously, dropped his hands to his side and crammed them into his jeans pockets. "In the interest of research. That's all. And on second thought, I think we'd better forget it. Okay?"

Ad campaigns often required unconventional working conditions, and Liz was used to it. Her personal motto—know it before you sell it. Only a month ago she'd spent the better part of a week eating mustard in every conceivable manifestation to get to know the product—a necessary step in the advertising process in order to convince the shoppers that the client's mustard was better than every other mustard on the market. Before that she'd doused herself in male aftershave and strutted through the office giving all her female co-workers a good whiff just so she could more vividly describe their reactions to its scent. Then there was that time with the hemorrhoid product...getting to know that wasn't so pleasant, but it was well worth the effort when she earned credit for an assist on a brand-new account. So Charlie's request didn't cause her to miss a beat as she replied in the most decisive voice she could muster, "My grandmother had bosoms, Charlie. I have breasts. Plain, straightforward word. No confusion. No thoughts of grandmotherly bosoms and nurturing, unless that's the image you're trying to achieve." She folded her arms across her chest, even though Charlie's eyes were focused squarely on her face.

"And if I ask you to run across the office so I can observe your *breasts* you'll sue me for sexual harassment. Plain, straightforward lawsuit."

"Maybe you could go to the park. Lots of runners there. You'll be able to observe those bosoms much better in sports bras."

He smiled, and nodded. "Good idea."

"Great idea, and I'm ready to help you with this project, or whatever you're calling it. I need another notch in my advertising belt. So tell me what *we're* working on and what else I can do to help, other than running and bouncing across the office for you."

"JACKIE SAID YOU WERE a go-getter." Charlie picked up a notebook then rifled his drawer for a pen. Nope, he still wasn't going to fess up to the romance novel he was writing. Not even to Liz, because she probably wouldn't understand this long line of brother-sister dares he was involved in, and losing more of them than he cared to admit. Last time, he'd dared Charlene to write an ad for doggy, bad breath biscuits knowing there was no way to sell the product graciously. But she did, and her ad was now on the sides of busses, all over TV and on billboards, making millions for the owner. Next month, they were filming a very hip infomercial about the product he didn't think was promotable. And his penalty for losing the bet to sister dearest, was that new Mercedes SL500 she was driving. *His* Mercedes SL500, with less than five thousand miles on it. And he'd loved that darn car.

The next dare—the romance novel. Sure, he'd heckled her about her job a few times. She was a book editor—romance novels. But apparently he'd heckled one time too many because she'd dished out a challenge to write a book that's up to publishing standards. Actually, three chapters due in three weeks, and based on that, winner takes all. Meaning if those chapters had real publication potential—and Charlene claimed that any good editor would be able to tell that well within three chapters—he won full claim to their great-great-grandfather's Civil War sword. If she won, meaning the verdict on the book was the ol' thumbs down, the sword was hers forever. Right now they shared joint custody, and while the sword's value was only about thirty grand, in sentiment, it was the family's pride and joy, and something he'd wanted all for himself since he couldn't remember when. To keep all things fair, they'd agreed that Charlene wouldn't be the judge. One of her co-workers had valiantly stepped forward to referee this round of the Charlie—Charlene games and make the final decision.

So now with Charlene's challenge off and running...

he smiled, thinking how the sword would soon be all his!

"Jackie was right, Charlie. I *am* a go-getter. So now, what about getting a piece of this *bosoms* campaign you're working on."

"Like I said, it's not a campaign," he stated, suddenly feeling guilty about misleading Liz. "Not in the way you think of a typical campaign, anyway." Her eyes were so eager, almost twinkling in anticipation, and he just didn't have the heart to lead her on. He was a game player for sure, but he didn't play people. And something about Liz compelled him to be totally honest here. Maybe it was the innocent enthusiasm she exuded, or the forthright ambition she didn't try to hide. Whatever the case, he wanted to be fair, and raising her expectations groundlessly wasn't fair. "It's a personal project—nothing to do with the agency."

"And whatever it is, I want in," she countered without missing a beat. "You've already taken my suggestions twice in ten minutes, and that should be enough to prove that I'm the right one to work with you on this *personal* project." Forgetting her caution, she walked across the room to his desk, stood opposite him, leaned forward and placed her palms down on the slick, mahogany surface. "And I *am* the right one, Charlie. You know that, or you wouldn't have asked me to prance in the first place."

"They were good suggestions, Liz, and I appreciate your help, but it's nothing I can involve you in, or I would. Believe me, if I could take anyone on, it would be you." As he spoke, he watched her movements. He wasn't sure when he'd ever seen anyone emanate with such poetic grace. And her bosoms...breasts didn't wiggle and heave with each step. They bounced a little, at best. Nice bounce. Beautiful. Hypnotizing. He allowed his eyes to feast for a second, at least he hoped it was only for a second, then blinked back the ogle. Jonquil never moved so seductively. He doubted she could because she wasn't anything like Liz. Jonquil was still ambiguous, but Liz Fuller was a lady who knew who she was and what she was about. There were no subtleties, and no mistaking her motives. She would do whatever it took in achieving what she wanted, and he liked that. Liked it a lot, in fact. "It's a family situation, but I appreciate your offer."

Another daring smile crossed her face and her arms went back up to cover her chest. "I think you're just trying to crowd me out of something you know I'd be perfect for. Whatever it is, I can do it."

"This?" he asked, impulsively spinning his computer screen around for her.

She looked down at the words. *Jonquil stood across from him panting and fanning her flushed, sweaty face, waiting for his capable mastery of her. Her ample, wet lips—lips the color of ripe tomatoes—quivered in desperate anticipation of the performance he was pulsing for. Her bosom heaved again, uncontrollably, in rhapsodic confusion, inviting him to make it his own. And the pounding in his groin multiplied with her each and every signal of want and need.* "What *is* this?" Liz sputtered, fighting back a laugh. *"Her bosom heaved again, uncontrollably, in rhapsodic confusion…"*

"I'm writing a romance novel," Charlie defended sullenly. "Men do that, you know."

"Of course they do. And some of them are very good, but I'm not sure this…" She couldn't stop the laugh, and it bubbled out like a wellspring. Tears followed, and she took the tissue Charlie yanked grudgingly from the box in his drawer and waved impatiently at her. "I'm sorry," she said, dabbing at her eyes, trying to collect herself. "I've never read anything like it before, and…have you ever considered writing comedy?"

"Comedy wasn't an option."

"Option?"

Charlie cleared his throat then whipped the screen

back around to face him, and hit the computer off switch.
"Good luck with Sporty Feet."

"What's rhapsodic confusion got to do with breasts,
Charlie?" she asked, still trying to wrestle with the re-
sidual laugh left inside.

"And I'd appreciate your keeping the details of my
book to yourself."

She started to nod, but the dam broke and the laughter
poured out again. "I'm sorry," she finally managed,
dabbing at a new sally of tears. "I just can't get a couple
of your more *vivid* images out of my head."

"Go ahead, laugh away. Doesn't hurt my feelings."
Even though he was offended that she didn't even try to
hide her laughter, especially since it had taken him the
better part of two hours to write the opening paragraphs.
He did like the way Liz laughed though. It wasn't Jonquil's nervous little titter, but a bright and loud gust,
nothing held back, with a couple of hearty snorts thrown
in for good measure. "In fact, feel free to make yourself
comfortable and carry on laughing." He stood, pulled
out his desk chair and gestured for her to sit, then without a word, marched out of the office, slamming the door
behind him.

3

"I OFFENDED YOU, DIDN'T I?" Liz sat down on the park bench next to Charlie, making sure to keep the greatest amount of distance between them. He was busy scribbling something into his notebook, and she decided to play it smart by not asking him if it was about bosoms, since he was a bit surly on the subject—rightfully surly, she conceded, considering how she'd laughed at him. "Look, I'm sorry. I didn't know you were serious about writing a romance novel. I honestly thought you were trying to put me off on an ad campaign. You know, telling me it was one thing when it was really something else."

"Lying?" He looked over the top of his reading glasses at her, arching his black eyebrows in mock dismay. "You thought I was lying to you?"

Liz smiled. "Let's call it protecting the integrity of your work."

"In other words, lying," he said, his voice firm.

"Lying," she finally agreed. "And after I read what you wrote, I...um..."

"Hated it."

"Not exactly hated it. Maybe something more like..." She scrunched her nose, searching for the right word to use here, a word that wouldn't hurt his feelings any worse that she'd already done. "More like doubted its technique in terms of what you were trying to accomplish."

"You're diplomatic, Liz. I'll give you credit for that." His voice softened a touch, and he twisted to look at her.

"And what I'm trying to accomplish is to win a bet with my twin sister. She's a book editor—romance novels—and she bet me that I couldn't write one that she'd think was good enough to publish. Remember Bowser Biscuits?"

Liz nodded. "Great campaign. It's doing a lot better than it was projected to, isn't it? I know everybody said you pulled a rabbit out of the hat with it."

"Thanks to Charlene—my last bet, by the way."

"Really?" Liz chuckled. "*She's* the one who came up with it? Wow. I'm impressed."

Charlie expelled the smallest hint of an exasperated sigh and focused on a clump of curvaceous joggers going by. "Which is why this thing is so serious to me."

"She must be a pretty mean competitor." Liz nudged over a little closer to see if he was jotting down what she suspected he was, but he snapped shut the notebook.

"Let's just say that she wins more than I'd like," he replied without a hint of emotion. "But not this time."

"So how often do you put on the gloves and step into the ring with her?"

"Lately, too often." Three losses in three months—way too often. Charlie finally unwound a little and settled back against the bench, his stare still on the generous fare of women in tight tops running by. "Way too often."

His stare was subtle, Liz thought, and surprisingly not lecherous, as were the stares of most of the other men sitting on benches, presumably there to take in the magnificent view of Lake Michigan, but in actuality to take in the abundance of females coming to the Lake Michigan shoreline. Charlie actually looked studious, even on the verge of being lost in thought. Curious, she thought. It wasn't what she expected from someone with his reputation.

"We've done it ever since we were kids," Charlie continued. "You know, like anything you can do I can do so much better than you ever dreamed. It started out with our allowances and candy and went on to, well, bigger toys, I guess you could say."

"Trying to establish the pecking order, maybe playing catch-up?"

"Or fight boredom. But Charlene is three minutes older, which could probably have a whole lot of psychological implications, if you get into that kind of mumbo jumbo. Which I don't, which brings me back to the boredom theory."

Liz chuckled. "Well, I know boredom, and I also know about playing catch-up. I have a lot of experience at both."

"And have you ever beat them?"

A wistful sigh escaped her lips. "I'm still working at it, but things seem to be shaping up and I have high hopes. And I'm sorry that I laughed at your work."

"So tell me, Liz. Were you right to laugh? Was it really that bad?" His eyes went to another shapely young jogger who was decked out in a very nice, tight sports bra, and he opened his notebook and made a few notations.

"Have you read a romance novel, Charlie?"

"Sure I have. Parts of a lot of different ones. Charlene used to bring her work home for the weekend—we have a weekend house up in Lake Geneva—and I looked at some of the manuscripts she was editing."

"Parts?"

"Yeah, enough to pretty much figure out what it's all about."

"And pretty much figuring out what it's all about is all the expertise or background you need to write one?" She snorted. "That's like saying that if you read an ad in a magazine once, you're ready to go right out and write one, and you, of all people know better than that."

"Apples and oranges."

She yanked the notebook out of his hand and opened it. "Leaping, wiggling, jiggling, bobbing, oscillating bosoms?" she read, and started to giggle. "She pranced across the floor, her bosoms oscillating. Is that oscillating, as in like a fan blade?''

"Be fair. We cut out *prancing* back at the office.''

"Apples and oranges, Charlie. And I'll guarantee this won't come anywhere close to Bowser Biscuits.''

"So what do you suggest?''

"Change the terms of the bet.'' She closed the notebook and handed it back to him, and saw, from the deep frown on his forehead, as well as the bullheaded look in his gray eyes, that he'd already rejected that suggestion. Charlie was dead set on winning this thing, and big sister was locked in his sights. "Or not,'' she added hastily.

Charlie nodded mechanically, his interest obviously held elsewhere—probably by the excessively well-endowed twenty-something sprinting by in a top and short shorts. He watched until she turned the bend and disappeared, then jotted some notes. His world, at the moment, was clearly so far away that he'd probably forgotten where he was, or who he was with.

Yep, he's sure good-looking, Liz thought, watching him lose himself in the creative process. All the single gals, and most of the married ones in the office talked about him, using terms like dreamy and beautiful and breathtaking. And he was all of those, for sure. Tall, well-muscled, with casual, wavy hair the color of onyx, and only a couple of years older than she was, Charlie had certainly caught her eye a time or two. After all, she *was* human, and gorgeous was gorgeous, and looking didn't mean anything other than casual interest. At this stage in her life though, a private opinion and a casual glance were as good as she'd allow. So when the hormone-driven office chitchat turned to Charlie Whitaker's sexy smile or his sensual, deep voice, or his spectacular, to-die-for derriere, she recommitted herself to lusting after career, not the boss's son.

"I don't suppose you happen to have a plan B handy, do you?'' Charlie capped his pen, casually crossed one leg over the other, then squinted up at the sun. "Maybe a romance ghostwriter in your closet? Or an unfinished romance in your drawer that I can just buy, tack my name onto and send to Charlene?''

''Plan B—well, I suppose you could start by reading a few romance novels before you try writing one. It's always nice to have an idea of what you're doing, and that's as good a way as any, I think.''

''Uh-huh,'' he responded, nodding his head in distinct disinterest.

''And you could go to the library for some books on how to write books.''

''Anything else?'' he prompted, still clearly not interested in her suggestions. The yawn he tried to stifle was a dead giveaway.

''Maybe you could get some expert advice.''

That caught his attention, snapped his eyes wide-open and made him sit straight up. ''A romance tutor? You've got to be kidding. I've had some pretty extensive experience in that department, and I've never had a complaint, thank you very much,'' he snorted.

''Well, I'd sure complain if you unbuttoned my blouse and told me what beautiful bosoms I have. 'Ah, beautiful bosoms, my dear. Succulent, like ripe cantaloupes.' After you uttered something like that to me in the heat of passion, I'd sure have some serious doubts about your...'' she raised her hands and squiggled quotation marks in the air ''—*extensive experience.*''

''I never said ripe cantaloupes.''

''But you probably would have.'' Liz caught herself tracking, with the astute interest of an ad woman in the research mode, a shapely young jogger who'd snatched Charlie's attention away from her, and she immediately shifted her gaze to the girl's feet to see if she was wearing Sporty Feet shoes. She was not, so Liz's stare fell to the asphalt. ''And you probably will, now that I've planted that visual in your mind. A combination of power of suggestion and grasping at straws.''

''You think I'm grasping at straws?''

She nodded.

"Then tutor me, Liz."

"Tutor you? How?"

"Talk me through it. Give me input just like you've been doing. Lead me out of the cantaloupe patch into…well, wherever it is I need to go to get this thing done the right way—the way that will help me win the bet."

"Spoken like a true romantic." She stood, and smiled down at him. "Maybe you should wait until you've fallen in love and experienced real romance before you write the book."

"You're assuming I haven't," he protested.

"Based on the evidence I've seen, I'd say you've kept yourself at an arm's length."

"Does a brain surgeon have to have his head cut open before he can operate successfully on a patient?"

"I've got to get back to work, Charlie. Good luck with your book." As she walked away, she felt the burn of his eyes on her back. But she resisted the urge to turn around, because she knew he was observing the motion of her hips, and recording it. "This one's for you, Charlie," she chuckled under her breath, pumping all the sway and swagger into her gait that she could manage and still stay upright.

"Teach me, Liz," he yelled. "Teach me the difference between bosoms and breasts and cantaloupes."

"Don't be impertinent, young man," a seventy-something jogger snapped as she passed by him. "Sex. That's all you young people have on your mind these days."

WITH THE THREE O'CLOCK meeting of department heads finally over, everyone was scrambling out of the conference like a heard of cattle on stampede. Everyone except Liz, that is. Lingering there in the aftermath, she was enjoying something that every other Whitaker executive considered dull. But she hadn't considered the meeting dull. Not in any way, and she figured it probably showed since she took ten pages of notes—longhand. No one else even jotted so much as a single word. But she'd been excited to take her place in the company's inner sanctums for her first time, with her very own temporary spot at the farthest end of the oval walnut table that seated thirty. Granted, she was barely in the same room with the agency movers and shakers and other senior staff, and she'd been forced to strain to hear more than one comment from that end of the room, but she was close enough to be considered part of it all, and that's what counted.

Now, in those few moments in which she dawdled, her mind went over the details of the plan that would keep her in that position permanently…she hoped.

"Meeting's over," Charlie prompted from the other end of the table. He was in his normal seat—not his dad's—even though Charles Senior was on a short vacation. Charlie's temporary bump from the right-hand side of the head seat to the head seat itself would probably have been acceptable, but Charlie refused when directed to the spot by his dad's secretary. He'd stayed in his place. Liz noticed that. And she noticed the easy way he abdicated his authority when the senior vice president took over. "Back to work."

"In a minute."

"Enjoying the view from down there?"

"Enjoying my life from down here, actually." She picked up a brown paper bag, stood and walked slowly to Charlie's end. "This is where I've wanted to be from the moment I was hired, and I want it to be permanent. And I'm willing to work harder than anyone else to make it happen, but I need a little help."

Charlie laughed. "You sound like a lady with a mission."

"Big mission, and it took me a long time to realize I could have one of my own, instead of sitting on the sidelines watching someone else's. Or worse, building my life around someone else's mission. Which is what I was doing.'' Reaching Charlie's spot at the conference table, she lifted the paper bag and dumped its contents in front of him. Books. Paperbacks. At least a dozen. ''So as part of *my* mission, I have a proposition for you.''

Charlie picked up a book and took a look at the cover. Man, woman, smiles, embraces. ''Sounds promising.'' The next one he looked at was similar. Better-than-real-life models, outstanding design, lots of sex…a real champion in the ad world. ''So proposition me.''

''Excuse me…'' Dolores Keifer, Charlie's secretary, poked her head in the door. ''I don't mean to interrupt, but you have an appointment in ten, Charlie.'' She fired a deliberate scowl at Liz. ''Business,'' she emphasized. ''And you asked me to remind you to go over your notes before the clients arrive. Which is what I'm doing.'' She fired yet another scowl at Liz, then pulled the door nearly shut behind her. ''Nine minutes now, Charlie,'' she called from the outer office.

''Wow,'' Liz sputtered. ''She's…''

''Efficient,'' Charlie supplied.

''I was going to say she's convinced I'm going to seduce you.''

''If that's the case, the walls stand a better chance of talking than Dolores. She's careful about these things.'' Charlie picked up another book, studied it, and arched his eyebrows in flagrant insinuation. ''Very careful.''

''That's what you think,'' Liz muttered almost under her breath. Apparently Charlie hadn't been to the water cooler lately. The sea of eager listeners parted when Dolores approached—parted and hushed in reverence, lest any one of them should miss even an ounce of the juicy office news she was so generous to share.

''So, my proposition?'' Liz prompted.

''Why do I get the feeling it has to do with bosoms.'' An articulate choking reverberated from the other side of the door, and Charlie stood, casually strolled over to the door, then pulled it shut. "So like I said before Dolores interrupted us, proposition me."

For a smooth-talker with a quiet, sensual voice, his words came unusually loud and Liz could only guess he suspected that Dolores's ear was still pressed to the wood, and this was one of his games. The Charlie Games, as they were referred to at the water cooler. And all the females wanted to play them. But not Liz. And just to let him know that she wouldn't be a part of them, she blurted, "Since I know, Charlie, that you're having some pretty big problems in *that* department, I really do want to help you. Especially because I know how important *that* part of your life is to you. And I promise I won't tell anybody, like you asked. Oh, and I bought some books I thought might help you with your problem." Her face radiated pure command of the moment, with a little dose of *I gotcha* confidence. "They'll teach you things you don't already know, fill in some of the finer details you've been missing, help polish your technique, give you new ideas, demonstrate what a woman really wants from a man, show you how to…"

"Yeah, yeah. I get the picture," he cracked, raising his finger to his lips to quiet her as he glanced uncomfortably at the door. "So what's the deal?" Dropping back into his chair, Charlie waved for Liz to sit at the head of the table, in the chairman's chair, then observed the natural way she accepted that position.

"No more games?"

He looked at his watch, then shook his head. "Not in three minutes."

"Then let's get down to it." Charlie certainly did have a disarming way about him, she had to admit. All the office discussion was truly unexaggerated about that fact. And she'd have to watch it, because he drew people in so easily they didn't even know they were being drawn until it was too late. Of course, they all went willingly. And when he turned on that perfect pearly smile, or let loose the twinkle in his sterling eyes, it was a come hither combination hard to resist by any clearheaded standard. Liz physically shook her head to purge herself of the mirage trying to take hold, and drew in a deep, girding breath. "In a nutshell, I'll be the tutor like you asked me to be before. I'll give you that romantic input you need, if you give me the input I'll need for the Sporty Feet campaign. I know that Marc Wells is up for the new senior executive spot even without Sporty Feet, and he's your dad's favorite, but I want that job, and I'll do it every bit as well as Marc will. Better, since he's hardly ever here anymore anyway, what with his book tours and motivational speaking. So a good promotion would be wasted on him, in my opinion."

"Okay, let me get this straight. You point me in the right romantic direction in exchange for my sage advice on Sporty Feet? That's all? You don't want me to recommend you to Dad, or ask him to give you the spot?"

Liz shook her head adamantly. "Your dad will notice me if I land Sporty Feet, then I'll be in the running for the next opening on my own merits—right along with Marc Wells. That's all I want. A chance to prove myself, and to have my work recognized. So, I just want to make sure that I'm on the right track with the campaign since this is my first solo, and because you're a senior executive, your part of the deal will be to keep me on track. That's all."

"And in exchange, I get…"

"More of what I've given you, already." She picked up a book with a broad-chested good-looker in a clinch with his stunning, long-haired lady love and waved it under Charlie's nose. "This is your objective, but I'll guarantee that heaving bosoms aren't mentioned in here, not even one time."

"So you'll steer me away from the heaving bosoms and I'll steer you toward Sporty Feet." Charlie opened the first page of one the books in front of him and read the first sentence of the prologue. Then he shook his head, let out a resigned sigh, closed the book and dropped it back into the bag. "Deal. Anything you want."

4

MEMORIAL DAY WEEKEND, and Liz had big plans for her three and a half days away from the office. Big plans in the professional sense, anyway. Sporty Feet was at the top of the list for sure, with tutoring Charlie right after it. And the back seat of her dented, teenaged Toyota was stuffed full of everything she thought she could need workwise, from an easel to sketch pads to her Power-Point paraphernalia. Not that she knew why she needed them, but she had them with her, just in case. Better to be prepared... And she also came prepared with a few more romance paperbacks just in case Charlie got really diligent in the next few days and plowed through the others she'd bought. She chuckled. Fat chance of that, but that hope eternal thing was springing in her...bosom.

"This is crazy," she said to the image in the rearview mirror. "Expecting someone like Charlie to settle down and write a publishable book—a romance...after what I already saw. What was I thinking when I agreed to help?" *Professional notice, promotion possibilities, for starters.* And spending a weekend away with Charlie. Nah! "Of course, it doesn't matter to me whether he wins or loses, as long as I win. Right?" *Well, not really.* She didn't like failing at anything. "But it's not going to be easy." *I guess we'll see.*

The drive up to Lake Geneva was as pleasant as it could be, considering that she was escaping the big city blahs of Chicago on a perfect midafternoon Friday, at precisely the same time that everybody else was trying to escape them. The Interstates in all directions were lined up, bumper to bumper, with trunky holiday jump-starters impatient to take advantage of the gorgeous day. But the sluggish traffic, and the fumes from the idling cars, and the horns from querulous motorists didn't bother her because she was looking forward to getting away for the first time in...how long had it been? Months? Maybe a year? She couldn't remember, which was the point. She'd been all work and no play for so long, she couldn't even recall the concept of play. And even though this was supposed to be a working holiday, working at the Whitaker family estate in the same neighborhood as Chicago's rich and famous was something to which she was looking forward. Just being out of the office was a nice reward, even if it was still work. Spending some time with Charlie was the bonus—in the utmost professional capacity, of course, since business and pleasure...

Stranded in a completely knotted vehicular standstill for five minutes now, Liz finally shut her eyes, leaned her head back against the headrest, and thought about Charlie for a moment. He was so easy to be around. Pleasant, witty, nice to look at, too. Not like Brian in any way, all dark and brooding and grumpy. Unlike her ex, Charlie was good-natured and considerate, and there was nothing not to like about him. Nothing at all. And any one of the twenty-six women working at Whitaker and Associates would testify to that in a heartbeat.

A wistful smile was just beginning to nip at the edge of her lips when an annoying horn from directly behind blurted into the middle of her...well, it wasn't a fantasy exactly. She didn't allow them. So, it was a mental assessment. Yep, a mental assessment, she convinced herself. Necessary, since the two of them were going to be working so close together for a while. Job-essential, that's all, and that dratted horn cut it right down the middle. Opening her eyes, she found herself straggling five car lengths behind the one in front of her, an indefensible sin on any Chicago Interstate, so she pulled forward to rejoin the inch-by-inch move groove with everybody else.

An hour later, Liz turned up the woodsy, winding driveway to the Whitaker's weekend getaway and was surprised to find a cedar-logged lodge nestled on a nearly rustic scrub of woods and wildlife. Not the image the Whitakers projected around the office, but...well, she liked it. For a moment, she even fancied herself settling down in a place like that. "Business, Liz," she reminded herself, climbing out of her car. "Don't go getting any stupid ideas." But a flash of Charlie and her cozying up on the porch swing she could see from the driveway shimmered through her mind before she could catch and squash it.

"Liz," Charlie called from the front door, waving. "Glad you could make it." He was flanked by a huge, bib-overalled man with a bulldog sort of face who hurdled down the steps and grabbed her suitcases from the back seat.

"Nice house," she said, trying to avoid looking at the porch swing, its likeness still so vivid she could almost hear the squeak of its rusty chain as it glided back and forth. "I didn't expect anything quite so..."

"Rustic? That's what everybody says the first time they're here. But Dad got it from a client who reneged on payment years ago, and he just left it like it is. Between you and me, I think he likes to simulate the rugged image—thinks that owning a lodge strikes a certain aggressive appearance. But he hardly ever uses the place, which leaves it available for Charlene and me as often as we want it."

"They made a TV show here once, ma'am," the big man remarked. His voice was thick and loud, and as deep as he was massive. "I was in it. Patrol Cops, airs every Wednesday at nine. You've seen it, haven't you?"

Liz nodded slowly. She'd never even heard of it, but she didn't want to hurt his feelings, and it was plain that she would if she let on how she didn't know a thing about the show. "Awesome," she exclaimed, satisfied that a hint of genuine interest was shining through. "I may have seen it. What part did you play?"

"Corpse."

"Practiced his part for days," Charlie said, winking at Liz. "Every time you turned around, Joe was right there on the floor, holding his breath, rehearsing. Sometimes he was so lifelike—I guess that would be deathlike, wouldn't it. Anyway, sometimes he looked so dead I almost had to feel for a pulse to make sure he wasn't."

"Did you start out dead, Joe, or did someone murder you first?" Liz followed Charlie and Joe up the steps and inside, and stopped just past the threshold. Lodge furniture, animal heads, a taxidermied black bear standing on its hind legs in the corner, its front paws extending out and ready to mutilate something—Liz shuddered as she took a quick look up at its face. Sure enough, its yellowed teeth were bared.

Other than the animals though, it was a wonderful room. The overall effect comfortable and warm. And surprisingly not pretentious. Enormous library shelves at one end, a tucked-away office alcove across from the stairs, an intimate seating area by the hearth with comfortable snuggling-in furniture for reading or... What she saw there was Charlie and her all cuddled up, maybe reading to each other or perhaps settling into the prelude for what would come later... Shaking her head and blinking her eyes, Liz snapped her attention to the long, wooden dining table sitting close enough to the fireplace to create a homey, toasty dinner nook, and fixed her wandering attention on counting the chairs. One...two... three...twelve, and by the time she was done counting, her retreat into fantasy was done, too.

"I was dead already when the program started," Joe continued, dragging her back into the conversation. "Just a DB—that means dead body. Right over there." He pointed at the hearth in front of a wall-length stone fireplace. "Face up. Shot in the heart. We'll watch the tape later," he added in low-pitched matter of factness, as if every newcomer to the Whitaker lodge was treated to the experience, like it or not.

Charlie came up behind Liz and whispered, "And if you tell him how true to life dead he looks, he'll be glad to replay it for you again…and again."

"Dead, like all these…trophies," she remarked, trying to avoid the inert-eyed stare of a beaver sitting on the fireplace mantle, poised to chew a three-inch thick stick. "So did these come with the house, or did Mr. Whitaker actually…?"

"Did Dad hunt?" Charlie chuckled. "Not animals, anyway. He just buys this stuff at auction. His wife at the time had it all frilled up—checkered curtains, throw pillows. She always called it adding the feminine touch, and it was pretty much all lavender. When he dumped her for wife number three he went the way of a macho motif—everything wifey two would have hated, and wifey three would never complain about, seeing as how she was too enthralled with her newfound wealth and status to rock the boat. Not that it did her any good," he chuckled. "Ditto for wives four and five. But no…Dad's a lover, not a hunter."

Joe let out a rumbling snort. "Guess it's all in how you define hunting, isn't it? So, which room do you want these in?" he asked, plodding toward the stairs.

"The main guest room," Charlie said.

Joe let out another rumbling snort, tromped on up to the second level muttering something they couldn't understand, then slammed a door at the end of the hall.

"He's a little rough around the edges, but…"

"He thinks we're sleeping together, doesn't he?" Liz interrupted. "And you let him."

"He thinks I sleep with every woman I've ever known. And I let him think whatever he wants. I mean, the man lives here with a bunch of…" He gestured to the overhead chandelier made of shed antlers. "So if he wants to believe that you'll come sneaking into my room later tonight, what's the harm? Especially since after this weekend you'll probably never see him again unless it's in the form of another dead body.''

"The harm is in not taking the arrangement seriously, Charlie. I have a lot at stake here, and apparently you do, too, since you want my help. But you're treating this like it's some sort of weekend date. And it's not a date. It's work. That's all!''

"And business and pleasure don't mix. Right?'' Charlie stuffed his hands into his jeans pockets and shrugged in conspicuous indifference. "Believe me, if there's one thing you've made perfectly clear about this weekend, there's nothing personal here, one way or another. And you don't have to worry because I'll honor that.'' His voice turned so cold it almost cracked. "Upstairs, your room is the last one on the left. Martha will help you settle in.'' Pivoting sharply, Charlie stalked out of the room, his footsteps so hard on the wood floor they rattled the entire series of British fox hunt prints hanging on the wall. Even the riders in their scarlet frock coats bounced up and down on their mounts.

The dismissal was so abrupt, so unfriendly and uncharacteristic, it caught Liz off guard, and Charlie was already long gone before she regained her wits enough to yell, "So when do you want to get started?''

Her answer was the slam of the door in the distance, then a lodge full of nothing but quiet.

"Sure don't know what you did to get that out of him,'' a quiet, sweet little voice piped up from somewhere in the hallway through which Charlie had exited. Liz couldn't see its source. "It takes a lot to get him so cranky—usually only happens when he loses one of those silly bets with Charlene. They're always doing them, you know. Have been as long as I can remember, and the bets just seem to keep getting bigger and bigger. I've been telling them both they've got too much time on their hands, but it doesn't do any good since they just keep on betting.'' The shadow shook her head. ''Way too much time...'' A short, round woman sprung into the lodge's inherent dim light and flittered her away across the floor to the stairway. She wore an old-fashioned white lace apron tied around her ample waist, over a floral-print cotton dress reaching down to a prim, midcalf length. Her glasses were granny-style wire rims, and her perfectly white hair was permed into tight curls that clung close to her scalp like a cap, without a single strand out of place. Martha carried a plain wooden cane hooked over her left arm, too, but she moved so swiftly it never seemed to have enough time to touch down. ''But never you mind about Charlie,'' she said, trotting right past Liz and on up the stairs. ''He gets over it pretty fast. So come on.'' She turned around and gestured for Liz to follow. ''We've got to get you settled in before...''

Before Martha explained *before what,* she was gone, leaving Liz to wonder how a seventy-something could be so spry. And by the time Liz reached her room, Martha was already unpacking her bags. ''Your bed,'' she said, pushing up and down on the mattress. ''And it's comfy. I'm sure you'll like it much better than Charlie's. His is too firm, if you ask me. Hard, like a board.'' She smiled. ''But if you like them hard...'' Martha fluttered on over to the bathroom and opened the door. ''It's a small one,'' she explained, ''puny shower, but I'm sure Charlie will let you use his. It has a hot tub—for two. Much better for the atmosphere, if you know what I mean. Of course, two people crammed together in a puny shower like this one can be lots of fun.'' She winked. ''Tried it a time or two myself.''

''We're not...'' Liz started. Now she understood what *before* meant!

''Oh, my dear. You don't have to explain to me. Believe me, I've worked here long enough to know how the Whitaker men are.''

"No," Liz said, shaking her head. "Charlie and I work together, that's all."

"Of course it is, dear," she said, scurrying over to the dresser. "And here are your welcome gifts, courtesy of Mr. Whitaker. We like to make sure all the guests are well taken care of." She handed a basket of scented soaps, lotions, bath salts and gels to Liz, then winked as she pulled aside a puff of pink tissue paper. "A variety pack in assorted colors and textures. If you require more, or find you have a particular fondness for one over the others, please don't hesitate to ask me." She smiled up at Liz. "I keep a supply on hand. And don't be shy about it, my dear. Like they always say, it's better to be safe than sorry, you know."

"I don't need condoms," Liz sputtered, removing the box like it was a venomous snake. "We aren't…you have the wrong idea." She looked at the box and saw the diagram for something that seemed more like a kitchen utensil than a condom, and dropped the box on the bureau. And from the looks of a couple of the condoms illustrated there, they probably could do double duty in the bedroom and kitchen. "Look, Martha. *Like I said,* this is a business arrangement. That's all. I'm here to work, and to help Charlie with a project. I'm not one of his…whoever it is that requires those." She pointed to the boxed prophylactics and wrinkled her nose. "And these are not for me."

"Whatever you say, dear." Martha's voice conveyed the explicit inscription that she didn't believe a word Liz was saying, which told Liz that she wasn't the first *guest* Charlie had brought to the lodge. Not that she expected she was, but the telltale evidence was a little unsettling, glaring up at her in its rainbow array from the welcome basket. "But just in case…" She raised her cane and nudged the box toward Liz. "And by the way, I'm preparing an intimate little dinner for this evening. Charlie said you two need to work undisturbed." She winked. "There's an antique glove box sitting on the table next to the sofa. If work becomes a bit more intense than you anticipated, you'll find inside it a nice assortment of..." She leaned toward Liz, wrinkled her nose and whispered, "Emergencies is what I like to call them. There are a few in the desk drawer, too. Like I said, better to be prepared." Martha gave Liz another wink then skittered out the door.

5

CHARLIE CLICKED SHUT THE LID of his laptop, and leaned back in the deck chair. Too nice of a day to waste on this, he thought, as Jonquil transformed from a nearly living, breathing creature into one who was locked up tight in his hard drive. The curtains in Liz's room were drawn now, and he couldn't see in, but he imagined what she was doing up there. Work, in some form. Plotting, designing, drawing, composing, whatever. And she was probably still dressed in her characteristic office clothes. Two-piece suit, black, or was it navy-blue? White blouse, or maybe she was living large today in a little off-white number. He hadn't noticed, since there was usually nothing new to notice. Same clothes, same hair—always pulled up and fastened in some sort of a librarian do. It could be gorgeous, though, if she wanted it to, which apparently she did not. He closed his eyes for a moment, and pictured her pulling out the pins, letting it down. One pin at a time, and ever so slowly…her beautiful golden tresses finally released, she shakes her head to let them fall free, then runs her hand through her hair to sweep it into place.

A sensual smile meant only for Charlie brushes her lips and she unbuttons the top three buttons of her blouse, then drops her suit jacket into a crumpled heap on the floor and kicks it away with her…two-inch spikes. No, make it three inches. Legs as gorgeous as Liz's deserved three inches. His gaze skims up her legs to just above her knees where her hemline threatens to stop the journey, and he waits while her fingers move slowly to the skirt's zipper and begin to pull it down with deliberate leisure…

Wow! Now that wasn't an image of Liz he had every day…any day. A bead of sweat broke his brow, and it definitely wasn't from the heat.

"Great," Charlie muttered, opening his eyes. She wasn't his type and he had no business trying to fantasize her into something she wasn't. No business at all. Even so, something about Liz Fuller brought out the fantasy in him. Probably just the challenge. Uptight, all business all the time lady in need of a little loosening. "That's all," he said resolutely. "Just another challenge." Still staring up at her window when the curtains parted and the sash windows were pushed out, he instantly averted his gaze to Joe, who was running through some skewed dialogue from Hamlet as he pushed a wheelbarrow filled with potting soil across the lawn.

"To plant or not to plant…" Joe bellowed, apparently practicing a voice projection technique, not that he needed it. Charlie took one final glace at Liz's window, grabbed his laptop and headed to the side of the house *without* the view, or the fantasy.

STILL A COUPLE OF HOURS before dinner, Liz debated her attire. Totally casual might work, she thought, shaking the wrinkles out of a pair of capri pants. Add a nice little T-shirt and Charlie…well, knowing Charlie he'd probably think casual meant she was ready to play. Which she wasn't. Then there were her everydays, but truthfully, she hated the look. Drab, boring, utilitarian—simple, effective and not for this place. "Come on, come on, come on…" she muttered impatiently. "This is a working dinner. Work, Liz. Nothing to get into a wardrobe tizzy over." But she wanted to look…what? Good? Sure, she wanted to look good. But good in what sense? Professional? Casual?

"Stop it," she hissed, plodding to the closet, feeling silly for the churning in her stomach. "This is Charlie, for Pete's sake. We're working. Period!'' Intellectually, she was convinced, but that still didn't make the churning stop. Sliding back the closet doors only part way to hang her clothes, she brushed against something with... feathers? "What?" she murmured, pushing the door all the way in. Sure enough...feathers! And a whole lot more. Negligees, peignoirs, see-throughs, and other assorted scanties. A tidy little row of them, in all colors, no less. Black, hot pink, white, and red. Lots of red. Charlie must really like red, she thought, trying to force back the irritation fighting to push its way to the surface.

"So what do you have in mind, Charlie?" she asked, pulling out the one with feathers. "Not that I can't guess." Thong panties, of course, but with some sort of garter belt to go over them. "Really comfortable," she muttered sarcastically, wondering where the black, fishnet stockings were. Getups like this had to have the fishnets.

Pulling the top off the hanger she held it up to herself. A barely there, see-through, feathered wisp of a thing, it came down to just below her...well, it barely cleared everything she kept covered up. And it came with an even skimpier bra, with stays substantial enough to push a modestly endowed B cup, which she was, into a full-out C with a little left over in the cleavage department. She held the bra up to herself, and choked when she saw that it would scarcely skim the tops of her nipples—B, C or whatever—if she were to try it on.

And the price tag dangled in plain view, so there would be no mistake that this was brand-new—one of those welcome gifts Martha mentioned. "You certainly think of everything, don't you, Charlie?" she said aloud, grinning. "Well, maybe not everything."

LIZ STEPPED INTO THE HALL and sucked in a deep breath. Looking down at the red nightie she was wearing, she checked to make sure that everything needing hidden was hidden. Compared to the standards of everything else she'd found in the closet, this little number was conservative. Red floral stretch lace, with a cami top stopping two inches above her belly button and a boyshort starting two inches below, she was mighty glad the floral parts were placed strategically because the film wrap that went over the ensemble was more revealing than concealing. Thank heavens she had a flat tummy, she thought as she ventured over to the top of the stairs. And that she'd shaved her legs this morning.

Sucking in one more deep breath, she took the first step down the stairs then she tossed a handful of other filmy nighties out over the railing into the common area below, where they drifted down in an almost ethereal scene, with delicate poofs of assorted colors wafting gently on the breeze of the ceiling fan. The people downstairs looked up at the spectacle, too astonished to comment beyond a single, "Well, would you look at that," from Joe, who immediately launched into the dance of a jumbo, bumbling ballerina trying to grab the slinky garb as it fluttered down. The grizzly bear in the corner snatched up a hot pink peignoir, tolerating its obtrusive dangling from his huge right paw in muted indifference. Three discriminate colors—midnight-blue, cherry delight and purple-passion—commandeered the chandelier and veiled the lights that mingled among the antlers, resulting in an eerie bluish shadow cast over the entire room. And the beaver laid claim to the basic red with the price tag. "You know, Charlie," Liz began as she maneuvered the stairs, still bestowing the closet goodies on her way. "I'm not even here for an hour and your intention is already coming through loud and clear." She passed Joe scrambling up the stairs, scooping up an armful of garments scattered over the steps and handrails. He smiled sheepishly as he dove in front of her to retrieve a pair of red stockings. "It's a business arrangement, and you knew the terms when you asked me to spend the weekend. I agreed to give you what you need, and you agreed to do the same for me. And at no time did we mention

these…these…I don't even know what to call them because I certainly wouldn't *sleep* in them.'' Stepping over
a strip of fabric that resembled a bra, she continued.
''Considering all the other little welcome goodies you
left in my room, I guess the terms of this arrangement
weren't as clear as I thought they were.'' In her right
hand Liz clasped a gold lamé garter belt, and when Charlie came into her view she snapped it, like a slingshot,
at him.

He reached out and plucked the garter from midair
then handed it to Martha, whose arm was draped with a
collection of tiger stripes and snake skins as she speared
yet another naughty with the tip of her cane. ''Liz, I
don't think this is the time to go into…''

She stopped halfway down the open staircase, shook
her head, and held out her hand to stop him. ''Is this
what you want?'' She spun slowly and seductively, like
a runway model in a celebrated fashion show, her hands
running provocatively over the lines of the apparel to
emphasize the obvious pleasures. ''But were afraid to
ask for?'' Resuming her purposely slow pace, she drew
in a deep breath to resteady her nerves. Not too bad so
far, she thought. Granted, Charlie looked a touch
stricken. Not exactly the response she expected from him
considering what he expected from her, but maybe she
was finally beginning to get through to him. She sure
hoped she was, because this relationship was way too
important to mess up with whatever he thought might
happen once she slipped into her negligee du jour. ''You
know, I'm trying to be reasonable here, because I understand that we somehow ended up with different expectations.'' On the landing that topped the last dozen
steps, she paused long enough to toss him the box of
condoms, then finished her descent. ''But the point is,
it's business. No matter what else you're thinking you
might get out of it…''

Charlie arched his eyebrows and shot her a commingling expression of *I don't believe my eyes* and *The sky is falling.* "Liz, I really think you should…"

"No," she interrupted. "I think you have a choice to make here. We have three days ahead of us, and we can go at this arrangement the way we'd originally intended, or we can…"

"Liz," he hissed, tugging at his collar. Even in the dim blue light the scarlet tinge to his face was becoming obvious. "Not now!"

"I'm just trying to earn a promotion here, Charlie. You know that. And I want it bad enough that I'm still willing to do whatever it takes. But without the games. Okay?" *Good*, she thought. *He's not so comfortable now.* She had him just where she wanted him. "Okay?" she repeated, walking away from the stairs, heading straight to Charlie. "So how about we just forget this whole sordid little incident and get on with the weekend?" Out of the corner of her eye, over in a dim-lighted spot in the room, she caught the toes of a pair of black oxfords. The right one appeared to be tapping, almost frantically.

"Liz…do you remember Barry Gorman, senior vice president of Sporty Feet? Barry's a neighbor." Charlie backed away from Liz, his eyes shifting to the stuffed bear. "He and his wife, Ellen, stopped over for drinks. Ellen's father, Lou West, in case you've forgotten, owns the shoe company."

Liz twisted around just enough to see that the balding, bespectacled fiftyish man seated on a lodge bench was draped in a fluffy, lime-green boa. *Oh no, oh no, oh no…* She found a spot on the floor—a knothole in the pine plank—and prayed for a way to crawl right into it then plug it up behind her. But no knothole—only the conspicuous shuffling from the area of the black oxfords, shuffling that sounded distinctly like a senior vice president, and his wife, scrambling to their feet, either to greet her on the pretense that what had just happened hadn't, or to run out of the room and never, ever look back.

"Barry, you remember Liz…Jackie's assistant." Charlie drifted over to Barry and removed the lime boa from his shoulders, all the while taking great care to focus his gaze on the bear rather than on any of the parties involved. "She's taking over for Jackie while she's out on maternity, and we've put Liz—" an almost pained look spanned Charlie's face as he squeezed out the rest of the words "—in charge of the Sporty Feet campaign. We have a lot of, um, confidence in her abilities." He nodded decisively. "Lots of confidence."

"I'll bet you do," Barry snapped, nabbing his wife's elbow on his flight to the front door. "Sorry we stopped by at a bad time, Charlie. Maybe I'll give your dad a call next week, after I've sorted through a few—" he looked over the top of his glasses at Liz, exhaled irritably, and shook his head "—a few details of the proposal from Whitaker. It seems that we might have just had a change of heart and stay where we are, after all."

"*Where you are, Mr. Gorman?*" Liz piped up, surprised to find her voice. Quickly, she cast Charlie a warning bullet glance, then walked across the room with all the confidence she could fake in so little clothing, directly to the man who still hadn't bothered to right his glasses in order to look squarely at her. And he was definitely looking squarely at her, frowning so hard that his eyebrows joined into one long, angry, horizontal slash above his narrowed, furious eyes. Stopping two feet in front of him and meeting his leveling stare, Liz took in a deep breath and felt the adrenaline start to surge. "I'll tell you where you are. You're still in bed with an ad firm that hasn't distinguished your company from any of the others out there, aren't you? Any of the hundreds of others out there. When you came to Whitaker, I believed that you were looking for an advertising firm that would save you from mediocrity, which is why you selected us—because we're never mediocre, as you can see.'' She gestured to her outfit to prove her point, glad more now, than ever, that it was the most modest one in the bunch. ''And your current campaign is mediocre, to say the least. Nothing at all that makes a person take notice. *Sporty Feet for Sporty People.* Come on, Mr. Gorman. You have a product that deserves better than that, and so far, you haven't given it everything it deserves. You haven't even come close.''

''Young lady, when I came to Whitaker I expected professionalism, not…not this.'' He grabbed the boa from Charlie's hand and waved it at Liz. Then finally, he righted his glasses. ''And those…'' He grabbed the box of condoms his wife had picked up from the floor.

''But they sell, Mr. Gorman. They reach right out and grab your attention, don't they? Not only do they grab it, they hold it. Right?''

''Smut.''

''Sex,'' Liz corrected. ''Charlie and I came here to work on the campaign this weekend, Mr. Gorman…to try to find a way to get your image in line with the footwear images that sell. Your profits were down eighteen percent last quarter, weren't they?''

Barry Gorman squirmed, then shoved both the condoms and the boa at Liz. ''That's beside the point.''

''Not if you want to stay in business it's not,'' Liz defended. She turned around and handed the accoutrements to Martha, who in turn handed an oversized trench coat to Liz as she flitted on by, still gathering unmentionables. Before turning back to face Gorman, Liz shrugged on the coat—Charlie's coat, she thought, catching the faintest trace of his scent lingering in the fabric—then cinched it at the waist and allowed herself one quick look at Charlie, expecting thunder from him. Surprisingly, he responded with a wink and just the tiniest promise of a smile.

''Economy slumped. Everyone took a beating,'' Barry snapped. ''Everyone!''

The adrenaline rush still coming, Liz's pulse was picking up and her nerve endings were beginning to tingle. This was what she'd been waiting for, to be a real part of the ad game and not simply the assistant who shuffled documents and clicked the PowerPoint remote for someone else. This was it. Sink or swim. She was the someone else she'd dreamed of being. *Welcome to your life, Liz Fuller. It's time to show them what you're made of.* "Not everyone took the hit, Mr. Gorman. Sure, some of your minor competitors felt the bite along with you, but not the big boys." She folded her arms across her chest, raised her chin in defiance, and shook her head in righteous bewilderment. "And I don't understand how you can disregard that kind of a hit because down eighteen percent means you came in under the little guys, and you know that." She cut him a challenging smile. "Dead last in your market, Mr. Gorman. By three percent."

"Is that right, Barry?" his wife chimed in. "You were dead last?"

"It's been worse," he snorted. "And these things go in cycles. Our new autumn line is bound to…"

"Your new autumn line doesn't make a bit of difference if you can't sell it," Liz stated. "And since you were down fifteen percent the quarter before last, that tells me you *can't* sell it without some major help— without a new image, which is exactly what Whitaker intends to do for you. Update your image. Give you a new appeal. Find your market and lock it in, once and for all."

"Are you going to let her get away with this, Whitaker?" Barry sputtered. He was beginning to sweat. His glasses slipped down his nose again. "She works for you, can't you control her?" Grabbing the white handkerchief from his coat pocket, he dabbed at his forehead. "Your father would have fired her…"

Charlie threw his hands into the air in mock surrender. "Hey, I'm just an ad exec, Barry. Liz doesn't work for me. But in my opinion, she's doing one heck of a job trying to pitch a concept. I'm mighty impressed. Problem is, you're not cooperating. And as far as I'm concerned, she's got some pretty good selling points.'' Charlie stepped up behind Liz and gave her a squeeze on her shoulder. ''Like I said, we have a lot of confidence in her ideas, Barry. That's why we saved her for you. Sporty Feet deserves our best, and Dad did handpick her, after all.''

''Good ideas, if you'd listen to them,'' Ellen hissed at her husband.

Barry glanced at his watch. ''One minute, Miss…''

''Fuller, Elizabeth Fuller,'' Liz supplied. ''And I don't need a full minute, Mr. Gorman.''

''That sure of yourself, are you?'' he sneered.

She nodded. Creating on-the-fly had her stomach twisted in fist-sized knots, her head banging a topsy-turvy rhythm and her lungs punching back at her for every breath she tried to draw out of them, and she loved every last jolt of the assault. More than that, right now she wanted the promotion harder than anything she'd ever wanted in her whole life. Problem was she'd pretty much just shot down everything she worked on for Sporty Feet so far, since *her* concept was all just a higher concept of the same ol' same ol' athletic angle. Which meant she was out there on her own, with no safety net in sight. Worse than that, with no idea in sight, either. Zilch! Nada! Nothing!

''Yes, I'm that sure, Mr. Gorman.'' She lied. Sure that this time tomorrow she'd be reading the want ads.

''So let me have it.'' Jamming the damp hanky into his pocket, Barry folded his arms across *his* chest and raised *his* chin in defiance, as Liz had done. ''Your time's running out.''

''Sex.''

''What?''

''Sex, Mr. Gorman. That's it.''

''Sex? That's your selling point for my shoes?'' He shook his head in solid disdain, then turned to his wife.

"If we hurry, I think we still have time to get home and have the Ashtons over for bridge."

"Fifteen percent down last quarter, then eighteen percent this, Mr. Gorman. You're on track for what next quarter? Twenty-one percent, then twenty-four after that? Can Sporty Feet weather that kind of a loss? Will your *position* withstand it?"

"I know you've never cared much for sex, Barry," Ellen said quietly, patting him on the arm, "but I like it and I think Miss Fuller...Liz is on to something." Her gentle pat turned into a threatening squeeze. "So listen to her!"

Barry shuddered. "That's not what Sporty Feet is about."

"No, it's not, and look what's happening," Liz continued. "Your market's flat, which means your advertising isn't working. Actually with those numbers, it's way beyond not working. Your advertising is dead, and the image you want to resurrect won't do diddly for you."

"Diddly?" Barry snorted.

"Diddly. And you'll be out of business by year's end if you don't come up with something to pull you out of the downtrend."

"And you think that's sex, young lady?" Barry asked. "Simply add a little sex to Sporty Feet and we're off and running again? Give up the established image that has carried us for decades for...for...*sex?*" He squeaked the word out, then swallowed hard and smacked his lips to rid himself of the taste. "No," he muttered, shaking his head skittishly. "I don't like it. Not one little bit. Not for Sporty—"

"But sex sells, Barry," Liz interrupted. For the first time, she felt the earth under her feet go solid. Her footing was equal to the client's right now because he was countering with emotion, not reason. That meant he was venturing into her territory, instead of forcing her to wallow in the middle of his. "You took notice the second those little nighties started floating out over the room, didn't you? You knew exactly what they were and what they represented. Instant recognition. Right?''

He nodded stiffly, his stubborn body language a dead giveaway that he was not in sync with the sales pitch. "But I'm trying to sell shoes—running shoes, and there's nothing sexy about that, Miss Fuller. We want to emphasize good fit, outstanding performance...athletic performance, not..." Clearing his throat in marked discomfort, Barry folded his arms securely across his chest. "Not sexual performance."

Nope, he wasn't in sync yet, Liz knew, but he was getting closer. After all, he was still there, listening, wasn't he? A tiny smile crept to her lips. "Not sexual performance, Barry. Sexuality...sex appeal...sexy. Something that says, 'Hey, look at me. If you own me that makes you sexy.' And sexy reached right out and grabbed you, which means it will grab your customers, too."

"What grabbed me, young lady, was a green boa," Barry spat.

"And you won't forget it, will you? Which is the premise behind the campaign I'm designing. Something that will grab and hang on."

"Meaning boas and...whatever else the rest of these things are?" Barry snatched a thong from Martha, who was dashing through to retrieve a pair of purple panties from the corner of great-great-grandpa Whitaker's portrait, and waved it at Liz. "This is what you're proposing?"

"No. I was just catching your attention with it. That's all. What I have in mind for you is something that's really high concept, especially for athletic shoes. And not nearly so blatant as what you're seeing here today. And I promise that after next Friday, you won't be sorry that you kept your appointment with us."

"Big words, Miss Fuller.' Barry shook his head, still not giving in to his own defeat. "So I suppose we'll see if you're as good as you think you are," he muttered.

"And it had better be good, young lady. Do you understand? Damned good."

Standing directly behind her husband, Ellen smiled pleasantly as she tucked the gold lamé garter into her purse.

CHARLIE WAVED THE GREEN BOA in the air, and Martha darted out of the shadows, swiped it and scurried away. "I'd say it went fairly well," he commented casually, his eyes glued to Joe, who had dragged in a stepladder for the purpose of retrieving the pink thing still in the grizzly's grasp. "All things considered."

Liz was fuming now, so angry she was pacing in literal circles. He liked the red flush to her cheeks. Bold. No mistaking the meaning. And her red blush went so well with the red nightie, it was a treat to which he'd never dreamed he'd be treated. If nothing else, it certainly put Liz in a whole new light for him—a light he'd let shine on him anytime. She wasn't saying anything yet, however. Not one word since Barry and Ellen had left ten minutes earlier. "So what's your take, Liz?" he finally ventured, forcing back a smile. He'd never seen this side of her before, and he liked it. Of course, he was seeing pretty much every side of Liz for the first time, and he was beginning to wonder why she'd never been more than a casual observance before. His mistake. A big one, it seemed.

"My take? Do you really want to know my take, Charlie?" She stopped dead in her tracks, raised her head slowly and locked onto his gaze. The figurative smoke was billowing from the top of her head. "Do you really want to know what I just did here? Do you really want to know what will happen to my job if Barry Gorman walks away? Do you really want to…"

Words failed her, and she began pacing again. Back and forth, seething and fretting, ranting and raving. Wow, he liked her in the heat of the moment. All sex and fury and so provoked there wasn't a vestige of her usual businesslike prim and proper to be found. Not what he wanted in *his* girlfriends, per se. They were a little more docile and willing...but in Jonquil... Now that would certainly make her leap right off the page. That is, if he could translate every little ingredient of Liz's explosion into words. "Could you just hold on to that mood for a minute?" he asked, practically running to the mission oak desk in the office alcove. There he grabbed a yellow legal pad, perched himself on the edge of the desk and began writing as fast as his hand would allow.

Catching *his* frantic endeavors to catch *her* mood on paper, Liz turned slowly, like a hungry animal sizing up its next meal, then watched him for a moment before she pounced. "I know what you're doing, Charlie, and it had better not be a verbatim account! Charlie? Are you listening to me?"

"Mmm...hang on." The ideas started flowing so quickly, he was thoroughly unaware that Liz was closing in on him, little by little. When she arrived at the desk, she looked over the top of the pad to see what had commandeered his attention, and encountered the name Jonquil, with a flame etched around it. Her name was next to Jonquil's, with an even bigger flame, and a descriptive word list—blazing, passionate, explosive, provocative...

"I like provocative," she said, continuing to read.

Fiery, fervent, tempestuous, hotheaded...

"Hotheaded? You think I'm hotheaded?"

"Did I say that?" He looked up, noted the red still in her cheeks, then added to his list—sultry, aroused, electrified, hot, torrid...

"You wrote it right there." She jabbed her finger on the word. "Hotheaded, and it's under *my* name."

Smiling, Charlie turned his pencil over, erased, then rewrote—hot-blooded. "Better?"

"How can you sit there and doodle adjectives after what just happened? Your dad's going to fire me if Barry Gorman doesn't strangle me with the boa, first."

His response was a distracted nod—one that pronounced the fact that he wasn't listening, that something in another time and place was summoning him. And he scribbled for another five minutes before he looked up and realized he was completely alone in the room. The bear had been disrobed and Joe was gone, Martha wasn't loitering in a corner somewhere, and Liz was... He dropped the legal pad back on the desk and stood. Liz was... A smile crossed his face. Perfect.

6

IT'S SO BEAUTIFUL HERE, LIZ THOUGHT, as she strolled through the grounds trying to calm herself. So calm and peaceful, and she needed it. She was still shaking, her reflexes yet snapping to fight off something, or someone. And if there was one thing she didn't need at the moment, it was the preoccupation of everything that had gone wrong so far. It was over, time to move on. But the move wasn't easy for her, even in the short time Sporty Feet had been hers, since she'd already invested so much thought in her first real account—thought that wasn't anything like the reality that had just played out. And nowhere in that investment was there even a speck of room for a green boa. "Jeez," she said, kicking at a pebble. "Just when I was beginning to like the job."

So now she was walking it off, and Charlie was tucked away in his office adding a little umpf to Jonquil, umpf ala Liz Fuller, she guessed. She'd already spotted his pattern—he watched her for a while, then wrote something down. Then he watched some more, and wrote some more. Flattering, she thought, and also amazing in the way he went from the most disastrous meeting anyone could ever imagine to calmly shaping a character for his book. She couldn't even change her lunch decision without due debate, because switching midstream wasn't her style, or strength. Nothing in her could simply go with the flow if the flow turned into something other than what she'd mapped out. But Charlie was awesome, the way he could turn it over like that without missing a beat. No pretense, no hidden agendas, no trappings and no sweat. That was Charlie, though. And she admired his self-confidence, and even envied it since hers was still on frail footing. However, just a while ago, thanks to Charlie, she'd felt her first real booster of professional confidence. Or maybe just a little of his rubbing off on her. Whatever the case, she'd taken hold of it, embraced it, and was even so bold as to call it her own. And it felt so good having that little bit of power and control, knowing that Barry Gorman wanted what she had to offer him even if he wasn't about to admit it yet. Not yet, anyway. Sure, he may have kicked at the idea initially. Maybe he was still kicking. But he'd walked out of the room with an idea in his head that she'd put there, an idea she *knew* he'd think about for the next week. That was confidence like she'd never, ever had before today, and she savored the sweet taste of it.

And she wanted more.

"Sex sells, Liz," Charlie said, taking his place on the garden bench next to her. "And you certainly did a good job of merchandising the heck out of it. Except for that green boa, I don't think poor Barry had a clue what hit him."

The brush of his shoulder to hers as he sat sent a shiver up her spine, and Liz scooted away from him. She knew what that tiny sensation could mean…could do to her, and she didn't want it. Not now, not since she was finally on her way. "Well, if sex wasn't the selling point before that fiasco, I guess it sure is now, isn't it?"

"You're good on your feet." He chuckled. "And out of your clothes. You nailed the hard part—selling the concept. The rest is the easy stuff."

"I wasn't completely out of my clothes, and that wasn't my concept, Charlie. You know it." Liz twisted around and glared at him. "Why *were* those clothes in my closet, by the way? I mean, what gives you the right to assume that a weekend at the lodge includes sex?" She wasn't angry anymore, but disappointed, and maybe a little blue over the failed prospect for something be-

tween them that she didn't want to happen in the first
place. Sure, putting on one of those nighties *for real*
would have been the easy thing to do—there were plenty
of girls, and a couple of the guys back at the office who
would have seized the moment in a heartbeat. But that
wasn't the moment she wanted, or needed, from this relationship. She'd had it once in another life, and it had
cost her precious years. So now, never again. "And what
makes you think that I'm the kind of person who would
fall for that anyway?"

"I don't suppose you'd believe me if I told you I don't
have a clue where those things came from, would you?"

"Charlie…" she sighed. "I've been around that block
a couple of times. Believe it or not, I know the next line.
You tell me they were left over from the previous resi-
dent, or your brother…"

"I don't have a brother," he interrupted.

"Or your dad," she continued.

"I *do* have a dad."

"That's not the point here. The *point* is I want what
we agreed on, and if that's going to be a problem, I'll
head on back to the city right now." She stood, and
walked to the edge of a small reflecting pond, then
looked down at her image. It was distorted by tiny ripples, not so much that she didn't recognize herself, but
enough so that any other stirring would have made it
difficult for her to tell for sure who was staring back at
her. And Charlie clearly owned the power to be that stirring, if she let him. But she couldn't let him. He was all
fun and games, as evidenced in his welcome gifts, and
he was a distraction she could not afford in any way,
shape or lethally gorgeous body. "So, what's it going to
be?" she asked, letting out a deep, disheartened sigh.

Charlie followed Liz to the pond, and stopped just
behind her, winding his arm around her waist, then pulling her closer, but not so close that she would confuse
it for something more than a friendly cuddle—not that
she could see him in the same friendly cuddle with his

secretary Dolores, or Gooch Griswald, the three-hundred-pound pro linebacker-turned-sports-ad-guru. Surprisingly, though, she didn't resist. And she didn't understand why, because she knew she should resist.

"Sex sells, Liz," he whispered into her ear. "And you're the salesman."

Not a bad feel, she thought, as she relaxed ever so slightly into the texture of his touch. Not bad, so long as she kept it in its proper balance—colleague to colleague. "Just as long as you're not the customer."

JONQUIL STOMPED AROUND THE room rattling the prisms of the lusters sitting on the fireplace mantel. Her hair swished over her face like the tail of an angry steed swatting away the biting flies. Her nostrils flared in indignation, and her breath came as a hissing radiator. Suddenly, her eyes slithered back and forth like the tongue of a snake sensing its adversary until all at once she discovered her quarry groveling in the dark corner. "He's mine," she screamed. "All mine." Her breasts heaved…her chest rose and fell in animosity…pugnacity…fury. "Leave him alone, I tell you. I shall conceive his child this very night. His heir. And you…his mother…will not thwart me in his boudoir, for at last, I have loosed him from the tethering string of your apron, old woman."

Charlie sat back and smiled. Not too bad, considering that he'd had only ten minutes in which to write it. And Liz would be pleased to see that he changed the heaving bosoms. Maybe he'd add another paragraph or two later, but dinner was ready, and after what he'd been through so far today, he was hungry. He could hear Martha in the kitchen scurrying Joe to the dinner table with the plates, reminding him to wash up first, after working outside in the garden all afternoon. And he could hear the floorboards creaking in Liz's room, probably as she slipped back into her everyday puritanicals. Too bad. Dinner with Liz in that nice little red nightie would have…would have gotten him into a whole bunch of trouble. But he could fantasize it, which is what he did, with his eyes closed, until he heard the sound of her footsteps on the stairs.

"Is dinner ready?" Liz asked.

Charlie opened his eyes and stared frankly at her. His desk was at the perfect angle to catch her every move, and for a moment the breath caught in his throat, and wouldn't be sucked in, or let out. Her hair was down…not just down, but flowing to her shoulders. And she was dressed in capri pants and an almost to the belly button knit shirt. Pink. Soft. And feminine in a way he'd only imagined Liz could be. "I got in some writing while you were changing," he sputtered. Even to him his voice sounded odd, strained. Or just a bit anxious, suddenly realizing that beneath the austere exterior was a woman he could really be attracted to, or much, much more. And the second *much* in that description caused a hard lump to form in his throat, a lump he couldn't swallow away. Still, he wasn't nervous, exactly. Not that he would admit. Surprised, definitely. Pleased, possibly. Maybe even stirred in the natural male sense because she was as gorgeous as any woman he'd ever laid eyes on, and that kind of beautiful did tend to stir a man, but he wasn't nervous. This was Liz, after all. Dour, self-disciplined and downright uptight Liz Fuller, his co-worker and temporary partner, and pretty in pink didn't change those facts…much.

But she was exquisite, no doubt about that. Soft in a feminine way he didn't expect from her. And the reaction begging to be let out in him wasn't anything he expected, either, so he shook his head in hopes of clearing away the carnal images doing the cha-cha there. Jonquil and Ralph…he could see them in a passionate embrace…erotic, lustful with so much need between them they could barely contain it…Wait! It wasn't Jonquil, it was… Oh, great! It was Liz and… He broke into a cold sweat. Liz and him. Another fantasy in pink, but this one was so perfect, so real, and his hands were shaking too hard to type it into his document. *Get a grip,* he ordered, rubbing his forehead. *A big grip.* But when he looked up, the real life fantasy was heading right for him—no grip to be found.

"You look like you've seen a ghost," Liz commented, crossing the room. Stopping at the desk in the office alcove, she glanced down at his open laptop the instant he hit the save button and all the words disappeared. "Or some pretty bad writing, maybe?"

"What I've seen is the calendar, and I'm a little concerned about getting Sporty Feet ready to go in time." He gathered up the nerve to look at her, and the image came pounding right back. "Especially since you're starting from scratch." He switched his focus to the blank screen in order to blot out the effigy of Liz trying to burn its way into his brain. "Don't you think you should go put your hair back up the way you usually wear it, or something?"

She instinctively reached for her hair. "You don't like it down?"

He loved it down. That was the problem—a big problem, it seemed. "It doesn't look right on you. Neither does…pink."

"Pink?"

"Don't you usually wear brown?"

"Navy-blue, sometimes black."

"Navy-blue's good. You should go put on navy-blue."

"Charlie, what's wrong with you?"

"Stress," he muttered, standing. "Lots and lots of stress."

"And my wearing pink agitates you?"

The word was not quite agitate, but he wasn't going to tell her. Instead, he headed for the dining area, stopping halfway across the wide open room and turning to her. "Martha doesn't like us being late." Then he hurried by the fireplace and on over to the table, taking his place at the head of it. Seeing Liz's place setting right next to his, he scooted it all the way down to the other end and was holding her chair out for her by the time Liz reached the table. "So make yourself comfortable," he said as she sat. The he returned to his end of the table, five chairs away from her end.

Dinner was basic, but large. The first course was cream of broccoli soup. "Could you pass the salt, please," Liz asked, eyeing the shaker down on Charlie's end.

Nodding, he stood and carried it to her. And as he returned to his seat, she added, "And the pepper?"

Nodding again, he carried the pepper grinder to Liz's end of the table, then waited a few seconds before he asked, "Anything else?"

"Not that I can think of." She smiled up at him as she turned the handle on the pepper mill.

Back at his end of the table, Charlie discovered the basket of rolls and took one out for himself, then automatically carried the basket down to Liz. Returning to his seat, he realized his oversight—the butter! So he took his own pat from the plate then made the trek to Liz's end of the table once again.

"I can see how you stay in such great shape," she commented as he settled himself back into his place. "All that exercise. You burn off the calories before you can even consume them." She winked at him. "Efficient plan." Then she returned to her soup.

The salad was simple, with no back and forth transfers, but the main course...Charlie almost groaned aloud when Martha set it on the table. Sauce for the asparagus, gravy for the potatoes...way too much activity for one meal, so he finally gave in and moved his food down to the other end with Liz. "I always did prefer TV trays," he muttered.

"Actually, at home I just pull a stool up to the kitchen counter. I mean, why bother going to all the effort of setting up a TV tray when you've got a perfectly good counter ready to use. I used to have TV trays, though, when I was married. But Brian preferred a formal table." She laughed. "Even for his oatmeal and prunes in the morning."

"Oatmeal and prunes?" He shook his head and wrinkled his nose in disgust. "Give me a good ol' breakfast burrito from the arches any day."

"And hash browns?"

"Two orders."

"Brian would have divorced me had I served him a breakfast like that. Come to think of it, maybe I should have. It could have gotten me out of that mess a whole lot quicker." She took a bite of chicken and watched Charlie go for a second helping of mashed potatoes. "You ever married?" she asked.

"From your assessment of my romantic scholarship, you should know the answer to that one. No, never married. Never even engaged."

"Confirmed bachelor, then?" She looked directly into his eyes.

"And you a confirmed divorcée?" he returned, his stare meeting hers.

Instead of answering his question, Liz skewered her last spear of asparagus and dragged it through the Hollandaise sauce. By the time she had swallowed it, Martha was lavishing strawberries atop a shortcake she'd placed in front of Liz, and Joe was right behind Martha, dolloping on the whipped cream. "What I am, Charlie, is a confirmed workaholic." She dipped her finger into the whipped cream, then held it up for him to see. "The more, the better." Then she licked it off her finger.

"So get out your pen and paper and let's work," Liz said, kicking off her shoes in front of the fireplace, then snuggling into the oversized couch. A little too warm this time of the year for a fire, but Joe had laid one anyway, a little one, he'd said, and she was glad he did because she liked the sound of the crackling and popping. Back in Chicago, the only crackling and popping she ever heard came from the water pipes in her warehouse condo, and this was nice. Cozy, comfortable, and yes, romantic.

"Laptop," Charlie said, settling into the chair across from Liz. "Much more efficient for me than the mighty pen, which I'm sure a workaholic such as yourself will appreciate." He looked over the top of his glasses at her, his face poker straight. "So tell me, Liz. What's romantic? I'm ready to make a list."

"Hmm…a list of what's romantic."

"Workaholics *do* take time out for romance, don't they?"

"On rare occasions." She pulled her feet up under her and tucked an overstuffed pillow behind her back. Tonight, of all nights, she wasn't in the mood for work. She'd thought she was earlier, even penciled it into her planner, but now that the moment was there, a good book and a glass of wine would have been a much better way to end the day. Or some settling-in conversation—*tell me about your day* or *you tell me your dreams, I'll tell you mine*. With the right person, of course, and Charlie…well, she could discuss her day with him for sure, but her dreams?

"Rare occasions when?"

"Rainy nights…that's always a good place to start. Or snowy nights, even better because it's cold outside and that can lead to a…" She looked at the fire and smiled. "A cozy, romantic fire. They snuggle together, sip wine, listen to music…"

"What kind of music?"

"Let me see what you have," she said, jumping up and sprinting to the entertainment center across the room. "I like Chopin personally, but…" She scanned the hundreds of CDs in the rack and finally selected one. "But jazz…George Winston is good. Of course, for Ralph and Jonquil, I suppose Chopin is better…" The strains of the mellow piano music drifted over the room as Liz settled back into the sofa. "He is good," she said wistfully, shutting her eyes. "Gosh," she whispered, drinking in the pure, sensual tones, "I guess I'd forgotten how wonderful he is…"

"The plight of the workaholic," Charlie commented, clicking away on his computer keys. "People like you feed on Muzak, don't you?"

"People like me would prefer to feed on a glass of wine," she responded.

"And that's romantic?"

"Could be, combined with George Winston and a nice fire."

"Clothed, or naked?"

"Who? George Winston?" She watched him stroll to the kitchen, then called to him just after he entered, "Champagne is even more romantic, if you're looking for real authenticity here."

Charlie stepped back into the great room, carrying a grocery list pad of paper and a pen. "And is there anything else madame wishes this evening?" he asked. "A nice beluga, maybe some brie. Or perhaps beluga on brie?"

"Beluga's too salty to be romantic," she said. "And brie a little too strong if you have something in mind for after the brie." Her eyebrows arched into intentional suggestion, and her lips pursed into a near kiss. "That's my opinion, anyway. And if I'm the one who's to be seduced, my opinion is what should matter to the one trying to seduce me."

"But what if I'm the one who's going to be seduced?" he asked, heading back into the kitchen.

"Wet T-shirt and a cold beer would do it, I bet," she called.

"Skip the beer," he called back. "No need for overkill." Charlie stepped into the great room carrying a champagne bottle and two flutes. "So where's the wet T-shirt?" he asked, handing the glasses to Liz. "It's domestic, by the way. Hope that doesn't kill the mood."

Liz watched him pop the cork, then pour the flutes half full. Instead of returning to his own little corner of the conversation area, however, he sat down next to her, so close in fact that she had to wiggle over to allow herself enough elbow room to tilt the glass to her mouth. "Domestic works," she said nervously, raising the glass to her lips. It wasn't that she didn't like the feel of him pressed up against her, but that she did. And while her logical brain was screaming that the proximity between them was merely a part of the arrangement, another part of her brain was screaming back *What kind of arrangement are we talking about, Lizzie?*

"Shouldn't we entwine our arms or something?" he asked. "That's what two people in a romantic situation would do, isn't it? Entwine arms to sip from their glasses?" He leaned into Liz, and raised his arm, awaiting her response.

With a timid smile, Liz lifted her arm and snaked it into his, then discovered that in order to actually drink the champagne without spilling it this *romantic* maneuver had to be accomplished in such closeness she could feel his breath on her cheek. "I've never actually done this before," she whispered as she touched her glass to her lips.

"Neither have I, but it sure has possibilities, don't you think?" As he pulled his flute toward his mouth, he bumped Liz's arm and somebody's champagne spilled all down the front of her pink top. "So is this where it gets romantic and you take off your shirt?" he asked, unhooking his arm and backing away.

Looking down at the mess, Liz smiled, then reached over to the coffee table holding the bottle and poured herself another drink. "This is where I take off my shirt and he licks the spilled champagne from my breasts. *If* this is a romantic evening, of course. Which it's not. It's only romance school, and stripping for the students is strictly against the rules."

"But what if I bring an apple for the teacher?" He

looked over the top of his glasses at her, and winked. "Do bribes work in romance?"

Liz took a drink of champagne, then set the glass back on the coffee table, and stood. "In romance, bribes aren't necessary. The teacher doesn't need an apple to take off her clothes if the student is someone she wants to be naked with. All the student need do is look in her eyes, and he'll know the answer without going down to the grocery and springing for a piece of fruit." She looked down at the wet splotch that seemed to be spreading by the second all over her shirt. As revealing as it was, hugging to all the outlines and protuberances, she might as well have been naked. Something she was sure Charlie was enjoying. Something, surprisingly, she wasn't scrambling to hide. "Night, Charlie," she said casually, turning to the stairs.

Charlie drew in a deep breath, let it out slowly, then grabbed his laptop and started typing while the vivid detail was still hot in his mind.

"ONE IN THE MORNING," she muttered, pacing by the window for the twentieth time in the last hour. She'd gone to bed by eleven, and was up trying to work by eleven-thirty, and now, here it was heading into the wee hours and she was inclined to neither sleep, nor work. "Sex sells, Liz." She'd muttered that simple, two-word phrase over and over for the past hour, struggling to lock in on the visual detail of exactly what kind of sex would sell Sporty Feet. Annoying as it was, she simply couldn't get past the mental picture of the klunky-looking shoes. Good to wear, to walk in, but that wasn't sexy—didn't even come close—and each time she tried to doodle out a concept on her sketch pad all she ended up with were the same old klunky shoes, sans sex appeal. "Sex sells...sex sell...come on, Lizzie, sell some sex here."

She picked up the sketch pad she'd thrown on the floor three times in the past hour, and looked at what she'd done...an embryo of something...anything salvageable.

It clearly wasn't there, and if she couldn't figure that out for herself, the tightening muscles in her neck were there to remind her. "So maybe I don't belong in advertising after all," she moaned, throwing her sketch pad back on the floor. "Maybe I'm a washout before I even get started," she said, bending to pick up her pad yet again.

"Close your eyes, Lizzie. Empty your mind, then take a fresh look." She did shut her eyes, although the part where she cleared her mind didn't work since it was corner to corner angst in there, and when she did manage that fresh look…

Charlie! "What?" she gasped, plowing through to the second, third and fourth sketches. Charlie everywhere. Always with two or three women on his arm, always the center of attention.

And undeniably selling sex.

"So he's a handy artist's model," she said, throwing the sketch pad down on the floor one more time. "What's the big deal?" Then she looked down at the sketch staring up at her…

Every line, every detail about him—pure sex. And the responses from the girls she'd drawn with him—those hussies! They just slithered all over him, clinging like a second skin when they got the chance.

Curiously, Liz nudged the hussy page back with her foot and bent to look at what came next. Charlie pecking away at his laptop, his glasses slipped down his nose. Charlie laughing. Charlie scowling. Charlie eating chicken for dinner. By the time she kicked through her evening's work, one page at a time, the portfolio of Charlie scenarios totaled ten in all, each and every drawing some way etched in glaring sex…overt, casual, intentional, unknowing…

"Hey, what's one more Charlie in the scheme of things, anyway?" Here a Charlie, there a Charlie.

Two hours since Liz had gone upstairs, and Charlie was still sitting by the fire, trying to type something, anything. But a vision of Liz was searing indelibly into his sanity, keeping his mind far, far away from what he should be doing. It wasn't the red nightie she'd modeled earlier, although the brief glimpse was a pleasant surprise. It wasn't even the outline of her breasts straining against her wet T-shirt. Of course, that was nice, too. He chuckled. Real nice! No, it wasn't the way that she dispelled, for him, the myth that underneath that austere surface was still another austere surface. It was the way she reacted when her walls came tumbling down, even if by accident. She'd stayed focused and calm. Never flustered, never fazed, not even a little. And he couldn't think of any other woman he'd ever known who could have been so composed when the outer shell cracked unintentionally. And that's what he couldn't get out of his mind.

Charlie looked down at the words on his screen and saw the list of descriptions he'd started earlier. At the top he added *stalwart*, then deleted it for *sexy*. In caps, no less. "But you don't ever come out to play, do you, Liz? All work and no play makes Liz Fuller…apparently happy." Pity, he thought, picking up his phone. Because Liz would make a great playmate.

LOOKING UP AT THE SWORD hanging above the fireplace, he punched the numbers and waited.

"Giving up so soon?" was Charlene's response instead of *hello*, when Charlie's number came up on the caller ID.

"Nope, just wanted to tell you I want it wrapped in a red ribbon. Makes a gift seem that much more special, don't you think?"

"Maybe I should send you a book on reality awareness, little brother."

Charlie chuckled. "Keep it. You'll need it."

7

AN HOUR BEFORE DAWN, Saturday morning, and Charlie was glad the pool was heated. The days were warm but the evenings cool enough to chill the water right down, and as much as he looked forward to his workouts, he didn't look forward to doing them in the cold.

Ribbons of light were beginning to stream across the unbroken surface of the water as he slipped out of his clothes and slid noiselessly into the pool to put away some laps. Twenty on a good day got him started, thirty revved him up. But he was already revved, with thoughts of Liz still niggling in the back of his mind, so he opted for twenty. And with the way he'd tossed and turned all night, they were going to be leisurely ones.

At ten laps, Charlie paused briefly on the side of the pool to catch his breath, and as he shook the water from his hair a tiny penlight flipped on and a quiet voice from the opposite side startled him. *"Her heart pounded, her breath caught in her throat. For an instant, she thought of turning and running, but instead found herself giving in to his touch, even demanding it.* See how simple that is Charlie? Nothing heaving, bouncing or even flaring."

"So she's always reluctant?' he asked. "She wouldn't just think *go for it* and leap into his arms?" Before Liz could answer, Charlie pushed off from the tile wall and started his next set of laps. Five behind him, he slowed to listen for her, but she was silent. "Liz? You still here?"

The penlight came on again. *"His doeskin trousers hugging the taut muscles of his thighs, and bare chested,* he looked glorious silhouetted in the grays and golds of dusk.''

"The men are always bigger than life, aren't they? Suppose the muscles in his thighs aren't so taut…I mean, mine are pretty good. Pretty great, actually, if you care to come in and have a feel, but I wouldn't really describe them as taut. Couldn't I get away with something less demanding, such as competent… *His doeskin trousers hugging the competent muscles of his thighs.*"

"Competent implies capable, which is fine if that's the image you want to create, but taut or sinewy or even hard implies power and ruggedness." Liz let her robe slide to the ground, revealing a black, sensible, one-piece swimsuit that somehow Charlie knew was a black and sensible one-piecer even without seeing it. Sitting on the side of the pool, she dangled her feet into the water.

"Which is what you like in your men?" he asked. He swam up next to her and rested his forearms on the pool's ledge. Her toes were wiggling in the water, causing tiny ripples he could see even in the near darkness. Sexy feet… No way. Women like Liz stomped on men with feet like those. They didn't arouse them. But then her toes wiggled again… Charlie swallowed an unintentional moan that was fighting its way out, and pushed off the side to finish his laps. Right now he needed some good, hard physical exertion to take his mind off of Liz, her foxy feet and just about everything else about her.

"Actually, been there done that with the taut thighs," she called. "They definitely are a bonus, but it's hard to make a relationship work when all you get are taut thighs or a taut butt."

"He had a taut butt?" Charlie called back. Two laps to go, but he decided to tack on another five to quell the restlessness suddenly building up in him.

"Rock hard, just like his head."

At the end of his extra laps, Charlie swam to the edge of the pool and splashed a little spray of water over Liz's legs. "So what you're saying is that you'd go for something a little less taut next time around?"

"Who said there's going to be a next time around?" she asked, kicking some water back in his direction.

He moved closer and splashed her again. "From what I can see, you came out of your divorce pretty unscathed."

"I came out of it taut, Charlie. And in your own words, capable. I had to fight darned hard to get that way, and I'm not willing to go back."

"But does that preclude a next time around? Suppose you find a man who likes his woman taut and capable?"

She kicked back, this time with both feet, and the fine water spray turned to deluge. And she kept kicking until Charlie ducked under the surface. When she finally quit, he grabbed her by the ankle, pulling her in. Both stayed under for a second then bobbed back up, and Charlie shoved off the side of the pool in his getaway attempt before Liz gained her bearings enough to retaliate. And he expected her to retaliate…wanted her to retaliate…looked forward to it.

"Charlie," Liz sputtered, spitting out the chlorinated water. "Where are you?" She thrashed around in the dark for a few seconds, splashing, kicking, then she went quiet. Ten seconds…twenty…not a sound.

"Liz, are you okay?" He ventured away from his side of the pool. "Liz?"

No answer. Only the same quiet.

"This isn't funny, Liz." Suddenly, a mild sense of urgency turned to panic, and he swam back to the place where he'd pulled her in and immediately began to dive blindly under the surface. "Liz," he spluttered, coming up for air. He grabbed hold of the pool ledge to steady himself before he plunged back in, and in that instant, a hand clamped down on his ankle from below and dragged him under. By the time he surfaced, she was sitting on the edge of the pool above him, laughing.

"Captain of the girls' swim team, Pioneer High

School." She kicked water in his face as he approached. "Two years in a row. State champions, too, by the way."

"No fair," he growled, making a lunge for her legs. But she slipped back into the water and escaped him silently once more. So he hung on to the edge, watching as the morning light crept slowly in, until he finally detected just the faintest trace of movement on the opposite side of the pool. Then he took a deep breath, held it and dove just below the surface of the water for the short distance. When he bounced to the top at the other side, he was almost under her and he literally skimmed the whole way up her back side, then locked his arms around her waist. "Wrestling team, Belmont Academy. Captain, three years. State champs twice."

"Private school," she laughed, struggling to get away. "One of those preppy boys. It figures." Lunging forward, in an almost stationary jackknife dive, she broke his grip and headed for the opposite end of the pool with every last speck of strength she had left in her. Halfway there, he caught up and swam alongside her, shoulder to shoulder, but there wasn't enough speed left in her to fight the fight all the way to the end, so she stopped, waited for Charlie to pass, then did an about-face. By the time he was at one end of the pool, she was at the other, her breath already returning to normal.

"You're good," he called, gulping for air.

"You're not half bad, for a boy from private school."

Charlie's pace back to Liz's end of the pool was slow, and by the time he reached her she was floating easily on her back, staring up at the dawn. He couldn't make out her details in full yet, but her silhouette was beautiful, her body lifting with the gentle current coming from the movement of two people churning the water. He liked her when she was relaxed. "I would have beaten you," he said, holding on to the pool edge. "By at least a quarter of the length of the pool."

"Not a chance."

"And what makes you so sure of yourself?"

"Years and years of not being so sure of myself."
She drew in a deep, calculated breath that escaped as a
wistful sigh. "I was a trophy wife, Charlie. He was
twenty years older, in need of a nice appendage. I
couldn't cook, but I looked good hanging on his arm,
which is all he wanted from me."

"Doesn't sound like you."

"Well, it *was* me. All the way." A hint of regret crept
into her voice. "Nothing expected of me, and I lived up
to that quite nicely, thank you very much. A marvelous
asset to my husband, but not an asset to myself."

"So what got you here?" It was getting chilly in the
water, even though the pool was heated, and Charlie
pulled his shoulders under the water to keep the cool
breeze off his skin. It was time to go in, past time actually, but he wanted to hear everything she wanted to
tell him and he knew that once the moment was interrupted, it might never happen again. She would reset her
barriers and put her hair back up, metaphorically speaking. So he set his teeth to the early day chill, and continued. "How did you end up as a tooth-and-nail ad
man...excuse me, ad person?"

Liz turned over in the water, then submerged herself.
When she came back up, she wiped the water from her
eyes and moved in so close to Charlie he could almost
feel her breath on him. "After the divorce, I decided it
was time to get a life, so I went to college, got my degree, and targeted Whitaker and Associates."

"Simple as that."

"Nothing's ever that simple. I couldn't get an intern-
ship because...well, I'm assuming I was a bit over the
typical age your father preferred. Then I couldn't get a
job because I was a couple years away from thirty and
greener than grass, and at Whitaker most people my age
are at the top of the career track instead of the beginning.

"But I kept going back because this was what I
wanted. And finally I got a job in the photocopying

room. That's all I did for my first four months, Charlie. I made photocopies. And I'm not complaining about it. I'm telling you just so you'll know how much I wanted to be there." She laughed. "I'll bet you never knew that Kleinschmidt and VanderBeeck offered me an associate's position before I was out of college. And Matheney Mendenhall came after me, too."

"Somehow, that doesn't surprise me. They're two of the best in Chicago."

"But Whitaker was *the best,* so I wanted it, and I never expected that I couldn't get it. And look at me now, having a swim in the boss's private pool."

"Expectations aren't always what they're cracked up to be, you know. I was practically swaddled in expectations from the time I was born, and I used to think it would be great if no one expected anything from me. But they did, here I am, and look at *me*…having a swim in the boss's private pool, getting ready to challenge a champion swimmer to a race to the end of the pool."

"You never know when to quit on these competitions, do you?" Liz laughed.

"Quit? Me, quit? Not a chance. How about making it interesting?"

"Depends on how you define interesting."

Charlie assumed the position to push off the side of the pool and waited for Liz to do the same. "You know that green boa? Last one to the other end wears it to the Fourth of July company picnic."

"Deal. And you'll look spectacular in lime green."

The race was off and Charlie didn't have to work too hard to stay up with Liz. In fact, he enjoyed staying right with her. There was a relaxed intimacy swimming next to her in the hushed, dim hours of early morning. And as they neared the halfway point, when he could feel her last-minute drive to push ahead and win starting to intensify, he glanced to the end of the pool to see Martha standing there, waving a pair of swim trunks at him.

"Yoo hoo, Charlie," she chirped. "You forgot these

again. You know I've been telling you ever since you were a little boy that you should wear swimming trunks.'' She bent, and laid them next to the pool edge, along with a towel and a shirt. ''And you'll catch your death of pneumonia, out here in the cold, so make sure you dry off good, and put on a clean shirt, too.'' She bundled up Charlie's discarded clothing, turned and scurried back to the house.

Liz paused a moment, glanced over at Charlie, who was moving out in front, and sure enough, there was finally enough light to show that hers was the only swimsuit in the pool. ''Charlie,'' she yelled, trying to pick up the race again, but it was too late. He hit the edge of the pool just a length ahead of her, then popped out of the water, scooped up his towel and ran for the house. Liz watched his naked backside as far as she could see it, and when he finally disappeared in a side door, she climbed out of the pool, threw on her robe and strolled back to the edge just for a second, his image sticking to her thoughts like hot summer humidity. Looking down at the trunks he'd decided not to wear, she saw a foil packet sitting next to them, and shook her head. ''I know,'' she said. ''Better to be safe than sorry.'' Then she went back to the house.

''Hey, Charlie. I think you underestimate yourself,'' she said, as she mounted the steps to her bedroom. ''From what I could see, it looked pretty taut to me.''

Across the room, in the office alcove and fully clothed now, Charlie watched her climb the stairs. When he heard her bedroom door click shut he turned on his computer and began to write. *She appeared to him, a vision in red, and he opened his arms gladly, to welcome her, to return to her that which she offered so lavishly to him.*

8

———

"YOU JUST MISSED HIM, MA'AM. He's headed to the links. Said he'll be back by two, but between you and me it's usually closer to four or five. Charlie's a good golfer, but he's slower than a three-legged turtle." Joe patted the last of a dozen hostas into the soil in the shade of the gazebo, rubbed his hands together to brush off the dirt, then looked up at Liz. "And the other three he's with play just like he does—slow. Which is why they play together—'cause no one else will go near 'em." He chuckled. "They gotta triple the caddy fee just to get anybody willing to go out there. It's ugly, ma'am. Real ugly." Joe reacted with a mock shudder, then reached for a flat of lilies of the valley. "But he asked me to bring you to the club so you two can work between holes. If that's okay?"

Ten minutes later, book in hand, Liz spotted Charlie and his friends sitting in collapsible chairs alongside the green, basking in the shade of a row of pines, eating chips, drinking colas, and watching another foursome play through. "What are they doing?" she asked.

"Club rules. They're only allowed to play here if they let everybody else go ahead of them." Joe wheeled the golf cart to a vantage point on a knoll overlooking the lush course, then stopped. "That's why they bring the chairs. They could end up sitting there half an hour or more."

Liz thought about all the time her ex-hubby spent on the course. For him there'd never been any relaxation, probably no fun, either, since he hated the game. His world, including his leisure, had been about pressure and image—being seen at the right place with the right people. Watching Charlie enjoy the day, enjoy the company, she wondered if Charlie ever felt any pressure about anything. A nice way to spend your life if you can get away with it, she thought. "Well, I hate to interrupt his fun, but he's got a deadline…" Always a deadline or an agenda, she thought. Never enough time to sit back and let someone else play through. "So we'd better get started."

CHARLIE WAVED AS THEY MOVED down the grassy hill toward his group. "Hope you fellows don't mind, but I'm involved in another one of my little bets, and…"

Lyle Horton, one of Charlie's golfing buddies, watched Liz climb out of the cart, then poked Charlie in the ribs with his elbow. "Don't know what kind of a bet it is, but if she's involved, can I get in on it?" He turned to his pals and laughed. "Or are you keeping it all for yourself?"

"She's helping me with a writing project," he said, surprised to find that he was a bit annoyed with his friend's insinuation, and even more surprised to find that he was annoyed because his friend was staring at Liz in the way any man stares at a good-looking woman. Not that Charlie was threatened by it or anything. But this was Liz, and…well, Lyle had no business giving her the once-over. He was married, happily—according to Lyle.

She was looking awfully good, though, he had to admit. Capri pants, again. But white, and a white T-shirt. Her hair was pulled back into a ponytail…nice…soft… No wonder they were looking. He took a glance at his friends, and they were all wide-eyed at her approach. At least they weren't drooling. Of course, this was a business relationship, which meant it wasn't any of Charlie's business the way other men looked at…or even drooled over Liz. He glanced at Lyle, who was still staring the hardest, and stepped into his line of vision. "Hey, Liz," he called. "Thought you might like some fresh air. Hope you don't mind spending a couple of hours out here."

"I think the man's trying to block my view," Lyle complained, winking at the other two men in the foursome. "Makes you wonder, doesn't it? Has Charlie gone proprietary or something?"

"I haven't gone proprietary," he snapped. "I'm just under a little pressure to perform…"

"I'll bet you are, judging from the looks of her," Pete Finley, another of the foursome razzed. "She's certainly not your garden variety good-time girl, is she?"

Charlie frowned at Pete. "Don't you have a ball to go hit, or something?"

"From what I hear," Liz commented, approaching the site under the tree in which the men were huddled, "a couple of hours is being awfully optimistic."

"Ouch," Lyle replied, stepping up to introduce himself. Pete followed suit, and so did Hector Diaz, the fourth of the foursome, while Charlie stood back, arms folded across his chest, and watched. Such an easy exchange between them, he noticed. She was attentive to them, she laughed at their lame attempts to impress her, she made just the right contact so they would walk away remembering her. She had everything that added up to a good…no make that a great ad executive. The image of Liz seated at *his* desk in *his* office leaped into his mind, and he didn't try to blink it away. Liz belonged there…and if she belonged there…*where am I?* he wondered, pushing aside the question since the answer was too complicated. "Okay," he said, "time to get this show on the road. Read to me, Liz."

Liz turned to Charlie and opened her book. "*Suddenly, Clayton understood the excruciating look of fear he'd seen lately in Deirdre's eyes, and his anger raged. 'How dare you?' he choked in a hoarse whisper. He whipped around to face Trent. 'Bloody hell, how dare you?' Crushing the torn muslin of her petticoat in his trembling hand, the blazing fury finally erupted within him and he…''*

Looking around at Liz, Charlie raised a shushing finger to his lips, winked, then spun back around and pulled a ball from his pocket. Bending, he placed it on the tee, then stood to survey his handiwork. He stared for a full half minute before he bent back down, rearranged the same ball on the same little wooden tee, then stood again. It was another half minute before he repeated the process, this time wiping the ball with a cloth handkerchief he pulled from the pocket of his yellow polo shirt. When he replaced the ball for the third time, he smiled, stood, then took the six-iron from his caddy, held it up and looked down the shaft of it to the hole, some one hundred fifty yards down the fairway.

"If you're plumb-bobbing," Liz said, referring to the practice of measuring a slope with the shaft of a golf club, "the club is vertical to the ground, not horizontal. And you usually save it for something a little closer. You know…a putt."

Shaking his head, Charlie held the club back out for the caddy, who slapped a five-iron into his palm. Raising it as a compass to the hole, he studied the distance with all the precision of a surveyor, and finally nodded. The caddy, a nervous-looking boy of about fifteen, dropped back to the golf cart, pulled out a water bottle and squirted his face.

"Okay," Charlie said under his breath, lining up his shot. He took a couple of practice swings, realigned the club's shaft with the hole, took a few more practice swings, then stepped back to shake the tension from his shoulders. After a quick look at his friends and a nod and a thumbs-up, he stepped to the tee again, bent down, twisted the ball until the manufacture's logo was perfectly aligned with the hole, then from his squatting position lined up his club yet one more time.

By the time he stood back up, Liz was ready to jump out of her skin, amazed that someone trying to play through hadn't thrown Charlie's clubs, and Charlie, into the water hazard. She moved away as Charlie raised his club for the swing, then dug her fingernails into her palms when he broke the swing and raised his hand to his brow to take another look at the hole.

"It's still there, Charlie," she snapped. "The hole hasn't moved an inch in the past twenty minutes."

Turning around, he raised a shushing finger to his lips once again, winked, then stepped away from the tee and repeated the tension-shaking ritual. This time the caddy came running with a chilled, damp towel Charlie used to wipe his face.

"For heaven's sake," Liz snapped, tossing her book to Joe. "How many more ways can you come up with to stall this shot? Just get it over with, will you, so I can get back to my reading."

In answer, Charlie whipped the cotton handkerchief from his pocket and wiped the leather grip on the club. Then he folded the cloth back up, tucked it away, and for the third time shushed Liz.

"No wonder it takes nine hours to play eighteen holes," she muttered, glancing to the sideline, where Charlie's three buddies, all four caddies and Joe were lined up shoulder to shoulder, watching. Lyle was rubbing his forehead while the one named Pete was shaking his head in disbelief. Charlie, in the meantime, stepped away from the tee once again, to measure the distance, and as he raised his club to look down its shaft, Liz lunged forward, yanked it out of his hand, spotted the hole, assumed the stance, and swung.

The ball sailed high and long and straight, all the way down the course, and stopped within fifteen feet of the hole, then rolled half that distance to it. She watched it come to a stop, spun around, slapped the club back into Charlie's hand. "Your caddy was right. A six would have been better." Then she smiled. "Bored wife, gorgeous hunk of a golf pro, daily golf lessons, Meadowdale Country Club." And marched back to her own golf cart, as the men and boys on the sideline applauded—all but Joe, who was engrossed in the book.

Lining up his putt, fifteen minutes later, Charlie shook his head and stepped back from the ball. "Can't do it. Got the yips," he muttered. Meaning he was too nervous to make the shot. Tossing his club to Liz, he walked off the green. "Guess you'll have to take it for me."

"She kissed his mouth, his chin, his nose, and then his mouth again," Joe boomed in his best basement-deep voice. *"Her back arched to him as his fingers fumbled with the tiny pearl buttons of her bodice."* He looked up at Pete, who stood alongside Lyle and the caddies, listening to Joe's reading. "A bodice? That's like the top part of her dress, isn't it?"

"Yeah, and it's very tight, at least it should be, since this book takes place when? A hundred fifty years ago? They liked them real tight and low-cut back then," Hector Diaz answered, settling back into his folding chair. He popped open a cola and propped his feet up on the cooler to take in Joe's zesty performance. "Makes you wonder how they could breathe, doesn't it?"

"This isn't a competition," Liz hissed at Charlie. "You don't just get the yips in a friendly game! *Nobody* gets the yips in a friendly game!"

"So what you're telling me is that it's form-fitting?" Joe asked Hector. "I'm trying to get the mental picture right. It sets a better mood for the scene that way."

"Well, Liz, it seems I've got the yips, whether or not I'm supposed to get them," Charlie said, shrugging. "Not much I can do about it, either. Sorry."

"Skintight," Pete supplied. "And cut down to here." He traced a just-barely-above-the-nipple line on his chest, then grinned. "At least that's what I've seen on the covers of those books my wife reads. Great covers, too. Really lifelike."

"So you just want me to take the shot?" Liz asked. "Why? It's not proper." She looked at the group huddled around Joe, none who were paying attention, in the least, to the game on the greens. "They might not like it."

Charlie extended the putter to Liz. "I'm not sure they'll even notice who takes the shot. And if they do, they won't care. We're casual that way. Just here to have a good time." Charlie moved back to the ball, bent down and twisted the manufacturer's logo to face the hole, then backed away. "So go for it. Have a little fun."

"She strained to be closer," Joe read, his thick voice sounding like a foghorn over the fairway. *"To be one with him, to band her heart to his. 'Please,' she cried. 'Hold me.' And his arms pulled her to him, then slid down her back to cup her buttocks."*

Liz aimed her shot.

"Her fingers dug into his flesh as he pulled her even closer."

And she took one final look at the hole.

"The full weight of him on her, crushing her to the bed, the feel of his hot breath on her face…" Joe paused and wiped the back of his hand across his forehead. *"With an urgency she didn't recognize in herself, she pulled at him to force him deeper inside…"*

Reaching up, Liz dabbed at a spot of perspiration beginning to bead her brow, and assumed the stance.

"And moved to wrap her knees even tighter around…"

Lowering her club, Liz's attention fixed on the ball.

"Then she surrendered a cry of elation as he thrust into her, deeper and deeper, her cry fusing with his shudder of release." Joe grabbed the can of cold cola Hector was holding up for him, pressed it to his forehead first for a quick cool-down, then popped the top and took a long swig. Pete and Lyle, in the meantime, relaxed their lock-kneed stances while all four caddies shut their gaping mouths.

Liz sank her putt in a single stroke.

And Charlie smiled.

LIZ SMILED UP AT THE WAITER who slid the tall flute of orange juice in front of her, then she scowled across the café table at Charlie. "Would you mind telling me what that was all about?" Outside, under an oak tree near the edge of the club house terrace, Joe was still reading to his entourage, which had grown by another five people.

"The love of the game isn't always about sinking the putt. Sometimes it's about the friendships, or the little bit of time spent away from everyday life."

"So you dally on the course hours longer than you need to and get in the way of serious players, for what? To escape everyday life?" Liz shook her head. "You waste a whole day *not* playing a game of golf?"

Charlie pushed his iced, sparkling water aside and leaned forward. "We're not all as hard-driven as you are, Liz. Some of us actually like to take a little time away from the daily grind."

"But you know how to play, Charlie. That's what I don't understand. Why not just play the game, then do the rest of your daily grind avoidance here, in the clubhouse?"

"You just don't get it, do you? It's not about the game. It's about this thing we do once a month where Hector can forget about those open-heart surgeries he performs every day, and where Pete can get away from the drudgery of running a car dealership and Lyle can play hooky from being a daddy to the eleven kids he and his wife have adopted. These were my best buddies when I was a kid, and we just get together, as simple as that. And sure, I could probably beat any one of them with one hand tied behind my back. They know it and I know it. But that's not the point. The point is letting down for a day. Being with friends. Enjoying life for a little while, because come Monday, Pete will be selling cars again, and tomorrow Hector will be on call at the hospital, and tonight Lyle will go home to eleven children who need him. And they wouldn't trade those lives for anything, but occasionally the escape is vital. And me…I can delay the game and give my friends just a few more minutes of that escape.''

''So in the winter…''

''Bowling.''

''Captain of a bowling team?'' she asked, smiling.

Charlie shook his head, and reached for his water. ''Nah…I barely break one hundred on a good day, and that's for real.''

9

JONQUIL FLITTED INTO THE room... Charlie looked at the words, then scratched his head. "Does flit work here? I think it has a nice delicate image. You know, moving quickly. But since the association is butterfly..."

Ensconced in the sofa across from Charlie, her bare feet propped up on the arm rest, Liz looked up from her sketch pad and absently removed her reading glasses. "I like the image. I know that Jonquil is kind of a free spirit, but she does have a nice delicate feeling about her, doesn't she. So I'd say stick with what you have."

Liz had that delicate quality, too, in unguarded moments, he thought. He'd spent the past hour watching her work, trying to capture part of her for Jonquil. And the more he watched, the more he didn't want to stop. Not that Jonquil was turning into Liz, because she wasn't. Jonquil was all reaction and emotion, Liz was anything but. But the way her toes wiggled when her attention to her work was drifting off, or the way she scrunched her nose when she was concentrating—they'd become part of Jonquil, along with so much more. Too bad Jonquil's zest for squeezing everything out of every moment couldn't be siphoned into Liz. But every single one of Liz's roads led to work, and while all work certainly didn't make her dull, it did make her rather inaccessible most of the time. Of course, there were those moments when she let down—few and far between—but when he was fortunate enough to catch one...well, suffice it to say he looked forward to them...watched for them...hoped for them. "I think it's time to call it a day," he said, shutting off his computer. "Wanna go into town and grab a beer?" he asked, surprised by his invitation. "Maybe a pizza, too." He already knew the answer, and wasn't sure why he'd asked the question.

"Extra cheese," she stated firmly.

"And no romance novels." Pleasant eye-opener, he thought. All those ideas he'd preconceived about Liz were splintering away a little at a time. Definitely a pleasant eye-opener.

Liz picked up her sketch pad and headed to the stairs. "Give me five."

"It's a dive," he called after her. "Dark, loud…but the pizza is worth the ordeal to get it."

"Ordeal? Better make it ten."

Exactly ten minutes later Liz descended the stairs smiling, decked in tight jeans and a tight, white T-shirt. Her hair down, her usual rigidness dissolved, the sight of her caused his breath to catch in his throat because he didn't expect this from her. He appreciated it. More than that, he liked it…really liked it. But looking the way she was looking, he wasn't sure if it was safe to take her to *that* kind of place. "Would you rather stay in?" he asked, suddenly visualizing what all the men at Rhoda's would do when Liz walked in.

"Hey, I squeezed myself into my ordeal outfit, and I'm expecting a pizza that's worth the effort." She bounded down the stairs with the agility of an athlete. "So what's it gonna be? Pizza or work?"

THE FLASHING RED NEON SIGN in Rhoda's front window strobed the fact that the place was open, and another that flickered blue let passersby know there was cold beer inside. Once through the door, for those who braved the gauntlet of motorcycles and pickup trucks to get there, and didn't mind the squeeze of overly familiar strangers, the ambience was expected. Seedy, loud and very active. And as Charlie dreaded, when he pulled Liz by the hand through the commotion, the shouts and whistles of bawdy appreciation swelled even louder than the piped-in honky-tonk music and the rest of the racket hanging thick in the smoky air. It was all friendly, in a coarse sort of way. No one tried to grab her, no one even really approached her other than the occasional *Hey babe, why don't you dump him and come take a ride on my bike.* And when Charlie and Liz finally reached a tiny table so far away from the main event that even the cigarette smoke in the air was thin, Charlie was grateful to drop down into the wobbly chair next to Liz and clear a spot on the table among the leftover beer bottles for the extra cheese special he'd ordered. "Like I said, the pizza's terrific," Charlie leaned into Liz so she could hear him. "Almost worth what you have to put up with to get it."

"I like it here," Liz shouted, her gaze fixed on a big man, six feet tall, three hundred pounds, with a braided beard halfway to his waist and a shaved head. He was attempting to stand up on a table, but his balance was a little skewed, probably from too much beer, and he missed his footing, which landed him face first over the top of the table. It splinted under his weight and he took three people, a half dozen bottles of beer, an order of greasy nachos and a couple of part-eaten pizzas to the floor with him. "A little out of the ordinary for me, but it's okay," she continued, kicking one of the bottles rolling toward her back to its original party. "Want to dance?"

Charlie eyed the line dance of sorts happening out on the floor, and frowned. "Don't know how."

"Want to know how?" she asked.

"Is it romantic?"

"Are you stalling, Charlie?"

He shook his head skeptically, and forced himself to his feet. "Not stalling…exactly. Just weighing my options for humiliation."

"If Jonquil wanted to dance, would Ralph hesitate, or would he do the gallant thing and agree, even if he didn't want to?"

"I can't see Ralph line dancing."

"But can you see Jonquil teaching him?" Liz grabbed Charlie's hand and pulled him away from the table. "It's pretty easy. Just take a couple of steps to the side…like this…" She did a couple of sidesteps, kicked her heel to the floor, then slid back to Charlie. "So try it."

"That's all?" He repeated her motions and smiled. "Guess I can line dance."

"Well, there's a little more to it. But watch me, I'll call out the steps as I dance, and you repeat them." She listened to catch the beat of the music, then began. "Left foot forward, then pivot half around to the right. Then a quarter pivot to the right, and two left sidesteps. And keep your thumbs in your belt loops."

Charlie watched her go through the dance steps, much more interested in her body movements than her instructions, and when it was his turn, he simply shrugged and asked, "Will you repeat that?"

And she did, twice. "Now, after that, you bump hips with your partner, left to left, then pivot into a right to right."

"I like that part," he said. "Can we practice it?"

"After you do the first part."

"Always a catch, isn't there?" He hooked his thumbs through his belt loops then followed her instructions— left foot forward, then pivot half around to the right. Then a quarter pivot to the right, and two left sidesteps. "Now do we get to bump hips?" he asked.

"In a minute. But first, try hitching up your left knee then turning a quarter turn to your right on your right foot, then touch your left toes…" As she was in midstep, Charlie sidestepped right into her, bumping his left hip to hers, then he pivoted around and did the same with his right.

"As far as I'm concerned, that's all you need to know to do a line dance," he said, smiling. "Think I'll do it again." He hooked his thumbs back into his belt loops, moved his left foot forward, then pivoted half around to the right. As he attempted the next pivot, a quarter to the right to be followed by the two left sidesteps that should have led into the hip bumping, he pivoted a little too far and was halfway into an out of control bump when he looked up and saw that the object of his bump was not Liz, but the big burly guy, who bumped back with his ample belly, sending Charlie sidestepping and knee-hitching onto the top of the table.

"Well, I think this dancing lesson's over," Liz laughed, holding out her hand to pull Charlie off the table. "Your dancing partner's a little too rambunctious for me."

"You should have warned me it could turn into a contact sport." Charlie tipped the bartender to send a bucket of brews the big guy's way, grabbed their pizza to go and hurried Liz out the back door. Two minutes later, the blinking neons of Rhoda's were nothing more than an embarrassing memory.

"SO WHERE DID YOU LEARN TO dance like that?" Charlie handed Liz another piece of pizza, and took one more for himself. Line dancing and bikers had stirred up his appetite, or maybe it was simply something about the stone garden bench they shared, or the moonlight, or the shadows cast off from the muted pathway's lights that softened everything around them. Or perhaps it was just that the two of them were home tonight, without the accompaniment of Martha strewing condoms along the path or Joe sprawled all over the path practicing his DB routine. Whatever the reason, he couldn't think of a person he'd rather be there with. Liz, much to his amazement, was smart, funny, gorgeous and full of surprises—a textbook case for tossing out the stereotypes, especially since a couple of days ago he'd braced himself for spending a long, dull weekend with someone whose idea of fun was kicking off her shoes under her desk. Boy, had he been wrong about that one. Big time!

"My ex traveled a lot, and I got lonely." She picked

up her bottle of beer and took a swig. "There was a little country-western place a few blocks from my house... dancing filled in some of the lonely nights, and I got pretty good at it." Smiling, Liz drew in a wistful breath. "Even taught a few classes...until Brian caught on. Then he reminded me that no wife of his went in for that sort of lifestyle. Whatever that sort of lifestyle was."

He envisioned her dancing, doing the sidestep, pivot, hip bump thing, and it stirred something in him, the same something that stirred when he saw her making her grand entrance down the stairs in that red nightie. And that explicit male awaking...for Liz, of all women...was definitely unexpected, to say the least. And quick. It just up and bolted before he knew what was happening. Not in a bad way, he told himself. But in a way that could sure complicate things if he wasn't careful. One more hip bump in his mind, though, and he was afraid that *careful* would fly right out the window. "Apparently your ex never saw the way you dance, because a man would have to be out of his head to put a stop to something like that."

"You like the way I dance?"

"Well, let's just say that if I hadn't been so busy doing the two-step with the big guy, you'd have been my next choice as dancing partner."

"Second choice?" She laughed, reaching over him to toss her uneaten crust back into the box. "Guess that means next time I'll have to try harder."

"You have a little pizza sauce..." He pointed to the left corner of his mouth.

She wiped it with a napkin.

"No, a little more to the left...down...no, you're missing it." Without thinking, he picked up his own napkin and dabbed it away. And when his hand brushed her face the spark that passed between them was perceptible...almost visible. He pulled his hand back and looked down at the pizza box, suddenly not hungry for another bite. Just the end of a long day, he reasoned. But when he looked back across at Liz, she was studying him and he knew the reason his appetite vanished. Her eyes wide, he saw in them an expression he couldn't read. She wasn't exactly smiling, but she wasn't frowning, either. And she didn't avert her eyes when he looked back at her. She didn't even try to conceal the fact that she was staring at him. "I...I um.... think..."

Impulsively, he returned his hand to Liz's face and brushed her cheek, then leaned forward to kiss her. It was short and tender, the tentative first kiss that comes when the emotions are still unsure. Lips barely meeting...the urgency to press for more outweighed by the fear of going through with it. The growing spark... He pulled back, but not so much that he could no longer feel the warmth of her breath on his face, and when her eyes opened to seek him, he was caught there for an instant, hanging in limbo between the second kiss and the more sensible retreat he knew he should take. But the kiss caught him and pulled him back to her, this time demanding so much more. Hard, and full of passion, she opened her mouth willingly to the probe of his tongue, and delivered the same journey back to him. And when her arms snaked around his neck to hold him there, to pull him even closer, he went willingly. But when his hands began a journey of their own—down her arms and almost to her breasts, he pulled back, sucked in a deep breath, and ran his left hand through his hair. The moment already long gone, he was as unsure as he'd been at the first moment of their kiss. "I think I'd better get on back and write it all down while it's still fresh in my mind," he blurted.

"Write it down?" she asked, scooting away from him.

"For Ralph and Jonquil...the book."

"The book," she said firmly, nodding her head in resolution. "Yes, I think you'd better write it down before you forget."

Forget? No, he'd never forget. And he'd never write it down, either. Ralph had no right to the feelings Charlie was feeling at the moment. "Good night, Liz," he said, standing.

"Good night, Charlie," Liz said, remaining seated. "Oh, and maybe you should start carrying a notebook with you, so when these *book* moments pop up you can write them down immediately."

An hour later, still awake, and pacing his room like a caged animal, trying to put a definition on what had just happened between the two of them—book research or real life—Charlie finally pulled a pair of swim trunks out of his dresser and put them on. Maybe some good, hard laps would tire him out, or at least take the edge off. Laps with trunks on this time. Trunks off, with Liz in close proximity, was too risky.

THE ROOM DARK AND NOT A sound in the house, Liz stared up at the ceiling for what seemed like hours. Not even a shadow danced there…nothing on which to concentrate, and she desperately wanted to concentrate on something other than the kiss. But she shut her eyes and saw it, and opened her eyes and thought about it. She even forced Sporty Feet front and center, but the only thing that marched into the limelight with those sneakers was the streamer reading "Sex Sells!" and that wasn't exactly what she wanted to think about, either.

Once, she almost relegated the kiss to the spirits of Ralph and Jonquil taking command of that fleeting sprig of time. That fairy tale almost did it, almost lulled her to sleep. Then the glaring truth popped right back in when she was teetering on the edge. The more she was around Charlie, the more difficult it was becoming to resist his charm. And he was charming…no doubt about that whatsoever. For sure, every word ever spoken of him at the water cooler was true, every innuendo, every vivid little detail. And here she was, girded in iron resolve and wanting something so reckless, something she wouldn't...couldn't yet admit.

"Tread lightly, Lizzie," she said, her eyes still fixed on the ceiling. "*That* kiss was just a kiss, but the next one..."

10

"DOES SHE LOVE RALPH?" Liz asked, slathering cream cheese on a breakfast bagel. Her new resolve this morning—all work. "Or is it just a physical attraction?"

"Don't have a clue yet. Haven't written enough of the book to know." He looked at the Bloody Mary sitting in front of him, the one Martha had scooted onto the wrought-iron veranda table along with a breakfast fit for a small army—bacon, eggs, fried potatoes...heaps of it—and instead chose a bagel, like Liz, and a glass of orange juice. "At times she seems to respond very favorably toward him, but at other times..." He shrugged and popped a bit of bagel into his mouth.

Liz looked over at Martha and Joe, settling in on the opposite side of the veranda, preparing to do the reading. It was a lazy Sunday, the kind meant for spending half the day in bed reading the Sunday paper and doing the crossword puzzle. And she was feeling lazy today. "Does Ralph love her? I know there's a physical thing happening between them. That's pretty obvious, but there has to be something more to sustain the story. So deep down inside, does he have anything going on other than lust?"

"Now, that's a loaded question if I ever heard one. What do you think?"

"It's hard to tell. I think he likes her, likes being with her, maybe even likes being with her while she's got her clothes on. At least I hope so, but I haven't seen an indication that anything else is going on."

Charlie picked up his juice glass, contemplated it for

a moment, then set it back down. "Shouldn't there be some indication of her feelings for him before he makes that kind of a commitment? I mean, how would it be if he declared his love to her and her intention was something completely different, like…"

"Being promoted to head chambermaid?"

"Sure. Or maybe she's been burned in the past and not confident that she wants to get involved again. That would make it pretty awkward for both of them—especially for Ralph, if he's developing real feelings for her and she's not returning them. And it could make it pretty awkward for Liz, too, if her only motive is to further her career. Don't you think?"

"For Liz?"

"What?" Charlie asked.

"You said it could be awkward for Liz?"

Charlie picked up his glass of juice again and this time downed the OJ in one big gulp. Then he grabbed a paper napkin and wiped his mouth before he responded. "I said Jonquil."

"You said Liz."

He shook his head, and shoved the pitcher of Bloody Mary halfway across the table to her. "I think you need something a little stronger than OJ to get your morning going."

"I heard you say Liz," she muttered, reaching out to pull the pitcher the rest of the way across. For an instant, her fingers brushed over Charlie's, causing her to shiver slightly—a shiver that wasn't the result of a cool, late spring breeze. Her fingers rested briefly atop his, and neither she, nor Charlie, moved to amend the touch. Nice fingers. Long, soft. She fantasized their touch on her skin, down her face to her neck, across her shoulders…bare shoulders… And she shivered again as the fantasy of his fingers moved downward.

Suddenly, Charlie twined his index finger up over hers, shocking her back from her fantasy, and she instantly broke into a cold sweat, then jerked her hand away from his as if she'd been stung by a bee. She yanked the pitcher toward her with such a force the early-morning picker-upper inside sloshed out over the edge.

Martha's radar blinked on instantly, and she bustled across the porch to wipe up the spill. By the time the table was tidy again, the iron resolve Liz had girded herself with last night was back in place. "Business and pleasure don't mix, Charlie," she said. "If what Jonquil wants is to become the head chambermaid, she should be trying for the position based on her merits. Not sleeping her way to it."

"So maybe that's how they started out—all business, or...well, sex. But what if somewhere along the way they fall in love? Doesn't that add some real texture— maybe a twist we didn't expect at the beginning?"

Instead of answering, Liz poured herself a generous Bloody Mary and grabbed another bagel. She didn't want texture, or even texture with a twist. Then she looked over at Charlie and he was sitting there grinning at her. Grinning! Teasing, taunting, tempting...and darn it. Twisting! "You said Liz," she muttered, cramming a large bite of bagel into her mouth, trying not to watch for his response. But she wasn't fast enough. In that fraction of a second where she was suspended between looking at him and looking away, he winked.

And she knocked over her Bloody Mary.

"*'YOU SMELL SO GOOD, CECILIA,'*" Joe bellowed, following the passage from the book with his sausage-sized finger. "*He spread her legs with his knees, and lowered himself to her.*"

Martha took in a deep breath and continued, "*'Martin, I've never...'*" Then she stopped and looked over at Charlie, who was settling into a lounger in the yard. "How old is this girl, anyway?" Martha called. "Because she's either a child or a ninny."

Charlie shrugged, and looked back up on the porch at

Liz, who was sitting in the glider, arms locked so tight across her chest even a pry bar wouldn't get in, studying something about Sporty Feet. "Liz," he called. "Did you catch her age?" She was sure in a mood this morning. And it was kind of cute, in an idiosyncratic sort of way. The awkward morning after, when two lovers see each other again for the first time since... The tension was so thick between them... They held each other in cool reserve...disdain...contempt..."Not bad," he muttered, grabbing his notebook—the one Liz had suggested he always carry. He took one more look at her, and smiled before he jotted down his ideas.

"She's seventeen," Joe volunteered. "And she loves Martin, even though she's betrothed to Paul. Paul abuses her, and if he ever discovers..."

"*Martin, I've never been with a man this way,*'" Martha cut back in. She clutched her hands to her breast. "*And it frightens me, my darling. To think that the two of us...*'" She paused and frowned. "What about protection?" she asked Joe. Then to Charlie she called, "You're going to use protection, aren't you?"

Charlie looked up, frowning. "What?"

"In your book. Protection."

He shrugged, then called to Liz. "Should I use protection?"

Liz looked over at Charlie, shrugged back, then returned to Sporty Feet.

"Well, if they don't consummate until after they're married," Joe intervened, "then it won't matter."

Martha chuckled, then leaned forward and whispered, "And you really think they're going to wait that long?" She and Joe both turned in perfect alignment to look at Charlie, then at Liz. Then they both shook their heads and smiled.

"*I'll never hurt you, love. Please believe me...*'" Joe's voice trailed off quietly in the sensitive moment. "*Please.*'"

"*I do,*'" Martha cooed in return. "*I truly do.' She

reached up to pull his face to hers. 'With all my heart.'"
Martha looked over at Joe, who was still lost in the moment and poked him in the arm. "Come on, it's your
turn. If you get any slower at this these two are never
going to make it to bed before Paul comes back and
shoots someone."

"It's a tender moment," Joe defended, "and it can't
be rushed."

A knowing smile crossed Martha's face, and she
laughed, "Apparently you never met my late husband.
Five minutes tops, and that included the cigarette."

Joe yanked the book from Martha's hands and continued to read. *"He made love to her with restrained desire…"*

LIZ LAID HER FOLIO ASIDE and watched the interchange
at the other end of the porch. Not exactly the way she'd
planned for Charlie to immerse himself in a romance
novel, but they'd been going at it for well over an hour,
Joe and Martha reading, and Charlie intermittently listening and writing, and no one was complaining. Of
course, after what had happened between Charlie and her
last night, no matter how hard he explained it away as
book research, it was better that Martha and Joe were
doing the romance coaching right now. She'd wanted
that kiss from Charlie, wanted the taste of him on her
lips, maybe even sent out the signals, and that was dangerous. Not just dangerous because it didn't have a place
in her career plans at Whitaker, and she certainly did
have plans there that couldn't afford an affair with the
boss's son, but dangerous because of Charlie's reputation—all that water cooler prattle about how his body
didn't have a serious bone in it when it came to his
relationships. That would have been fine ten years ago
when she was looking for something different in a relationship—something idealistic, something with a certain fashionable image, something with more surface
than depth. But she wasn't the same person with the

same needs now. Who the person was, well…she was pretty sure of that part. The needs were another matter. Still in the forming stage, she wasn't sure how they'd turn out. There were some convincing clues, though.

With a long, wistful sigh, Liz looked at the man listening to the intense love scene between Martha and Joe, and picked up her sketch pad to add yet another rendition of Charlie to her collection.

"So how much more of this do I have to endure?" Charlie asked thirty minutes later, plopping down next to her in the other half of the glider. "Those two make for one really strange visual image, if you know what I mean."

Liz laughed. "I guess you can have some time off for good behavior." She flipped shut her sketch pad and set it to her side. No way she wanted him to see the Charlie gallery she'd been creating for the past couple of days. Actually, her intent wasn't to stick Charlie in every sketch, and there were times when she was positive that her latest creation didn't catch him, but when she went back later to look…there he was. One more time. "Are you going to let me see what you've been writing?"

"You show me yours first." He reached across her for the sketch pad, and nabbed it away from her before Liz could protest. "Sporty Feet, I hope. I got a call from Dad this morning, and Barry's being pretty obstinate about the whole thing. Which means Dad's getting a little testy, too."

She reached to yank the pad back from Charlie and toppled sideways into him. "That's personal property," she sputtered, trying to manage a graceful exit from his lap. "And it's not complete yet, so give it back!"

"It's an ad concept, and I promised to help you with it. Remember? So let me have a look," he teased, holding the pad away from her as she stretched for it.

"*I said* give it back," Liz snapped, making another grab.

"Hey, I've let you see mine several times already, so

why can't I see yours?" He grinned, waving the sketches at her.

"The difference is you needed to have me see yours, but I don't *want* you to see mine." She lunged across Charlie once more; however, he jerked the pad out of her reach and opened the book to the first sketch.

"We can set up a meeting for Tuesday morning and go over everything then," she suggested, holding her breath. He was looking pretty hard at a sketch of himself, and there was no way she wanted him to find out that he'd been her subject, forty times now. He would certainly read something into it that she hadn't intended, or at least hadn't consciously intended. Then he'd heckle and try to wheedle himself in where he wasn't wanted—well, not wanted in the way he wanted to be wanted, but the way she was afraid she might really want him. Way too complicated, and all because every time she put pencil to paper the result was Charlie, even when she tried to turn it into someone else.

"Not bad," Charlie muttered, holding a sketch of himself up to view. "I like the girls hanging all over him. Nice touch, and I like the mood. It's really coming across. Definitely a sexy quality in the way they're gazing at him…that is gazing, isn't it?" He looked at Liz, a mischievous glimmer in his eyes. "They seem to be fixed on his every word, like they can't get enough of what he says. Is that right?"

Doesn't he recognize himself? she wondered, trying physically to force back the blush that was beginning to warm her cheeks. *Maybe if he doesn't… Please, oh please, oh please don't let him recognize himself.* "It's all about an attitude," she offered.

"What?"

"My slogan. *It's all about an attitude.* The shoes look like every other athletic shoe on the market and they wear pretty much the same way. So the way I see it, we can't sell the shoe." Cautiously, she slid her fingers over across to the pad and pulled it out of his hand. Once it was back in her complete grasp she shut it and tucked it between herself and the side of the glider. "Instead of the old slogan—*Sporty Feet for Sporty People,* we change it to *It's all about an attitude* and promote the attitude with the sex you keep telling me sells."

"You mean an attitude like those three women in your sketch who all want to take that lucky guy to bed?" He laughed. "That's an attitude I'd sure like to buy into."

"I'll bet you would," Liz said defensively, "but that's not what it's about."

"Don't kid yourself, Liz. That's the *only* thing it's about, whether or not you want to admit it." Charlie reached across her, grabbed the pad back and opened it to the sketch. In the picture, the man's back was turned to the observer, with only a hint of his profile visible. And his women were entwined around his body as if he were a snake charmer and they were the charmed. In a sense, they were almost a part of him, an extension—no distinction where one stopped and another began. "If you don't think this sketch isn't about someone wanting to take someone to bed, then what we're looking at is something completely different because it has blatant lust…"

"Desire," she corrected.

He tossed her a quick, perceptive glance then smiled. "Okay. It has blatant *desire* oozing out of every pencil stroke. And you can see it, Liz. Admit it." Taking a long, hard look at the drawing again, he nodded his approval. "Good start. You've certainly caught the essence of something—lust, desire, whatever you want to call it, it's going to grab the attention of every man who sees it." He chuckled. "Three women. That's pretty bold, and you're right, it *is* all about an attitude, isn't it. Or at least someone's interpretation of an attitude."

"And what do you mean by that?" she challenged.

"The sketches *are* all me, aren't they? And you're inferring that my attitude at the time you sketched me was all about sex. At least, that's what your drawings are saying."

"You?" she gasped.

"In an abstract kind of way. Although I'll admit, I don't think of myself as that muscular. But hey, if that's the way you see me…"

"In your dreams," she snapped.

He arched his eyebrows suggestively. "A couple of times. So, how about your dreams? Anything good in them lately? Anything…or anyone I know?"

"I think you're confusing this campaign with real life." She tilted her chin in resolute defiance to stare him straight in the eye. "And as far as I'm concerned this arrangement is, and always has been, about work."

"You think so, do you?" He flipped to a particular sketch, then held it up for her to see. "Well, you do have a certain way with attitude. Amazing how those women slinking all over *me*—excuse me—slinking all over *him* look like…wait a minute. They wouldn't be you, would they? No, they're having a good time—enjoying themselves, smiling, laughing…*lusting*. And to me it looks like they're open to just about anything he wants. Or maybe it's the other way around. He's open to what they want." He shook his head as he handed the drawings back to Liz and reached over to brush his thumb across her reddening cheek "Definitely not you, Liz. Although I think you'd be stunning with a little of their attitude. So, are you ready to read what I've written?"

"I'm ready for lunch," she replied, pulling away from him. "A working lunch."

"Not according to what I saw in your sketches." He leaned over and touched a kiss to her cheek, then got up and wandered over to Joe and Martha, who were still reading aloud.

Raising her hand absently to that spot, Liz turned

away from him and stared down at her sketches. She could deny it to Charlie until she was hoarse, but he was right. Every single one of them was Charlie and...good grief...her.

11

Ralph scrutinized her luscious breasts. His eyes, and his potent manhood bulging to full capacity, he licked his lips in lascivious anticipation of the feast to come. Her breasts were the size of ample…generous…humongous muskmelons pushing right up to her chin and leaping out of her bodice, begging his lips. And his lips quivered and pulsed to suckle the supple, mouthwatering nipples that strained to hurdle from their captivity into his manly welcome. "Strip for me woman," he grunted, dropping his drawers to his ankles, "and come administer to my considerable virile need." Charlie hit the save button, then stretched back in his chair and smiled, pleased with his latest efforts. "Perfect," he said. He couldn't wait for Liz to read it. More than that, he couldn't wait for her reaction. That little flash of irritation in her eyes, the tiny huff of impatience she couldn't hide, the bite of the lip while picking the words she'd use to tell him how bad his writing is and still trying not to offend him, then another tiny huff of impatience when she couldn't bring herself to say them…it was almost exhilarating and absolutely sexy, and he liked the feel of it. Even craved it. Liz, in all her moods and manners, was exciting to the point that she was tenaciously becoming the best part of his day. Sure, it was a little deceptive, writing the bad stuff for her to critique since the *real* writing was coming along nicely, and way too fast. But it was the only thing he could think to do in order to spend more time with her. And the more time he spent with her, the better his odds of…well, he wasn't quite sure what he wanted at the end of those odds, but one thing was for sure. He wanted to be with Liz while he was figuring it out, and he was sure that if she thought her end of the deal was over, she'd run right back to business as usual, with a starched-to-the-eyebrows attitude.

I need a little more time, he kept telling himself as he typed yet another awful passage from the exploits of Ralph and Jonquil. The only thing he couldn't tell himself, though, was what he needed it for.

"I've been giving it a lot of thought, and I've decided to go back early tomorrow," Liz said, approaching Charlie's desk. "I want to spend the day on Sporty Feet... without interruptions, and I'd feel more comfortable working at home."

Charlie looked up from his computer screen and watched her sit down in the straight-backed wooden chair across from him. She was as rigid as the chair was straight...had been that way all afternoon. Her hair was even pinned up, which meant Liz was being typically Liz once again. All locked up tight and ready to work. This was the Liz he'd expected to spend the weekend with, but not the Liz he'd enjoyed being with these past couple of days. He knew she'd worked on Sporty Feet throughout the entire afternoon without taking a break, and read pages from his book through dinner. And now, as the evening wore on, there still wasn't an inch of give in her. "You're welcome to stay here," he offered, even though he knew her mind was already made up. "Then follow me back into town Tuesday morning."

Liz shook her head, and smiled. Her first smile in hours, Charlie noted. "Thanks, but I need to give it my full attention, and that's hard to do here. Not that I haven't enjoyed the weekend, because I have...really. But I want to be by myself for a while. See what I can do without, well...help." She scooted forward in her chair to turn the laptop around to face her. "I want to spend the rest of the evening working on your book, if that's okay." Looking at the first line on the screen, she read aloud, *"He grabbed her by the arm and jerked her onto his lap."*

Liz read the passage again, this time to herself, then frowned. "Couldn't she simply go to him willingly, instead of always being forced or jerked?"

"I don't know," Charlie snapped, his mood suddenly dark. It wasn't like he should be annoyed that she was leaving…leaving early at that, but for some unexplained reason, he was. Somehow, he'd pictured their ride back into town together, stopping at Starbucks for a coffee, complaining about the bumper to bumper traffic, going over his ideas for the book and her ideas for Sporty Feet. It was a cozy scenario that he hadn't known was part of his plan until her plans ruled out his. "Could she go to him willingly, Liz? You tell me."

"I think that occasionally she'd like to. Maybe sitting in his lap is even her idea."

"I doubt it," he grumbled.

"She'd approach him from behind and wrap her arms around his neck."

"Nope." He shook his head belligerently.

"Then bend down and kiss his ear."

"No way." And he folded his arms across his chest. "Not the Jonquil I know. She'd rather be upstairs cleaning the toilets."

Liz smiled. "They didn't have inside toilets in those days."

"Cleaning anything that will further her career then."

"Are we having an argument, Charlie?"

"It's all business, Liz, so that would be a difference of opinion, not an argument. And no, we're not having a difference of opinion. You say she wants to go to him willingly, so I'll take your word for it, because I certainly can't find it in her motivation anywhere." He turned the computer back to face him and typed in a few words. "There. How's that?"

She walked up to him and dropped her rigid body

straight into his lap. Liz read the passage then shook her head. "Shouldn't you add *with a thud* onto the end of that?"

"I think it's fine," he argued.

"And so romantic," she replied, shaking her head. "The only thing that should be rigid is his..."

"Maybe we should make this an early night so you can get an early start tomorrow," he interrupted. Clicking off his computer, he swivelled around in his chair then headed into the great room. By the time he reached the stairs, Liz was right behind him.

"Charlie," she said, reaching out and grabbing his arm. She gave him a hard jerk, causing him to spin around. "If Ralph jerked Jonquil that way, he'd bruise her."

"So how should he jerk her?" he snapped.

"Look, I know I've been preoccupied with Sporty Feet. I'll admit it. And when I do make time to help you...well, you haven't progressed very much. Not as much as you could have if I'd taken more time. And I know that everything I have to say comes out sounding critical, which I don't mean for it to, and I'm sorry. I know this bet's important to you, and believe it or not, it's important to me."

"It's important to you, why? Because I want that sword, or because you don't like to fail?"

A tiny smile crept across her lips. "I would be lying if I said it doesn't matter if I fail because it does. I hate to fail. But I'd like to see you get that sword, too. So if you were planning on spending tomorrow working on your book, then I can stay here and we'll..."

He reached out and placed his index finger over her lips to silence her. "You go home tomorrow, Liz," he said, his voice suddenly soft. "I know how important Sporty Feet is to you." And he did know, and understood. In a way, he even envied her the passion she had for something so new and exciting in her life.

"Thank you," she whispered.

Their eyes met, and lingered in an understanding that came without words. And they stood at the base of the stairs, locked in that single moment for what seemed an eternity, until Charlie finally broke the spell with a nervous throat clearing. The moment had gotten far too intense for him. Another few seconds and…well, he wouldn't be getting ready to head upstairs alone, and he was definitely going up there alone tonight. Liz, for one, wasn't ready to head up the stairs with him. More than that, he wasn't sure he was ready for what would happen if they did go up together. And this had nothing to do with anything that would take place after the bedroom door closed. "Night," he said, beating a hasty retreat, vaulting two steps at a time. Anything less would have led to the kiss that should have happened between them, the kiss that just plain scared him.

At the top of the stairs, when he looked back down at her, she looked up at him. "See you in the morning," she said. And those few simple words clutched his heart as he realized how nice it would be to hear her say them every night.

THE RIDE HOME THE NEXT morning was over before Liz even realized that she was sitting in the underground garage of her converted warehouse condo, brooding. She'd purposely put all thoughts of Charlie out of her mind for the hour-plus drive, choosing instead to concentrate on Sporty Feet. But Sporty Feet kept slipping away in unguarded moments, and Charlie was always there, ready to creep in. And when he crept, he was hard to shake loose. Especially since every image of the campaign implanted in her mind dragged Charlie into the mix, one way or another. *Stupid,* she thought, giving in to the distraction all alone there in the garage, with Charlie still plastered to her brain. *Really stupid.*

It wasn't like she needed a man. She'd been without for quite a while now, and she was doing very nicely on her own, thank you very much! It wasn't like she wanted a man, either. Abstinence makes the heart grow stronger and all that nonsense. Been there, definitely done that one before, and that whopper of a mistake still had her hustling to catch up to where she would have, could have, should have been. So why all this restlessness about Charlie? Her biological clock wasn't ticking yet. There were still several good years ahead of her for that one. And she didn't have a driving need for companionship. These past few years all by herself had been just fine—no one else to worry about, no one else to plan around. No one else to call her shots.

But Charlie was entering her picture way too much these days. Problem was, she liked it. And him. And the way she liked him was really beginning to worry her. Sure, the physical thing was there, and if she hadn't recognized it before, the kiss had sure done it. In fact, on her part the physical thing was alive and well, she discovered, much to her surprise. Last night…at the stairway… That look they shared… She was ready to follow him anywhere, even to bed. At least, at that moment. She had this sneaking little hunch, too, that the moment wouldn't be too difficult to duplicate.

In the clear light of day she was glad she hadn't followed him, but twinges of regret for what might have been—last night, tomorrow, next week, next year—were wiggling their way back in. That's what scared her even more than the little sparks she'd felt zipping between them most of the weekend.

Once inside her condo, Liz tossed her suitcase in a corner, leaving the unpacking for another day, and went immediately to work. Spreading her sketches out on the hardwood floor in a circle, she sat cross-legged in the middle of the harvest of her artistic endeavors looking at the way Charlie encroached from every angle, in every thought, in every breath she drew in. "Oh, no," she moaned, collapsing on top of her sketches and staring up at the ceiling. "You never were very good at falling for the right guy, were you?"

12

"No, I'm not ready to give in," Charlie said, hitting the save key on his computer. He read the last couple of sentences to himself, and smiled. "For once, I'm going to win this one."

"I hear you have a little help," Charlene replied. The tease in her voice was loud and clear over the phone. "Martha said it was quite the weekend."

"Business, sis. Only business."

"You two skinny-dipping in the pool sounds like anything but business."

"Tell Martha to get her facts straight next time. I was skinny-dipping. Liz was in a swimsuit."

"Something Dad left in the closet for one of his guests? Something red, maybe?"

"Martha doesn't miss a thing, does she?"

Charlene laughed. "I hope it works out for you, Charlie."

"The bet?"

"No. The girl. Wanna make a little wager on that front?"

He let out a long sigh. "Long shot, sis."

"Only if you want it to be, little brother."

"Dolores, would you ask Miss Fuller to step in here, please?" he requested over the phone intercom. "Tell her it's urgent." Three minutes later Liz appeared in his office, her hair pulled up and knotted as usual, her more-for-effect-than-need reading glasses in place, and her navy-blue business suit as starched and rigid as ever. "I wanted you to have a look at this," he said, motioning her over to the desk. "I think I may finally be on track."

"And I think I'm on track with Sporty Feet, too," she said rounding up the most businesslike voice she could find. Smiling awkwardly, she moved to the desk to swivel the monitor around to her, and knocked over his desk clock which set off the domino effect. First, a stack of file folders hit the ground, followed by desk caddy that spilled pens and paper clips everywhere, and finally the phone, which never exactly hit the ground but dangled a few inches above it, swinging back and forth on its wire. Grabbing the phone, Liz sat it back on his desk, unintentionally pushing most of its buttons in her rescue attempt, and a round of automatic dialing started. But Charlie clicked it off before the first full rotation was complete, and escorted Liz to his chair before she could cause any more damage. "Sorry about that," she muttered, dropping a handful of paper clips back into the caddy Charlie was holding. "But I was up all night, trying to come up with a way to give Barry the kind of sex he didn't know he wanted."

"And?" Charlie asked, bending down to pick up some file folders.

"And I can't wait to try it out on him. He'll probably complain at first, but once he grasps what I'm trying to do, I think he'll like it. Naturally, I want to try it out on you first, to see what you think."

The crowd gathering in the reception area outside Charlie's office was totally quiet as they listened to the exchange coming across the intercom. Dolores tweaked the volume a bit so the newcomers in the back of the crowd could hear everything.

"Sure, but I'm kind of anxious to go first, since you turned me down yesterday."

"Okay, so show me what you've got."

Charlie twisted the screen to Liz after she sat and cued up the document. "After last weekend, I've really been working hard to get it right this time." He flipped through the pages. "So start here…aloud."

"Aloud?"

"Listening to it always gives me a better idea of how good it is. Feedback. And at this point, I think feedback is crucial since we don't always agree on what's proper."

Liz scanned the first paragraph, then began, "*'I want it from you, baby. Oh, yes, oh, yes. More, please let me have more, oh baby, baby.'*" She paused for a moment, pondering what she'd just read, shook her head, and let out that tiny huff of impatience he knew was coming. "Charlie, this really isn't too…"

"Just keep going," he urged. "There's a lot more, and the further I go the better I get."

"Are you sure? I mean, we could start over later. Wait till we have more time to grind out the details, because I think this is going to take some work."

"I've really been waiting for this…"

Another sigh of impatience, this one a little louder than the last, escaped her as she continued to read. "*'Don't keep it from me, I beg of you, kind sir. I live for your mastery, for the fondle of your hands on my immense breasts, for the squeeze of your stiff manliness against my aching woman's place…'* Charlie, I can't keep doing this."

There it was, the flash of irritation in her eyes. "Don't stop now, Liz. It's getting better."

In the outer office, Roger, in accounting, pulled a handkerchief from his pocket. His hands were plainly trembling as he wiped his sweaty palms.

"Look, I have a meeting in ten, Charlie. Maybe we should finish this later."

"At least tell me if what I've done so far is better than last time."

Yolanda, the head of research, clamped a hand over her mouth to stifle a giggle and ran from the office. Robbie, from the mail room, discreetly untucked his shirttail, then slunk out the door right after Yolanda.

Liz shook her head skeptically. "Let me jot down a few notes—maybe some areas where you could make a few changes...improvements...and I'll get them to you later this afternoon. You can go over them and maybe work out some of the details on your own. You know, practice your technique or something, so it won't be quite so rough next time. Okay? Oh, and Charlie, like we talked about the other day, I really don't mean to be so critical all the time. You'll get the hang of it, I promise. It just takes practice." Walking to the office door, she laid her hand on the knob, then added, under her breath, "Lots and lots of it."

With those last words, Dolores clicked off the intercom and shooed everybody away, and so by the time Liz departed Charlie's office, the reception area was empty except for Dolores, who couldn't bring herself to look up at Liz, and Fred Perkins, a senior account executive who was breathing a little hard as he presumably read last month's company newsletter still pinned to the bulletin board. "I'm going to need some time with Charlie later," Liz said to the secretary. "Is he free around four?"

"He has a four-thirty," Dolores snapped.

"Great, then that should give me plenty of time, since I think we can finish what we need to do in about ten or fifteen minutes."

Fred, a short, round-bellied, flabby man, expelled a sound, something between a choke and a gurgle, and ran from the office with the speed of a Kenyan sprinter. Liz watched him until he hit the hall and was out of sight, then turned to Dolores, "I wonder what's wrong with him?" she asked. "Do you think maybe someone should go after him?"

"Moral turpitude," Dolores spat, scribbling Liz's name onto the schedule.

Liz shook her head, surprised. "Fred? I guess you never can tell, can you?"

"Humph," Dolores snorted, finally making eye contact with Liz—prolonged, glaring, outraged eye contact. "You're penciled in," she cracked. "Fifteen minutes!"

Liz nodded an acknowledgment then headed into the hall, only to find several of her water cooler co-workers converged in a tight clump, whispering amongst themselves, with Fred in the center of the conversation. They all shut up when Liz approached them, and remained tight-lipped as she walked on by. But she could feel their collective surveillance imprinted on her back all the way down the hall, and halfway to her office the whispering commenced again. The farther she moved away from them the louder it got, until finally, just a few feet from her door, she spun around to face them and amazingly, they were quiet, each and every one of them. Quiet, and looking in opposite directions.

Turning away, Liz hadn't gone more than three steps when the buzz began once more, and she whirled around to take another look, but like the first time, they were quiet. *You're just being paranoid,* she told herself as she scooped up her drawings to take to art. To prove the point, she poked her head into the hall, only to discover that the clump had grown by several people. And when they caught her looking at them, they all shut up as if on cue. *Well, maybe a little stranger than usual,* she concluded, looking down to make sure her shoes were on the right feet, that her panty hose weren't bagging around her ankles, or toilet paper trailing off her heels.

"SO TELL ME HOW IT WAS?" Charlie knew how it was. He'd worked hard to get it that way. Edited and rewritten until it was the epitome of awful. And he could tell from her agonized expression that Liz wasn't effervescing with high praise. That little flash of irritation in her eyes, that tiny huff of impatience, biting her lip while grappling for just the right words with which to crucify him—all the typical Liz mannerisms were there, there like he'd hoped for. "Any progress at all? Maybe I could have made that scene a little longer, added more detail or action. What do you think?"

"It reads, well…unnatural in some places, I guess you could say. I'm still not sure you've captured the essence of…um…romance, or anything else that would really interest a romance reader, for that matter."

"So what you're telling me is that you didn't think the dinner scene was romantic?" Charlie asked, so wide-eyed unassuming he almost had to bite his own lip to hold back the laughter punching to break loose. "I paid what I think was some nice, graphic attention to their interactions with each other, especially in the parts where they're actually eating."

"You call that romantic, Charlie? She was ripping meat off of a bone with her bare teeth. And you're right, the detail was vivid. So vivid, in fact, I could almost hear her doing some territorial growling. I guess that might have a certain earthy appeal, especially for a cave-man type, but you had Ralph dabbing the grease from her face. In romance novels, the women don't get greasy from the food they eat, and if somehow they did manage it he certainly wouldn't clean her face. Not with the sleeve of his shirt, for heaven's sake. Maybe he'd wipe away a tear with his shirt, or brush a smudge of dirt, but not grease! Oh, and they would never eat from opposite sides of the same leg of lamb, either, even if their lips did come together briefly over the mint jelly. But he might have cut her a bite of the food from his plate and fed it to her with his fork, or fingers. Fingers are good Charlie, and the sensuality of a finger slipped between her lips should never be underestimated. That would have been so much more romantic than their locking eyes over the shank of flesh they were gnawing to-gether."

Charlie shut off his computer and stood. "So what

you're saying is that if I get rid of him reaching over to…''

"Were you even listening to me?"

"Sure. The primitive undertone isn't sexy?"

"Maybe in bed, but not at the dinner table."

"So tell me about this finger deal then," he said, taking off his reading glasses. "You said a finger slipped between the lips is sensual? Like this?" he asked, raising his index finger to her lips. At first he traced the line of her bottom lip slowly and methodically, as if to memorize every contour. Then he moved to the top lip and followed the delicate outline from corner to corner, hesitating over every detail of the curves. "Would she like this?" he asked, his voice so hushed it blended into the electricity sparking between them. "Is it romantic enough, or would she prefer something more like this?" Before she could answer, his finger slipped between her lips to the soft, fleshy part just inside. "Would she suck his finger?" he asked. "Or simply tease it with her tongue."

In answer, he felt her tongue stroke a fragile line over the pad of his finger, then seek to draw in more. And as her teeth parted and her need for more turned from delicate to demanding, his own need elsewhere was becoming uncomfortable, and way too obvious to be arising in the office. But her eyes were wide-open, watching him, challenging him to the next degree, and he couldn't pull away. No male response in him was prepared to do that, but no male response in him was prepared for the way she drew in his entire finger, either, and licked and sucked as hungrily as a starving woman.

Suddenly weak in the knees, with an increasingly uncomfortable tightness in his groin, Charlie finally forced himself to pull away from her. He dropped down into his chair then spun away, not so much to look at the clock he forced himself to look at, but to break the entire spell. He was sweating like a man who'd run a full marathon in a three-piece business suit, hard like a man on the verge of the sexual encounter of his life, and sitting in the stupid office in the middle of a perfectly ordinary business day with his secretary just outside. And for a moment there…actually for a few moments there, he'd forgotten the reality of the situation and slipped into a place where he and Liz could have come together and… This wasn't good. Not good at all. And she was standing there unfazed, checking her wristwatch, no doubt thinking about her next meeting. "I get the picture," he said, his voice a little too thick to sound normal. "And I'll tweak the scene later. Okay?"

"Good, because you've got a four-thirty, and I have a four forty-five. So, let me know when you get it done and I'll go over it. And maybe I can bring you up to speed on Sporty Feet, too."

"Dinner?" he managed.

Liz nodded. "If you promise not to wipe my face with your sleeve."

Charlie watched her leave, remained seated, and took a drink of water once she was gone. Something stronger would have been better, but there were office rules—no alcohol on the job, no smoking, no sex… He let out an audible sigh and told Dolores to give him five extra minutes before his next meeting. Then he flipped on the screen and re-created every detail—with a few notable exceptions—and by the time he got to the part where Ralph's hand trailed down from Jonquil's lips to her breasts, he was a composed man once again. Composed and ready to take his meeting.

As Vic Riker trooped into the office carrying a car muffler, Charlie wondered how long the pretense with Liz would work before she caught on. She was too smart not to see through what he was doing now. Although…*he* wasn't totally sure what he was doing because Liz wasn't his type. Not that he had a type, but if he did it definitely wasn't Liz. Probably someone closer to Jonquil, actually. A cross between a hot-blooded vixen ready for sex at the wink of an eye and the housewife greeting him at the door with his slippers and meat loaf after a hard day's work. Not that he ever wore slippers or even liked meat loaf. But Liz had made it abundantly clear there was nothing domestic in her, and there probably wouldn't ever be. And suddenly he missed that homey quality in his life, although he'd never particularly thought about it before this, much less cared.

Of course, there *was* the other thing, he thought, looking down to make sure he was presentable when he stood to greet his client.

Lately, though, as he sat down to write about Jonquil, there seemed to be less and less of her on the page, and more of Liz. And he was already beginning to dread the day when she wouldn't be looking over his shoulder, critiquing his romantic proclivities. Well, one day at a time, he thought, and one purposely bad scene after another. Not the best plan to prolong the experience, but it was still all he had. And maybe, just maybe, by the time these three chapters were in the mail to Charlene, he'd have a better idea of what to do next. "Vic," he said, rising slowly as the man dropped the muffler across Charlie's desk. "Nice to see you."

OUTSIDE CHARLIE'S OFFICE, in the empty hall, Liz clung to the wall, too wobbly to go anywhere. Skip, the errand boy, gave her a thumbs-up as he rolled past on his in-lines, and she thought about asking him for a piggyback to her office. But instead, she sucked in a deep breath, put one foot in front of the other, and started that long journey back to her own sanctum, the slight salty taste of Charlie still on her lips.

What in the world will happen when Charlie finally gets the writing right? she wondered. Thinking back to the last passages she'd read, she smiled. Not much chance of that, which meant she didn't have anything to worry about for another couple of weeks. But then what? *Hey, you're a creative person. You'll come up with something.*

THE DINER CHARLIE HAD chosen for their dinner date was cozy and plain, and Wanda, the owner, a robust, baby-booming platinum blonde, bustled out from behind the counter, handed Liz a menu and pointed to a booth in the corner. "The usual, Charlie?" she asked, giving Liz the once-over. "We've got homemade apple pie for dessert, too." The food was on the table before Liz had settled in—stew, biscuits and pie—and before Liz took her first bite, Wanda was already back behind the counter, beaming from ear to ear at Joe, who'd tagged along with Charlie and Liz, promising not to sit with them. Settled on a stool at the other end of the diner, Joe gave Wanda a nod, and apparently that's all it took, because in a flash, she plunked a bowl of stew and a platter of biscuits in front of him, then stepped back and watched him dig in. After a couple of bites, he gave her another nod, and she returned to her other customers, a dreamy, woman-in-love look all over her face.

"They're in love, aren't they?" Liz asked, spearing a chunk of carrot.

"Joe probably is, but I don't know about Wanda."

"Believe me, she's a woman in love." Sliding down in the booth to make herself comfortable, she brushed Charlie's leg under the table. Even that slight touch caused a shiver to slide up her leg to her back, and she looked over at Charlie, sure he was experiencing the same reaction, since she'd felt it so intensely. But he was cutting a piece of stew beef in half, unaware of everything else. "Just look at the signs, Charlie. She's ready to follow him anywhere, anytime." Lucky Wanda.

"Signs? What signs?" He turned around to look, but Liz immediately reached out and grabbed his arm. "Don't let them see you looking."

"So how am I supposed to look at them if I can't look at them?"

She scooted over in her seat and patted the spot next to her. "Come over here, so you won't have to turn around to do your gawking."

"I wasn't gawking," he protested.

"But you would have, if I hadn't stopped you."

"So when you do it, it's a casual observation, and when I do it, it's gawking." He grinned. "Now I understand. It's a gender thing."

"It's not a gender thing," she whispered. "When they fall into your line of vision, it's a casual observance. And when you have to go out of the way to look, it's gawking."

"So the fact that you haven't taken your eyes off them in the past five minutes, even though they fall into you line of vision, makes this a casual observance, not a gawk…stare…gape…leer…ogle…" he teased. Sliding into the seat next to Liz, he *casually* glanced over to the counter where Wanda was stirring sugar into Joe's coffee. "So go ahead. Tell me what you've discovered in your casual observances."

The light banter between them was fun, the silly arguments stimulating. She'd found herself looking forward to it these past few days. More than that, she'd found herself looking forward to essentially everything about Charlie. Sure, it would have to be sorted out eventually, but not now, not until the chapters were written and Sporty Feet over with. So she leaned into him, placed her hand on his knee and whispered—not that Wanda and Joe could hear her over the "Nights in White Satin" blaring from the radio. "Look at the way she's stirring, for starters. It's subtle, but if he's attentive he'll figure it out."

Charlie shrugged. "Looks normal to me."

No reaction from her hand, not like she'd hoped, so she looked under the table to make sure it was on his knee and not some other entity under there, and sure enough…"Has she ever stirred sugar into *your* coffee, Charlie?" She inched her hand up his leg just a little. "Or have you ever seen her stirring sugar into anybody's coffee, for that matter?"

"Come to think of it, Joe doesn't even take sugar."

Charlie smiled, and slouched casually into the seat, bringing his arm up over the back of the booth to practically drape around Liz's shoulders. He glanced down to her hand on his thigh and to her crossed leg, watching her foot move gently to the sway of the music. Then he slid his leg over in that direction—just enough so their legs barely touched. "And I think he prefers tea."

Was he noticing, or only getting comfortable? She couldn't tell, but she still settled into Charlie a bit more, molding her body to his. And when it was apparent—to her anyway—that her positioning was more than chance, she finally breathed in a tiny sigh of contentment. At least one of them was getting something out of the encounter. "And look at the way she doesn't take her eyes off him when she's doing it. I don't think she even blinks."

"Is it romantic?"

"Very romantic."

"But he doesn't have a clue, does he?" Charlie's arm slipped off the back of the seat to her shoulders, and his finger grazed over the bare skin of her arm, eliciting a slight shiver from her.

"Not a clue," she answered, wondering if Charlie was finally picking up on a clue himself, or if he was as oblivious as Joe. She pressed her foot to Charlie's leg as "Nights in White Satin" played into "Born to Be Wild," and nudged its beat deeper into him this time. "Not a single clue."

"Well, maybe someone needs to tell him what he's missing."

"How long's it been going on?"

"Six, eight months, I think." He pulled a biscuit out of the basket and broke it open to slather with butter, then handed her half. "Hasn't asked her out yet, though."

"So what's he waiting for?"

"A sign he recognizes, I suppose."

"From God?"

"From Wanda. He's afraid she'll turn him down, so he's biding his time, hoping for some clear indication that she's interested, too." "American Pie" was playing now, and slowly dying along with the nimble tap of her foot. By the time the good old boys were drinking whiskey and rye her foot was slipped back into its shoe and planted solidly on the floor.

"You gonna tell him?" she asked. "I'm mean, look at the expression in her eyes. It's obvious, even from way over here. See? She's crazy about him."

"Well, if it's that obvious, he'll see it, won't he?"

Liz shook her head and snatched Charlie's piece of apple pie away from him. Someone so oblivious to the obvious didn't deserve dessert.

13

"I'VE GOT FIFTEEN MINUTES AT nine-thirty, about twenty minutes at noon, and I'm completely free from three-thirty until four. Would you block out those times in Charlie's schedule, and tell him I'll come to his office, since it's larger than mine. We need the room to spread out. And Dolores, I know he's busy, but *he* asked me to make the time, and since I don't really have a lot of it today, tell him he's got to be prompt if he wants me to..." She stopped. Dolores didn't know about the book, and she couldn't. Part of the deal. "Just tell him to be on time. Okay?"

Dolores didn't say a word as she penciled the three appointments in Charlie's schedule, but the instant Liz was out of the office she was on the phone.

Back in her office, Liz plopped down into her chair and turned on her computer screen. The images there were getting better each and every day, the concept finally with enough detail that her confidence was starting to flourish just a little. She'd been buried for the past couple of days, working twenty and sleeping four, and she was on the final lap here. What came as a surprise though, was how much she was enjoying her squeezed-in moments with Charlie, and even looking forward to them. Five minutes here to discuss Jonquil's proclivity toward kissing with her eyes open, and ten minutes there to argue Ralph's rambunctious, *Woman, come here!* appetite. "Ginny," she said to her temp, "would you make sure that whatever happens today, you keep me on schedule. I've got a full day, and I can't afford to get behind. So stop me, interrupt me, drag me out, or do whatever it takes, will you?'' She laughed. ''And don't take no for an answer.''

''You betcha,'' Ginny replied, her inch-long acrylic, purple nails clicking a surprising speed on the computer keys. She looked up at Liz through thick spider lashes, and the dull office fluorescent picked up the glint of her nose stud. ''Anything else I can do to help, just let me know. I really like this job, and I wouldn't mind hanging on to it.''

Liz caught herself staring at the fingernails, and smiled. Career women came in all makes and models these days. No more rules, no more restrictions, finally! And fuchsia hair notwithstanding, Ginny was excellent at her job—a keeper, if Sporty Feet came through and Charlie Senior decided to keep *her*. ''Well, right now, it's all about the Sporty Feet deadline, so keep me on track until it's over, Ginny, and I promise I'll see what I can do.''

Ginny smiled and gave Liz a purpled-nailed thumbs-up. ''The files for your meeting with legal are on your desk, right side. Contracts on top. Triplicate. Budget's on the right. Drawings are over on the worktable, in order. Plus the trademark research...''

Five minutes later, Liz sat down at the small conference table in legal and began to plow through some of the contractual aspects of Sporty Feet, not that contracts were part of her responsibility, but she wanted to make sure she was versed on every aspect of what might take place in the client meeting. And secretly, she hoped that Barry Gorman might be willing to talk deal, even though Whitaker policy wasn't to press for a deal at the first meeting. But preparation was the better part of advertising, and she would be prepared—fully. Of course, no matter how good her presentation, Barry's best reception, she already knew, would most likely be the lighter side of loathing, but she was prepared for that, too. She'd personally invited Ellen Gorman to the meeting, a smart tactic, she thought. A little familial push from Barry's side of the table couldn't hurt…any ally in the sales storm. Still, Liz wondered if crossed fingers and a four-leaf clover tucked behind her ear might help. Maybe a horseshoe taped under her chair, too.

The conference room bustled around Liz's campaign. Two attorneys, a legal assistant, Georgia from art, Roger from accounting, a couple of interns, and Sebastian, a twenty-year fixture at Whitaker who no one really knew what he did other than to show up at the right place at the right time to either approve or disapprove. They all spaced themselves out along the table and Liz took her place at the head. Her first time there, and she wanted to come back. In fact, for the first time since she couldn't remember when, it was all about her accomplishment. She wasn't in the shadow of someone else now, nor was she standing in line waiting for her turn. This was it! Here and now. And as the bustle turned into commotion when accounting didn't jive with the budget from art, legal didn't gel with legal, and Sebastian sat with his arms folded neatly across his chest frowning over the proceedings, Liz drew in a deep breath of pure satisfaction and watched the blaze of nervous anticipation impel the meeting into near frenzy. She loved it, every last little bit of hustle and confusion. It was everything she'd ever wanted…everything she'd aspired to, even during the days when she didn't know she was entitled to an aspiration. And she didn't want to walk away from it, ever.

Then she thought about Charlie, and a bleak ache caught her breath. *What about Charlie?* He was everything she'd ever wanted, too. Charlie…career at Whitaker. To have one meant to walk away from the other. Office policy. One and one could never equal two at Whitaker and Associates. Rules wouldn't permit it, and someone would be fired—her. And that black mark at the beginning of her career would end her career, or at the very least send her right back to the beginning. *She slept with the boss's son to earn a promotion,* people would gossip.

Liz shook her head sadly. So close on all accounts—work, romance—but so far away.

"Liz? Will it work?"

Roger's nasally voice shook her out of her momentary lapse. "What?" she snapped, realizing how grumpy she sounded.

"Cutting about ten percent out of electronic media and adding it to print. Do you think we could shift the projected cost over to them, then when they need it let them take it out of..."

"Miss Fuller," Ginny blared from the doorway. "It's time. You've got that quickie scheduled with Mr. Whitaker in five minutes, and you don't want to keep him waiting. He called and said he's ready whenever you are, and not to be late, that he has an appointment in fifteen minutes."

"Qui...quickie?" Roger stammered, dropping his ledger. Georgia, who was arranging her department's spreadsheet on the table for Roger and Sebastian to peruse, tripped over Roger as he stooped to grab up his book. Both ended up in an unsightly clump of bodies on top of the table, with Roger facedown and Georgia sprawled indelicately over his back. Except for Sebastian, who merely moved the spreadsheets aside then went to pour himself a glass of water, no one else seemed to notice the disturbance, inasmuch as every one of the wide and disbelieving eyes in the room was focused on Liz, awaiting, of course, a logical explanation.

Oblivious to the innuendo of Ginny's words, as well as the not-so-diplomatic undertones of shock beginning to register in the conference room, Liz didn't even look up from page twelve of the contract she was reviewing—errors and omissions. "Thanks, Ginny. Tell him I'm on my way."

One of the lawyers, a starched and polished fifty-something in a gray suit, dropped his two-hundred-dollar fountain pen on the table then slapped at it with such force that the palm of his hand on the wood grain sounded like a pistol shot. Liz looked up, smiled, then scooted the contract back at him. "I'm not an attorney, Mr. Wallingford, but it looks fine to me. Maybe an additional couple of weeks in the extensions clause might be good, since we're cutting this thing so close already. I don't want to lock us in so tight that we find out we've shortchanged ourselves. Oh, and see if you can get away with a two-year option instead of one. It's worth a shot." She looked at Sebastian for approval, and when he nodded, she stood up. "Thanks for coming, everybody. Now if you'll excuse me..."

Mr. Wallingford tucked his pen away, handed the contract to his legal assistant, then watched Liz leave the office. Once she was gone, he pulled out a white handkerchief and wiped his forehead. Sebastian poured Wallingford a glass of water then left.

"I think we'll be ready," Liz said, shutting Charlie's door. "Everybody's working pretty hard, and I think we've covered just about all the bases Barry might anticipate, plus one or two he doesn't."

"Georgia showed me the sketches this morning," Charlie commented, his attention fixed on his computer monitor.

"And..."

"And they look fine."

"Just fine? I've been working almost around the clock, and that's all you have to say? They look fine. I thought part of the deal was that you would give me suggestions, or at least input." She walked to the chair Charlie had positioned adjacent to him, then sat. Irritated that he wasn't paying attention, she continued. "What do you think about the one where she's wearing Sporty Feet and a red negligee, you know, like the one I found in your closet. The one with all the feathers."

Turning away from the monitor, Charlie looked over the top of his reading glasses at her. "For starters, you didn't have one like that in the layout, and if you had I'd have probably suggested to Dad that he pull you off the assignment. And as far as what you did have, I looked, I liked and they're fine. What else do you want me to say?''

"Sorry. I'm just nervous since this whole thing's been happening so quickly. Usually I like a little more time and a lot more order, and there hasn't been much of either. And all these little five and ten minute quickies, as Ginny calls them, are beginning to get on my nerves. We need some time to really get into it…'' She let out a deep sigh, and smiled. ''And I don't have time.''

"Do you want time?'' he asked.

"Yes, I do,'' she said earnestly. ''I like it when we're…plotting the cavort. I just wish I had more time for you right now, but I don't.''

Outside, Dolores turned away from the door, rubbed her ear and whispered to Mr. Reynolds, the janitor. ''She's playing hard to get, and Charlie's falling for it.''

"Well, five minutes here and five minutes there do add up,'' Charlie replied, his face melting into a genial smile. ''So I guess I'm stuck with taking what I can get when you can give it to me.''

Liz laughed. ''It's tough, isn't it. With two such different focuses—me trying to stay focused on Sporty Feet and you trying to learn how to rip off a bodice in the easiest way.''

"She's holding out on him,'' Dolores said to Mr. Reynolds.

"But I'll make it up to you,'' Liz promised Charlie, ''because I know how important your sword is.''

"Something about his…sword,'' Dolores spat. ''She calls it his sword.''

"It gets easier. I promise,'' Charlie said to Liz. ''Once you've been doing it as long as I have, you'll learn to roll with the punches. And believe me, you'll get punched just about every day. But what you've done so far is just fine. Sorry, it's good…great…fantastic.''

"Okay, okay. I get it."

"So, when can I get it?"

"He's telling her how good she is," Dolores announced to Mr. Reynolds, this time not even bothering to whisper. "And he wants to know when he'll get it." She staggered away from the door, flopped down in her desk chair and fanned herself frantically with a manila file folder. "He wants more. I think she's making him beg, poor thing."

"I've got about ten minutes," Liz laughed, "so you'd better make 'em count."

JONQUIL, BABY…

"Skip the baby." Liz sat back in the chair and crossed her legs. "I don't think that Victorian women responded positively to baby. Try my love, my sweet, my darling—something endearing."

Charlie hit the Delete, then stared blankly at the screen. His focus was anywhere but there, and Jonquil and Ralph were so far away right now he knew he wouldn't be able to reel them back in, not in his few allotted minutes. "Joe finally asked Wanda out," he said absently. "That night, after we left. I told him what you said, and he went back at closing. They rented a movie and went to her place."

"And?" Liz twisted around to face him, her leg nearly touching his. "Come on, Charlie. There's got to be more. Did he have a good time? Are they going out again?"

"I think they're going out again Friday. And he said that her apartment is nice. She has a poodle, apparently. Apricot. Fifi."

"That's it? A nice apartment and a poodle named Fifi?"

Charlie looked down and saw that the chasm between his knee and hers was only an inch, but as much as he wanted to, he refused to cross that tiny gap. Office rules, and sure, he could break them and get away with it if he wanted. And with Liz he wanted. But it wasn't right.

Anyone else would be fired, and being next in line didn't exempt him—at least not ethically. People would talk, too. Boy, oh boy would they talk. And that kind of gossip was never in the best interest of the company. So instead of crossing the gap, he widened it. "She made him popcorn."

"Popcorn…"

"You know, I'm a little concerned about Jonquil," Charlie said abruptly. "She seems oblivious to Ralph in some ways…a lot of ways. I mean, she always has this agenda, and it gets in the way of anything that could happen between the two of them. And she's just not willing to open herself to the possibilities, even though there are times I get the sense that she might want to."

"But Ralph wants it to happen between them. Right? He wants something more from her than simply a sexual relationship?" Liz leaned forward to twist the computer screen to a better angle and her knee *pressed* into his, and she *did* leave it there when she leaned back in her chair. "Is he doing anything to let her know how he feels, because all I see is that it's the same old thing between them. He summons her, she heads straight to the boudoir. And after a while that's pretty predictable, and boring. Especially if there's some other undercurrent going on here. Maybe he should start dropping some hints to see how she feels. A few hints about the way he feels about her won't hurt, either."

"Won't the fact that he's the boss and she the employee get in the way? Suppose he's had this code of ethics until now—not to have an affair with the hired help. Is he going to have to fire her in order to sleep with her?"

In the outer office, Dolores, back at her post, turned to Garvey, from computer assisted design, and whispered, "Something about Ralph wanting sex, too. Couldn't hear it all but I think Ralph wants more of it, and Liz is getting bored with him. Guess that's why she's going after Charlie. And he said he may have to fire her if he wants to sleep with her. Company policy.'' Garvey turned to whisper the latest development to Stacy, from the secretarial pool, who whispered to Amy, also from the secretarial pool and on down the line until Georgia from art finally turned and reported to Mr. Reynolds, who'd stepped into the hall for a breath of fresh air, ''She can't make up her mind between someone named Ralph, and Charlie. So Charlie's demanding more sex from her right now, which she's happy to do since Ralph is pretty boring in bed.''

''Ralph?'' Mr. Reynolds choked. ''You mean Ralph McMasters? Isn't he on the Board of Directors?''

That word spread back up to the front of the line at twice the speed the last little tidbit had spread to the back, and Dolores shook her head in unabashed repugnance as she took an empty glass from Garvey and pressed it to the door in her try for enhanced acoustics.

''There's a bigger issue here than just sleeping with her, Charlie. Sex is sex, and if that's all Ralph wants, you don't have a story. You need something more from Ralph—some true feelings, a commitment, if not to her, then one he makes about her to himself until the time is right. And like I said before, dropping hints isn't a bad way to do it until someone screws up the courage to be completely honest about *his* feelings, or the ethical employer-employee dilemma is resolved.''

''Or *her* feelings?''

Liz nodded grudgingly.

''So what kind of hints are we talking about here?'' Charlie asked Liz. ''Flowers and chocolates?''

''Too ambiguous. Anybody can order flowers and chocolates without any thought. Ask my ex. He was the master of the apology speed dial, and when the florist actually started carrying Godiva to cater to people like Brian, one-stop apologizing made him a very happy man. Of course, that's just a personal opinion. Maybe Jonquil is the type who'd like those kinds of things. Although I really haven't pictured her as the material girl.''

Mental note, Charlie thought. No flowers and chocolates for Liz. "And what do you picture her as?"

"I think she's someone who would much rather have a nice, romantic evening with the man she loves. You know, sharing time."

"Popcorn and a rented movie, like Joe and Wanda?"

"Popcorn and a movie could be the most romantic thing in the world. Or soft music and dancing, or a picnic, or a 2:00 a.m. swim…" She stopped and shut her eyes, and a tiny smile captured her lips. "It's not the what so much as the who, and maybe Jonquil is the type of woman who'd love to just sit and eat popcorn with him. They're sharing a bowl, and their hands accidentally meet as they both reach in at the same time…" Her eyes snapped opened and she practically lunged from her chair. "Time's up. Got to get back to work."

"Think we could go over some details of a nice, romantic evening later on?"

"How about after the Sporty Feet meeting, when I won't be so preoccupied. Everything's ready to go for the meeting, but I really need to polish my pitch since I haven't done one before."

Charlie smiled. "Want some help? Tonight, my office, about seven?"

Outside, Dolores turned to Garvey and whispered, "Apparently Ralph sends her jonquils and Godiva chocolates, and she doesn't like them. She wants something else from Charlie. I'm not sure, but I think she wants popcorn."

"Oh, Charlie…" Liz cried. "That would be great. And after I get through this thing I promise I'll give you everything you need."

"First time's always the roughest, but it gets better. Oh, and if I'm late, don't give up on me. I'm having drinks with Bellamy at six, but it could run over a few minutes. So just in case you get here first—" he tossed her a spare office key "—make yourself comfortable."

"She's claiming that she's still a virgin," Dolores

choked to Garvey, not even trying to be quiet. "And he's telling her it gets better after the first time. Men! They'll say anything it takes to get a woman to go to bed with them."

"But I thought she said that Ralph McMasters is boring in bed," Mr. Reynolds piped up from the back of the line. "So how could she know if she's still..." He shrugged his shoulders and reached up to scratch his bald head. "Women! They'll say anything it takes to get the right man in bed with them."

ALONE IN HIS OFFICE, Charlie closed the alternate copy of his book and clicked on the real one. Three chapters almost completed now, and he'd show them to Liz when they were done. He wanted Liz's real reaction because he valued her opinion, more than that he needed it. But he dreaded that moment, too, because it would be an end to their working together, and that had become the best part of his day—something he caught himself anticipating at odd times. Putting on his glasses, Charlie began to read. *An afternoon so beautiful and bright, and so perfect it should have been captured on canvas, Jonquil spread the blanket on the soft meadow grass and motioned for Ralph to join her there. He approached, carrying with him a sprig of fully-blossomed jasmine, its scent finer than that of any exquisite French perfume, and he tucked it behind her left ear. "The right side is for a woman who has not been taken," he whispered, stroking his fingers over the delicate white petals, then continuing downward along her delicate face. "The left is for the lady who has been taken, and you, my lady, are taken."*

Charlie smiled as he clicked shut the story. Liz would like that.

And she would be so stunning in jasmine...

14

THE AFTERNOON WHOOSHED BY so fast that Liz was stunned when she looked at the clock and saw that it was after four. Just a little less than three hours until her final meeting with Charlie before Sporty Feet. He'd been awfully good about letting her out of their agreement, if only for the next day, and she was feeling a little guilty because he really wasn't coming along as well as she would have liked. In fact, each and every time he asked her to read his latest writing, it seemed worse than the time before. Probably because her best efforts were concentrated on Sporty Feet. But a deal was a deal...and except for the presentation, which Charlie would help her with later on, she'd gone about as far as she could go on the shoe campaign.

Suddenly, inspiration hit. Two birds, one appointment. "Ginny, could you make a couple of calls for me. I need to run home for a little while..."

ALMOST SEVEN, AND LIZ finished lighting the last of the dozens of white candles. Slipping the CD into the player and adjusting its volume to a soft, sensuous level, a little George Winston and some candleglow had successfully transformed his office into a secluded little romantic rendezvous. All for the deal, she reminded herself while she checked to see that the champagne was chilling sufficiently in the sculpted silver champagne bucket.

She'd asked Ginny to order in a nice dinner for two, something romantic. And by the time she'd returned to Charlie's office, it was filled with flowers and candles, and an elegant table was set with sterling and crystal, and a chafing dish was warming two lobsters. So much more than she'd expected, she was pleased, if not a little nervous at the whole suggestive ambience. But Charlie wouldn't read anything into it other than a show and tell. *This is the way we do a romantic dinner, Charlie. First you take some candles, then some nice champagne...*

But her dress...hip-hugging, breast-cleaving and sequined. A leftover from married days, when she thought that looking good was all it would take to get her wandering hubby's attention back. She'd never had the courage to wear it for him, and in retrospect, she was glad because he wouldn't have noticed. Consequently, it had hung in the back of her closet all these years, with its tags still attached. And tonight...well, maybe Charlie wouldn't read anything into it other than an attempt to show him...what? Seduction? No, she hadn't been sending out those kinds of signals. "I hope, I hope, I hope," she said aloud, crossing her fingers at the same time. "Stupid hormones, anyway," she muttered.

Liz slumped into Charlie's leather couch and looked down to make sure nothing had popped out of place, then cringed. The darned slit up the side of the dress came almost to her hip. One little cross of the leg and Charlie would be treated to more of her than she intended to show any man. "So I'll stand," she muttered scooting to the edge of the couch.

"Liz..."

The door pushed open and Charlie entered. Framed in the doorway, silhouetted against the candlelight, even dressed in his standard business casual of jeans and sport coat he was stunning—so stunning he robbed her of breath for a moment.

"Are you in here?"

"Over here, Charlie," she said, her knees so wobbly she had to grab the couch for support. "By the couch. I thought we'd kill two situations with one appointment and go over the presentation and also have a romantic dinner at the same time—for your book research, of course—if that's okay with you. Since we're both running a little short on time…''

CHARLIE STEPPED FULLY INTO the office, closed the door behind him and leaned against it until his eyes grew used to the dimness. His first impression was of the candles—candles everywhere. Dozens of them, all casting a warm glow over the otherwise dark office. His second impression was the sweet aroma of the flowers…jasmine? No, maybe roses. And in sensuous dimness he discerned the elegantly set table, and the bottle chilling next to it. It would be champagne. Liz wouldn't forget that romantic detail. ''It's amazing,'' he said, his voice so hushed it sounded strange even to him. ''Beautiful. If you'd have said something…I mean, I didn't expect…I would have dressed more suitably.'' He finally allowed his gaze to trail to Liz, who was standing almost behind the couch, clinging to it for what looked to be dear life. In her own little corner of the room, the lighting didn't permit him much more than her casual outline, but as he moved toward her, what he saw…or maybe it was what he envisioned that he saw…robbed him of every last relic of composure. There, hiding in the shadows of his office, was the most stunning woman he'd ever seen. ''Beautiful,'' he murmured, moving slowly toward her. ''Absolutely beautiful.''

''Ginny did a super job, didn't she?'' Liz forced out nervously. She tugged up the bodice of her dress, even though it didn't go anywhere, then tried to pull her leg in under the fabric, which didn't work since the slit was long and the fabric deliberately skimpy.

''What?''

''My temp. She's responsible for most of this.''

Charlie held out his hand to Liz, to draw her from the corner. ''Believe me, Ginny couldn't be responsible for everything. From what I'm seeing, nature had a big hand in it, too.'' He paused for a moment, just to watch. Liz was nervous, unsure of herself. And he liked that. It made her seem so vulnerable and soft. And the only thing on his mind was how to get her into his arms. "Care to dance? Anything but line dancing," he chuckled.

"Good," Liz gulped, still holding on to the back of the couch.

"What?"

"Asking me to dance. That's a nice touch. Romantic." Her voice almost squeaked with nervousness and she cleared her throat. "Jonquil would definitely respond positively to this."

She took his hand and allowed him to lead her to the middle of the office, and the single touch of his hand instantly sculpted into an intimate press of his palm to hers. And as his fingers entwined with hers, he wove his left hand around her until it came to rest on the bare skin in the gentle sway of her lower back. Then he pulled her into him until their two bodies were tight together as one, and began to move ever so slowly to the music. "And how would Jonquil respond to this?" he whispered, kissing her jaw, just below her ear. "And this?" he continued, pressing his lips to that same spot and running his tongue lightly over the soft flesh there, cherishing the slight shudder coming from her.

"She'd love it."

Liz's whisper was so husky it made *him* weak in the knees.

"In fact, I think she'd beg him to not stop, if he tried to." Her hand slid to his shoulder, and curled around the back of his neck, then addressed him with feathery fingertip caresses in that sensitive place there that roused his own shudder.

"And would she like this?" he asked. In return, his hand skimmed up her back until he encountered her neck, where he placed a row of kisses from one side to the other. Then he reached to pull the pins that held her hair in its place, and as it sprang free, he smoothed his hand through the silky strands to sweep them into place. And once it was down, he lifted it off her neck to lavish another row of kisses there. "I've always liked Jonquil better with her hair free of its constraints."

"I think she'd love it," Liz gasped, tilting her head slightly at the press of his lips now to her throat. Holding her breath to keep from crying out, she moved her hand up his neck to run her fingers through his hair. "And would he?"

The music changed tempo and Charlie's cadence matched its beat as he dropped his hand back to Liz's waist and swirled her around. "I think Ralph loves just about everything Jonquil does to him…"

"This?" she asked, pulling her face to his. She brushed her lips to his so quickly and lightly the spark ignited in that brief instant surprised her. Their shared reactions didn't, though, as they wrapped their arms around each other and surrendered the deep kiss that had been imminent between them for days. And as she opened her mouth to the probe of his tongue, and shivered at the exploration of his fingers along the contours of her breasts, the niggling reminder of where they were and what they were supposed to be doing assailed her and she pulled away, fumbling to tug the fabric of her now indecent neckline back into place.

"What are we going to do about this, Charlie?" she asked, reaching up to smooth her mussed hair.

Charlie stepped back to take in a bracing breath, then walked to the dinner table, popped the cork on the bottle of champagne and with all the ease he could improvise at the moment, poured it into two flutes. Apparent ease on the outside, maybe, because inside he was wobbling. A lousy kiss had never caused that kind of reaction in him before, and *that* kiss had been anything but lousy. Quite the contrary. Holding out a glass for Liz, he checked to see that his hand wasn't shaking. "You're the one with all the romantic notions, so you tell me."

LIZ REFUSED THE CHAMPAGNE, and turned her back to silence George Winston, whose sensual strains only moments earlier were now intrusive. "I want this job," she said quietly, her back to him. "And I want…" She wanted him, but the words were too complicated, and she couldn't even find the courage to turn around, to face him, to see the look on his face. And she wasn't sure she wanted to see the look there, because the look she so desperately wanted didn't have a place in her future, and the look she so desperately didn't want to see would surely break her heart. "Lobster's getting cold…" Darn, she could feel the tears so close behind her eyelids. "Asparagus with hollandaise…" And this was nothing to cry over. Besides, she'd given up tears for any occasion years ago. "Rice pilaf…" And if they flowed now, nothing would ever be the same. Not her relationship with Charlie, not her job. "Cheesecake…" And she wanted…what her heart demanded? What her logic dictated? She didn't know, which scared her because until this moment her focus had been so sure.

Now, nothing was.

"Liz," Charlie interrupted, stepping up behind her. He pulled her into his arms, her back to his chest, and held her tightly to him for several seconds, allowing her body to relax into his. When he felt the rigidness in her finally loosen, he let out a soft sigh and said, "What they've all said about me at the water cooler isn't true. I've never dated anyone from the firm. I can't…"

"You haven't?"

"Never even wanted to."

"So what I've heard…"

"Rumors." He chuckled. "And the negligees…they belong to my dad. The family secret."

"He's a transvestite?" she laughed, wiping away the stray tear that had escaped.

Charlie laughed out loud, and spun Liz around to face him. Bending, he placed a light kiss on her nose, then pulled her face into his chest. "He married stepmom number seven last week, or is it eight? She's twenty-two, and I'm guessing you stumbled into Dad's little wedding gift for her. He likes his women…I guess the word is desirable.''

"And the basket with the condoms?''

"I don't take women to the lodge, so I guess that was Martha's way of looking after me.'' He reached down to tilt her face to his, and placed a tender kiss on her lips. But the kiss was brief and she pulled away.

"That still doesn't mean we can do this,'' she said, moving to blow out the first of the candles. "I want to work here, Charlie, more than you know. And if anybody thinks that we're even…that we almost…it won't work.'' She moved across the room to the next candle grouping and blew them out. "I'll admit that I feel a certain attraction to you. And I think it would be really easy to just let something happen between us. I mean, I may be pretty job-focused most of the time, but I am human, after all.'' *And his body so experienced…* She blew out another grouping and the light level in the office dropped from sensually dim to downright dark. "But people will talk, and you know that, and there would always be gossip and speculation attached to my promotion—and I'm assuming that once I land Sporty Feet I'll be in line for a promotion.'' *And his kiss so soul-shattering…* She whisked across the dark room to find the light switch and halfway to the door Charlie caught her by the arm and pulled her roughly into an embrace, and the kiss that sprang up between them was hard and demanding. Everything she'd ever wanted, and couldn't deny herself.

"Charlie,'' she purred as their lips parted, then she opened her eyes and saw the reality. "No!'' she cried, pushing away from him so hard and fast she propelled him backward into his desk.

"What the…'' he sputtered, fighting for his balance, but before the words were out, the first trickle hit. "What the…'' he sputtered again, looking up at the precise moment the water began to pour down.

"The sprinklers!" Liz groped her way toward the light switch, grabbing a file folder to cover her head, not that it made any difference. Soaked was soaked, and she was completely, down-to-the-skin drenched within seconds. "The smoke from blowing out the candles set them off," she called over the horn starting to blast from the outer office. Before Liz could slip slide the rest of the way to the door to turn on the light, it flew open and Mr. Reynolds, the janitor, rushed in clutching a fire extinguisher.

"Where's the fire?" he shouted, his cylinder aimed and ready to douse.

"Fire!" Roger from accounting screamed from the hallway. "Charlie's office is on fire! Everybody out! I'm the floor captain—follow me!" He ran down the hall to the stairs, but no one followed, and he didn't look back before he slammed into the stairwell at full speed.

Dolores, Georgia from art and Garvey from computer design scurried into Charlie's outer office and huddled in a cluster, straining to steal a peek into the inner office, and when the lights came on, the first sight to which they were treated was Liz, with her hair hanging in soggy strings, standing in a soaked, now nearly transparent clingy dress in the middle of the room, with her hands crossed over her chest for modesty's sake. The skirt of her dress was so twisted and bunched that every inch of her left thigh, all the way up to her hip, was exposed, and she was looking down pitifully at the leggy display, realizing there was nothing she could do to cover herself.

The water still coming, Charlie stripped off his wet jacket and gallantly draped it around Liz's shoulders, then led her to the outer office. "Mr. Reynolds, would you see to it that the sprinklers are turned off immediately. And Dolores, call the fire department and tell them there's no fire. Cancel my meeting, too," he said, glancing at the crowd of ten now gathered in the hall to watch.

"You had a meeting tonight?" Liz choked.

Charlie took a quick look at his watch, thank heavens a waterproof. "In half an hour. Everyone came back in because we all wanted to give you some presentation pointers, since this was your first time. Whitaker likes to support its rookies." He kicked off his leather loafers then bent down to remove his soppy socks. "But you'll do fine. Don't worry about it."

"I'm afraid I have some bad news," Mr. Reynolds announced, emerging from the flooded office holding the lobster. "This poor little fellow didn't survive. Guess he drowned—didn't know lobsters could do that. But I found him lying on the floor, belly-up."

"Don't worry about it?" Liz forced a stiff laugh to keep herself from crying. "What makes you think I'm worried?"

15

THE FIRE AND WATER restoration crew arrived at six the next morning, and by eight, Charlie's worst nightmare was confirmed. His office was pretty much a complete disaster instead of the partial one he'd hoped for. Some of the furniture was salvaged and dragged into the hall, and a couple of workers were busy trying to dry it before the mold set in. His books were a total loss, the same for his computer. Luckily the fireproof safe in which he kept his backup disks was also waterproof, and when they carried it out of his office, holding it up like the sole trophy in a long, hard foot race, he instructed Dolores to find a safe, *dry* place for it. Funny thing was, he wasn't sure what he was happier to find unharmed—his business accounts, or his book.

Liz was locked in her office, not taking phone calls, not letting anybody in, not coming out, not answering through the door. Though he hadn't seen her yet this morning, he knew that what happened between them the night before was now slammed shut in her emotional vault, and the combination was long lost. For those few moments it had been pleasant. More than pleasant, actually. He'd convinced himself that Liz was his perfect fit. And in some strange way, he was more sure of it this morning than he'd been last night. But would she ever let down just the tiniest bit of her guard again? He shook his head in exasperation, let out a frustrated sigh, and headed to the hall. "Dolores, tell my dad I'll see him after I've talked to Liz."

"But he said he wanted to see you now, and he wasn't sounding any too happy."

"Just tell him," Charlie snapped.

Ginny was busy clicking through the PowerPoint presentation when Charlie tramped into the office. "Tell Liz I want to see her *now*."

"She's still not…"

"I don't care," he interrupted. "She has the most important presentation of her life in an hour, and I'm not leaving here until I see her. So tell her to open up or I'll call someone from maintenance to come up and do it for me. Understand?"

Ginny nodded, then scooted across the tiny office and knocked on Liz's door. "He says he's going to have maintenance open your door if you don't…"

"I'm busy," Liz shouted.

"So am I," Charlie shouted back. "And I'm not leaving until we talk."

The door suddenly swung open and Liz stood there, arms folded across her chest, the expression on her face as hard as the wood in the door frame. "What do you want?" The ice in her voice was so unmistakable it was nearly visible.

"What do I want?" he snapped back. "This hasn't exactly been the best morning of my life, and I'm not in the mood for *your* mood. We've got less than an hour, and right now, I'm not even sure a huge dose of sex will sell this thing."

"I'll be fine."

"Will you? Go take a look in the mirror. Then come back and tell me that what you've seen there will be able to pull off this sale, because judging from the dark cloud you're wearing, I'm not convinced."

"So you're here to do what, then? Take it away from me?"

Charlie shoved past Liz into her makeshift office and gestured for her to shut the door. "I'm not taking anything away from you," he growled. "In spite of your mood, which I'm chalking up to first-time jitters, I came here to see if you needed any last-minute help, because believe it or not, I want you to nail this thing. You *need* to nail this thing.''

''As in, if I don't I'll *need* to look for another job?''

''That's not up to me, but right now Dad's not very happy. In fact, he cut his honeymoon short and flew back in last night, which isn't a good thing since his marriages rarely last past the honeymoon.''

''So garnish my wages to pay for the damage.''

''It's not about the office, Liz.''

''Then what is it?'' She dropped down into her desk chair and slid a disk into her hard drive. Immediately, the Sporty Feet presentation came onto the screen. *It's all about an attitude.* The words spiraled their way from oblivion into view, and wrapped themselves across the presentation field in such a beguiling, sensuous manner they captured even Liz's attention, and she'd seen this opening dozens of times. Bold and suggestive, they were almost one with the voluptuous voice that spoke them— a voice that faded into the quiet seduction of the saxophone music playing in the background.

''That's good,'' Charlie whispered. ''I guess I didn't know how good.''

''I tweaked it last night. Couldn't sleep, obviously.'' She stopped the program and pulled out the disk. ''It's the best I can do, and if it doesn't sell the client, your father will have my resignation at the end of the day. Okay?''

Charlie smiled down at her. ''Whether or not it sells the client, Dad won't accept your resignation after he sees your work. He may be a little irritated that you didn't land the account, which I don't think is going to happen, but he's got a pretty shrewd eye for ad talent, and I'm betting he won't let you walk out the door, if for no other reason than he won't want the competition to snatch you up. And they will, Liz, because you've got what it takes to become a major threat to us." He smiled. "And me."

"Nobody's going to want me unless I come with flood insurance," she replied, the glums not gone.

Still vulnerable behind that facade this morning, he knew she didn't want anybody to see it. That's the way Liz was, but he saw it, and he wanted to put his arms around her, maybe hold her for a little while. He had to allow her that little bit of resistance to which she was clinging, though. Her lifeline. This was pure Liz, one hundred percent, down to her stubborn core, and so much a part of what he loved. But loving her meant backing off, and as difficult as that was going to be, he had to do it. For now, anyway. "Good luck," he said simply, then left.

LIZ WATCHED HIM GO, and she felt a little empty, or disappointed. Maybe both. No, she wasn't going to allow a replay of last night to happen, at least not the part where he kissed her and she was so darned willing to be kissed. Charlie would be so very easy to get lost in, and she was halfway there when that fateful cold shower called a propitious halt to it. This morning though, she was having a tough time fighting her way back to her original footing. Partners, co-workers, maybe friends. Unquestionably the wisest choices for the relationship, and certainly what she'd intended from the start. Disappointing, though, and yes, she could admit it to herself, but never to Charlie.

"Ginny, are you ready?"

Ginny popped into the office and gave Liz her customary thumbs-up. Today, her nails were black, as was her hair and her knee-high lace-up boots. Perfect match for her black miniskirt, black turtleneck sweater and her black tam. "My mother always said basic black is the most sensible thing you can wear," she grinned. "Especially when you want to make a good impression. And together, look at us! We're awesome, don't you think?"

Awesome? Liz looked down at her black skirt and jacket, much more conservative than Ginny's outfit, but black all the same. Together, they looked like a couple of undertakers, and she sure hoped they weren't heading for *her* funeral.

THE CONFERENCE ROOM WAS surprisingly packed, Liz discovered as she took her place at the head of the long, mahogany table. She would stand for the meeting, Barry Gorman and his people would sit to her right and Charles Senior and his people would sit to the left of her.

Today, Barry was flanked by Ellen, who gave Liz a cheery smile as she wiggled into the first seat nearest Liz, which was normally reserved for the client who would be doing the buying. But Barry yielded his place to his wife without so much as the questioning arch of an eyebrow, and slid easily into the second spot. Somehow, this didn't surprise Liz at all as she guessed that quiet little Ellen Gorman was the real boss in the family when it mattered.

Charles Senior leaned back in his chair, folded his arms across his chest and adopted an attentive look as the lights went down. Charlie, on the other hand, looked almost miserable. His face wasn't exactly locked into a frown, but he wasn't demonstrating the usual pleasant expression people expected from him, and suddenly, Liz realized how much she needed that silent shot of confidence she'd come to count on. A cramp formed in the pit of her stomach as the lights dimmed to presentation level, and of all things, her hands began to shake. Finally, after so long, this was her moment. Hers alone. And Charlie was allowing her to have it. No thumbs-up, or go-getum winks from him this time. Not even a squeeze on the shoulder or an assuring smile. Simply center stage, because Charlie trusted her to do it.

And she trusted Charlie's trust with all her heart.

Smiling, Liz signaled Ginny to cue up the introduction. *This one's for you, Charlie,* she said to herself, shutting her eyes for a moment to fix his image in her mind. Not so surprising, it was already there, every last detail, and the last thing she saw as she turned toward Barry Gorman was Charlie's bare backside streaking for the house. Then she took in a deep breath and saw Sporty Feet. "It's all about an attitude, Mr. Gorman." Liz walked away from the customary front-of-the-room position and moved to a spot just over Barry's shoulder. Laying a pair of Sporty Feet on the table in front of him, she continued. "And shoes alone can't flaunt an attitude. But for you, Whitaker wants to flaunt a whole new attitude. Something new that no one expects from you."

She strolled casually to the head of the table. "And the new attitude is simple. Sex. It attracts attention, and it sells. And that's the premise of our campaign. To attract attention to Sporty Feet and to sell the product. Quite simple, really. While all the other shoe companies are focusing on high energy and sweat, we'll be focusing on sexual energy and plain old seduction. And I can promise you that when you turn typical industry descriptions like *grips your feet* into something sensual like *hugs your feet,* people will notice. And they'll buy."

Ginny cued up the program and the new slogan curled across the screen. Sixty seconds later, when the commercial prototype played itself into a sunset, the last images remaining were those of two pairs of Sporty Feet kicked off hastily into the grass as a gorgeous pair of female legs stood on tiptoe with a gorgeous pair of male legs. And as her leg started to entwine itself intimately with his, the camera trailed off to the shoes and the slogan curled across the screen once more, with one slight change. *Sporty Feet…it's all about your attitude.*

The lights came up, and Ellen Gorman burst into zealous applause. "That sure makes me want to go out and buy something!" she exclaimed, jumping up to give Liz a hug. "Isn't it wonderful, Barry?"

Barry Gorman pushed his glasses up, and looked

across the table at Charles Senior. "It's certainly not what I expected from you," he said stiffly. "Not at all."

"You understood the premise last weekend," Liz defended.

"I'm not saying it's bad," Barry continued. "It's very…suggestive, and maybe suggestive is good. I don't know."

"So what if we put it before some consumers, a focus group?" Charles Senior asked. "If you have any concerns, that would be the next logical step, I'd think."

"That will take too long," Charlie stated. "Sporty Feet is hurting now, and waiting another few weeks until we can get this thing out to test won't help their profit margins in the mean time."

"And if you look in my package, you'll see statistics on how sex has turned a dozen other companies around," Liz added. "It's a proven winner, and the numbers bear it out." She stepped over to the display of sketches—a before and after array of the Sporty Feet advertising already out there now and what she proposed to put out there in print, all propped up on easels, neatly running the entire length of the conference room wall. An impressive collection, and she glanced at them to make sure none of the Charlies had slipped through. Satisfied that they were what she needed, she clicked on her laser pointer and aimed at the first drawing. "Look at the difference. What you're seeing is a pair of flat shoes. *Sporty Feet for Sporty People*. Nothing there to draw you in, and who really cares about the shoes, anyway? But look at this." She switched the beam to a drawing of a very sensual couple dancing in the sand—their shoes once again lying off to the side. Her cotton T-shirt was slipped dangerously over her shoulder and his lips were pressed to her neck while one hand was sliding suggestively down her backside. "That's an image of something much bigger than plain old shoes. And the one thread of continuity in everything you see here is that the shoes are always off, which implies something better to come—a huge association in advertising terms. And that's what we're selling here—the promise of something much more when you buy the shoes. In a manner of speaking, the shoes are simply along for the ride.''

Liz drew in a deep breath, then let it out slowly. ''That's the proposal, Mr. Gorman, and I've included contracts in the packet I gave to your attorneys earlier.''

Charles Senior suddenly snapped to life. ''Contracts? Sorry, Barry. We usually give the client some time to think things over, but…'' He looked blankly at Liz, her name obviously gone from his mind.

''Liz,'' Barry supplied. ''Elizabeth Fuller.''

''Just off a honeymoon,'' Senior chuckled. ''You know how that is. Anyway, Liz is new and perhaps she didn't realize that we don't necessarily bring up the contract issue until later in the negotiations.'' His gaze floated over to Ginny, who gave him a wink. ''So maybe Miss Fuller's assistant…what's your name?'' he asked Ginny directly.

''Ginny Kowalski,'' she said, puckering her fire-engine-red lips—the only color on her entire body—into something resembling a kiss.

''So maybe Ginny could take the contracts back,'' Senior continued, ''and we'll get to those in the next meeting.''

Liz strolled to the front of the table, picked up the white sneakers sitting there and carried them over to Senior. ''These are your size, Mr. Whitaker. I checked. Would you mind putting them on?''

The dozen other people around the table started murmuring and squirming while Liz unlaced one of the shoes for her boss. Charlie, though, gave her a wink of affirmation and even unlaced the other shoe for his dad.

''Why?'' Senior asked, not budging.

''It's all about image,'' she returned, holding the shoe out for him.

Senior glanced over at Charlie, who merely shrugged and offered the other shoe, and he grudgingly bent down to unlace his thousand-dollar custom-mades. He was mumbling something indecipherable as he went through the effort, and a minute later, when he straightened back up, he barked, "Now what?"

"Walk around," Liz prompted, stepping back to let him up. Across the table, Barry Gorman's glasses were in their proper place, the first time Liz had ever seen them there on purpose, and he was leaning forward in his chair, straining to see the floor on the opposite side of the room, where Senior was parading up and down. Good sign, she thought. Actually, a great sign! "So now, tell me what you think."

Senior stopped and scowled. "I don't get it."

"Are they comfortable?"

"Sure."

"As comfortable as the rest of the shoes in your closet?"

"Probably."

"So what distinguishes them from anything else?"

Senior started to pace again, this time concentrating on the shoes. Finally, after a minute of back and forth he stopped, and shrugged. "Damned if I know."

"Exactly!" Liz slapped the table with an open palm and startled everyone back to attention, including Barry, who was so baffled by the events he actually looked to Ellen for an explanation. "*Damned if I know* is not exactly a glowing endorsement for Sporty Feet, is it, which is why I'm prepared to go forward with this deal today. And for Sporty Feet's sake, we don't have a minute to waste."

Across the table, Ellen Gorman nodded her approval.

16

"A LITTLE HIGHER." Wonderful hands. Easy to get used to. The incredible feel of them massaging her neck, after the Sporty Feet ordeal had stretched every last muscle and tendon to its limit, she kept reminding herself that this was only a friendly neck rub among colleagues. Charlie would have done the same for...well, she couldn't think of anybody right off hand. But it was a professional courtesy, nonetheless, and as he kneaded out every last kink and knot, and she forced herself to stifle the groans of pure ecstasy begging to get out, she was sure she wasn't the first to have this touch. His hands were too experienced. They'd dealt this wonderful magic before, and for a minute she wondered about all the lucky recipients before her, and frowned when she thought of any lucky recipients in the future. "Can you believe how long that took? And it wasn't Barry's side of the table asking all the questions. In fact, Sporty Feet was pretty quiet, all things considered."

Charlie chuckled. "I think Ellen had a lot to do with that. In case you didn't notice, she was hanging on every word you uttered." He slipped his hands down to her shoulder and continued. "You sold her that day at the lodge, and I think the rest was a foregone conclusion that they'd buy whatever you were selling." He trailed his fingers over the front of her shoulder to the sensitive area around her collarbone, and his deep massage turned light, almost feathery. "Did I ever tell you how bad my first solo was?"

"Oh...gosh that feels good," Liz moaned in response.

"Dad turned me loose, and I wasn't nearly ready. And I didn't even remember the client's name. Kept calling him Mr. Hoover...it was Hooper, and he walked out in the middle of my presentation after I accidentally dropped a jar of his wart remover on the table and it began to eat through the varnish. He simply got up and left without a word."

"A little to the left...keep going...a little more. There, that's it. Perfect." Better than perfect. It was a touch she could get used to, grow old with, never get enough of..."And you didn't convince him that a double marketing approach might work—wart remover slash varnish stripper?"

Laughing, Charlie moved his thumbs up to the base of her skull and began a gentle knead. "You're a lot faster on your feet than I am. And not only did I *not* convince him to buy the campaign, he turned around and sent us a bill for wasting his time. Dad took it out of my salary."

"Ouch!"

Charlie jerked his hand away in response. "Did I hurt you?"

"No," Liz laughed. "Your dad's punishment did, though." As much as she wanted him to continue the massage, and as much as she would have loved for it to go even further, she seized the opportunity to break completely free of his spell, and stood up. Time like this with Charlie was dangerous. It sent her spinning in all sorts of directions she couldn't afford to go...home, family, golden wedding anniversary... Something about him dredged up a need that stung of a discontent she couldn't, and wouldn't define. Besides all that, the timing was way off. It was *her* turn, at long last, and she'd worked too hard to throw it all away. And even the small taste to which she'd been treated told her more powerfully than ever that she could never, ever be only an extension of someone else's life again.

But it would be so easy to be an extension of Charlie's

life. That little bite of reality was becoming more apparent all the time.

"I never thought of it like that." Charlie chuckled. "I guess that's another of the reasons why I love this job *so much.*"

"Am I detecting something here? Maybe some discontent?"

"Oh, yeah. Every Friday. But it goes away by Monday…or Tuesday."

"And what happens when it doesn't go away until Tuesday or Wednesday, or Wednesday or Thursday?" She moved to the tiny window and looked out to the gravel rooftop of the building next door. Charlie's office had a wonderful view of Lake Michigan. Even Mr. Reynolds, the janitor, had a nice view of the lake's parkway from his work area. She would have loved a view like Charlie's but settled for a view like Mr. Reynold's. Someday soon, she hoped.

"It's what I do, Liz. If I burn out, I'll take a couple months off and go lie on a beach in Hawaii or somewhere. And I don't hate it, even if I sound that way sometimes. But hey, it's Friday. I'm entitled."

She shook her head. Even if he couldn't hear that vague longing in his voice, she did. And she knew it oh so well. Funny, how different they were, but so much alike. "Your dad wasn't exactly thrilled with the way I handled the presentation today, was he? Did you see him turn his back on me while I was speaking, and call for a dinner reservation?"

Charlie followed Liz to the window and slipped his arm around her waist. A natural fit there, he pulled her to him until her head tipped instinctively to his shoulder. "You're the new guard, Liz. Time's are changing, and he's not. But the good news is that Barry agreed to let us represent him, barring any unforeseen problems with the contract. And that kind of success is something Dad won't argue with, even if he doesn't necessarily agree with the proposed campaign."

"Do you think he liked anything I did, other than the fact that I landed an account that'll bring the firm about half a million dollars?" Her voice betrayed a mixture of fatigue and pure relief, and as much as she wanted to fight the intimacy brewing between them, there was no fight left in her today. She liked being so close to him, feeling his support and strength, and she needed it, if only for the moment. And no, she wasn't deluding herself. She wanted Charlie. Oh, how she wanted Charlie. She just couldn't have him. And as soon as his book was finished, and she was knee-deep in her first real publicity campaign, this little *thing* she was feeling for him would go away. Or be replaced. Or be consigned to a dusty yearning that was never meant to be.

"Does it matter? You did a good job, the client was happy and the firm gets more money. Win, win, win."

"Did you like what I did?" she ventured, her voice betraying a hint of insecurity.

"Does it matter," he whispered.

"Yes."

"I loved what you did… I love…"

"She's in a meeting…" Ginny yelled from the outer office. "Please have a seat and I'll see if she can…"

Charlie pulled his hand away from Liz only a split second before the door banged open so hard it crashed into the wall, and a tall, big-boned, mulish-faced woman stormed in. "Are you Liz Fuller?" she screeched. "*The* Liz Fuller I've been hearing so much about?" The woman marched straight to Liz, but Charlie bolted away from the window and managed a body block that separated her from her target, and took hold of the woman's arm.

"Calm down, Eleanor," he said. Attempting to maneuver her to a seat on the opposite side of the cramped office, she struggled until she was able to pull away from him, and she was halfway back to Liz's desk when he caught her again. "I don't know what this is about, but why don't we sit down and talk about it—quietly."

"Quietly? You want me to be quiet around this... this...hussy?" Yanking free of Charlie, she tromped across the room and jabbed a finger at Liz. "Hussy!"

"Eleanor..." Charlie lunged for her and tugged her back from Liz, which wasn't easy since she was digging her heels into the carpet and holding on for dear life to a built-in book case.

"Hussy!" she screamed again.

"You can't just come in here like this," Liz fumed, lunging for the security of her desk. "Ginny, call security," she shouted. "Tell them we need help up here, now!"

"Security?" Eleanor yanked her arms out of Charlie's grip again and pounced on the desk. "Do you know who I am?" Leaning so far across the desk she looked more like she was stretched out across it, she raised her pointing finger at Liz one more time, and shook it. "You... you...tramp! I ought to call security on you!"

"Stop it, Eleanor!" Charlie grabbed the sixty-something woman by the waist and tried to pull her back from the desk, but she spun around, clobbered him with her purse, then spun right back to Liz, pointed, and screeched, "Slut! Do you really think you'll get away with sleeping your way into the job? How dare you!" In one gigantic sweep of her amazingly well-muscled arm, she cleared the top of Liz's desk, sending papers, books, paper clips and everything not attached flying to the floor.

Liz scrambled back and pressed herself as flat to the wall as she could get herself. She didn't have a clue who this woman was, and she didn't want to. Twice Liz's size, she looked like a strapping combination of a lady wrestler and a Roller Derby queen. And even at twice Liz's age, Liz recognized that one blow from the woman's bowling ball fist would set her up for ice packs and stitches. "Charlie..."

"Eleanor! Are you out of your mind?" Charlie circled

around the desk and stopped in front of Liz, to protect her. "What the hell is this about?"

"Don't you know, Charlie?" she shrieked. "Everybody else does. They've been calling me, telling me all the sordid little details."

"Know what?"

"My husband, Charlie. She's sleeping with my husband, and she's not even trying to be discreet about it."

"Vaughn? No way! Liz wouldn't..." He turned slightly, and asked, "You aren't, are you?"

"Who's her husband?" Liz choked. "I mean, no, I'm not sleeping with anybody!"

"Who's my husband? What do you mean, who's my husband? How many men are you sleeping with, that you have to ask?" Eleanor raised her purse up over the desk, then dumped its contents...pill bottles, sample packets...Viagra! "Recognize the pills, Miss Fuller? Now do you know who my husband is?"

"Security's in the hall," Ginny announced from the doorway. "With about half of the people who work here. So what should I do next?"

"Tell security to wait," Charlie shouted. "And for God's sake, tell everybody to go back to work, will you?"

"Miss Fuller," Eleanor bellowed, reaching into her jacket pocket, "there's no excuse for what you've done, and I'm going to make you pay for this."

Seeing what Eleanor was about to do, Charlie latched on to Liz and pulled her to the floor. "Get under the desk," he ordered, pushing her head down to keep it out of the line of fire. "And don't come out." As soon as she was safe, he stood back up to challenge the angry woman. "Don't do it, Eleanor," he warned, holding his hands up in surrender. "It's not worth it."

"Not worth it, Charlie? Do you know how much these pills cost me?" She pulled her hand out of her pocket and waved the receipt at him. "And if she thinks she can sleep with him while *I'm* paying for the pills, she's out of her mind. I'll take her to court, if I have to.''

Charlie let out a relieved sigh, and nudged Liz with the toe of his shoe. ''You can come out now,'' he said. ''It wasn't a gun.''

''A gun? You're carrying a gun, pumpkin?'' A tiny, elfish man with flappy ears appeared in the doorway, then darted straight to the side of the mountain of a woman who overshadowed him by a good half foot.

''Vaughn,'' Charlie said, stretching his hand down to help Liz to her feet. ''She seems to think you're sleeping with Liz...Liz Fuller.''

Liz's head rose above the top of her desk, eye level with the Viagra, and that's as far as she went. ''Mr. McMasters... She thinks I'm sleeping with Mr. McMasters?''

''Not only sleeping with him. You told everybody at Whitaker that he's boring in bed, which he's not, after he takes his pill.''

''You don't think I'm boring, pumpkin?'' the mousy little man piped up. A diminutive smile squiggled across his face. ''Really? Do you mean that?''

''I didn't tell anybody at Whitaker anything about Mr. McMasters, since this is the first time I've ever met him.'' Liz raised up a little higher, but not so high she had to abandon her safe place behind the desk. ''So who's saying that I did?''

Vaughn McMasters suddenly discovered the supply of his potency pills on the desk, and scurried to tuck them into his pockets.

''I heard it from Peggy Anderson in the mail room,'' Eleanor barked. ''And she said that Melba from purchasing heard you two together with her very own ears.''

''And I heard it personally from Ramon...you know that real cute maintenance guy who works for Mr. Reynolds,'' Ginny called from the outer office. ''And he told me that he heard it personally from...well, I thought he said he'd heard it personally from you, Miss Fuller, but

I'm guessing that's probably not right, so it must have been from your secretary, which is…me,'' she giggled.

"I didn't tell the janitor I was having an affair with Mr. McMasters,'' Liz defended. "And if I were having an affair with him, or anyone here, my confidant certainly wouldn't be…well, anybody in the office since it's strictly against office rules.''

"So, are you, or aren't you?'' Eleanor boomed at Liz. She didn't even look at her husband, who was trying to slip, unnoticed, from the office. "Are you sleeping with my husband, trying to earn your promotion on your back? I've heard you're pretty ambitious, and that you've got Charlie lined up if Ralphie won't give you what you want.''

"Ralphie?'' Charlie choked. "Who the hell's Ralphie?''

"My husband! Ralph Vaughn McMasters. What's *she* done to you, Charlie? Pickled your brain with so much sex you can't think right. You used to be so much sharper than that.'' She pointed her finger at Liz yet again. "So who's next? Sebastian? Charlie's dad? Are you working your way through all the top people until you find one who will promote you?''

"Charlie,'' Liz hissed. "Get this woman out of here.'' Dropping back to the floor, she crawled completely under the desk, and collapsed into a resigned slump. Four more hours until quitting time.

"WELL, I'D SAY THAT WENT smoothly,'' Charlie commented, scooting in next to Liz. Tight fit, and there under the desk with her it was a little too low to sit up straight, but she'd refused to come out and at the moment she was simply settled in there, eating a banana, offering half to him.

"I have a headache,'' she replied, flicking a wayward sample pack of Viagra out of her cramped quarters. "My back aches and I'm getting a cramp in my…that's none of your business.''

"Mr. Spinoza from Sporty Feet on line two," Ginny said, holding the phone down to Liz. "He's an attorney, I think."

"Tell Mr. Spinoza I'm in an important meeting. Can't be interrupted." Trying to wrestle out of her jacket, Liz got it halfway down her arm then couldn't maneuver it any farther, and she was trapped in it like a straitjacket. "Just cut it off me, will you, Charlie? I'm tired of black, anyway."

Charlie laughed. "I think you should take the rest of the day off."

"Why would you say that?" she snapped.

He chuckled. "I'd tell you that you deserve some downtime since you just landed a big account, and your nerves are a little on edge, but you'd get all defensive and…"

"Edgy?" Liz interrupted. "Me edgy? I ruined your office last night and got accused of sleeping my way to the top today—sleeping with a board member whose ears are bigger than my…" She looked down at her chest. "You're darned right I'm edgy, and I've earned it!"

"Mr. Spinoza said they've decided they're so happy with the new concept they want a new logo to go with the new slogan. Something sexy." Ginny stooped to pick up the banana that had slipped out of Liz's fingers, and handed her a bottle of water. "Your three o'clock canceled, and someone named Jackie called to congratulate you, even though—quote—you're making a total mess of the whole Whitaker firm—unquote. Whatever that means."

"I'm taking the afternoon off, Ginny. No more calls, no more irate wives. Give me thirty minutes, then I'm out of here."

"And I'm going with her. Ginny, would you ask Dolores to step in here for a minute." He reached across to Liz and took her hand. "I think you need another weekend at the lodge, don't you?"

Ginny smiled, turned and gave a thumbs-up to Ramon

who was loitering at her desk. Ramon, in turn, did the same to Georgia, who flew from the office into the welcome of a half dozen people who weren't intrepid enough to maneuver into earshot to take in, for themselves, the next chapter of the Liz Fuller saga.

"I hope Jonquil and Ralph are coming, too," Liz said. "We're getting pretty short on time."

"Ralph. Think I'll change that name to Rafe. Don't want to picture *Ralphie* every time I write." He grinned, and gave Liz a teasing wink. "Ralphie and Viagra."

"Ralph, Rafe. Same name," she snorted. "And I hate both of them."

He reached to her face and brushed back the hair that had sprung loose from her no-nonsense do. Then gently, his thumb stroked her jaw line and traced its way to the corner of her mouth. But he stopped short of running his fingers across her lips. In her mood, she'd bite him. "Anyway, Jonquil and Ralph will be there, if you're up to it."

"Oh, I'm up to it, if you are."

"You wanted me, Charlie?" Dolores asked, stepping around the desk and looking down at Liz's feet sticking out from under. "Is she okay? Should I call 9-1-1 or something?"

"I'm fine," Liz answered. "Peachy."

"Let Dad know I'm using the lodge this weekend," Charlie told his secretary. "And cancel the rest of my day."

"Congratulations on Sporty Feet, by the way." Dolores said, bending down to Liz. "You know, we have an old partners' desk in storage. More room underneath, if you're interested, dear."

"Have 'em move it on in, Dolores. I have a feeling I'll be spending lots of time down here, if I don't get fired first."

"THE LODGE," DOLORES TOLD the anxious crowd. "And she wants..." Dolores clutched her hand to her chest and dropped into her chair. "She wants other people there. But she's worried that he might not be up to it."

17

JONQUIL LAID BACK IN THE grass and the sun reflected off her perky peaks like a shining mirror. "You are too kind to me, Ralph," she cooed. "I don't deserve all this. Please, take what you will from me as your due." Charlie set the page aside and gazed up at the late-day sun. It wasn't exactly reflecting off of anybody's perky peaks, but the day was beautiful and he was glad to be there with Liz, no matter what the pretense, although all pretenses were soon coming to an end.

"Shouldn't she be polishing his boots, too?" Liz asked, her voice so even it gave away no hint of emotion or reaction. "Maybe strewing her shawl along the path he walks?"

"Hey, she's grateful. What can I say?" Charlie turned his head to hide the smile. "Just trying to show him some of that indebtedness, which I think, is appropriate, under the circumstances."

"Circumstances?" Her eyes went wide. "Care to explain that?"

"You know, like the gifts and extravagances he gives her that she could never afford as a maid. That kind of a thing."

"Oh, and don't leave out sex. She should be grateful for that above anything else, shouldn't she?" Liz popped open the cooler and pulled out a stem of grapes. "Would you like for me to peel one of these for you?" she asked casually. "After I grab the palm frond and fan you for a while?"

"Well, now that you bring it up…" A wicked smiled

touched his lips. He loved to tease her. Loved to see that spark of fire ignite in her eyes. Loved the healthy challenge he'd come to expect from her. Loved just about everything…"And do it slowly so I can take notes."

"Is there anything else you'd like me to do for you, while we're on the subject of subservience." She gave him a saucy little smile, then wrinkled her nose. "Anything that doesn't have to do with bosoms?"

"That's pretty restrictive, isn't it? If Ralph wanted bosoms, Jonquil would be falling all over herself to provide him with that enjoyment. That's just the kind of girl she is."

"In *your* fantasy, maybe. But not in Jonquil's." She popped a grape into her mouth, and playfully threw one at Charlie. "She's smart, and strong, and you may try to pound her down into a menial position, but I'll guarantee that she won't stay there for long."

"Not even for the man she loves?"

Liz's smiled broadened. "*Especially* for the man she loves. And if he loves her, he won't put her there." Kicking off her shoes, she laid back on the blanket and ate another grape. "So why don't you rewrite that scene while I just lie here and rest," she suggested. "And see if you can write it as Jonquil—not as Ralph."

"You want me to be Jonquil?" he asked, raising his voice an octave until its pitch was in the female range. "So does that mean you'll be Ralph?"

"Sure, and Ralph's taking a nap right now." Closing her eyes, she let out a relaxed sigh and within seconds her breathing turned even and deep.

Charlie studied her for a minute. White short shorts that cupped her backside so gloriously they could have been designed exclusively for her, a white midriff T-shirt that kept creeping up, and those gorgeous long, bare legs leading all the way down to those gorgeous, bare feet. She was so soft in the unguarded moments, and so hard in all the rest. And he liked both parts of her. No, he loved both parts. Earlier this morning, during Sporty

Feet, he'd never wanted to land an account as badly as he'd wanted her to land that one. And afterwards, when she'd simply shaken his hand and offered a cordial thanks, her composure so guarded she didn't even allow the slightest trace of excitement to break through, he'd been so excited he'd wanted to leap over the conference table like a tennis player over the net. But her cool reserve was turned on and working hard, and he wouldn't have cracked it for anything.

"I thought you were working," she said, squinting up at him.

"I am," he lied. "In my head. And I thought you were sleeping."

"I did. I'm pretty fast at it. Now, read me something...something new, something romantic." She raised her arms and laced her fingers together under her head, causing her creeping T-shirt to creep up a little more. "Make *me* fall in love with Ralph. Tell me something about him that will surprise me, that will make me realize, beyond the shadow of a doubt, that he's the man for me."

"Ralph? What would make you love a man like him? A great physique, maybe? How about this? *His pecs bulged under his shirt, almost so much that the tight stretch of the fabric was ready to rip right open.*"

Liz giggled. "Do his pecs flex as he walks?"

"Very funny. *And his thighs, with the iron girth of a century-old oak, were so powerful they protested against the confines of his...breeches.*" Charlie glanced sideways to gauge her reaction, and saw the laugh just bubbling to get out. So beautiful, so downright ravishing, and here he was hiding in a book. "*Jonquil craved the feel of his mammoth hands on her—rough, brawny, with the grit of sandpaper. A man's hands.*" He glanced down at his own. Not even a callous. Which would Liz prefer—rough or smooth? "*With digits so mightily-versed in the aptitude of fondling a woman...*"

"Whoa...What do you mean digits?"

"Fingers." He waved his at her, then continued, "*...so mightily versed in the aptitude of fondling a woman that they were legendary, yea even craved throughout the land. And Jonquil melted into a puddle of surrender each time she was the recipient of that oft celebrated and immeasurably manly touch. 'More, please more, she always begged.' And he would look down from his lofty six-foot-eight height upon her buxom bounty and bestow that for which she had a hankering.*"

"Give me your hand," Liz said, sitting up. "Just hold it out."

Shifting a little closer to her on the blanket, he obliged, and the delicate way her flesh touched his, even if only hand to hand, was almost more than he could stand. Right now, the manly part of him was beginning to strain, definitely protesting against the confines of his breeches. He pulled one knee up to keep from feeling like the thirteen-year-old boy unable to control himself while dancing with the prettiest girl at the junior high dance. "So what do you see there?" he asked.

"For starters, no sandpaper," she said, running her fingers over his palm. "They're strong, gentle—certainly not mammoth, but large..."

Charlie's mind began to wander as she analyzed his hands. She was so distracting—everything she did, or even when she was just lying there doing nothing. He couldn't write when he was around her, could barely think, that much was becoming undeniably clear. And he really needed to write. More than that, he wanted to write. There were so many things, so many vivid details of her that he had to get down on the page.

She loved him, he thought. He'd been attentive to those signs she talked about—like right now, when she was tracing a delicate line up one finger and down the other. At least he hoped he was reading the right signs. But she was so determined to ignore them, which was actually what he expected from her, because Liz always did the right thing. By the book... Then he smiled.

You're a challenge, Liz Fuller, but I'm willing to bet that…

"And a callous from hard work is acceptable—women like that kind of ruggedness in a man's hand, but not sandpaper, Charlie. It connotes chafing and rough and…"

A contented sigh escaped him. For the first time in his life, the stakes of a bet truly mattered. Problem was, he hadn't come up with a way to win it yet, and Liz certainly wasn't throwing out any hints.

DINNER WAS BRIEF, and Charlie beat a hasty retreat to his computer immediately afterward. This was the first time Liz had ever seen him so eager to write that nothing else mattered, and she was fascinated by the change from procrastination this afternoon to enthusiasm this evening. Remarkable, and it made her wonder what had happened out there on the blanket—what she'd missed. An energized muse, maybe? Or the realization that he had to kick it in gear to win the bet. Whatever, she sat and watched him write for a while after dinner, watched his fingers fairly fly over the keys. And each time she'd tried to tiptoe around the desk to catch a look at what he was doing, he clicked off the computer screen and smiled sheepishly. After a while, she took the hint and went for a walk, and now, here it was, well after one in the morning and he was downstairs, still hard at work, and she couldn't sleep.

Maybe a swim? Just a few laps to work out the tension, to make her tired enough to sleep the rest of the night. And she really needed the sleep, because soon, she was going to have a heart to heart with him about his writing. There was no way around it, and no way around the fact that she dreaded telling him that it was awful, especially since he seemed to be working so hard at it lately, and even enjoying it. But he trusted her to be honest, and because she loved him, she couldn't do otherwise no matter how much she wanted to spare his feelings. Being dishonest in a relationship—and she surely hoped they could salvage something out of this for a relationship—simply wasn't in her.

After slipping into a swimsuit, a brand-new, risqué little number hanging among all the lingerie in the closet, Liz took the back stairs so as not to disturb Charlie, and headed straight to the pool. Once there, she slipped silently into the water and simply relaxed in the gentle ripples as it cradled her, floating away all the stress and strain of the past week. Once or twice, she heard a noise and looked up to see what it was, but nothing was there except the near darkness. And once or twice she turned to glance at the house…hoping, maybe? No, she wasn't hoping for anything, since this time there would be no turning back. There was nothing in her that could, or would turn back. And she was desperately relying on Charlie to be the strong one, because what she didn't want, she truly wanted with all her heart.

Suddenly, a muted splash on the opposite end of the pool caused her to suck in her breath and hold it in sweet and agonizing anticipation.

"Caress," he stated, swimming up behind her. "I've been trying to come up with better word choices and that's a nice word, don't you think? Much better than grope or pat. It's soft, gentle…" He ran his thumb over her lips, then moved to place a kiss there. "Suggestive," he whispered. "And suggestive can be deeply romantic, can't it?"

"Suggestive of what?" she gasped, shutting her eyes.

"Of this, maybe." Pressing himself to her back, his hand skimmed over the brief fabric of her swimsuit. "Nice," he said, tracing the line of her French-cut thong from her backside to her waist, then around her to her belly button—an inny. His finger lingered there for a moment, to explore the exquisite circle, then moved upward. Halfway to her breasts, he was diverted by the outline of her ribs for a moment, then ducked under the

water to endow a line of kisses there, from her left side
to her right.

"That's certainly a caress," she gasped, as he surfaced. Turning around to him, she bent her knee upward
to press into his hip, and he was naked, as she expected.
Naked and hard, and exciting in a way she'd never
known before. "In every sense of…oh…" Her voice
trailed off to a tiny moan. "Charlie…"

His hand continued its slow, soft journey over her skin
until it reached the scrap of fabric posing as a top, and
he untied the string quickly then, and tossed it into the
middle of the pool.

"Jonquil would like that," she gasped, squirming
against him just enough to press her bare breasts to his
chest.

"And what would *Liz* like?" he growled, pinning her
back to the tiled wall with his hips. "Tell me, Liz."
Sliding his body down the length of hers until he was
fully submerged, he playfully licked his way from just
below her inny all the way up to the hollow of her throat.
"How would Liz respond?" he asked when his face met
hers.

"Liz would remind him that was only one part of her
swimsuit." She tossed her head back to draw in a deep,
steadying breath. It was now, or never. "And that it
looks so lonely out there in the middle of the pool all
by itself."

Without a word, Charlie slid back down the length of
her body and pulled the petite-sized swimsuit bottom
over her legs, then kissed a trail of hot, staccato kisses
from her toes back up to her inny. "And then what?"
he rasped, bobbing up out of the water for a breath of
air. The rest of the swimsuit went flying into the middle
of the pool.

"Something like this," she said. Her back still to the
wall, Liz's legs floated up to circle his hips, and she
pressed herself exuberantly against him, thrusting to feel
as much of him against her as she could. "Or this."

Suddenly, she slid down his body, pressing every inch of herself to every inch of him, until she was the one under the water, kissing a serpentine path from his chest down. Reaching his belly button, also an inny, she allowed herself a slow trip back to the surface, her breasts rubbing along the path her lips had taken. And when she pushed herself out of the water, she pinned him to the tile pool side with her hips and let the ripples of their combined movements design a subdued thrusting between them. "She would tease for a while, then invite him, I think."

"Invite him? Sounds suggestive."

"Very." Moving away from Charlie, Liz pushed herself up out of the pool and stood boldly in the moonlight. Holding out her hand to him, she watched as he emerged hard and ready for her. And they made it to a deck chair, where she pushed him down and lowered herself to him. Then she kissed her way downward to his flat stomach, stopping just above his erection, and looked up at him. "And she would say that she wants everything he has to give." Moving back up, Liz wrapped her arms around his neck and looked adoringly into his eyes. "Now, Charlie," she whispered.

"Liz," he murmured, his voice charged with raw longing. He opened his mouth against her lips, his tongue smoothed over hers. With one hand he brushed her breast in a soft caress. Her nipple went hard, tempting his fingers to play there. Then he bent down and took one between his teeth, rubbing the nub with his tongue. "Did you hope I would come for a swim?" he panted minutes later. "Were you waiting for me?"

"Yes," she admitted boldly. "I was waiting." The sensation almost more than she could bear, Liz pressed harder into Charlie, kneading her hands across his chest and all the way down the rippling muscles of his abdomen to feel his imposing hardness, and she lingered there, teasing and taunting and stroking him to elicit the moans she was desperate to hear. "And I knew you would come," she laughed, bending to follow the path of her hands with hard, demanding kisses.

"That sure of yourself," he gasped.

She stayed there, pleasuring every sensitive spot on his body he was aware of and some he wasn't before tonight, until he could stand it no longer, then he rolled her off him and underneath, and looked down at her in the moonlight. "You're so beautiful," he said, his hands beginning the exploration over her belly and down to that sensitive spot between her legs, the identical spot she'd only just pleasured so vigorously for him.

"Charlie," she gasped, lifting her hips to his touch. Each stroke, each carnal path he traced sent a building tremor through her, over and over, until she was racked with a hard climax like nothing she ever dreamed could exist. And in a while, as her moans diminished into a contented sigh, she watched Charlie's hand trail down to his robe pocket and return with a familiar variety pack. "Remind me to thank Martha later," Liz laughed, selecting something plain.

"She knew you were a lusty wench right from the beginning," he teased.

"Did you?"

"I hoped. God, I hoped." Rolling off her, he moved to his back and pulled her atop him once more. "And was I right?"

"Let me show you." Rising up slightly, she lowered herself over him, and when all of him was in her, she remained still for a moment. This was all she wanted, no matter what the cost. And the cost was going to come high.

The rhythm between them came in a frantic cadence that needed its release immediately, and she thrust hard onto him, driving herself downward for everything he had, until his moans equaled hers. And in the moment when she thought she was spent, that she could go no further, Charlie grabbed her around the waist, rolled her over, found his place between her legs, and drove himself into her with a demand that bettered hers. And they climaxed together, in a furor of nighttime heat and sweat and satiated gasps.

"Well?" Liz panted, his spent body still atop hers.

"Well, what?"

"Credits? You know, blue ribbon winner or something."

He raised up and kissed her forehead, then winked. "Elizabeth Fuller invitational."

She smiled up at him. "Charlie Whitaker, first place." First place in her heart.

18

"WELL, I DON'T KNOW WHAT it was about, but she left without notice, son. Came in early, packed up her office and told Ginny to tell me she'd send over a formal resignation later on. And she went straight to Kleinschmidt and VanderBeeck, our competition. So you tell me. What's it all about?" Charles Senior reared back in his chair and looked around Charlie to Ginny Kowalski, his new personal secretary. "Did she say anything to you, honey?"

Ginny shrugged. "Just like I told you last night, sweetie, and that's all I know."

"What did you tell him last night?" Charlie quizzed, spinning around to Ginny. "What do you know about Liz leaving here?"

"Well, not much, but I think it probably has something to do with what the two of you were doing, well…in the office. Doing it a lot. And it being against the rules, you know."

"Doing what a lot? I don't know what you mean." He turned back to his dad, who was busy lighting up a fat Cuban cigar. "But apparently you do, don't you, Dad."

"Sex, son," he said, gesturing a thumbs-up. "You and what's her name in your office. Seems you weren't very discreet about it. It got broadcast. And I suppose she took the smart way out and left before I had to fire her."

"Broadcast?"

"Yep, seems just like everybody here heard just about

everything you two did here. Over the intercom, or something. So there's no use denying it." Senior flicked his lighter a couple times to no avail, and Ginny jumped up and nearly fell across his desk to help him, her mini-skirt hiking up so high, Charlie turned away. "Good girl," Senior cooed, eyeing her long, red fingernails in lustful expectation. "And from what I hear it was pretty…well, I'm not sure what kind of word I want to use here, since on one hand you're my son and a father takes pride in his son's accomplishments if you know what I mean, and on the other hand I'm your boss and there is an office policy against this sort of thing on company time."

"It was wild," Ginny supplied eagerly. "And bois-terous. Dolores said…"

"Dolores?" Charlie shouted.

"Your secretary," Senior offered.

"I *know* she's my secretary, Dad."

"Well, she heard you, Mr. Whitaker." Ginny backed away from the desk, and wiggled her fingernails at Sen-ior as she scooted back onto the couch. "Right through the office door. And so did the others…Georgia, Garvey, Mr. Reynolds…"

Drawing in a deep breath to steady himself, Charlie shut his eyes against the headache starting to pound and rubbed his forehead. "It's a bet, Dad. With Charlene."

"Having sex with a co-worker in your office is a bet with your sister? That's really stretching it, don't you think?"

"Not sex. A book! I'm writing a book and Liz is helping me. It's a romance novel and she's my…she *was* my tutor…writing tutor."

"You write romances," Ginny squealed. "I read them all the time. So does my mother. Can I have your au-tograph?"

Senior dropped his smoldering widow-choker into an ashtray and spun around in his leather swivel chair, one that more resembled a throne than a piece of office furniture, and reached for a bottle of Scotch in the cabinet behind him. He removed only one glass, and poured himself a generous shot, then swigged it down in one gulp. "And the prize this time?" he finally asked, spinning back to face Charlie.

"The sword."

Senior arched his eyebrows, then picked up his cigar. "Well, fix it, son. What's her name's too valuable to hand over to Kleinschmidt and VanderBeeck, especially since I was counting on her to step into senior executive this week. Oh, and next time you write a book, keep it out of the office. Okay?"

"Liz," Charlie said on his way out the door. "Her name is Liz Fuller."

"Whatever." Senior winked at Ginny, then took another puff of the Cuban.

"TELL HIM I'LL CALL HIM this evening." Liz looked at her secretary, Antonio, and let out a deep breath. Efficient, male model material and the desire of every female at the water cooler, he was only a small part of the total Kleinschmidt and VanderBeeck package she'd been offered when she'd made that call to accept the job, the job that came her way ten minutes after word was out on how she'd landed Sporty Feet. So far, three hours into her new job, she really couldn't say that it was bad. Because it wasn't. Expense account, car, office with a view, secretary with a view—not bad at all.

But she already missed Whitaker.

Business and pleasure, she reminded herself. And she was right. It hadn't worked. But she'd fixed it. And now it was time to see if there really was a relationship with Charlie in the mix. Also, if a relationship between competitors could work. She shook her head skeptically. Everything about the two of them getting together had worked against them so far. Now here she was, at the top of another big hurdle. He would own the company one day, and if things went according to plan, she'd be a partner…here. She shook her head again. "Really stupid."

"Excuse me," Antonio said, stopping at the door.

"Not you." Liz's voice was quiet, and she was fighting with everything inside her to keep the sadness out of it. "Me. Just thinking about a big mistake I made, am making, will make…take your pick."

"Would a little vanilla hazelnut coffee help? Maybe with a nice scone?"

So gorgeous and so shallow, Liz thought. Just what she should have gone after this time. Gorgeous, shallow, no fuss, no muss, no conflicts…no Charlie. "Thanks, but I'm fine."

"And that call from Mr. Whitaker, the one you said you'd return later… He made it from the outer office."

Liz looked up and smiled. "He did?"

Antonio nodded. "And he said he's going to make one every five minutes until you can squeeze him in."

Just then the phone rang, and Antonio scurried out to answer it. Then he buzzed Liz. "It's him again, and he's standing right outside your door."

As if on cue, Charlie poked his head into Liz's office, still holding the phone to his ear. "Nice office," he commented. "Great view."

Her heart caught in her throat. "Antonio," she said into the phone, "please tell Mr. Whitaker to come in."

Antonio blew into the doorway. "You may go in, Mr. Whitaker." Then he waited until Charlie was seated across from Liz before he blew back out, closing the door behind him.

"We had a deal," Charlie said, crossing one leg casually over the other. "Remember the deal? And I fulfilled my part of it. But I don't recall that you did."

Liz spun around in her chair to face her view of Lake Michigan—the view she'd wanted to see every day from Whitaker and Associates. "I'm your competition now. Can you live with that? Because I'm good, Charlie, and you know that. We'll be fighting for the same accounts."

"So you got your promotion. That's what you wanted, and here you are. But a deal's a deal, and I still expect you to stick to your end of it."

She continued to stare at the lake. "You know why I had to leave?"

"Before we get into that, I want you to take a look at a few pages. Read them, offer your opinion, and when you're through, after you listen to what I have to say, we'll talk about it." He pulled several pages from his canvas case and waved them at her. "Five minutes, Liz. Then the deal's over."

"Do you really think we can settle this in five minutes, Charlie?" she cried.

She reached across the desk for the papers, but Charlie snatched them back. "Just listen," he said. "I read faster, and this way you'll have plenty of time to make your next appointment."

Liz opened her mouth to argue—the natural thing to do with Charlie—the sexy thing—the thing that she wanted so badly to do again. But instead, she remained quiet, folded her hands on her desk, and nodded.

Charlie put on his reading glasses. *"She was beautiful to his eyes—so exquisite was the mere glimpse of her that even the fairest of all the flowers in his gardens could not compare."*

"That's beautiful," she whispered. "Remarkable."

"He loved her in a way that had not existed in the heavens, or on the earth, until that day when first he gazed upon her. And he knew in his heart that it was a love for time and all eternity."

"Oh, my..." Liz choked. "Charlie, I don't know what to say. I've been so afraid I was going to have to tell you how awful your writing was, but this...it's wonderful."

"So it's getting better? "

"Better? It's incredible. Every word so perfect. And the way the emotion flows through it all... I think you could do this for real. You know, write books, maybe romance novels.''

''You said I should fall in love, first. Remember? Experience it firsthand.''

A deep scowl suddenly spanned her face. ''I'm beginning to sense something suspicious going on, Charlie Whitaker. Even love can't turn the worst writer into the world's best. So what happened?''

A typical Charlie grin slid effortlessly across his face. ''Well, first I did fall in love, and you were right, that helped.''

Liz's scowl softened a little.

''And I did read all those books like you wanted me to, and saw how bad my original style was.''

And her eyes softened.

''And I started writing from the heart.''

''But I read what you were writing, Charlie. It was awful...horrible...dreadful...''

''That was writing from the hip,'' he interrupted. ''I wanted to hold on to my tutor, and that was the only way I could think of to do it.'' His eyes twinkled the twinkle she loved—the twinkle that was Charlie Whitaker through and through. ''And I thought it was a pretty good plan,'' he continued. ''Write something bad, and she'll hang around to help me get it right—long enough, I hoped, to come up with a real way to hang on to you. I knew if you saw my real writing, the writing which was all about you, by the way, you'd be back to work, business as usual, and our deal would be off.''

''All about me?''

''Every last word, except for her bosoms, maybe.'' He tossed her a devilish wink. ''I may have endowed her just a little bit better.''

''Charlie!''

''What can I say? I'm a writer—vivid imagination—speaking of which...'' He shoved another paper across her desk. ''Read this.''

Putting on her glasses, she studied the first few lines

then looked up at him, her expression bursting with astonishment. "They want to see the whole book, Charlie? I don't know what to say—congratulations, maybe?"

"Say yes," he said.

"To what?"

"Do you love me?"

"I'm your competitor."

"Yes, but do you love me?"

She sat back in her chair and folded her arms across her chest. "Do *you* love *me?*"

He smiled. "Turning this into a business negotiation, are you? Well, before I tell you that I love you, which I do, I want you to know that when a man loves a woman, he doesn't want to control her. He wants to support her in what makes her happy. He wants to be part of those things, to be part of her. And if he can't be all that, if he can't be happy for her successes, and willing to do what it takes to help her achieve them, he doesn't love her. And I love you, Liz, more than anything else in the world. I have from the beginning. And right after you— well, pretty far down the ladder actually, since nothing comes close to the way I feel about you—anyway, way down there after you is my writing. I loved writing those chapters and I think I've known from the first paragraph—the first *real* paragraph—that I was going to be a writer. That's what makes me happy.

"And I'm about to ask you to marry me, but you'll have to understand that you'll be marrying an author, not an ad writer anymore. Which means as a struggling new writer I may have to live off *your* earnings for a while." He grinned. "And you'll also have to take my place at Whitaker, since I handed in my resignation half an hour ago and they're in desperate need of a senior ad executive right this very minute. You'll also have to get used to a new lifestyle with me as a stay-at-home, and you as the business suit, because if you say yes, that's our life. So will you?"

"Yes," Liz shouted. Pushing herself back from the desk, she jumped up and leaned over the desk top, her palms flat against the wood. "Yes, Charlie, I love you. I fell in love with you the day you asked me to jiggle my bosoms all the way across the office, and I haven't stopped."

"I didn't ask you to jiggle." He stood and leaned over to Liz, his palms flat on the desk, too. "But I certainly would have loved it." He kissed her lightly across the nose, then whispered, "And in case you're interested, you've been a mighty difficult client to sell on the concept."

"But now that I'm sold," she teased, brushing her lips over his, "I think it's time to talk contract." She pulled back, and smiled. "Nothing legal, mind you. Just something to spell out the details…"

"Legal," he stated emphatically. "Legal and binding—forever."

"Yes!"

"Oh, and about the sword. I've sworn off bets since I'll be having better things to do with my time. And I'm giving it back to Charlene, since I've just won the best prize of all."

"Now, that's romantic," Liz murmured as she walked around the desk to Charlie's arms.

"Isn't it," Charlie agreed.

OUTSIDE, IN THE SECRETARIAL office, Simon, Matilda and Fritz all waited in line to hear Antonio's version of what was going on inside. "All I can make out is something about jiggling her bosoms at him," he said.

Epilogue

CHARLIE LOOKED AT THE SWORD hanging over the fireplace, a baby gift from Aunt Charlene for the twins, Rafe and Jonquil. "It does look pretty good hanging back up there," he said to his sister.

"And in about thirty years they can make a bet to see which one gets to keep it."

He laughed. "Or maybe I'll give it back to you so you'll have to deal with it."

"But look what that one little bet got you into." She gestured to the fireplace, then to the entire great room in the lodge. "If I'd known then what I know now, the stakes would have been much higher," she teased. "It was nice of Dad to let you buy this place from him."

"You mean nice of Ginny, don't you. She's city—won't step foot out of the city limits. And now with their new baby…" Charlie laughed. "Charlotte, our little sister…he's so preoccupied with his new life I don't think he's even given this place a thought."

"Well," sighed Charlene, "maybe number seven, or is she number eight, will be the keeper. He sure seems to be in love this time."

"Take it from someone who knows. There's nothing like it."

"Oatmeal this morning," Liz called, dashing down the stairs, tugging her business blues into place. She tossed her sensible shoes down ahead of her, and stepped over Joe, who was sprawled out on the floor, taking time off from his gardening duties to rehearse his part as an unconscious shooting victim for an upcoming TV episode of *Patrol Cops*. He was a regular DB on the show now...dead body, or a nearly DB, as in this case. And he rehearsed each and every time he got the call. "And I think you can add a little of Happy Baby Bananas to it. I left some samples out on the counter—a new account I'm going after."

"I already did," Joe said, trying not to move his lips.

Life was working out well, Charlie thought. Much better than he believed he'd ever have, and he was happy. More than that, he was fulfilled as a full-time writer and stay-at-home dad. Even better, Liz was the full-time career woman she needed to be, and these days his dad not only remembered her name, he was shifting, a little at a time, control to the only other Whitaker in the firm as he became more involved with his new family. And Liz was thriving on it, much more than he ever would have.

Life in the lodge now, without the dead animals, was everything Charlie wanted, especially since Liz had discovered that one of the joys of commuter trains was extra time to work on the way to and from the office. And having Martha, and the newlyweds Wanda and Joe, all helping with the babies was a godsend since he tended to lose himself in his work. Always busy, sometimes hectic, it certainly wasn't the ordinary life, and he and Liz often joked about it. But then, what was ordinary anyway?

"Liz, tonight I'd like to go over a scene with you— one between Armand and Graziella. It seems a little stilted to me, and I want your opinion before I get too far with it. And since my editor's got me on such a tight deadline with this book..."

"Hey, I stuck you with the best editor we have, next to me." Charlene tucked Rafe under one arm and Jonquil under the other, and headed to the former office alcove now turned nursery, since Charlie had commandeered Joe's old room for an office, after Joe moved into the garage apartment with Wanda. "So if you'll excuse the three of us, I think we'll go discuss the ins and outs of being a twin.''

Liz kissed the babies as Charlene rushed by, then she greeted Charlie by wrapping her arms around his neck and snaking her stockinged foot up his leg. ''Want to drive me to the city today? I'm wearing that little red cami and boyshort under my blues,'' she said, pulling his face to hers. ''The one you like so much. And I have some ideas for a car scene that just might work, but I think we need to try them out first, if you know what I mean.''

''The story takes place in 1830,'' he said, lowering his lips to hers.

Tilting her chin to receive his kiss, she winked. ''I know, which is why I think we should try it out first.''

* * * * *

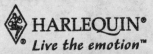

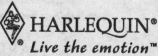

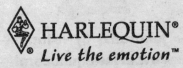

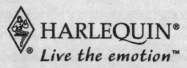

Is your man too good to be true?

Hot, gorgeous AND romantic?
If so, he could be a Harlequin® Blaze™ series cover model!

Our grand-prize winners will receive a trip for two to New York City to
shoot the cover of a Blaze novel, and will stay at the luxurious Plaza Hotel.

Plus, they'll receive $500 U.S. spending money!

The runner-up winners will receive $200 U.S.
to spend on a romantic dinner for two.

It's easy to enter!

In 100 words or less, tell us what makes your boyfriend or spouse a true romantic
and the perfect candidate for the cover of a Blaze novel, and include in your submission
two photos of this potential cover model.

All entries must include the written submission of the contest entrant, two photographs of the model
candidate and the Official Entry Form and Publicity Release forms completed in full and signed by
both the model candidate and the contest entrant. Harlequin, along with the experts at
Elite Model Management, will select a winner.

For photo and complete Contest details, please refer to the Official Rules on the next page. All entries
will become the property of Harlequin Enterprises Ltd. and are not returnable.

**Please visit www.blazecovermodel.com to download a copy of the Official Entry Form and
Publicity Release Form or send a request to one of the addresses below.**

Please mail your entry to: **Harlequin Blaze Cover Model Search**

In U.S.A.
P.O. Box 9069
Buffalo, NY
14269-9069

In Canada
P.O. Box 637
Fort Erie, ON
L2A 5X3

No purchase necessary. Contest open to Canadian and U.S. residents who are 18 and over.
Void where prohibited. Contest closes September 30, 2003.

HBCVRMODEL1

HARLEQUIN BLAZE COVER MODEL SEARCH CONTEST 3569 OFFICIAL RULES
NO PURCHASE NECESSARY TO ENTER

1. To enter, submit two (2) 4" x 6" photographs of a boyfriend or spouse (who must be 18 years of age or older) taken no later than three (3) months from the time of entry: a close-up, waist up, shirtless photograph; and a fully clothed full-length photograph, then, tell us, in 100 words or fewer, why he should be a Harlequin Blaze cover model and how he is romantic. Your complete "entry" must include: (i) your essay, (ii) the Official Entry Form and Publicity Release Form printed below completed and signed by you (as "Entrant"), (iii) the photographs (with your hand-written name address and phone number, and your model's name, address and phone number on the back of each photograph), and (iv) the Publicity Release Form and Photograph Representation Form printed below completed and signed by your model (as "Model"), and should be sent via first-class mail to either: Harlequin Blaze Cover Model Search Contest 3569, P.O. Box 9069, Buffalo, NY, 14269-9069, or Harlequin Blaze Cover Model Search Contest 3569, P.O. Box 637, Fort Erie, Ontario L2A 5X3. All submissions must be in English and be received no later than September 30, 2003. Limit: one entry per person, household or organization. Purchase or acceptance of a product offer does not improve your chances of winning. All entry requirements must be strictly adhered to for eligibility and to ensure fairness among entrants.

2. Ten (10) Finalist submissions (photographs and essays) will be selected by a panel of judges consisting of members of the Harlequin editorial, marketing and public relations staff, as well as a representative from Elite Model Management (Toronto) Inc., based on the following criteria:

Aptness/Appropriateness of submitted photographs for a Harlequin Blaze cover—70%
Originality of Essay—20%
Sincerity of Essay—10%

In the event of a tie, duplicate finalists will be selected. The photographs submitted by finalists will be posted on the Harlequin website no later than November 15, 2003 (at www.blazecovermodel.com), and viewers may vote, in rank order, on their favorite(s) to assist in the panel of judges' final determination of the Grand Prize and Runner-up winning entries based on the above judging criteria. All decisions of the judges are final.

3. All entries become the property of Harlequin Enterprises Ltd. and none will be returned. Any entry may be used for future promotional purposes. Elite Model Management (Toronto) Inc. and/or its partners, subsidiaries and affiliates operating as "Elite Model Management" will have access to all entries including all personal information, and may contact any Entrant and/or Model in its sole discretion for their own business purposes. Harlequin and Elite Model Management (Toronto) Inc. are separate entities with no legal association or partnership whatsoever having no power to bind or obligate the other or create any expressed or implied obligation or responsibility on behalf of the other, such that Harlequin shall not be responsible in any way for any acts or omissions of Elite Model Management (Toronto) Inc. or its partners, subsidiaries and affiliates in connection with the Contest or otherwise and Elite Model Management shall not be responsible in any way for any acts or omissions of Harlequin or its partners, subsidiaries and affiliates in connection with the contest or otherwise.

4. All Entrants and Models must be residents of the U.S. or Canada, be 18 years of age or older, and have no prior criminal convictions. The contest is not open to any Model that is a professional model and/or actor in any capacity at the time of the entry. Contest void wherever prohibited by law; all applicable laws and regulations apply. Any litigation within the Province of Quebec regarding the conduct or organization of a publicity contest may be submitted to the Régie des alcools, des courses et des jeux for a ruling, and any litigation regarding the awarding of a prize may be submitted to the Régie only for the purpose of helping the parties reach a settlement. Employees and immediate family members of Harlequin Enterprises Ltd., D.L. Blair, Inc., Elite Model Management (Toronto) Inc. and their parents, affiliates, subsidiaries and all other agencies, entities and persons connected with the use, marketing or conduct of this Contest are not eligible to enter. Acceptance of any prize offered constitutes permission to use Entrants' and Models' names, essay submissions, photographs or other likenesses for the purposes of advertising, trade, publication and promotion on behalf of Harlequin Enterprises Ltd., its parent, affiliates, subsidiaries, assigns and other authorized entities involved in the judging and promotion of the contest without further compensation to any Entrant or Model, unless prohibited by law.

5. Finalists will be determined no later than October 30, 2003. Prize Winners will be determined no later than January 31, 2004. Grand Prize Winners (consisting of winning Entrant and Model) will be required to sign and return Affidavit of Eligibility/Release of Liability and Model Release forms within thirty (30) days of notification. Non-compliance with this requirement and within the specified time period will result in disqualification and an alternate will be selected. Any prize notification returned as undeliverable will result in the awarding of the prize to an alternate set of winners. All travelers (or parent/legal guardian of a minor) must execute the Affidavit of Eligibility/Release of Liability prior to ticketing and must possess required travel documents (e.g. valid photo ID) where applicable. Travel dates specified by Sponsor but no later than May 30, 2004.

6. Prizes: One (1) Grand Prize—the opportunity for the Model to appear on the cover of a paperback book from the Harlequin Blaze series, and a 3 day/2 night trip for two (Entrant and Model) to New York, NY for the photo shoot of Model which includes round-trip coach air transportation from the commercial airport nearest the winning Entrant's home to New York, NY, (or, in lieu of air transportation, $100 cash payable to Entrant and Model, if the winning Entrant's home is within 250 miles of New York, NY), hotel accommodations (double occupancy) at the Plaza Hotel and $500 cash spending money payable to Entrant and Model, (approximate prize value: $8,000), and one (1) Runner-up Prize of $200 cash payable to Entrant and Model for a romantic dinner for two (approximate prize value: $200). Prizes are valued in U.S. currency. Prizes consist of only those items listed as part of the prize. No substitution of prize(s) permitted by winners. All prizes are awarded jointly to the Entrant and Model of the winning entries, and are not severable - prizes and obligations may not be assigned or transferred. Any change to the Entrant and/or Model of the winning entries will result in disqualification and an alternate will be selected. Taxes on prize are the sole responsibility of winners. Any and all expenses and/or items not specifically described as part of the prize are the sole responsibility of winners. Harlequin Enterprises Ltd. and D.L. Blair, Inc., their parents, affiliates, and subsidiaries are not responsible for errors in printing of Contest entries and/or game pieces. No responsibility is assumed for lost, stolen, late, illegible, incomplete, inaccurate, non-delivered, postage due or misdirected mail or entries. In the event of printing or other errors which may result in unintended prize values or duplication of prizes, all affected game pieces or entries shall be null and void.

7. Winners will be notified by mail. For winners' list (available after March 31, 2004), send a self-addressed, stamped envelope to: Harlequin Blaze Cover Model Search Contest 3569 Winners, P.O. Box 4200, Blair, NE 68009-4200, or refer to the Harlequin website (at www.blazecovermodel.com).

Contest sponsored by Harlequin Enterprises Ltd., P.O. Box 9042, Buffalo, NY 14269-9042.

HBCVRMODEL2